# THE BEST FRIEND BARGAIN

CRYSTAL KASWELL

# Copyright

This is a work of fiction. Similarities to real people, places, or events are entirely coincidental.

**THE BEST FRIEND BARGAIN**
Copyright © 2020 Crystal Kaswell.
Written by Crystal Kaswell
Cover by Melody Jeffries

# Also by Crystal Kaswell

### *Inked Love*

*The Best Friend Bargain* - Forest

*The First Taste* - Holden

*The Roomie Rulebook* - Oliver

### *Inked Hearts*

*Tempting* - Brendon

*Hooking Up* - Walker

*Pretend You're Mine* - Ryan

*Hating You, Loving You* - Dean

*Breaking the Rules* - Hunter

*Losing It* - Wes

*Accidental Husband* - Griffin

*The Baby Bargain* - Chase

### *Dirty Rich*

*Dirty Deal* - Blake

*Dirty Boss* - Nick

*Dirty Husband* - Shep

*Dirty Desires* - Ian

*Dirty Wedding* - Ty

*Dirty Secret* - Cam

### *Pierce Family*

*Broken Beast* - Adam

*Playboy Prince* - Liam

*Ruthless Rival* - Simon - coming soon

### **Sinful Serenade**

*Sing Your Heart Out* - Miles

*Strum Your Heart Out* - Drew

*Rock Your Heart Out* - Tom

*Play Your Heart Out* - Pete

*Sinful Ever After* – series sequel

*Just a Taste* - Miles's POV

### **Dangerous Noise**

*Dangerous Kiss* - Ethan

*Dangerous Crush* – Kit

*Dangerous Rock* – Joel

*Dangerous Fling* – Mal

*Dangerous Encore* - series sequel

### **Standalones**

*Broken* - Trent & Delilah

### **Come Undone Trilogy**

*Come Undone*

*Come Apart*

*Come To Me*

Sign up for the Crystal Kaswell mailing list

## Chapter One

FOREST

My phone sings with Gloria Gaynor's pained voice.
*I Will Survive.*
The breakup anthem to end all breakup anthems.
The song my little brother set for my ex-girlfriend.
The first line fades into the second.
The melody spreads through the empty room. It expands to fill the spaces in my head.
It pokes every single bruise.
Tears at every stitch in my heart.
This is nothing. A prank. My little brother fucking with me.
It's not Mack calling me.
That's not possible.
I suck a breath through my teeth. Turn off the faucet. Place the clean mug on the counter.
For a second, *I Will Survive* fills the silence. Then the call ends and the room goes quiet.
Nothing but my shaky exhale.
My strained inhale.
In. Out. Easy.
Then my phone lights up again and I lose track of my breath.
Gloria Gaynor repeats her refrain.

She's strong enough to get through this.

She still knows how to love.

She's going to be okay.

Whereas I—

Fuck, it's been two years. She doesn't have a place in my heart.

Not anymore.

I wipe my hands on my basketball shorts. They're too slick. Good for a scrimmage against my little brother. Shit at absorbing sweat.

The room is empty. The house is empty. My brother is no longer shooting hoops. My sister is no longer savoring a decaf chai. My family is no longer here to back me up.

It's five steps to the dinner table.

No more plates. No more lasagna dish. (My sister's favorite). No more mugs of tea and coffee.

Nothing but my cell.

*Incoming Call From Mackenzie Davis.*

Mack to her friends. To her enemies. To whatever the fuck I am.

I answer the call. "Hello."

"Forest." Her voice drips with surprise. "Hey."

My stomach churns. Her voice is familiar. It tugs at the stitches holding me together.

Which is ridiculous.

I'm fine.

Yeah, I'm not running into another woman's arms. I'm not ready to trust. Or kiss anyone. Or accept more from a woman than casual sex.

Not that I'm fucking anyone.

Or thinking about fucking anyone.

Only Skye. And that—

Not happening.

"Hey." I swallow the nausea that rises in my throat. Push away the images that flit through my head.

His hand in her red hair.

Her lips parting with a sigh.

Her groan bouncing around the room.

Okay, my love life is D.O.A. So what? I don't need love. Not the romantic kind.

"Is everything okay?" There's no reason for Mack to call me. We've barely spoken since I caught her with Mr. Valedictorian. Unless she's calling about—

Fuck.

"Is Skye okay?" I swallow hard. Mack isn't just my ex. She's also my best friend's cousin. And she—if something happened to Skye.

I pull my cell from my ear. Check the screen for missed texts. Something from her parents. Or her.

There's nothing. Just some teasing from earlier today.

"I don't know." Mack's voice is soft. Caring even. "I haven't talked to her. That's actually… why I'm calling."

My shoulders relax. "Oh."

"I guess I should tell you first." Her voice gets stronger. Surer.

My head screams *hell no. Hang up. Call Skye right now. Make sure she had dinner. Insist on feeding her leftovers if she didn't.*

*Ask her to pick out a movie. One of those movies that's all talking. They're slow, but it's worth it to watch joy spread over her face.*

"Yeah?" I ask.

"Diego and I are getting married."

My stomach drops.

"It's soon. A month. I, uh… I've already sent the invitations."

"Right."

"I'm not pregnant. If that's what you're wondering."

"No—" That's not what I'm wondering.

"I hate to ask you this, Forest. I know you've had a hard time moving on. And I… I don't want to make it harder." Her voice is soft. Sweet. Like she really does care.

Like she really does hate the idea of hurting me.

Is it true? Or a put on?

I can never tell with her. I could once. Or maybe I couldn't. Maybe that was why we didn't work.

"I'm fine." The words feel like a lie. But they aren't. I am fine. I don't need love. I'm surviving like this.

"It's amazing you and Skye have become such good friends. I never expected that."

"Yeah."

"She's just... so different from you, don't you think?"

There's the Mack I know. The girl who has to win every competition. Who sees everything as a competition. "What do you mean?"

"Nothing. Just a vibe," Mack says. "Well... there is her Instagram. Doesn't it bother you? How much she wants attention? You hated when I did that."

Maybe. Or maybe she's fucking with me. Either way, I'm not letting her insult Skye. "What is it you need to know?"

"Are you sure it's okay I ask?" That caring tone drops into her voice. "Are you sure you're over me?"

No. "Go for it."

"If you're sure... I... I want to invite her. But I don't want her to feel bad. She's been single for so long. And with how everything went. She's on your side and there is that... well, no, that's our secret. I shouldn't say anything."

Okay...

"I just... I don't want her to feel like a loser."

Fuck her for suggesting that. "She won't."

"Oh."

"Yeah."

"She's been single for three years now."

So what? Why does my best friend need a boyfriend? She's happy enough. She has love in her life. She doesn't need romance.

That shit ends in pain.

She's better off without it.

"I hope she's okay." Mack feigns concern.

For a second, I believe it. "You're worried about Skye?"

"She's always had trouble with guys. You know how they are. She has a pretty face, but with her size… a lot of guys won't go for a bigger girl."

Fuck. There isn't a tinge of sarcasm, insult, mocking in her voice.

She really believes this.

That she's helping Skye by calling her fat.

"Guys aren't into girls with perfect tits?" I ask.

Fuck, the image of her in that tiny bra, the one from her Instagram—

Black lace spread over light skin. Barely covering her massive tits. Begging for my hands.

Her dark hair falling over her eyes.

Her wine lips parted with a groan.

My cock is already standing at attention.

It's a bigger traitor than my heart. It doesn't care that Skye is the most important person in my life. That she's my best friend. That there's no way in hell I'm fucking that up.

It only cares about her lush tits, her thick thighs, her crimson lips.

Fuck, the thought of those thighs against my cheeks—

Mack lets out a hell of a forced laugh.

My dick deflates. Talk about opposing forces.

It's what I need at the moment. I close my eyes. Push away mental images of my best friend in lingerie.

Focus on my ex's bullshit. "Have you heard something? About guys no longer liking girls with amazing tits?"

"No… Um." Mack's laugh gets faker. "You're right. She is… voluptuous. Lots of guys like that."

"Yeah." Fuck yeah.

"But, uh… she is still single. Isn't she?"

"No."

Jealousy creeps into Mack's voice. "Really?"

"Yeah."

"Oh. That's great. I'm glad she found someone." She pauses for a moment. "Do you think she wants a plus one? Is he the type who'd come? Do you know him?"

"No." There isn't a boyfriend. There isn't anyone. Which is for the best. I want Skye to be happy. And love makes you unhappy. Besides, there's no one who deserves her.

"Oh." Her laugh is soft.

Fuck, I can see her smiling. I can hear her whisper. *Poor Skye. Single again. Loveless again. What a loser.*

No.

I'm not letting her do that.

No fucking way.

I shouldn't say this. It's stupid. Petty. Immature. But I don't care. "Skye's not dating someone else."

"She isn't?" Mack asks.

"It's me. We're together."

"What?" The politeness fades from her voice.

She's upset. Hurt.

Incredulous.

I need to sell this.

I muster up every ounce of enthusiasm I have. "She's the love of my life."

"Wow. That's uh… that's surprising."

It's bullshit. It's obvious bullshit. "It's been a ride."

"You and Skye… Wow… I guess, in a way… that's great, really." Her laugh is knowing.

It says too much. Things I can't stand hearing. "It is."

"I'm happy for you," she lies.

"Thanks," I lie back.

"I guess that makes my next call easier."

"Yeah." Shit. "You know what? I gotta go. Work." I slip my keys into my pocket. Move toward the door.

"It's nine."

"Early appointment tomorrow." I pull the door open. "I'll talk to you later." I end the call and I hightail it to my best friend's house.

## Chapter Two

SKYE

Cold air greets me as I step out of the car. Ah, Southern California spring. Warm afternoons. Cool evenings. Wild temperature swings.

Sure, the night sky is beautiful. This close to the beach, I can even see a few stars. But the air temperature at nine o'clock?

My cell claims it's fifty-eight degrees—and dropping every minute—but that has to be wrong. My arms are already covered in goose bumps.

I pull my sweater tighter. Not that it helps. It's a cropped sweater. It's not designed for warmth.

Why do I have this anyway?

I shrug my purse off my shoulder. Slip my phone into the front pocket.

The screen blinks with a text from Forest.

*Don't—*

The screen flashes, overriding the text.

*Incoming call from—*

"Skye!" Forest's voice booms.

He races across his parents' yard. To mine.

I retrieve my cell. Motion to Dad's car. "I'll come over after I change." I do not need the commentary from my parents. If I hear my dad insist I'm with Forest one more time, I'm going to go insane.

*I know he's your boyfriend. Why don't you want to tell me? You think your dad isn't cool enough to understand young love? You realize I was your age when I married your mother?*

Seriously, enough is enough.

I don't need the reminder that Forest and I are just friends.

That he is not interested.

That he will never be interested.

That I am completely and totally uninterested in anyone else.

It's agony every time our knees brush. Every time he smiles that *God, you're so difficult and I love it* smile. Every time he runs his hand through his dark hair and shrugs like he just can't explain himself with words.

Every time his dark eyes fix on me.

Or he says my name.

Or he hugs me goodbye.

It hurts being so, so close and so, so far at the same time.

But it's better than the alternative.

My phone's buzz pulls me into the moment. Someone is calling. I don't know who or why, but if they're calling instead of texting, it must be important.

I answer. Bring the speaker to my ear. "Hello."

"Skye, hey." Mackenzie's voice flows through the speaker.

My thoughts skip a beat.

What the hell is Mackenzie doing calling me?

I don't care that she's family; I don't want to hear from my cousin.

She stole my crush. Then she tossed him aside, broke his heart, and left him to stitch himself back together.

He's still in love with her. Or obsessed with her. Or unable to move on.

Something.

She did that to him. She promised she wouldn't go after him—

she knew I liked him—and she did it anyway. Then she didn't even appreciate what she had.

"You have time to talk?" Her voice is easy, casual, like this call is a normal part of our routine.

My veins buzz with anger. "I'm kind of busy actually."

"It will only take a minute."

I bite my tongue. I can't tell her to go screw herself. I'll hear about it every Thanksgiving and Christmas for the rest of my life.

I wave Forest away. I need to protect him from this. Whatever it is.

"Sure." I swallow the rage that rises in my throat. "What's up?"

"It's kind of weird." She laughs.

It's too familiar. I can hear her laughing over 'N Sync. Teaching me how to apply eyeliner. Offering gossip.

*Honestly, Skye, Forest is huge. Too much for your first time. You wouldn't know what to do with it.*

Shit, he's still moving toward me.

Running toward me actually.

"Hold on a second." I put my hand over the receiver. "Forest, I—"

Forest sprints up the stairs.

"What are you—"

He barrels into me. Pins me to the door.

The weight of his body sinks into mine.

For a split second, my eyes close. My head fills with delicious thoughts.

His strong hands on my thighs.

His soft lips on my neck.

His thick cock driving into me.

"Hang up." His fingers curl around my wrist.

Mackenzie's voice flows through the speakers, but the words blur together.

He pushes my hand into the door. "Now."

"Why?" My arms refuse to move. His touch feels too good. Possessive. Careful. Demanding.

What he's like when he fucks.

He must be.

He's a caretaker with everyone, always, all the time.

"Now, Skye." His eyes bore into mine. "Trust me."

I stare up at him. Try to find some response that isn't *please keep doing this. Don't explain. Don't expand. Don't offer any information that will puncture my fantasy.*

He pulls my phone from my hands. Ends the call.

He's still so close. We hang out all the time, but we're not usually this close.

There are flecks of amber in his coffee eyes. God, they're such pretty eyes. Deep. Impossible to read.

"Follow me." He steps backward.

For a second, my brain clicks on, then his fingers curl around my wrist and my thoughts scatter. "What are we—"

"She's gonna call back."

"And?" How does he know Mackenzie is the one calling?

"Come on." He tugs a little harder on my wrist. Not enough to hurt. Enough to say *I've got you.*

Or maybe I'm projecting. "I have to shower." I wrap my fingers around my gym bag. I'm still in my pole outfit. High-waisted booty shorts, sports bra, cropped hoodie. It's appropriate for the activity—I need bare skin to grip the pole—but for this?

It's funny. I'm not cold anymore. I'm on fire.

"And change?"

He glances back at me. Gives me a quick once over. Tilts his head to one side. "Why?"

Because he's the hottest guy on the planet—a man with actual abs—and I'm soft.

Because he sleeps exclusively with model-thin women and I shop in the plus-size department.

Because I want to.

"Skye?" His eyes flit to my exposed stomach. My bare thighs. My combat boots. "You look good."

"I…" Talking is hard. "I'm cold."

He nods *sure*. "I'll grab a blanket." He squeezes my hand. "I'll explain fast. I promise."

I try to think of some sort of logical response, but all I have is *please keep touching me*.

---

As soon as we're inside, Forest releases me. He slides my cell into the front pocket of his basketball shorts. Goes straight to the couch.

Grabs the purple blanket. Drapes it over my shoulders.

He raises a brow *better*.

No. I'm burning up. This is only making the situation worse. But I need the shield.

He's in his basketball outfit. His swishy shorts fall above his knee. Show off his muscular thighs.

His strong shoulders are on display. The black and grey sleeve on his left arm. The broken heart on his chest.

I... Uh...

Thinking...

I'm thinking.

I'm here for a reason.

I'm doing something besides staring.

Really.

Something buzzes against the table.

My cell.

Oh.

"Are you going to explain?" Something is happening. And it's something with Mackenzie. So it's bad news.

"Sit down." He motions to the couch. "You need something to drink?"

"Do I?"

"Water." His tone shifts to a paternal one. The one he uses with his siblings. *I know best. I'm taking care of you. Listen to my wisdom.*

"Okay." I sit on the middle cushion. Watch him fill two glasses, cross the room, hand one to me.

My fingers brush his.

God, his touch feels so good. It doesn't usually make me this fluttery. I usually have a better handle on my crush.

Today—

I don't know if it's the mention of his ex or the basketball shorts or the broken heart tattoo.

God, it's so fitting. A glass heart, shattered into a million pieces. Exactly what she did to him.

Exactly what I want to fix.

I want to glue him back together.

But that's not how it works. And even if it was, Forest is—

Well, he's not exactly happy being shattered. But he accepts it.

More or less.

"I said something stupid." His throat quivers as he swallows.

"That doesn't sound like you."

He nods *I know*. Crouches on one knee. Sets his water on the coffee table behind him. "Mack is getting married."

"Oh." My eyes bore into his. He's not crying or hitting something or screaming. Which makes sense. He keeps his feelings close.

He doesn't share the things that hurt him. Not usually.

But he must be upset.

His ex is marrying another guy. The guy she screwed behind his back. The guy he caught her screwing.

I want to punch her and she—

She betrayed me, but it's nothing compared to what she did to him.

"It's about a month away." He takes my hand between his.

"Okay." I swallow another sip of water. "Are you okay?"

He nods *yeah*. "She started talking about—"

"That's it?" I copy his nod. "Mackenzie is getting married and you nod?"

"I said I'd explain fast."

Okay…

## The Best Friend Bargain

His thumb brushes the back of my hand. "Make me a promise."

"What?"

"Give me twenty-four hours to figure this out."

"To figure what out?"

He takes my water. Sets it on the coffee table. Returns to that perfect position, crouching in front of me.

Like he's about to unpeel my blanket, slide my shorts off my ankles, pry my thighs apart.

He's not.

But, God, it's a beautiful mental image.

His nails on my thighs.

My hands in his hair.

His lips on my skin.

I bet he growls. I bet his voice gets low and deep. That tone that's somehow needy and demanding at the same time.

"Do you trust me?" Vulnerability streaks his expression.

I take a deep breath. *Think unsexy thoughts. Or at least semi-sexy thoughts. Sexy-romantic thoughts. About protecting him.* "Yeah."

"Then promise."

"Okay." Twenty-four hours isn't a long time.

"She said she was worried about you. Being single for so long. And guys—" His eyes flit to my chest. "She had this tone, like you were a loser because you don't want a relationship."

That sounds like my cousin. "And?"

"I snapped."

"You snapped?"

He nods *yeah*. "I told her we're together. That you're my girlfriend. That you're the love of my life."

"You told Mackenzie that we're together?"

"Yeah."

"That I'm the love of your life?"

"I did."

"And she..." I pinch my wrist. I'm not dreaming. I'm still here. On the leather couch at the Ballard's place. Covered in Ariel's purple blanket. Sitting across from my best friend. "She took that—"

"What do you think?"

"She wasn't even a little jealous?"

He chuckles *yeah right*. "It was stupid. A moment of pettiness."

"Maybe."

He raises a brow. "It *was* stupid."

"Yeah, but—"

"I'll walk it back. I just need to figure it out."

"Or not."

"Skye—"

"It hurt her, right?"

He looks up at me. "So?"

"So, if I don't go to this wedding, I'll hear about it for the rest of my life. And you—there are lots of people who want to see you melt down."

"Holden?" He refers to his trouble-making little brother.

"Yeah, but people who actually mean it."

"Skye—"

"It's a good idea." I stare into his eyes. "I protect you. You protect me. We both make her jealous."

"I don't know."

"Did she say something about how I struggle because guys are superficial?"

His lip corners turn down.

He doesn't have to say it. We both know. I've heard it from her so many times.

*It's too bad you're still single, Skye. One day you'll find a guy who can see past your size. You have such a great personality.*

He's right. This is stupid.

But it's perfect too.

"I think it's a good idea." I make my voice as confident as I can. "I want to do it. I want to convince her we're together. I want to pretend I'm yours."

## Chapter Three

SKYE

He stares back at me, his eyes wide, his breath steady.

It's written all over his face:

*This is the worst idea in the history of the world.*

Maybe he's right.

Maybe I'm mad with lust.

I've liked him forever. Since the day we moved in next door and he came over all sweaty and out of breath.

He was a cool older boy. A brooding athlete with dark eyes, tattoos, and a stoic disposition.

We became friends. My crush grew from *oh my God, you're hot* to *oh my God, you have such a soft center under that hard exterior. Can I please have the key that unlocks your heart? All the soft parts. And all the hard parts. Especially the hard parts.*

Then Mackenzie stayed with us for the summer.

He liked her.

She liked him too. But she promised me she wouldn't go for him. She said *sisters before misters. I'd never go after a guy you like, Skye. I wouldn't do that to you. Even if he's out of your league.*

Then she did.

And she acted like it was for my own good.

*Sorry, Skye, but he kissed me. What was I going to do? Tell him I didn't want him to kiss me? Do you really want me to lie to him? It was magic. Fireworks. Like something out of a movie.*

*He's so handsome. And tall. Too tall for you. And guys that hot—they never date the chubby girl. It wasn't meant to be. We'll find you someone. Maybe that guy in your bio class? He's cute.*

She can be horrible, yeah. But it's only obvious in retrospect. At the time, I believed her. I believed she was looking out for me. That she wanted the best for me.

Forest was hurting so much. He was still carrying around the weight of his mom's death, taking care of his dad, his brother, his sister.

With Mack—

It was like she lifted that burden.

I wanted that for him. Even if it killed me. Even if I hated her for betraying me. Even if the sight of them kissing made me sick.

He was happy. For a long time, they were happy.

There's an awful side to Mackenzie, but there's another side. This charming, cool, fun, popular girl. She shines under the spotlight. Her smile is dazzling. It really is.

There's just something about her.

I want her to like me.

Everyone wants her to like them.

Everyone wants to bathe in the light of pretty, popular, thin Mackenzie.

The girl with the cool tattoos and the bright red hair.

The girl with all the gossip.

God, the things I've heard about Forest.

*He's huge, Skye. I thought I was going to burst the first time.*

*He's not like my ex. When he goes down on me, I see stars.*

*He says I'm the best he's ever had. That he'll never want anything else.*

My veins buzz with righteous indignation.

Then desire.

Sure, thoughts of Mackenzie and Forest together hurt.

But the thought of his thick cock, his skilled mouth, his strong hands—

God, it's hot in here.

It's so hot.

His voice pulls me from my dirty thoughts. "I can't lose you."

I can't concentrate. Deep breath. Steady exhale. "You won't."

He shakes his head *don't be ridiculous*. "I'll figure something out." His voice is strong. Sure. "We can orchestrate a breakup. Find you a fake rebound guy."

"Maybe."

"Maybe?"

"She already believes it." I swallow hard. He's all I have. I shouldn't risk that. Even if I want to make my cousin jealous. Even if I want to protect him from her smug smile. Even if I want to prove we're both better off without her. "Right?"

"Yeah."

"And that…" Mackenzie may be the star of the show most of the time, but she can't stand when she's not. She gets jealous like *that*. And she always hated that me and Forest were friends. "Look me in the eyes and tell me you don't want to make her jealous."

"I'm twenty-eight."

"And?"

"I'm too old for this." His eyes meet mine. "You're too old for this."

I clear my throat. "Rude."

His laugh breaks up the tension in his shoulders. "See. You're fucking funny, Skye. The only person who always makes me laugh." His fingers brush my wrist. "I'm not risking that."

"We're old. Like you said. Wise."

He shoots me some serious side-eye.

"Mature."

"You want to pretend you're in love with me to make your cousin jealous."

I clear my throat.

"That's mature?"

"It's more than that."

He makes that *sorta* motion.

"It is."

His lip corners turn down. "I'll think of something."

"If you don't?"

"I will."

"Then there's no risk agreeing. If you don't think of something better, we'll pretend we're together."

Apprehension streaks his expression.

Okay, I need to sell this. But softer. He needs room. "Sleep on it." I hold out my hand. "You'll agree in the morning."

He stares at me like I'm crazy, but he still shakes.

## Chapter Four

FOREST

The hum of the shop is familiar. The buzz of my tattoo gun. The low murmur of conversation. The pained vocals of Chase's favorite band (my favorite album).

The poor singer can't get over his ex. Every song is about her, even the ones he insists aren't about her.

Hell, he makes *You're So Vain* look like the picture of apathy.

I let the familiar melody fill my ears. Let my head drift to its happy place.

This is a classic backpiece.

*Amor vincit omnia.*

Love conquers all, surrounded by wings.

Thin lines, soft shading, sharp angles. The perfect mix of vulnerability and defenses.

The moment you let your guard down, let someone in, give them the chance to hurt you.

Sure, I can't accomplish that.

Yeah, the thought of showing someone my broken heart makes me sick.

But I understand the sentiment.

If it's what this girl wants, well—

Good for her. I hope she's happy. I hope she finds a love that fills her soul. That lasts forever.

I trace the last line of the quote. "Hanging in there?"

"Uh…" Her voice is weak. Stilted. "Will you think I'm a wimp if I ask for a break?"

"Shoulder blades hurt."

"So it's going to get worse?"

"Yeah." I can't help but chuckle. She's a tiny thing. A thin girl with long blond hair and delicate features. She looks like she'd blow away in a strong breeze, but she hasn't made a peep so far. She's tough.

"You're laughing at my pain?" Her voice almost gets to teasing.

"It gets better after it gets worse." I turn off the gun. Set it on my tray.

She needs the break. I need to stretch. And toss aside the storm brewing in the back of my head.

Mack is getting married.

Skye wants us to fake a relationship.

It's stupid. Immature. Petty.

But I get it.

Maybe I can't erase Mack from my mind. Maybe I can't stitch my heart back together. But I can do what it takes to never see her again.

Skye can't.

She cares about her family as much as I care about mine. And Mack is family.

She's fucked.

She needs a shield. Something to keep Mack's backhand compliments at bay. To wipe the smug look off her face.

"How about some water?" I need to get my head in the game. At least for the next few hours. This is a great job, a great shop, a fucking calling. I've wanted to do tattoos since I was a kid. I tried to go to college, study something practical, make my dad happy. But I never got it out of my head.

This is where I belong.

Where life makes sense.

Hell, it's in my blood. My mom was an artist—an animator. She would have worried about my unconventional path, but she would have been proud.

She was always proud. Full of love and joy and life. Even when she was dying, she was full of life.

My client pushes herself up. She offers me a shy smile. "I think I want to get up."

"In that?" I motion to the tape she's wearing as a top.

Her cheeks flush, but I can't tell if it's modesty or desire.

She has nothing to be embarrassed about.

Her tits are small, but they're nice. They suit her slim figure. Even with the tape, they're perky.

"Don't leave me waiting." My client brushes her long hair behind her ear. Presses her lips into a sweet smile.

She's flirting.

She wants me.

It's not surprising. Or unusual. There's something about the rush that comes with new ink. Dopamine and adrenaline.

Men get friendly.

Women get flirty.

Half of my female clients proposition me. After Mack left, I accepted their advances.

It was fun for a while. But it was empty too.

Shit. I'm getting distracted again. It's Skye's offer.

I had a million dreams about it. About her hands in my back pocket, her soft body against mine, her lips on my skin.

Fuck, those crimson lips.

Do they taste as good as they look?

Does she taste like the honey and matcha she's always drinking?

My cock stirs.

Fuck. It's one thing getting excited at the thought of her curvy body. But this?

Uh-uh.

I haven't kissed in forever. I tried it with my first few one-night stands, but it was all wrong. Too close, too intimate, too personal.

It was easier keeping it wham, bam, thank you, ma'am.

"Hey." Chase nods from his spot at the counter.

I push my dirty thoughts aside. Move to the water cooler. Pour two cups. Down one.

Head in the game.

Memories of Mack locked in a box.

Thoughts of Skye far away.

I'm Forest Ballard, expert tattoo artist.

The guy who protects my family.

Who looks out for my friends.

Shit. My head goes to Skye immediately. The frustration in her blue eyes. God, her eyes are gorgeous. Bright. Full of life. Like the sky itself.

They're a little darker, a little deeper. Halfway between sky and ocean. A hundred percent intoxicating.

"You okay?" Chase asks. He's our official manager. And a good friend. I've known him forever. Since we were on the same basketball team in high school.

We still play once a week.

He's a good boss. He keeps the shop running like a well-oiled machine. And he still spends half his time on tattoos.

He's good at it.

He is exactly where he's supposed to be.

My friend used to be the picture of misery. He made me look well-adjusted. Hell, he made the miserable fucker singing about car crashes look well-adjusted.

For ages, he was obsessed with his ex-girlfriend. Unable to move on. Forgive her. Or himself. Or a single person in his family. (Not that I blame him).

Then he did.

He met someone who pushed him enough. He finally saw the light.

All right, that someone was my baby sister. And he did get her pregnant. It was what she wanted. They're both happy.

But it's hard getting past the whole *what the fuck, dude, you got my sister pregnant* impulse that rises in my stomach.

Ariel's almost twenty-five now. She's getting a PhD. She's self-reliant.

And now she has Chase to help her, protect her, take care of her.

I trust him to do it.

But it's hard letting go of my need to protect my baby sister.

Our mom died when I was a teenager. Dad fell apart, so I picked up the slack. I made sure he ate. I took Ariel to school. I kept Holden out of trouble, more or less.

For a long time, that was my life. It was taking care of other people.

I'm not complaining. There's something about making sure my family is happy, healthy, safe. It fills me in a way nothing else does.

I love taking care of the people I love.

With Ariel being pregnant with a little girl, a girl named after our mom—

It's amazing. I'm going to be an uncle. It's happening so fast. I'm still wrapping my head around it.

My kid brother Holden—he works here too—isn't nearly as sentimental. He's a born and bred troublemaker. Though it's hard to blame him. I did my best, but he did his best to slip through the cracks. Sometimes, he did.

It's amazing he ended up as functional as he is. He's always giving me shit, but it's well-intentioned.

Yeah, he sleeps with everything that moves.

He throws a ton of parties.

He takes nothing seriously.

But he's happy, he's employed, he's yet to get arrested (as an adult).

I shake off my concern—I can't help it; I'm always worried

about my siblings—as I refill my cup, cross the room, offer my client her water.

She pulls her legs onto the bench. Folds them over each other.

It's the same way Skye sits when she's watching TV on the couch.

Fuck, my head is swimming.

This girl is cute, yeah, but that doesn't matter.

The skin stretched over bone.

The words I'm etching onto it—

That's the only thing that matters.

Her fingers brush mine as she takes the cup. She stares at it for a moment, looking for confidence or comfort or something else it's incapable of offering. "You do a lot of these?"

"Wings?" I ask.

She nods *yeah*.

I can talk work. Hell, I can offer her a shoulder to cry on. As long as that's all it is. "Some. They're not as popular as they used to be."

"So my look is dated?" Her lips curl into a shy smile.

"Classic." I take a long sip. Set my cup on my shelf. Reach for a new set of gloves. "The last few years, tattoos have gotten more popular. It's not just punk rock babes and biker dudes. Moms come in with their kids. Honor students come in with their friends. Virgins come in with their boyfriends."

"Virgins?" Her eyes go wide with interest. She stares at me like she's waiting for me to launch into some *Penthouse* letter kind of story.

Fuck, it does sound raunchy like that. "Tattoo virgins." I give her a quick once over. "This is your first?"

She shakes her head. Peels her jean leg up, revealing a shooting star on her ankle.

It's small and messy. Perfect in its messiness, actually.

"I was seventeen and my boyfriend knew a guy who wouldn't ID," she says. "As you can tell, the work is impeccable."

"Scared you off, for what, a year?" I turn on the charm. Shoot her that *baby, we both know you're a hottie* look.

Her cheeks flush. "A few more than that." She finishes her water. Offers me the cup.

I take it. Nod to the bench. "You ready?"

The song fades into the next. An ode to the singer's apathy about his ex. He doesn't care about her. He doesn't miss her. He doesn't need her.

Why does she think he cares anyway?

I'm not sure which of us is less plausible.

I'm not over Mack, sure, but it's not that I'm still in love with her. Or that I want her back.

It's more that I don't know what the hell I want.

Mack filled this hole in my heart. There was this emptiness inside me. I didn't even know it was there until she filled it.

She made everything brighter, easier. For the first time, I wasn't a guy surviving, barely managing to take care of my family.

I was awake, alive, okay.

We had problems, sure. Plenty I let myself ignore. But we were happy. I thought we were happy.

Until I walked in on her with him.

After that—

Some part of me shattered. The world went back to being dark, ugly, hard. Only everything was different.

My dad was functioning.

My brother and sister were adults.

They didn't need me anymore.

No one needed me anymore. Not the way they did.

And I—

Gloria Gaynor is okay because she still knows how to love.

I've got no fucking idea. How can anyone let their guard down? It's the stupidest decision of all time.

I miss it.

God, there's something about letting someone in. About feeling completely understood.

Understanding someone else.

Showing them exactly where they can hurt you.

It's exhilarating.

But when I think about it now—

Fuck, the room is already getting stuffy.

"I think I'm ready." My client's stilted voice pulls me from my thoughts. "How much more will it hurt?"

It always hurts. But it's worth it. "You can handle it."

Her nose scrunches with distaste. "What if I can't?"

"You can."

"What if I can't? Are you going to make it up to me somehow?" Her eyes meet mine. They ask for comfort. Safety. Sex.

She's still playing coy, but it's clear what she's after.

It happens all the time.

Women see me as a tall brooding tattoo artist. A mysterious bad boy. The box they check before they move onto a real relationship.

It has its perks. I'm not complaining.

For a second, this girl's offer tempts me. I consider taking her home, peeling her out of her tight outfit, pinning her tiny body to the wall—

But I don't see her. I see Mack. I see her hazel eyes filling with pleasure. Her red hair falling over her perky tits. Her lips parting with a groan.

His name filling the room.

*Yes, Diego. Harder, baby. Harder.*

My dick practically deflates.

Nothing kills the mood faster than my ex.

I keep up the charm anyway. "What are you looking for?"

She flashes me that same shy smile. "You could buy me a drink."

"If you wimp out of your tattoo?"

She nods.

"Sounds like I'm encouraging you to run."

"You think you're that irresistible?"

I shoot her a megawatt smile. "You don't?"

Her cheeks flush.

I swallow my surprise. It's hard to believe I still have it. I never use it. Not anymore. "A drink. If you make it through the entire thing."

She looks up at me. "You really think I can?"

"I know you can."

Her eyes fill with vulnerability. "How do you know?"

"You're tougher than you look."

"And you?"

"Oh, I'm way less tough than I look."

She laughs, even though it's a bad joke. Even though it's true.

Here I am, two years after walking in on my ex groaning another guy's name, and I still don't know how to love.

I'm still hopeless when it comes to romance.

But I know how to protect my friends.

And I will protect Skye.

Whatever it takes.

## Chapter Five

SKYE

Thankfully, my parents work long hours. Dad is a doctor. Mom runs a consulting firm.

For most of the day, the house is mine.

It's the only thing that keeps me sane.

I've lived at home since... always. During college, it was sensible. A way to save money. Sure, my parents would have helped with an apartment, but rents in Brentwood are ridiculous. The drive to UCLA is easy. I have tons of room here.

It was an easy choice.

Then, after I graduated, I struggled to find employment. When I did, it was temporary stuff. That's the film and TV industry. A few weeks as an office PA here. An unpaid internship there. An assistant gig that didn't pay anywhere near enough for my own place. A few more weeks or months of unemployment.

Rinse. Repeat.

Last year, I thought I made it. I got a job as a development assistant at a new reality TV company. Sure, it's not what I want to do, exactly. But it's film and TV adjacent. It's relevant to my degree in film studies. It's a job with a trajectory.

It was a slog sure, but it was a step in the right direction.

Then the company folded.

For the last five months, I've been looking for a new job with no luck.

Mom and Dad always tell me to follow my dreams. Hold out for a great job that uses my brain and somehow gets me where I want to go. But I don't know where I want to go anymore.

After three years of working shitty jobs with little or no pay, I no longer look at film with the same luster.

Sure, I love movies. There's nothing better than sitting on the couch and losing myself in two hours of moving pictures. Especially, when the movies are smart and naturalistic with snappy dialogue and excellent acting.

But I want it to be my couch. In my apartment. On my TV.

I want to live my life. To feel like my life is going somewhere.

And a constant stream of shitty gigs that don't pay or stimulate my brain—

Gigs that are insanely competitive because everyone wants to be a part of "the industry"—

That's not fun. Or stimulating. Or fulfilling.

It's certainly not going anywhere.

Yeah, I'm lucky. My parents offer me a place to crash. I make enough from on and off employment that I take care of myself.

But, goddammit, I want a real job. A career. A future.

All I have is my blog.

*Princess Skye's Plus-Size Fashions.*

Princess Skye on social media.

It started as a lark. Because there weren't enough people reviewing plus-sized clothing. And the women who were running plus-size blogs had more conventional tastes.

Forest says I dress like a goth princess. That's where I got the princess thing, actually. It's a good description. There's something about black corset dresses, combat boots, big eyelashes—

It feels right.

I feel like me when I'm wearing a bold black dress, thick eyeliner, crimson lipstick.

Maybe that's why I like pole dancing. It's not just fitness—though it is incredibly demanding—it's big and loud. A show. I can show up in stiletto combat boots, false eyelashes, and a sparkly black one-piece, and I get compliments, not *why are you wearing that* looks.

It's funny. Mack was the one who dragged me to a class. Who went on and on about how much she wanted to learn sexy moves. To entice her boyfriend.

She quit when she realized it was more about strength, flexibility, and pain.

It's literally painful. There's no getting around it. Holding onto the pole hurts. Period. End of sentence.

And it's necessary for any static pose, climbing, hanging upside down.

For the first six months, I was covered in bruises. But, somehow, my skin got used to the pressure.

I spend a lot of time at the studio. It's my main indulgence. Well, besides matcha lattes.

Speaking of—

My mug is empty.

I check my edits one more time. Me on the beach, in a gauzy black dress, fabric and hair blowing in the wind.

It's not my usual vibe—it's hard to mix beach and goth princess—but it works.

There. I tweak the color. Make it just a little brighter. Then I crop. Tag. Post.

My gaze shifts to the closet. The dress is still hanging on the edge. It's a beautiful dress. Well made. Sexy in a classy way.

And expensive.

But I don't buy my own clothes anymore. I did when I started. When I hit ten thousand followers, designers started sending me free stuff. Rarely at first.

Then all the time.

Now, I have more clothes than I could ever wear. I even make a little money from the ads on my blog. It's not enough to sustain me.

But it's enough to pay for shoes, haircuts, makeup, eyelash extensions.

I guess I'm an "influencer."

It's a horrible term, but it's not the worst thing in the world. Hell, it's the only thing I'm really good at. Well, the only thing with even a hint of career potential.

And the world could certainly use more plus-sized fashionistas.

More non-white "influencers." (Dad is Korean. Mom is white. The two of them are disgustingly in love. And all my friends think he's hot).

I close my social media. Head downstairs. Fix my second matcha latte.

Mmm, almond milk (I inherited Dad's lactose intolerance), green tea, honey. Sweet, creamy, rich. Just a little nutty.

A hint of vanilla extract.

The perfect mix of sweet and savory.

A rare moment of bliss.

I enjoy for as long as I can. Then my phone buzzes and my bliss vanishes.

*Mackenzie: Are you and Forest really together? That's great news, Skye. I'm so glad he got over his thing for thin women. Some people can't shake their type, you know?*

Bile rises in my throat.

I swear to God, every time we talk she reminds me I'm not thin.

It shouldn't bother me—I love my body, I do—but it does.

I shouldn't let her affect me. That's the only way she wins.

But I—

God, I hate her so much.

I can't let her do this.

I'm not letting her do this.

I don't think.

I pick up my cell and I text Forest.

*Skye: I want to do this. I'm not taking no for an answer. Tell me you'll do it. Promise me.*

## Chapter Six

FOREST

My phone buzzes against my thigh.

A text from Skye.

But I'm not ready to answer it.

I have half a dozen hours to think of a better idea. Of some way to protect her that doesn't risk everything.

One more appointment—some girl-power lyrics—then I can devote all my brain power to figuring this out.

Right now, I need a clear head. No thoughts of Mack's smug smile. Or Skye's hurt frown.

Or Skye's perfect tits for that matter.

I'm concentrating.

Working on a mock-up.

Something.

I reach for my sketchbook, but the *bing-bong* of the door interrupts me.

My kid brother, Holden, saunters through the door.

He hugs something to his chest as he shakes his head *this is a real tragedy.*

From his spot behind the counter, Chase glances at Holden. He shrugs *Holden is Holden.* Returns to his mock-up.

My brother's gaze shifts to me. "Fifty bucks says you have a meltdown at the ceremony." He holds up a square envelope addressed to *The Ballard Family*. "A hundred says you show up at her room the night before the wedding, begging her to call it off."

"Nice to see you too." I roll my eyes, but I don't sell the apathy. The key to dealing with Holden is convincing him you don't care. He's like a toddler. He always wants more attention. Whether I'm trying to get him to back down for my sake or his, I always do it with a shrug.

My brother chuckles *okay, sure*. He looks to Chase. "You want in on this action?" He drops the envelope on the counter. Pulls out his wallet. Then two hundred-dollar bills. "I'll give three to one odds. Forest makes a fool of himself before that bitch walks down the aisle." He turns to me. "She invited all of us."

"And?" I shrug like I don't care.

He chuckles as he copies my shrug. He leans against the counter, the picture of cool. "Yeah. Sell that story." He turns back to Chase *can you believe this?*

Chase's gaze flits from him to me. Then back to him. "You think I'm on your side here?"

"Shit, forgot who I was talking to." Holden shakes his head. "You made it. You moved on. You were even more miserable than Forest."

Chase chuckles *fair enough*.

"If there's hope for you…" He looks to me. "You want to bet?" He holds up the bills. "Three to one odds."

"You want me to bet on myself?" I ask.

He nods *yeah*. "Yeah. Gotta get you at the ceremony."

"You're going?" I shrug my shoulders. Of course, he's going. He can pretend he doesn't give a fuck as much as he wants. I know better.

His methods are… unconventional, but he does try to help.

"You're pretty casual about Chase fucking our sister," I say.

"Yeah, 'cause I realize she's an adult who makes her own decisions." He rolls his eyes *obviously*. Looks to Oliver's suite. "You want to bet? Odds are dropping to two to one after the first taker."

# The Best Friend Bargain

The hum of Oliver's gun ceases. He stands. Shakes his head. "Can I bet on Forest giving you a black eye?" His chuckle is low. Deep. Knowing.

He and Holden are best friends.

Somehow.

It still doesn't make sense. Oliver is serious and moody. Holden is... not.

But they're two peas in a pod.

"Yeah." Holden reaches into his wallet. Pulls out another hundred-dollar bill. "Even money."

"So, he bets a hundred bucks, he gets a hundred bucks back?" Chase asks.

Holden nods *hell yeah*.

"What good is that bet?" Chase asks.

"He gets to enjoy Holden's pain," I say.

"That's cruel. You'd do that to me?" Holden winks at Oliver. "Can't believe you want to do me like that."

Oliver nods *uh-huh*. "I'm going back to work." He drops into his suite, turns on his gun, tunes us out.

Holden looks to me. "What do you say? Want to bet on my black eye?"

"You're gonna pay me to hit you? Not seeing a downside." I try to make my voice teasing, but it's not quite there. I'd never hit Holden. Hell, it's my job, as his older brother, to make sure no one hits him.

He doesn't make that job easy. But I still do it.

"Didn't think that one though." Chase chuckles.

"It's for you, Forest." Holden looks at me with a dead-serious expression. "You gotta work out that aggression."

"Do I?"

He nods *hell yeah*. "Look me in the eyes and tell me you don't want to hurt someone right now." He picks up the envelope. Pulls out the invitation.

*You are cordially invited...*

Fuck, it's hot in here. Stuffy. We need to turn the AC up. I don't care that it's a cool day.

I need air.

I need—

"Leave him alone," Chase says.

Holden shakes his head *no fucking way*.

Chase whispers something to him.

Holden shrugs *true*. "I got a lot of people willing to bet on you."

"Lucky me." My throat goes dry. *You are cordially invited to the wedding of Diego Flores and Mackenzie Davis.*

"Give me some inside info. You going stag? Showing up with a cousin you're passing off as a girlfriend? Hiring a sex worker? I know a girl with great rates," Holden says.

Chase chuckles. "You hire a prostitute?"

"I know her. I don't hire her," he says.

Chase looks at him like he can't tell if he's lying or not. Then his attention turns to me. His blue eyes fill with concern.

It's a normal look for him. Chase is more protective older brother than I am.

His family is more fucked up than mine is.

Though it's not *his* and *my* family anymore. The guy is marrying my sister. They're having a baby. A baby named after our mom.

Fuck, even that isn't enough to push away the nausea in my throat.

Something buzzes against my leg. My phone. A text.

An excuse for some air.

I look to the clock. Ten minutes until my appointment. Maybe I can cancel. Or ask Chase to fill in.

My hands are shaking. My entire body is shaking. And I—

Fuck, it's too stuffy. It's impossible to work with the air this still and suffocating.

"I need coffee." I move toward the door. Try to avoid my brother's gaze.

His bright eyes—he has Mom's eyes—fill with concern for a

## The Best Friend Bargain

split second. Then they're back to typical Holden Ballard *I don't give a fuck* bullshit. "You gonna call her? Beg her to call it off and take you back? I'll give hundred to one odds on that working."

From his suite, Oliver chuckles.

I guess he's not tuning us out.

Chase just shakes his head. "At this rate, I'm going to hit you."

"I'll sue you for creating a hostile work environment," Holden says.

"You think there's any jury who would take your side?" Chase teases.

Holden nods *fair enough*. He looks me up and down. Shakes his head *you're pathetic*. "You are going?"

"Yeah." Maybe. If I find a replacement fake boyfriend for Skye, it might be better for me to skip. To sell the whole *she broke my heart, I can't stand to be near her* story.

"Alone?" He raises a brow. "She's going to think you're still in love with her."

"I'm not—"

He holds up his hand *don't bother*. "I'm telling you, Forest. This girl is good. Discrete. Hot. Too hot for you."

"You don't think he's good-looking?" Chase asks.

"You do? Damn, you into freaky shit, Keating? Want to double team some siblings?" He shakes his head with mock horror.

"Jealous I'm not asking you?" Chase meets his level of ridiculousness.

Oliver's laugh gets louder. He turns off his gun. Stands. "Fuck, can I get in on this Forest punching Holden thing?" He nods something to his client then pulls out his wallet. "It's a long time coming."

Holden beams, proud of himself for inspiring this level of… confidence.

"I can recognize when a man is beautiful. Unlike some people, I'm secure in my masculinity." Chase winks at Holden.

"You think I can't?" Holden nods *hey* to his best friend. "Oliver is way cuter than Forest."

"Not as tall," Chase says.

Holden rolls his eyes. "'Course it's about height with you." He turns to me. Pretends to assess my attractiveness. "He does have that Ballard charm."

"Uh-huh," Chase says.

"Oh what, you don't like it?" Holden raises a brow. *Come on, you are dating Ariel Ballard, our sister.* "You aren't selling that."

"You don't have the Ballard charm." Chase chuckles.

Oliver does too.

I try to laugh with them, but it's impossible.

It's still so fucking hot in here.

I still don't have a good idea. A way to protect Skye. A way to hold my heart together for the next two months.

There's something I can do. Some way to survive this. To make sure Skye thrives.

I just need to get out of here. So I can think.

I take another step toward the door.

Holden stops me. "You do have a plan?"

"Yeah." All right, I need to see this. Whatever it is. I pull out my cell. Read my best friend's text.

*Skye: I want to do this. I'm not taking no for an answer. Tell me you'll do it. Promise me.*

*Forest: It's a bad idea.*

*Skye: Did you think of something better?*

*Forest: Not yet.*

"Earth to Forest?" Holden jumps behind me. Tries to read my texts over my shoulder. "You talking to the super bitch? Checking your bank account to see how much you're gonna have to convince any woman to put up with you?"

Chase shakes his head *you're such an asshole.*

Holden shrugs *and you're not?*

"No. I'm talking to Skye," I say.

"You're going to try to sell that you're dating Skye?" Holden chuckles *okay, sure.*

He and Chase exchange a look.

Oliver too.

"I thought you were convinced they're in love," Chase says.

"No. Only that he wants to motorboat her," Holden says.

A low chuckle fills the room. Then another.

"No, we're just—" Explaining will only make it worse.

*Skye: I'll meet you at Inked Love in an hour. And I'll show you that it will work.*

*Forest: What if it doesn't?*

*Skye: It will.*

## Chapter Seven

FOREST

The bell rings as Skye steps inside the shop. Her light eyes move around the room. Stop on Holden.

He's sitting at the counter, sketchbook open to a mock-up, attention on Skye.

He nods a friendly hello. "Nice to see you, Skye. Tell me you're here because you woke up and realized you can do better than Forest."

Skye opens her mouth to reply to Holden. Stops just in time to shoot him a serene smile. "How's work?"

"Good." He turns his sketchbook to her. "Kicks ass, huh?"

Her eyes meet mine. They ask for something, but I don't know what it is. "Subtle."

Holden turns the sketchbook to me. Shows off a traditional pinup. With Skye's thick makeup, dark hair, curvy frame.

Fuck, she's even wearing one of Skye's outfits. Only her cropped black cardigan—the one with tombstones embroidered on the Peter Pan collar—is unbuttoned. It's falling off her shoulders. Showing off her round tits.

The drawing's.

Not Skye's.

Not that—fuck, if anything, Skye's tits are bigger. Not that I'm looking.

All right, I'm looking now. But only because Holden put the idea in my head.

She's *wearing* that dress. A tight black thing with corset lacing. The neckline is low. And the lacing is tied in a bow right between her tits.

It begs for my hands.

The skirt is short. Some gauzy fabric that blows in the breeze. It shows off her lush thighs.

God, I need those thighs against my cheeks.

Shit.

I close my eyes. Will my cock to cool it.

Not that he listens to me.

Lakers lineup. Clippers line up. Skye's dad shaking his head *are you sure about Forest being your boyfriend?*

It's enough I catch my breath.

"Fuck, I think he's hard already." Holden winks at Skye. "You two gonna consummate your relationship here? I'll find my camera."

"Oh, Holden, you know I only invite quiet guys to watch." She blows him a kiss.

He mimes catching it. Pressing it to his crotch. "You can keep your lust for me a secret. I won't tell my brother."

"Tragically, I don't have time." She gives me a quick once-over. "I'm here for a reason."

"How about I buy you a tea?" I ask.

Her tongue slides over her wine lips.

Fuck, her lips look soft.

Kissable.

Which is ridiculous. I don't kiss anyone. I haven't.

But it's not leaving my head.

Skye is Skye. She always dresses in something black and sexy. She always wears her makeup dark. Always paints her lips some shade between wine and raspberry.

And those lace-up boots—

It flits through my head, an image of her in nothing but the boots.

Her legs hooked around my waist, boots crossed over each other.

The heels—chunky black things—digging into my back.

"Seems like you have time," Holden says. "He needs to go *relieve* himself."

Shit. Either I'm obvious or Holden—

No, it's Holden being an idiot. He's always like this.

And Skye is always a curvy goddess. A goth princess. A—

Shit. Not going there.

"Matcha?" Her eyes light up. Then it's her entire face. When she loves something, she does it at a hundred percent. "The place with the Hulk on the wall?"

"You want to walk there in those shoes?" It's close to our sister shop, Inked Hearts, but it's a twenty-minute walk from here.

"How do you think I got here?" She motions to the door. *Let's go.*

"On one of those scooters, skirt blowing in the wind?" Holden winks at her.

She ignores him.

"You know I'm gonna get some coffee. That place on Ocean," Holden says.

"No, you aren't." I shoot him a stern look. One that means *stay where you are.*

He plays coy for a minute, but he does nod. "I'll stay here. Do another one of these." He flashes the pinup. "But naked."

---

THE SUN BOUNCES OFF THE NEARBY SHOP WINDOWS, THE SHINY aluminum cars, the patent leather of Skye's boots.

Those damn boots.

I want to feel the weight of them against my back.

To pin her thighs to the bed as she—

Fuck.

What's wrong with my head today? Sure, Skye is gorgeous. And sexy as hell. She's always posting ridiculously hot pics on her Instagram.

Supposedly, they're for other women. To show off clothes.

But fuck if I can remember a single piece of attire.

The pics show off her curvy body.

The clothes are in the way. Not the focus.

There's way too much fabric—

Shit.

I try to push my thoughts to less dirty place. They refuse.

It's weird. I don't usually struggle to draw a firm line between friends and lovers. Yeah, I picture Skye naked from time to time. Think about her when I fuck myself even. But that's all it is. Me noticing a hot chick.

She's an attractive woman.

I'm a red-blooded man.

Who hasn't fucked anyone in the better part of two years.

Maybe that's it. Maybe I need to get laid. Maybe that's what will make it possible to look at Skye without picturing her naked.

Her eyes flit to me. She slips on her cat-eye sunglasses. Turns to Inked Love. Watches Holden spy. "You have to admire the balls."

"Do I?"

Her laugh is soft. Light. "If it was his ex, he would have told her to go fuck herself, then sent her a picture of him fucking another woman."

Probably, yeah. "Is that your plan?"

Her cheeks flush.

I think. With the makeup she wears, it's hard to tell. Not that I'm complaining.

The loud makeup, the blunt haircut, the black dresses—that's Skye. It suits her. It is her. It's impossible to imagine anything else.

"I don't know." She moves forward. So she's in front of the

boutique next door. And out of Holden's eye line. "Do you have pictures with anyone who could pass as me?"

"I've never been into pictures."

Her teeth sink into her lip. "Never?"

I shake my head.

"Too bad. That only leaves my plan."

"Skye—"

"Seriously, Forest. Don't tell me I did my makeup for nothing."

"You posted a selfie on Instagram."

"So?"

"You did your makeup for that."

She clears her throat. "You know what I mean."

"You do your makeup first thing in the morning."

"Sometimes."

I raise a brow.

She nods *it's true*.

Maybe, but I need to look her in the eyes. I reach for her sunglasses. Peel them off her face. "I can't talk to you like this."

She shudders as my fingers skim her temples. "I, uh…" Her eyes meet mine. "So… uh…"

"It looks good. Your makeup."

"I know."

"Your dress too."

"Are you going to spend the afternoon telling me things I know?" Her lips curl into a half-smile.

It warms me everywhere.

Right now, this seems like a good idea.

Whatever it takes to keep her smiling.

To protect her.

Help her.

"You're sure you're going to convince me," I say.

She nods. "I am."

"How?"

"It's simple." She pulls out her cell. Opens the camera app. "We take a few pictures. Post them on social media." She rests her head on my shoulder. Smiles at the camera. "When she gets jealous, you'll know I'm right."

Sure, there's a part of me that wants to make Mack jealous. That wants to make her beg for forgiveness. But it's not a part I like. Hell, it's a part I hate. "Skye—"

"You don't want her jealous? Really?"

"No."

"What do you want?"

"To protect you."

Her expression softens. "Be more selfish."

"I'll try."

She laughs. "Thanks." She motions to the camera *let's go*. "Just try it. You'll like it. I promise."

"I'll like it."

"Yeah."

"And you?" I ask.

"Will also like it." Her fingers brush my navy t-shirt. "Or we could go all in. Take this off. I unbutton your jeans. We imply we're fucking in the Inked Love bathroom."

"Get arrested and spend the summer in jail?"

She shakes her head. "There's no red lipstick in jail."

I can't help but laugh. "Is that really red?" *It's perfect on you. I want to taste it. Feel it on my neck, stomach, cock.*

"I think it's called Wine and Dandy."

*You taste like wine, princess?* My balls tighten at the thought of her soft lips. Which is another reason why this is a terrible idea.

I already want to tear her clothes off.

If we—

I can't even think about kissing her. About kissing anyone. It's out of the question.

"Do I need to reapply?" She glances at the screen. Blows her reflection a kiss.

"It's perfect."

She rests her head on my shoulder. "You ready?"

"I don't remember agreeing to this."

"You won't take a picture with me?"

"You know what you're doing."

"Trust me. You'll want to do it when she reacts."

"Skye—"

"Please. Give me an hour. That's it."

"Is this really what you want?"

She nods, the picture of confidence, and motions to the camera. *Right now.* "One hour. That's it. If you're still against it—"

"You'll keep asking?"

"We'll call it off." Her brow furrows with concentration. "And I'll… start fake dating Holden or something."

"No—"

"If you aren't going to be the one to help me, then—"

"Skye, seriously."

She motions to the camera. "Come on. You're going to drain my battery."

There's no way I'm letting her fake date Holden.

"Forest."

Shit. I'll give her an hour. That's fair.

Skye is headstrong. If she really wants a fake boyfriend, she's going to do it.

I need to take the position or find a suitable replacement.

Not fucking Holden.

My little brother holding Skye, touching her, kissing her—

No way.

No one is holding her, touching her, kissing her.

Only someone is. She's doing this, with or without me.

She moves closer.

Presses her body against mine. Wraps her arm around my waist.

Our reflections stare back.

She's perfect—comfortable, gorgeous, sexy.

I'm… not.

*Click.*

She snaps a picture. Studies it. "This isn't the spot." She slides her cell into her purse. Motions to Inked Hearts. Then in the direction of the beach. "Which is more annoying? Holden or beach crowds?"

"That's a tough call."

She laughs *right*. "How about this?" She motions to the coffee shop across the street. "We sit next to each other. Post something about the cold brew we're sharing. How it's our routine."

"Yeah…"

"You don't like it?"

"What are you trying to do?" I ask.

"Convince you."

I swallow hard. Fuck, my heart is still beating so fast. It's ridiculous. I'm not Gloria Gaynor. I don't know how to love again. I'm not going after Skye.

She deserves someone who can love her with every ounce of his heart.

Yeah, I think love is a bad idea. I tell her that. But if she disagrees, I'm not going to stand in her way.

Only the thought of someone else kissing her—

"Okay. We'll do the coffee shop," I say.

"Good." She steps sideways, breaking our contact. "You think it's enough?"

"How much does it need to be?" I study my friend's expression. Try to figure out what she's after.

Her cousin hurt her, sure.

And there's no way Skye's avoiding this wedding. Her family will remind her she skipped it for a long time.

She needs to do something to protect herself.

But there's something in her voice.

It's more than that.

"It needs to be enough she believes it." She moves toward the light. "Enough that she regrets what she did."

"Cheating?"

"Tossing you aside. Breaking my trust—"

"Your what?"

"Nothing. It's… all that usual shit. About how I'm not hot enough for a boyfriend."

"You don't believe that." It's ridiculous. I believe Skye when she says the goth princess thing scares off guys. But she's still a curvy goddess.

Fuck, I need to tear off that dress. Drop to my knees. Peel her panties to her ankles.

Do they match that lacy bra she posted?

I need to know.

"Forest?" The walk sign flashes. She moves into the crosswalk. "You think of something?"

My fingers curl into fists. She's right. Mack shouldn't get away with that shit. With constantly implying that Skye is lesser because she's not as small as Mack is.

I wish I could say that Mack isn't attractive, but she is. She's gorgeous. And her body is—was—appealing in a different way.

But so is Skye's.

Women are beautiful. I've never struggled with wanting the physical parts of a relationship.

With wanting a naked woman under me.

It's the rest of it—the intimacy, the connection, the vulnerability—that makes me nauseous.

"Will this make you happy?" I ask.

"I'm doing it."

"But will it?"

"It will satisfy me." Her gaze flits to the clean concrete as we step onto the sidewalk. It's strange how nice everything around here is.

Every shop on this block is clean, white, bright. Sure, Inked Love has the bright pink string lights, the red frames, the big black letters.

But it's still trendy, modern, sleek. Like a tattoo shop designed by Apple.

We stay quiet as we move into the clean coffee shop, order drinks, fix them, meet at the table.

She motions to the seat facing the window. "It's the best light."

If anyone knows, it's her. "Is that your secret?"

"Part of it." She pulls up her Instagram. Motions to her hundreds of thousands of followers. "You think this is easy?"

With her tits out like that, yeah. Any guy who stumbled across her page would follow.

Fuck, it's right there. The picture with the black bra.

She's lying on her bed, black satin falling off her shoulders, black bra struggling to cover her tits.

She tagged some lingerie company, but fuck if that matters.

The picture screams *I'm Skye Kim and I have perfect tits*.

How many guys fucked themselves to this?

If it wasn't Skye—

"Sit already." She taps the chair.

I should be thinking about her naked. It's what we're trying to sell.

It's not like it's a stretch.

Skye clears her throat.

I sit.

She slides onto my lap.

Fuck, she's warm. We're close all the time. But not like this.

Nobody has been here in so fucking long.

My heartbeat picks up. My throat quivers. My head spins.

The last time I had a woman in my lap—

A million things fill my head. Mack's long red hair. Her soft smile. The groan she made as Diego thrust into her.

Skye's soft thighs.

Her wine lips.

Her short hair.

"You ready?" She hooks her arm around my neck. Holds out her cell, camera pointed to us.

We appear on screen.

She's exactly where she's supposed to be.

I'm hopelessly out of place.

I turn toward her. Stare into her eyes.

Fuck, they're such a perfect shade of blue.

Like the fucking sky. Her parents say it's a coincidence, that her eyes were dark when she was a baby, but I don't buy it.

"Tell me if it's too much." Her voice is soft. Giving. She gets that I'm a mess. That I can't handle any kind of intimacy.

I wish I could. That things were different. That I could be everything she needs.

But I'm not. Things aren't different. There's no point in wishing.

I nod *okay*.

She slips her hand into my hair.

I press my palm between her shoulder blades.

Her lips part with a sigh. I know that sigh. It means *I need you inside me*.

Is it real? Or pretend?

No, it doesn't matter. Either way, I can't have her.

*Click*.

She leans in. Presses her lips to my cheek.

*Click*.

Her fingers dig into my hair. She tugs a little harder. Turns her head so her neck brushes my lips.

*Click*.

It's a second, fast, but I still taste her skin. Roses. Honey. Something all Skye.

She sighs as she slides out of my lap. Motions to the last picture. "You think?"

It's perfect. Her hair is falling over her eyes. Her lips are parting with a groan. Her fingers are digging into my hair.

It looks like we're fucking.

There's no mistaking this for a friendly chat at a coffee shop.

There's no platonic here.

This is a commitment. "It's a lot."

"I know."

"Hard to dial back."

She nods. "Is it okay?"

"Yeah." There's no getting out of my lie to Mack. We might as well sell the hell out of it. Even if I'm going to find her a replacement boyfriend. Someone she can leave me for.

Another woman leaving me for someone else.

It's fake this time, but it still hurts thinking of Skye in some other guy's lap.

Laughing at some other guy's jokes.

Groaning over some other guy's touch.

I can't stand it.

I don't want anyone touching her.

I sure as fuck don't want anyone kissing her.

But what choice do I have? Either I do this with her. Or I let her find someone else.

## Chapter Eight

SKYE

Mmm.

Matcha and macadamia milk.

Is there anything better?

For one beautiful moment, my world is green tea and sunshine.

Then Forest's hand brushes my knee and everything comes into focus.

I jerk up. Try to play it off as a desperate need for another sip.

Mmm. Sweet, rich perfection. Maybe I do desperately need another sip. Maybe my latte can actually erase all the ugly shit in my head.

"You should post that." Forest's gaze shifts to my lips. He watches as I take another sip. Watches my lipstick mark the lid.

It's not like he's thinking about my lipstick marking his neck. Or his stomach. Or his cock.

Not like I'd ever think that.

That would be…

Ahem.

"Only the audio. With a picture of my hand on your thigh." His gaze shifts to the hem of my skirt.

It falls to mid-thigh. Shows plenty of leg. Plenty of… flesh, I guess.

I'm lucky to have an hourglass figure. A very full hourglass figure. I have big boobs, yeah, but I also have round hips and thick thighs.

I love my body, I do, but I understand how other people see it. Especially in Southern California. Curvy isn't always meant as a compliment.

"Skye?" Forest's jean-clad leg presses against my bare thigh.

My skin buzzes from the contact. "Yeah?"

"Is that what you're going for?"

"This shop is loud." I motion to the line of people. "It will be obvious it's something else."

"Or sound like public sex."

"You're okay with that?"

He runs his hand through his dark hair. "You're really set on this? With or without me?"

No. Maybe. I don't know. I want her jealous, but nothing will make her jealous like Forest will.

And it will protect both of us.

How is she going to accuse him of being unable to move on? Or suggest I'm too fat for a boyfriend? Or say something snide about how guys love Asian chicks but only skinny ones?

Sadly, Mackenzie's claims are usually true.

I can't even call her a bitch for pointing it out. Lots of guys think I'm too big. Plenty of people comment shit about how Asian women are supposed to be skinny on my blog. Or something about how my white parent must be fat. Or how mixed girls are ugly.

I guess just as many talk about how mixed girls or hot. Or how bigger girls are hot. But, somehow, that's just as bad.

Like I'm an object that only exists for their dick.

Not that I—

I mean, I'm not exactly a slut, but I do enjoy said body part. In the context of a happy relationship. I've been in two. Neither was mind-blowing, but they were nice enough.

I never fell in love.

Never wanted everything in their heart.

Not like with Forest.

"Doesn't your dad follow you?" Forest asks.

"On Facebook."

"He sees this?" He taps his cell a few times. Brandishes an image from my Instagram.

I'm kneeling on the sand in a retro black bikini, my hands in my hair, my gaze faraway.

"What about it?" Sure, it's a bikini. That's what people wear at the beach. I have my insecurities, yes, but I don't let them get in my way.

"Your tits are spilling from that thing."

"So?"

"So, that's your dad."

"He doesn't have an Instagram, okay." I take another sip. Let out another sigh. "And I don't cross post on Facebook."

"'Cause you don't want him seeing it."

"No…" Of course. Who wants their parents' comments on their body?

My parents mean well. They say all the right things. It's just it's so obvious they're trying to say the right things. *You look wonderful, honey. I appreciate your bold style and your confidence. Your body is yours and we're proud of it no matter what. We're proud of you no matter what.*

I swear, they must have taken some seminar. *How to instill confidence in your chubby daughter.*

"Shit." Forest's eyes go wide.

"Don't tell me my parents are on there."

"No. This." He taps the screen a few times. Turns his cell to me.

*Mackenzie Davis: Hot! I'm surprised you're so bold in public. XOXO*

"So…" It is hot. And my pictures are always hot. And she's a heinous bitch for that snide commentary. I know what it means. It means *wow, how did you manage to convince someone as hot as Forest to appear in public with a troll like you?*

"She is jealous."

"Yeah."

"Does it feel good?" he asks.

It does. Victorious. But more than that too. Like I'm protecting him. Like he really is mine. "What about the comment?" I tap the rest of her comment.

He chuckles. "She was into the public sex thing, but I wouldn't do it."

"Really?"

"Yeah." His cheeks flush.

"Oh." A beautiful mental image flits through my head. Forest dragging me to the bathroom, pinning me to the wall, pulling my dress to my waist—

"I've done it since."

"Oh." It's so hot in here.

"It can be fun. But I don't get off on it."

"Oh."

"You okay?"

"Oh." Is that three? Four? A thousand? There aren't enough *ohs* for this conversation.

"You ever?"

"Did I ever—"

He motions to the bathroom. "In public?"

"Um, only second base."

"Second base?"

"I was in high school." And, I, uh… "There was a time at a party. But we were in a different room."

"And you—"

"No comment."

"You fucked a guy with your friends in the next room?"

"No, I…" I trip over my tongue. I want him to think I'm as cool and carefree about sex as he is. "It was more… hand stuff."

He chuckles. "Hand stuff?"

"What?" My cheeks flush.

"It's so rare you're shy."

"You have one disgusting pervert in your life."

He raises a brow.

"Holden."

"Oh." His chuckle gets louder. "True." He shakes his head with understanding. There's something he's not saying.

Something about how he's an even bigger pervert. How he wants to do truly filthy things to me.

Uh…

That's…

Yeah…

That's totally what he's thinking. Totally.

"Fuck." He pulls up his social media. Which is ninety percent tattoos. Or maybe ninety-nine percent. "You remember that time your date got sick the night before your friend's wedding?"

"Of course." I try to focus on my matcha, but my eyes stay on his hands. What the hell is he doing?

"I took you."

"You rented a tux and everything."

"Yeah." He chuckles. "I looked ridiculous."

A little. But he also looked super hot. Fuck, Forest in a suit. If we do this, he's going to wear a suit to the wedding. I get to put my hands all over that suit. "You looked good."

"We danced together all night," he says.

"Well, yeah. Holden tricked the DJ into playing your music," I say.

Forest's smile gets nostalgic. "A bunch of people snapped pics. When Mack saw them, she got pissed. Demanded details about what we did after. Exactly where we went, when I got home, what I did when I was there."

"What you did?"

"Yeah. She wanted to know if I thought of you. If I showered before I fucked myself."

"She did not." Sure, Mackenzie is the jealous type. But she never thought I was a rival. She never thought Forest actually wanted me.

"She kept going on and on about how she knew I was thinking about you."

I shake my head.

He nods *she did*. "She thought there was something between us. I guess... you think she was already fucking him?" His smile disappears.

"I don't know. She... she didn't tell me. If I'd known—"

"I know."

I swallow hard. "You saved me that night."

"It was nothing."

"It was a lot. And fun."

He nods *true*.

"This will be the same. Bigger, yeah. But the same idea." I try to look him in the eyes without blushing. "We'll kiss a little, hug a little, hold hands. But it doesn't have to be more than that. It doesn't have to be weird."

"I haven't kissed anyone in two years."

"Oh."

"I don't know if I—"

"We don't have to do that. It can be something else. As long as we seem intimate."

His eyes fill with vulnerability. "You're really doing this? With or without me?"

I cross my fingers behind my back. "I am."

"Who will you get? If it's not me?"

"You're my first choice."

"If it's not?"

"I don't know. Maybe Holden. Or Oliver."

His brow furrows. "You're sure?"

I uncross my fingers. "I am."

He holds my gaze for a moment, turning over my words. "Okay, I'll do it. But no more unilateral shit."

"It was your—"

"I know. From now on, we decide a story together. Plan together. Figure this out together."

I offer my hand. "Deal."

"Promise I won't regret this."

"I promise."

He looks at me like he doesn't believe me, but he shakes anyway.

## Chapter Nine

SKYE

We spend a few minutes picking out a photo.

The two of us staring at each other like we're madly in love. It's pure sweetness.

And it's clearly us.

Forest's chest piece—the shattered glass heart—is peeking out from his t-shirt.

His chin, mouth, nose, eyes, hair—his entire face is in the shot.

Mine too.

We look good together. The same dark hair, but his eyes are dark and deep, like a rich cup of coffee.

Mine are a vibrant blue.

Same light skin—I have more of my mom's pale complexion than my dad's tan coloring.

I'm in all black, wearing my makeup like a badge of honor.

He's in a charcoal t-shirt, wearing his tattooed arms like they're the only accessory he needs.

He holds his hand over the *post* button. Looks to me for approval.

I nod. "Do it."

He types a caption. Tags me. And her.

*Celebrating our invitation to the wedding of the century. Love it when family brings us together.*

"Oh my God." A laugh breaks up the tension in my shoulders. "You're an evil genius."

"I know."

"I think I love you."

He swallows hard.

"I only mean—"

"I know."

"You're going to be a great fake boyfriend."

"I sure as hell hope so." He taps the button. *Woosh*. The picture appears on his feed.

Her like appears instantly.

Then a comment. *I always knew you'd be perfect together.*

She knows.

She buys it.

She's jealous.

This is happening.

He's mine. For the next five weeks, he's mine.

## Chapter Ten

SKYE

It's right there. Parked in front of my parents' house.

Red Camry. *You got passed by a girl* bumper sticker. Hello Kitty air freshener.

Mackenzie's car.

My heinous cousin. Who stole my crush. Who acted like she did me a favor stealing my crush.

Who still holds everything—her size, her hair, her one hundred percent white features, her relationship status, her employment status—over my head.

Who tore Forest's heart from his chest and tossed it aside like it was nothing.

He follows my gaze. Stops dead in his tracks. "Did you talk to her…?"

"No." It's only been a few hours since we posted. Since she commented. (Okay, yes, I had a second matcha after the first. Then we grabbed dinner at the organic juice place. It's expensive, but the kale salads are amazing).

"She…" He rubs the space between my thumb and forefinger with his thumb.

"I…" I can't pull my hand away. That feels too good. I don't care that he's seeking comfort for the hurt his ex caused. I don't care that he's thinking of her. I only care that he's touching me.

"That's her mom's car." He motions to the red SUV in the driveway. In my mom's spot.

Of course, Mom moved the car for her heinous sister.

I motion to Forest's house. "They're going to see us."

He nods *right*, leads me to the front door, whisks me inside.

His posture stiffens. His jaw cricks. His shoulders rise to his ears.

I'm already losing him.

Fuck, this sucks. But I'm not dwelling.

This is a time for action.

I pull out my cell. Text Mom.

*Skye: Is Aunt Danielle visiting?*

*Mom: We're at dinner.*

*Skye: You didn't invite me?*

*Mom: We called three times.*

Oh, there are some missed calls here. But... well, my parents call all the time. They're involved. I can't pick up every time they want to ask if I'd rather have pork or beef for dinner.

*Mom: We're finishing up. Danielle wants to go to that wine bar in Marina Del Rey.*

She refers to her sister by her first name. Of course. She's not going to call her sister Mrs. Davis.

*Mom: Your cousin is here. And her fiancé. She's talking about your boyfriend. About Forest being your boyfriend.*

*Skye: Oh.*

*Mom: When did you two make it official?*

*Skye: Recently.*

*Mom: Hmm. Well, we can talk about why you felt the need to hide that later.*

God, kill me know. Mom loves talking about feelings and consequences and the way the world views women.

*Mom: You don't have to come, but I hope you do. You only get one family, Skye.*

Of course, they're going to Mrs. Davis's favorite wine bar. She loves her wine. And loves insisting everyone do things her way.

No wonder Mom's car is missing. They probably carpooled. She's probably smiling at Mackenzie right now, gushing over her massive engagement ring, sighing *if only my daughter was engaged. Employed. Normal.*

She doesn't say it. She says everything right. But I know it's in the back of her head. She was so happy that summer Mackenzie stayed with us.

"They're having dinner." I wrap my fingers around my cell. "We're invited."

"We're invited?"

"Yeah." I bite my lip. "I guess Mackenzie shared our relationship status."

"Fuck, that was fast."

"Yeah." Almost like she knows we're full of it. Like she's testing us. No. That's ridiculous. How could she possibly know? "Maybe…" I suck a deep breath through my teeth. We're doing this. It's happening. No second-guessing. "We should make it official."

"Official?"

"On social media."

He rolls his shoulders. "They're at your place?"

"A restaurant." I set my cell on the dining table so I won't reply *fuck Mackenzie*. "They're going to a wine bar."

His brow furrows with frustration. "Her mom is there?"

"Yeah." Neither of us has to say it. Mackenzie's mom is a high-functioning alcoholic. She's not interested in help. And you can't help people who don't want help.

"You want to go?"

"Shouldn't we?" I'd rather have a week of practice, but we need to start this eventually.

His eyes meet mine. He stares, looking for something. Finding it, I guess. He nods *yeah*. "We need a story."

I nod.

"How long have we been dating?"

"A few months," I say.

"Why haven't we said anything?"

"It's new. We don't want to mess it up."

He arches a brow *really*.

"Yeah, really."

"Your entire life is on social media."

"No. My style is on social media. There's more to life than clothes."

"Makeup and hair, yeah." His lips curl into a smile.

He's teasing me. God, it feels good. It's rare for him.

Sure, we're close, but he's kinda… stoic. His smile, his laugh, his teasing words—

They're everything.

"When have I ever mentioned a relationship on social media?" I ask.

"I've seen your Instagram, Skye. You have your tits out in every other picture."

My cheeks flush. "I do not."

He pulls out his cell. Shows off a photo from my page. A bralette I was sent a few weeks ago.

"I'm advertising the company." I motion to the tag at the bottom of the page. "It's for my followers."

"Well, yeah—"

"My female followers."

He looks at me like I'm crazy. "Fuck, Skye, I can't even say it's for a guy. 'Cause what guy is there?"

"Trust me," a bouncy voice interrupts us. "There are plenty of guys enjoying those pictures." Holden appears in the upstairs hallway. He lets out an over-the-top groan as he pretends to wrap his hand around his cock. "I know I did."

"If I believed you, I'd…" I don't know what I'd do actually. Much like Forest, I've learned to tune out Holden. The kid lives to cause trouble. Reacting is what he wants. Only… well, I'm a lot less cool and collected than Forest.

"Take me to your room and punish me?" Holden winks as he rushes down the stairs.

"How did you hear us?" Forest shoots me a *God, why is he here* look.

It's a good question. Why is he here? He has his own apartment elsewhere.

Their dad is out of town.

Ariel moved in with Chase a few weeks ago.

All right, I'm answering my own question. Why would Holden stay in his tiny studio apartment when he could crash at his dad's massive four-bedroom pad?

The TV is huge. The liquor cabinet is stocked. The basketball court in the backyard—

Well, I don't get sports, but Forest and Holden play all the time.

"Have you been waiting for us?" Forest shoots his brother a cutting look.

"You should drop to your knees and beg for my help," Holden says.

"Interesting fantasy you have there," I say.

Holden smiles, not at all bothered. "Oh, baby, you know I'm thinking of you when I say that."

"Oh yeah?" I challenge.

He nods *hell yeah*. "Whatever you're into, Skye. If you want to tie me up and spank me…" He raises a brow *I know you do*.

I clear my throat.

Holden is hot. Incredibly hot. Long limbs. Lean muscle. Colorful tattoos.

Devil-may-care attitude.

He even has Forest's nose.

But that only turns up the light on the neon sign flashing in my head:

*Holden isn't Forest.*

I wish my heart wanted someone other than Forest. It would make my life a lot easier.

But it doesn't.

It's Forest or bust.

"If you want to drop to your knees and beg…" Holden crosses the room to me. "We can take some great pics. No one will know it's not you and Forest." He winks.

"What about your new ink?" My eyes flit to the spot of said ink. He has a fresh tattoo right above his dick.

Okay, it's a little above that. But it's certainly in a noticeable location.

Not that I—

Oh God, why am I fanning the flames?

"You noticed?" He runs a hand through his wavy hair, suddenly coquettish. "I was hoping you would."

"What do you want?" Forest asks.

"Can't congratulate my two favorite people on their fake relationship?" he asks.

"We, uh…" Okay, I'm not selling this. Not to him. "Thank you, Holden. Really. I appreciate it. And I will think of your new tattoo when I touch myself later." I make a show of winking. "Don't tell Forest."

"Baby, I know." He blows me a kiss. "Think of yours all the time." He motions to the tattoo on my ribs. The one Forest did.

A lyric from the song Celine plays for Jesse at the end of *Before Sunset*. With the sunset in the background. It's watercolor—a style Forest hates—but he still did it for me. He did it perfectly.

Not that anyone can see it at the moment.

Holden continues, not at all bothered, "That picture on your Insta… mmm, lost track of how many times—"

"We appreciate the thought, Holden." Forest's voice gets gruff. "But we're busy."

"You're gonna try to sell this?" he asks.

I clear my throat.

Forest does too.

Holden just laughs. "All right, sure. Go. Convince them you're happy. And asexual. Nothing wrong with that. Aces deserve love too."

"We're not…" I clear my throat. "We look very—"

"Yeah, you look good together. But you'd look good with anyone Skye." Holden winks at me. He looks back to his brother. Blows him a kiss.

Forest rolls his eyes. "Do you have a point?"

"Yeah, actually," Holden says.

"That's novel," Forest says.

"Love you too." Holden turns to me. "I can see you're the smart one. So I'll talk to you. You're prettier too, so that's win-win."

"Gee, thanks," I say.

He nods *sure thing*. "You two make the worst fake couple I've ever seen."

Ahem.

"If you want to sell this, you need to sell the fuck out of it." He motions *come here* to his brother. "Go ahead. Kiss her. Convince me you're in love with her."

Forest stammers. "I…" He fights a blush. "I'm not… I…"

"If you can't convince me, you can't convince her." He stares into his brother's eyes. "So do it. Come here. Kiss Skye. Convince me you're in love with her."

## Chapter Eleven

SKYE

Yes.

Hell yes.

A million times yes.

My tongue slides over my lips.

My fingers curl into my thighs.

My breath hitches in my throat.

Forest's expression softens for a split second. Then his eyes fill with frustration. His lip corners turn down.

It's not about me.

It's him.

I repeat the words to myself like a mantra, but they refuse to stick.

I don't care about the logic. Or his perfectly reasonable boundaries. Or his somewhat less reasonable intimacy issues.

Only that he doesn't want to kiss me.

"Excuse me." I cut through the brothers. Go straight to the fridge. Ginger liqueur. Vodka. Ice. Club soda. Lime.

"Gotta drink your way through it, huh?" Holden chuckles. "It's not too late to kick Forest to the curb. Take me instead."

"Uh-huh." I bring my glass to my lips. Take a long sip. "You want one?"

"Sure." Holden smiles. "Fix one for Romeo over here too. Fuck knows he needs to loosen up."

"I'm fine." Forest's voice stays firm.

"You sure?" I hold up my Moscow Mule. "It's good." Sweet, spicy ginger. The sharp bite of alcohol. The tart kick of lime.

He shakes his head *no thanks*. "Someone has to drive."

I fix one for Holden. Leave it on the counter.

He takes a step toward me. "You gonna do this, Romeo?"

Forest's eyes flit from me to his brother. "After you leave."

"If you can't do it in front of me—"

"No, I—" Forest shifts his weight between his feet. "Are you going to stand there?"

"No." Holden crosses the room to the counter. Picks up his drink. Takes a long swig.

Forest clears his throat. "I don't know—"

I swallow hard. "We don't have to—"

"Yeah, you do. You're twenty-eight, not fifteen," Holden says.

"I don't know if I want to fake that." Forest slides his hand into his front pocket. "It's too much."

Holden looks to me. Raises a brow. *You believe this?*

"Yeah." It's sweet, actually.

"All right." Holden rolls his eyes *whatever*. "Come here, Skye."

"What?" My cheeks flush. I'm already here. We're both at the counter. He's two feet away.

"Gonna show my brother how it's done," Holden says.

"You're going to kiss her?" Forest asks.

"No shit, Sherlock." Holden's eyes meet mine. The playfulness fades into pure desire. He stares at me like he's about to pin me to the wall. Motions *come closer*. "Unless you want to lead."

Forest's fingers curl into fists. "She doesn't want to kiss you." Frustration drips into his voice.

Anger.

Envy even.

He's all stiff. He's staring at his brother the way he looks at pictures of Diego and Mackenzie.

## The Best Friend Bargain

He's jealous I'm kissing Holden.

It makes no sense.

He doesn't want me.

He can't bring himself to kiss me.

How can he be jealous I'm kissing someone else?

I nod *okay* to Holden. "I have high standards."

"Oh? Your ex was good with his mouth?"

"Yeah." I force a smile.

Forest's jaw cricks.

Holden's eyes flit from me to his brother, then back to me. He nods *you see this too?*

I shrug like I don't.

He nods *okay, sure*. "Just kissing? Or eating you out too?"

My cheeks flush. Then my chest. I'm hot everywhere. Nervous.

I barely remember my last boyfriend. It was a million years ago. College. A desperate attempt to get over Forest. An attempt that failed miserably.

But I did…

He did…

Ahem.

"You seem like a woman who knows what she wants." Holden wraps his arms around my waist. Pulls me closer. "You demand what you want?"

"I…"

"If you were my girl, would you climb onto my lap and demand to come on my face?" Holden asks.

Forest's eyes fill with envy.

Holden's expression gets knowing.

He cups the back of my head. Looks down at me like I'm everything he wants. "I ever tell you how much I want to fuck you?"

"Once or twice." I swallow hard.

He leans down. Presses his lips to mine.

My eyes close. My hands go to his hair.

His technique is fine.

He even tastes good—like ginger and vodka.

But it's weird kissing Holden.

Wrong.

Awkward.

I play my part. I tug at his t-shirt. Moan against his lips.

He groans back.

He groans loud enough to wake the neighbors.

Then he releases me.

I step backward. Turn to my fake boyfriend.

He's glaring like his brother is the scum of the Earth. Like he can't stand that Holden touched me. Like he'll kill anyone who touches me.

"That's a start." Holden nods to Forest's expression.

Forest looks down at his fists like he's not sure why they're curled. His eyes move over the room. Over me. "I—" He takes a step toward me. "How about this?"

He closes the distance between us.

One hand goes to my cheek.

The other goes to my waist.

He leans in closer. Turns so his lips brush my neck.

He runs his fingers through my hair. "Does it look real?" He drags his lips up my neck. Along my ear.

He's just barely touching me.

But, God, that hint of pressure—

My entire body buzzes.

He…

I…

This…

"Yeah." I barely push the words out.

"You two gonna fuck right here?" Holden asks.

"What do you think?" Forest's voice gets louder. More confident. He presses his palm into my lower back.

"I…"

His fingers brush my skirt. "You dress like a goth princess."

My blush deepens. "You say that—"

He pulls back enough to look me in the eyes. "I ever tell you how much I like it, princess?"

I shake my head. "No."

"I do." His eyes meet mine. "You're beautiful."

I swallow hard.

"Those pics on your Instagram drive me crazy." His voice is smooth. Like he means it.

Does he mean it?

Is he making this work by telling the truth?

Or is he a better liar than I think?

"I know they aren't for me. But I want them anyway," he says.

I stare up at him. His dark eyes are so deep, so full of hurt, so beautiful.

My eyelids press together.

"I want to strip you to nothing and fuck you senseless." He leans closer.

But he doesn't kiss me. Not on the lips.

He brings his mouth to my neck again. Pulls my body into his.

He holds me close for a moment, then he releases me.

"Damn, Forest, you're a fast learner," Holden says. "Think I should fuck Skye while you watch. So you can get the hang of that."

Forest rolls his eyes, suddenly without jealousy. "Are you trying to get a black eye?"

"Do it. I'll look tough. You'll cancel your appointments. I'll take those sloppy seconds." He blows me a kiss. "And these too."

"I'm not going to do it. But if you keep starting shit, someone is." Forest shakes his head. "You're gonna end up dead. Or in jail. You want a repeat of senior year?"

Holden's playful expression drops for a second. He shrugs it off. "I want to see Skye naked." He winks at me. "However she wants to show me."

"Goodbye, Holden," I say.

"You're leaving?" Holden takes in our attire. "In those outfits?"

"Yeah." I smooth my dress. It's fine. Appropriate enough.

"No, no, no. Skye, you're a goddess." He lays on the charm. "You look perfect. But my brother over here—" He shakes his head *I don't think so*. "At least put on a clean shirt."

Forest nods *fair enough*. He moves up the stairs, down the hall, into his room.

Holden waits until his brother is out of earshot. "It's a bold play, Skye."

"What?"

"What?" He copies my tone. Then my posture. Shrugs like he has no idea what I mean.

"Yeah?"

"You sticking with the coy shit?" he asks.

I clear my throat.

"He might not realize you're into him. But everyone else does."

"It's not your—"

"He's my brother."

"And you care?"

"Got money on it." He smiles, unfazed.

"You have money on…"

"Can't tell you. It won't be a fair bet." His eyes flit to the stairs. "He's into you too."

"He's in love with her," I say.

"He's not over her, sure. Doesn't mean he's in love with her." Holden raises a brow. "Don't get me wrong. I think you should ditch the loser. Get over him the fun way." He motions to his bedroom.

"With you?" I ask.

" You don't like me. No risk of catching feelings."

It's a good point, actually. He's full of shit, but it's a good point.

"If you come to your senses, let me know." He looks to the stairs as Forest reappears in slacks and a button-up shirt. "If you don't… good luck."

"Thanks."

"But I'll be here if you get your heart broken." He winks. Turns to Forest. "If you ever need an easy fuck, I've got you covered, Skye."

Forest's fingers curl into fists. He doesn't notice it. But Holden does.

I do.

My fake boyfriend is jealous of his brother's advances.

It's not much.

But it's something.

## Chapter Twelve

FOREST

The place is straight out of a home and garden magazine. Hardwood floors. Exposed brick walls. Happy family spread over square tables.

Mack in a short ivory dress, her red hair pulled into an elegant updo, shiny pendant hanging from her neck.

That feather turning into birds on her shoulder.

The heart on her wrist.

The one I did.

The one that now bears his name.

*Diego* in a curvy script. Right above the skeleton lock. The one that matches the key on my forearm.

Besides the fresh ink—there's something on her other shoulder, some mix of flora and fauna—she looks exactly the same.

Pretty brown eyes. Slim figure. Fire-engine red hair.

She stands. Shoots us a serene smile. "Forest." She extends her hand. "You look good."

I shake. "You too."

She turns to Skye. "You… It's been forever." She moves around the table. Offers Skye a hug.

Skye's light eyes fill with confusion. Then she blinks and presses her lips into a smile. "It has." She doesn't hug her cousin. She offers her hand.

Disappointment streaks Mack's expression, but she still shakes. She nods. Motions to the bottle of wine on the table. "It's not as sweet as a Moscow Mule, but it's not bad."

"Thanks." Skye motions to the chair across from Mack.

What the hell is she getting at?

She looks up at me. Kicks the leg of the chair. Motions *come on*.

Oh, fuck, I need my head in the game.

I need to sell this.

But my head is beating like a war drum.

My stomach is churning.

My mouth is sticky.

Mack is right there. Next to Diego.

He's dressed this time—in slacks and a polo shirt—but that doesn't keep my thoughts in line.

His hand in her red hair.

Her red nails on his back.

His name rolling off her lips.

*Yes, Diego. Harder. Harder, baby.*

Fuck, I'm going to throw up.

"Forest." Skye wraps her arm around my waist.

It soothes me. Pulls me into the moment.

This room is all different. Dimly lit, rustic, homey.

Not our bright bedroom.

There's no red comforter. No spinning fan. No stereo playing sexy pop songs.

I still can't listen to Britney Spears without—

"What do you want to drink?" Skye rests her head on my shoulder. Runs her fingers along my side.

It's over my shirt, but I still feel it everywhere.

Her touch feels so good. I need more of it. All of it.

And not the way I normally do. Not in a friendly way. Not even in a sexual way.

Something more than that.

"Whatever you're having, princess." I force the words from my throat.

"Princess, huh?" Mack raises a brow *that's unusual*.

"My goth princess." I pull Skye a little closer. But it's not for the ruse. It's because she's a life raft. Because I need her. "You look beautiful today."

She looks up at me with a warm smile. A real smile. "You told me."

"You don't want to hear it again?"

"I always want to hear it again."

I brush a stray hair behind her ear. It's funny. Her hair is usually neat—it's cut in a straight line, just below her chin—but today it's messy.

It's begging for my hands.

God, she feels so good. She's not supposed to feel this good.

"You look handsome too." Her fingers brush my button-up shirt.

I step backward. Pull out Skye's chair.

My body goes cold immediately. I miss the contact. I need it.

But I can't.

She deserves someone who can offer her everything, who can give her their heart.

Her eyes hold on mine for a moment, then she turns to her parent's table. Exchanges hellos with her dad—he's always asking me to call him David—and her mom.

Then Mr. And Mrs. Davis.

I nod my own hellos.

Skye takes a seat.

I follow her lead. Let the adults drift into the periphery.

Not that I'm a kid.

I haven't felt like a kid since Mom's diagnosis.

Fuck, I can't even remember what that feels like.

"I hear you're still looking for a job?" Mack's voice pulls me back to the room. It's pleasant, polite, empathetic even.

It's hard to imagine she really cares. That she isn't trying to rub

Skye's unemployment in her face.

Skye doesn't talk about it, but I can tell it bothers her.

I wish there were something I could do. Besides offering her the front desk gig at Inked Love.

She always turns me down.

She insists she doesn't want help. Not with employment. Not with her future.

"Yeah, I... uh..." Skye smooths her skirt. "I'm figuring it out. You?"

"Still at the gallery." Mack pulls her arm over her chest. She wraps her fingers around her upper arm, covering the watercolor butterfly.

Damn, it's nicer up close. Soft, twilight colors that bleed into each other. "That's good work."

"Thanks." Mack beams. "I designed it."

"She's being modest," Diego says. "She was working on it for weeks."

Mack shrugs like it's no big deal. But I know better. She wants people to take her seriously as an artist.

Only she's never had any success as an artist. She works at a gallery, selling other people's paintings.

Designing a tattoo—even her tattoo—that's a big step for her.

"Let's see then." Skye forces a smile. "It looks beautiful from here."

Mack actually blushes. "That isn't—"

"Come on. You can't tease us like that." There's a tinge of mocking in Skye's tone.

Mack doesn't notice it. "If you insist." She stifles a squeal as she stands. She turns to us, pulls her dress's strap toward her neck, leans closer.

Skye's eyes fix on the design.

It is beautiful. Butterflies against the twilight. Blue, purple, and pink bleed together. The watercolor sky sparkles with white stars. A solid black tree line sits beneath it.

A trendy twist on a classic.

Some would call it basic or played out, accuse Mack of being one of those girls who tries too hard to be cool.

That's Mack.

Always trying hard. Always concerned about appearances. But still beautiful, interesting, enticing.

Fuck, she looks so much like the girl I fell in love with.

That girl held me together when I was falling apart. When I didn't even know I was falling apart.

I thought she loved me. That she cared about loyalty and family and forever as much as I did.

Was I always wrong about her or did she change?

Did I change?

I don't know anymore.

"It suits you," Skye says. "It's pretty. Trendy. Delicate and bold at the same time."

Fuck, that's accurate.

Skye turns to Diego. "Do you have any tattoos? Any Mackenzie designed?"

"Well…" Mack's hazel eyes light up. Her smile gets wide. Huge. She's the same girl who loves talking about art. Who loves being the center of attention. Who shines when the spotlight is on her.

I should hate it. Find it repulsive. Roll my eyes.

But I don't.

Her smile still lights something inside me. Some piece of my heart that still belongs to her.

Mack continues, "there is one. We, uh… But, no, you don't want to see that, Forest."

"I don't?" I try to keep my voice even. Get most of the way there.

"It's intimate. I don't want to upset you with stuff you can't handle." Her smile is apologetic. Her voice is earnest. She really believes that she doesn't want to upset me.

That she isn't saying this in an attempt to hurt me.

That she isn't twisting the knife in my back.

Mack doesn't even realize what she's doing. It's hard to hate her when she's oblivious.

Not that I'm capable of hating her. I wish it were that.

It would be easy. To hate her, blame her, believe everything that happened was her fault.

That I was still capable of love.

But I'm not.

It's not.

Sure, she's the one who couldn't keep her pants on. But it means something about us. About me.

No one cheats when they're perfectly happy, madly in love, completely satisfied.

Mack clears her throat. She looks at us with that serene smile. The one that means she's exactly where she belongs. "Why don't you tell us about you? You're working at a new shop, right? Making more?"

I ignore her attempt to change the subject. "Let's see it." I don't care if the tattoo says *Diego's cock is my favorite thing in the world*. I can handle it.

"Forest." Her tone gets curt for a split second. Then she swallows a sip of wine. Shrugs it off. "Another time."

Skye looks to me. "I have one from Forest, but I can't show it off here. Not if I want to keep things PG-13."

Mack's eyes flare with jealousy. "Oh."

"Yeah. It's pretty hot too." Skye places her hand on the table. Nods *take it*.

I intertwine my fingers with hers. Turn to Skye.

It's funny. I look at my best friend all the time. But I never stare at her like this.

She's different up close.

Same bright blue eyes. Same thick brown eyelashes. Same short black hair.

Her dad's hair.

Her mom's eyes.

Her—

Fuck, I don't know where she inherited that body. Her mom is slim. Her dad is pure muscle.

But Skye is all soft curves. It's not just her perfect tits—fuck, they're unreal in that snug dress. It's her dramatic waist, her lush ass, her full thighs.

"Hey." She looks up at me, her bright eyes full of affection. "You look handsome today."

I don't know if she's faking it or not. I stare back anyway. Release her hand. Bring my palm to her cheek. "You look gorgeous."

Her eyelids flutter together. She leans into my touch. Let's out a soft sigh. "It's just—"

"You wore that dress to drive me insane, didn't you?"

Her chest heaves with her inhale. "Maybe."

"It's working."

Her lips part with a sigh. "Working how?"

"I want to undo this." My fingers brush the corset lacing. The bow. "See what you're wearing under it."

Someone clears their throat.

Mack.

It snaps me out of my trance. Or maybe into it.

Fuck, it's hard keeping this shit straight. This is pretend. I'm pretending I want Skye.

It doesn't matter that I want her.

She's my best friend. I'm not fucking that up.

Mack clears her throat. "You're very…"

"Sorry." Skye turns to the table. Lets out a coquettish giggle. "You know how it is when it's new. You can't keep your hands off each other."

"Yeah." Mack forces. "I do." She squeezes Diego's hand.

He leans in to whisper in her ear.

She nods *yeah*. Laughs.

He whispers something else.

Her laugh gets louder. Fuller. Realer.

It bounces around the entire fucking room.

My stomach twists.

My dinner threatens to make an appearance.

He makes her laugh. That's one thing I—

Skye is hilarious. I make her laugh, sometimes, but I'm not on her level.

I want to give her that pleasure. To set her at ease. To fill her with bliss.

Mack smiles wide as she turns to us. "This is weird, huh?"

Diego nods. "I should have reached out a long time ago." He offers me an apologetic look.

Mack turns to me. "Can we have a minute, baby?"

He nods. "How about we get a drink? At the bar?" His eyes meet Skye's. "I have a cousin who's into fashion. I'd love to pick your brain. Pass it on."

She shifts back in her seat. "You want to talk about fashion?" Her brow furrows with confusion. Then her eyes light up. Like she realized something.

He motions to the bar. "Yeah. I'll buy you a glass."

Her eyes flit to me. She stares at me, waiting for something. An okay. Or an excuse to say no.

I want to say *fuck no. Don't talk to him. Don't leave.*

*Stay with me. Hold me. Kiss me again.*

"Whatever you want to do, princess." I try to give her room to say no. "I'm getting tired. If we stay out any longer, I won't be able to fuck you properly."

Skye's eyes go wide. Her cheeks flame. "Oh, uh, well my parents are right there, so maybe less on the volume." She stands. Looks to Diego. "Sure, I have a minute."

"Riesling?" he asks.

She nods.

He knows her favorite drink.

Envy rises in my throat. I'm not even sure where it goes. I hate that asshole.

I guess it doesn't need explanation. The fucker slept with my girlfriend. I'm pretty sure that gives me free rein to hate him forever.

But that feels off. Like it's not enough. Like it's not the reason I don't want him talking to Skye.

Besides the cheating dickhead thing, Diego's a good guy. Handsome, smart, athletic.

A former baseball star.

A straight-A student.

He's in grad school now. Researching some breakthrough that's going to save the world.

I watch them move to the bar.

Then I turn to my ex-girlfriend.

She refills her glass of wine. Looks to her parents. They're stopping Diego and Skye. Gushing over his suit. Her dress. Some shit about school. How he's acing it.

How there's nothing he can't do.

I swallow the bile that rises in my throat. "You want another drink?"

"Thanks."

I refill her glass.

She leans a little closer. "She has a loud style, doesn't she?"

"Yeah." I don't know what Mack is getting at, but I know her tone. It's not a compliment. She can insult me if she wants, but I'm not letting her insult Skye. "Her tits look amazing in that dress."

"She does show them off." She does nothing to hide her judgment.

I shrug like I don't notice. "Lucky me."

Mack's eyes turn down. She's a lot like Holden. She wants a reaction. I'm not giving her one.

She's not happy about that. "They are… big." Insecurity streaks her expression for a minute. Then she swallows a sip of wine. "I guess that's a perk of being—"

"She's a curvy goddess, yeah."

"Right." Her smile is fake. "I'm glad we have a minute. There's a lot I want to say to you, Forest. I… I hope you're ready to hear it."

I nod *uh-huh*, but my eyes stay on Skye.

## Chapter Thirteen

FOREST

"You look good. Healthy." Mack's slender fingers wrap around the stem of her glass. She brings it to her red lips. Takes a long sip.

Her lipstick doesn't mark the glass. It stays perfect. It stays the same bright shade as her hair.

My kid sister, Ariel, used to tease her. *Can we trade names? You're the real Little Mermaid.*

Mack has the long hair and the narrow waist, but that's where the similarities end. She hates swimming. She won't sing. She's closed off instead of curious.

Ariel, the protagonist of the animated film, is so passionate about the human world that she's willing to give up everything for it.

Ariel, my little sister, lacks the Disney character's grace and singing voice, but has that same drive and curiosity.

My sister froze after our mom's death. I did what I could to bring her out of her shell, but I didn't exactly lead by example.

I was too busy trying to keep everyone healthy, happy, functional.

It took Dad years to get over Mom's death.

By then, I was in college. I was struggling to juggle school and family. I was tired, frustrated, scared all the time.

Mack was the only person who understood.

It was easy being with her. I didn't have to explain it or discuss it or look for cracks in her armor.

She just got it.

Her mom is an alcoholic. She knows what it means to take care of family.

She has a lot of other flaws, sure, but they seemed so insignificant in comparison.

My mom was gone. My dad was too depressed to get out of bed. My sister was lost. My brother was acting out.

What did it matter that Mack got jealous of girls who were thinner, prettier, more stylish?

What did it matter that she hated my favorite band?

That she liked pretentious movies and couldn't follow basketball?

I'd done the college experience. Hooked up with strangers, gotten drunk at frat parties, skipped class to get high.

It was empty. Pointless.

Don't get me wrong. I didn't exactly mind sleeping with hot women. But after it was over, it was over. I didn't feel better, fuller, more understood.

Sure, I was satisfied physically. But emotionally?

It was nothing like when I met Mack.

She was the first person who cared about more than the dark hair and the tattoos.

She knew exactly where I hurt. Exactly where to apply salve to the bruise.

I didn't realize she'd use that knowledge to rub salt in the wound.

"You, um, you still playing basketball?" She follows my gaze to her mom. Presses her red lips together.

"Yeah. Once a week with Chase. Once a week with Holden."

"Holden plays?" She clears her throat *please look at me. Please pretend my mom isn't drinking. Please make this go away.*

"He's not bad."

"But you kick his ass every time?"

"Chase's too." My eyes flit to the bar. Skye and Diego are sitting across from each other. Talking about something.

Her hand brushes his arm.

He laughs at her joke.

She clinks glasses with him. Laughs harder. Not that fake laugh of earlier. A real one.

I know all of Skye's expressions. I know her better than I know anyone.

"I'm worried too." Mack's voice is soft. "She's so pretty. Not that she's out of your league."

"Yeah." I don't know what she means by that, but I don't like her tone. "But no one compares to Skye."

Her brow furrows. "And he's…"

"You must like him. You're marrying him."

Her eyes turn down. "Forest, I… I don't know what to say. I didn't do this to hurt you."

Maybe. But I'm not about to tell her it's okay.

"It's not like I wanted to fall in love with him." Her gaze shifts to the bar. She watches as Skye swallows her last sip of wine. As Diego refills her glass. Leans in to whisper in Skye's ear. "I thought we were forever."

"What's it matter now, Mack?"

"I just… I thought maybe you'd identify."

"With worrying my girlfriend is going to leave me for someone else?"

She swallows her glass in two gulps. "Forest, you know I wouldn't have done that unless—"

"Seriously, Mack. Don't."

She sets her glass on the table. Taps the wood with her red fingernails. (Twenty bucks say she's wearing red heels too). "How are you?"

"How am I?"

"Yeah. Can I not ask that? Is it too sensitive a subject?" She reaches for the bottle.

"How many is that?"

"You're not my keeper anymore."

I was never her keeper. I looked out for her. That was all.

She needed more. She needed someone to take care of her for once. But whenever I tried—

Fuck it. She's right. It's not my problem.

If Mack wants to get drunk, she can. If she wants to stew in envy, she can. If she wants to interrogate her fiancé on his feelings for another woman, she can.

It's her life.

She's the one in charge of it.

She's the one who decided she was done with me.

"So…" Mack takes another sip. "How are you?"

"Good. Busy. We don't have enough help at the new shop. I've got a full schedule."

"Busy suits you." She presses her lips into a smile. "What else are you doing? Besides basketball and tattoos?"

"The usual."

She stares back at me, not at all following.

"What?"

"What usual?"

My brow furrows.

"The whole time we were together, you were with me, or you were working."

"No." I do things. I did things.

"Yeah." She nods. "Maybe not working at Oddball. But you were always making dinner for Ariel, or helping Holden with his homework, or cleaning up your dad's place."

"Holden never did his homework."

Her expression softens. "You know what I mean." She takes another sip. "I always thought you'd be a good dad."

What the fuck? I stare into her eyes, trying to figure out what she means, but I don't get there.

"You, uh… sorry. I think I'm a little drunk." Her laugh is messy. "Diego and I talk about it. We're not trying yet. But in a few years."

"Congratulations."

"Do you still want that?"

"Yeah."

Her eyes go to Skye. "Does she?"

"I don't think that's any of your business." Yeah, Skye and I sometimes discuss our future. She's pretty sure she wants a family, but not a hundred percent. She'd be a good mom. Open, loving, just tough enough to keep kids in line.

"Sure, yeah…" She takes another sip. "You… You know… it's funny. You look at her the way I always wanted you to look at me?"

"I look at her like I love her."

"Yeah. Right. And you do make a lovely couple. Such a contrast, you know? Her being so soft. You being so hard."

I'm not letting her make it an insult. "Skye's the most beautiful woman I've ever seen."

Jealousy streaks Mack's expression. She must be drunk because she's doing nothing to hide it. "Yeah." She forces a smile. "I'm just… I'm so glad you're happy. I didn't think you'd have that. I didn't think you'd move on."

"Thanks." I'm not sure there's any actual well-wishing in there, but I'm not giving her the satisfaction of taking offense.

"And, well… I get that we had a rough landing. I don't expect you to like me. Or love me. Or forgive me even. But I hope you can. I hope we can all be friends again."

"Yeah."

"I… uh… I guess someone should go talk to them, huh?"

"Why?"

Her eyes meet mine. It's all there, in her hazel eyes. *Because of how we ended. Because I don't trust him. How could you?*

Or maybe I'm projecting.

How can she trust him? How can he trust her?

How can anyone trust anyone else?

How can you give someone your heart? Show them exactly where they can press to hurt you the most?

"I just…" She pushes herself up. "I really am happy for you, Forest."

"Thanks."

"I don't know if you want to be here for this or not, but if you do… it would be really nice. I want you and Skye here. If you can handle being here."

"Yeah."

"I, uh…" She takes a step backward. Trips on her heels. (They are red). Catches herself. "Excuse me."

"Wait."

She freezes, deer in headlights.

I stand. Move around the table. Offer her my arm. "I'll take you home."

"I'm fine."

My brow knits. She's not fine. She's drunk. Very drunk. But she's right. I'm not her keeper. And, honestly, I don't want to be her keeper. Not anymore. "Make sure you call a cab." I nod *goodbye*. Cross the room to the bar.

Skye is still laughing.

Diego is still looking at her like she's the funniest person he's ever met.

She probably is. She's certainly the funniest person I know.

"Hey." She looks up at me with a hazy smile. "I think…" She holds up her glass. "I think I've had a few too many."

"Want me to take you home?" I ask.

"Yeah…" She swallows her last sip. Sets her glass on the bar. Shoots Diego a smile. "Thanks for the drink."

"My pleasure." He takes her hand. Leans in. Presses his lips to her cheek.

She turns bright red. "You… uh… Good night."

He nods *good night*. Turns to me. "I guess I should take my girl home too."

"Yeah." I swallow my hatred. "Take care."

He offers me an apologetic smile.

I ignore it. Help Skye out of her chair. Lead her to her parent's table, wish them goodbye, whisk her to my car.

She looks up at me with fuzzy eyes. "Are you okay?" Her fingers curl around my wrist. "What can I do?"

*Fuck me. Distract me. Convince me I'm capable of loving someone else. Convince me you don't want Diego. That you really do want me.* "Don't fight me about driving you home."

She shakes her head. "Not with them there."

"You can go to my place, but you're going straight to bed."

"To your bed?" Her wink is heady. Like she's demanding I fuck her in my bed.

But that's just Skye getting caught up in her ruse.

She's a great actor, even if she doesn't realize it.

## Chapter Fourteen

SKYE

"Drink." Forest pushes a glass of water into my hand.

I shoot him a *really* look as I take it. "Really? Do I need to hydrate after a few glasses of wine?"

"A few?"

"Judgy much." I am thirsty. So thirsty. My mouth is bone dry. My throat too. But I need to make him sweat it.

His dark eyes narrow. "Don't make me force you."

"You're going to force me to drink this glass of water?" I tap the glass with my pointer finger. "How?"

"You want to see?"

Kinda, yeah.

He stares into my eyes, dead serious. "Skye." His voice drops to something demanding and paternal. The tone he uses with his siblings. The tone that screams *I will take care of you no matter what you do*.

"Forest." I try to copy his whole *I am alpha protector grr* thing but I don't pull it off.

A chuckle breaks up his *don't fuck with me* stare. "You're not tough."

"I am too."

"Oh yeah? Want to guard me in pick-up basketball?"

My nose scrunches reflexively. "Do I want balls to fly at my face?"

"Do you?"

Oh. My cheeks flush. "No, uh… flying would be a bit much. How do you guard someone anyway?"

"I'll show you." He nods to the water. "If you drink."

"You think an offer to teach me sports is going to encourage me to bend to your will?"

"You're gonna drink it." His eyes flit to my mouth. "You always lick your lips when you're thirsty."

"I do not."

"Every time you get a matcha—"

"That's different."

"It's past midnight. I'm not making you a matcha." He pushes the water toward my chest. "Drink."

"It's not like I have stuff to do."

"Drink. Now."

I study his expression. It's a solid poker face, but there's the slightest curve to his lips.

God, his dark eyes are pretty. As interesting as his lips. Or his shoulders. Or his tattooed arms.

Or his cock.

Not that I've seen it.

I mean, I want to see it. In context. I don't salivate over random dicks. But a hot guy with his hand wrapped around his hard cock?

Forest with his hand wrapped around his hard cock?

Mmm.

My tongue slides over my lips.

Dammit.

"Where are you going, Skye?" He moves a little closer.

"Nowhere."

"All right." He smiles, victorious. "If you don't drink the water, I'm leaving."

Goddammit.

"Five." He shifts off the bed. "Four." He takes a step toward the door. "Three." He reaches for the handle. "Two." He raises a brow *this is your last chance.*

For a second, I hold his stare. Return it. *I'm a badass and you will bend to my will.*

Then he says, "one."

I swallow a sip of water.

He chuckles. "Why do you argue with me?"

"Why do you argue with me?"

His chuckle gets louder. "You start it."

"Maybe I can take care of myself."

"I know you can." He moves to the dresser. Pulls out a band t-shirt he got a million years ago. (He'd never go see his once favorite band now. He calls their new stuff "terrible pop shit." Every time it plays on the radio, he complains they sold out).

"I feel like a fourteen-year-old girl."

His cheeks flush as he tosses me the t-shirt.

It was black once. Now it's a faded grey. The screen print—a truly hideous Rubik's Cube bearing the band's name—is peeling.

He's had this shirt for the last decade. And he's offering it to me.

Okay, it's a shirt, not a declaration of love. It doesn't mean anything. Except that he's a gentleman.

"Help me with this?" I motion to the zipper on the back of my dress.

He nods *sure*, crosses to the bed, sits next to me.

His fingers brush my shoulder blades. The backline. The zipper. "Where'd you get this one?"

"It's a new designer."

"You buy it?"

"No."

"No?" he asks.

"Her dresses are like three hundred dollars each."

"She just gave it to you?"

"Of course."

"Of course?" He pulls the zipper down my back. Lower and lower and lower. There.

"Yeah, I, uh… I bought all my clothes when I started blogging. But now designers send me stuff all the time. In the hopes I feature it."

"That's a sweet deal."

"Yeah."

"The lingerie too?"

My cheeks flush. "That too."

"You have guys message you?"

"What guys?"

"Any." His fingertips skim my skin for a second, then he pulls his hand away. "I bet a lot of guys want to fuck you."

*Do you?* "Maybe."

"You've been single a long time."

"And?"

"Is that what you want?"

Well… uh…

"You must miss it."

"Sex?"

"Yeah."

"Oh. Yeah." I swallow hard. "Do you?"

"Yeah."

"But you… you could. You have opportunities."

He shrugs *I guess*. "I see someone and I think of Mack. Of walking in on them. Hearing her groan his name."

"It bothers you."

"Does it bother me that my ex was cheating?"

"Well, yeah." It's more than that. "It's just… you're so focused on the sex."

"Is that a question?"

"Well… Why?"

"Have you ever had good sex?"

"Uh…"

"Steve. Was he a good fuck?"

My cheeks flush. Fuck, the matter-of-fact tone of his voice. It's hot in here.

The air-conditioning is on high. I'm halfway out of my dress. But it's so goddamn hot in here.

"Did he make you come?" Forest asks.

My blush spreads to my chest. "Mostly."

"Did he make you see stars?"

No. But I... I clear my throat.

"Do you miss it? Miss the feel of his hands, the taste of his lips, the weight of his body over yours?"

I turn back to him. Try to find meaning in his expression. But his dark eyes fail to illuminate matters.

"It's not a trick question."

"I don't know... I guess I miss it. But not him. Exactly." It has been forever. So long since someone has touched me like they wanted to tear my clothes off.

Well, besides Forest—

And that's pretend.

The firm touch, the gentle kisses, the sweet nothings—

I do miss that. Badly.

But what am I going to do? I can't have Forest. And I don't enjoy casual *relationships*.

I tried a random hookup in high school. But as soon as the guy unzipped my pants, I froze. His hands were wrong. Invasive. Awkward.

I tried to grin and bear it. Tried to enjoy the manual stimulation. But it just didn't happen.

Eventually, he gave up on making me come, went back to the party, told all his friends I was frigid.

Which was probably for the best, honestly. Guys in high school assumed I was easy because of my ample... uh, everything. I don't know what it is about being a bigger girl. But tons of guys assume I'm desperate, willing to take their dick anytime, anyplace.

"Damn. You want it that bad." Forest's eyes turn down. "I didn't realize the situation was that dire."

"No… it's just… been a while."
"How long?"
"Well, since my ex… you know—"
"Fuck, that was three years ago," he says.
"Yeah…"
His eyes go wide. "That's forever."
"Well, uh… maybe three and a half. Toward the end, we weren't really…" I cared about Steve, but it was never passionate. It was nice. Then it wasn't. Our breakup wasn't passionate, angry, sad. It was a formality.
"It wasn't good anymore?"
"It wasn't anything. We just stopped." My eyes meet his. "You and Mackenzie?"
"We were still…" He runs his hand through his hair. "Fuck, we'd hit a wall about a year before that. She'd pulled away. A couple months after that, she started jumping me left and right. I thought… fuck, I guess I didn't think." He shakes his head *fuck, I was an idiot*. "He inspired her."
"Yeah, but she still wanted it from you."
He chuckles. "I'm so lucky."
"Do you think… would you rather the opposite?"
"Would I rather not be sloppy seconds? Is that your question?"
I clear my throat. "Of course, it sounds ridiculous when you say it like that."
"It is ridiculous."
"You'd have had nothing."
He stares at me like I'm crazy.
"Months without sex."
"So?"
"So… wouldn't you get horny?"
"What? I don't have a hand?"
My blush spreads to my chest. "I, uh…"
"Or porn?"
"You watch porn?"
His eyes fill with disbelief. *You're really asking this?* "You don't?"

"It doesn't work for me."

"Maybe you haven't found the right porn."

"Maybe." God, it's hot in here. I… uh… "I…" I hold up my shirt. Motion *turn around*.

Tragically, he does.

I finish unzipping my dress. Pull it over my head. Lay it flat.

Mmm. His t-shirt smells like his laundry detergent. It's soft from a million washes. It's against my bare skin.

The fabric that touched his bare chest is touching mine.

"What do you like?" he asks.

I clear my throat.

"You don't want to tell me?"

"It's just…"

"Is it freaky shit?" He turns around. Raises a brow. "I promise I won't judge."

"You sound like Holden."

"No, Holden would get in bed next to you, slide his arm around your waist, and whisper *baby, I'll give you the best show you could ever find*."

That's probably true. "Is your knowledge of adult entertainment so vast that you can find any content I desire?"

"I have been single for two years."

"Yeah, but you…"

"But I…"

"Slept with half of Los Angeles after things ended."

"It was a phase."

"And it ended because?"

"It got boring."

"Sleeping with beautiful, thin model looking women got boring?" I ask.

"Where they thin?"

Yes. He slept exclusively with skinny chicks. He has a type. The polar opposite of me. Sorority girl types. Conventional, thin, trendy. Like Mack. "And tall."

"Honestly, Skye, I can barely tell the difference between a five-foot-ten woman and a five-foot-five woman."

"You're just so tall it's painful?"

"Not as tall as Chase."

I can't help but chuckle. "Not that you're counting?"

"Not that I know he has exactly one inch on me?"

"Does he?"

"Does he… oh." He chuckles. "Is that what you want? A scene of two guys whipping it out and comparing?"

"No." I mean, if it's Forest and anyone, sure. But not as a kink or something.

"Okay, let's try this." His eyes shift to my strapless black bra. My dress. "I can hang that up."

"I will." I stand.

His eyes go straight to my bare thighs. None of his pajama bottoms or boxers fit my hips.

He's well built. Lean. Broad shoulders and chest. Narrow waist and hips.

It's super fucking hot.

But it also means there's no way in hell his pants are ever getting over my ass.

It is what it is.

It means I wear a t-shirt and panties when I spend the night.

He doesn't normally care. Or notice.

He doesn't normally stare at my thighs.

His pupils dilate. His tongue slides over his lips. Then he drags his eyes up my body.

He does it slowly. Like he's taking me in for the first time.

Finally, his eyes meet mine. For a split second, he stares at me like he's going to tear my clothes off. Then he blinks and his expression is back to normal.

"Let's try this, Skye. You tell me what you don't like about porn, and I'll find you a nice, ordinary video."

"Why?"

"It's been a while for you too."

Ahem. I hang my dress in his closet, between two plain black t-shirts. "I prefer reality."

Jealousy streaks his expression. "With who?"

"No one... just..."

"Is there someone you want?"

I clear my throat. "That's not important."

"There is."

Shit. I need a good lie. Something believable. "He's interested in someone else."

"And you—what? You're just waiting?"

"No, I... I'm not doing anything."

"Why not?"

"Because."

"Because why?" he asks.

"You always tell me to stay away from love. That it only ends in pain."

His eyes soften. "Well, yeah, but... if it's what you want—"

"I can't have what I want."

"Who is this guy?"

"It doesn't matter."

"How can he not see how amazing you are?"

"Forest, it doesn't matter."

His brow knits. "It does."

"Can we just..."

"You're not going to tell me?"

I shake my head. "I'm not pursuing it. That's all you need to know."

His frown deepens. "Why don't you want to tell me?"

Because it's him. But it's not like I can say that. "Let's just... what were we talking about?"

"Is it someone from school?"

I clear my throat.

"Someone at the shop?"

"Forest—"

"Is he the strong, silent type?"

"Porn? It was porn, right?"

He moves a little closer. "You'd rather discuss porn than—"

"Yes."

Understanding spreads over his expression. "Okay. Then let's shake on it." He extends his hand.

"On what?"

"Your new entertainment."

Jesus Christ, he's trying to kill me. "My what?"

"You trust me, don't you?"

"Of course."

"Then trust me." He motions to his hand. "I'll find exactly what you like."

He's not talking about fucking me, but, God, it feels good believing that.

## Chapter Fifteen

SKYE

I dream about Forest forcing me to watch porn—classy, beautiful, French film quality adult entertainment.

Wake sweaty and wanting.

Everything is different.

But everything is the same too.

His bed, his shirt, his music.

His favorite album. Of course. He plays it all the time.

Our taste in music overlaps to a large degree. I like more 90s in my rock—riot grrls, grunge, ska—but I enjoy his miserable punk-pop musicians too.

These guys—this guy in particular—are so maladjusted. They make me feel normal.

Sure, I'm not a millionaire with a multi-platinum album.

But I don't wish my ex would die in a car crash. Or a fire. Or…

It's mostly car crashes with this guy.

He's got some issues with automobiles.

And women.

The dude is basically the poster child for toxic masculinity. The guy's ex broke his heart, but he can't admit that, even to himself.

The poor guy doesn't see it. He insists he doesn't even think about his ex, even though every song is about her.

He's so intent on avoiding vulnerability his pain turns to hate.

Though… really, I'm not being fair.

The guy calms down a lot in his next album. (As Holden would say, a hundred dollars says that's next in the queue). He lets his guard down. Lets the vulnerability in.

It's kind of… appealing actually. The way he pushes you away then pulls you in. The way he finally admits how lost and alone he is.

Not that I stare at Forest every time he plays it thinking *do you see what's happening here? Are you going to follow in his footsteps? Are you finally going to let me in?*

I'm asking too much.

He's good to me. He takes care of me.

So what if he won't let me in? It's not like it consumes me.

It's not like my heart screams *please, tell me where you hurt, tell me how to fix it.*

Not at all.

I move to the bathroom. Go through my routine. Seek distraction in my cell.

Form response to a job application. Updates on three plus-sized blogs I follow.

Several dozen pictures of women in clothes.

Three Instagram PMs.

One *oh my God, I love your stuff.*

One *are you single, baby.* (That earns a block).

And one inquiry from a lingerie company.

Huh.

It's not like the usual requests—free clothes for consideration.

It's more.

*Dear Princess Skye,*

*We love your style—the photos and the clothes. And the sex appeal too. Who is that gorgeous male model? Is he available for a second shoot?*

*We want more pictures like that. It doesn't have to be him, but it simply must be you.*

*We're looking for influencers with a big following and a whole lot of style. Your photos are amazing. Sexy, classy, teasing. Give us more of that.*

*We're offering five thousand dollars for a series of five photos.*

*Let us know if you're interested, and we'll send a contract.*

*Sincerely,*

*Foxy Lace Lingerie*

No. That's not possible.

I'm reading this wrong.

There's some bizarre spelling mistake.

Someone wrote thousand when they meant to write nothing.

Only that's completely implausible.

And the lingerie company has a completely legitimate footprint. It's new and small, but it's real.

They're really offering me five grand.

Five grand to post pictures in my underwear.

Their underwear.

Pictures like the ones I took with Forest.

Only in lingerie.

We…

I…

Oh my God.

"Skye?" Forest's footsteps move closer. He knocks on the door. "You okay?"

"Yeah…" I read it again. And again. And again.

The offer stays the same.

Five. Thousand. Dollars.

That's just…

It's not…

Oh my God.

"You decent?" He taps the door. "I'm coming in."

"Yeah… I…"

Music floods the room. God, there's something so familiar about the singer's voice. I didn't like it at first, but now it's home.

"You don't look okay." His voice is steady. Caring.

"I am. Just…"

"Hungover?"

"No." A little. "That's not..." I force myself to look away from the phone. To look to him.

He's wearing pajama bottoms. Only pajama bottoms.

His torso is bare.

I can see every line of the broken heart tattooed to his chest.

The lilies spreading over his shoulder.

The Latin quote running down his ribs.

*ex nihilo nihil fit*

Nothing comes from nothing.

The perfect anti-nihilism quote.

Pure Forest.

And the lyrics on his hip.

Something about trusting someone enough to love them. Trusting them when they say you're good for them. About loving them enough to risk breaking their heart.

I can only see the top line. The top half a line. His pants cover the rest.

Mmm.

I want to trace it. Touch him. Take in every single letter.

"What?" His voice is utterly matter-of-fact. "I have something on my face?"

"No... I..." Must stop staring. Must bring my gaze to his eyes. Must look at something besides the ink on his hip.

"You..."

"That tattoo."

"Which one?"

The one driving me out of my fucking mind. The one begging me to rip his pants off. The one positioned so I *have* to think about his cock. "The..." I point to his hip. "It's this guy, yeah?"

"Yeah."

"Why would you... he's such an asshole."

He chuckles. Motions to the kitchen *come on*. "It's from the next album."

"Oh."

## The Best Friend Bargain

"I'll point it out when we get to that song."

It's the next thing on his playlist. Of course. He's so... I can't even laugh about it. I'm too transfixed by the ink.

He told me when he got it.

I've seen it a few times. The few times I convinced him to go swimming. (Forest isn't a beach guy).

But this is...

"Come on." His fingers wrap around my wrist. "I made you a matcha."

"Matcha..."

"You sure you're not hungover?"

"Yeah... I..."

He pulls me closer.

My body presses against his. God, he's so hard and warm and right.

It's a split second. He steps backward, pulling me with him.

My eyes go to the ground. Then his ass.

His pants are loose. I can't get a good view.

A tragedy if there ever was one.

But, uh...

He leads me all the way to the kitchen island. Motions to the stool. *Sit.*

"I'm okay." I force my gaze to the kitchen. It's the same as always. Clean (he's a neat freak). Shiny. New.

A carafe full of java in the coffee maker.

Scrambled eggs—with veggies, of course—warming on the stove.

A tin of matcha sitting next to a whisk.

"Sit." He turns, grabs the mug of matcha, holds it up. "Or no matcha latte."

"With almond milk?"

He raises a brow *who do you think I am?*

Mmm. Well, I am a little woozy. I want to sit anyway. It's not because he's issuing orders.

"Sit," he says again.

My legs obey his command immediately. My heartbeat kicks up. My veins buzz with desire.

He's just so... intense. And sexy.

It's not news.

But after being so close—

I can't deny the facts anymore.

I can't breathe in his presence anymore.

I can't think anything but *take off clothes now please* anymore.

"Are you gonna tell me what's wrong?" He sets the matcha in front of me.

I take a greedy sip. Let out a low, deep moan. Mmm. He's way too good at this.

"That sounds more like you." He chuckles.

"Thank you."

"My pleasure." He turns to the stove. Scoops eggs onto two plates. Adds extra green onions to mine.

My favorite.

He always fixes them just how I like them. I don't even have to ask.

He brings our plates—and the sriracha—to the counter. "Eat."

"I..."

"Can you not fight me one time?"

"Where's the fun in that?"

He chuckles *you're ridiculous* then he hands me a fork. He just knows I'm going to eat.

I mean, I am. He's a great cook. And I'm starving.

And, God, there are so many green onions. And tomatoes. Soft, juicy rich tomatoes.

Mmm.

I nearly inhale the food. It deserves better, but I'm starving.

And this is easy. Comfortable.

Breakfast with Forest.

The air-conditioning and music mixing into a familiar soundtrack.

No talk about lingerie or pictures or pretending.

He finishes his eggs. Stands. Collects our dishes. "I found you a video."

"A—" Oh. It hits me at once. "When?"

"Last night."

"You were looking at porn on the couch?" It's already back to normal. His extra pillow and comforter are already in the closet.

"For academic reasons."

"Uh-huh."

"You scared of cum on the couch?"

My jaw drops.

He laughs. "I didn't."

"You…" Since when does he talk about cum? With me?

Something is different with him too.

Seeing Mackenzie.

Or seeing Diego.

Or touching me.

God, I want it to be that.

For now—

Forest fucked himself on that couch.

It's a beautiful mental image.

It's perfection.

"Scout's honor." His lips curl into a half-smile.

"I trust you." But I don't want to believe it. I want to picture him wrapping his hand around his cock. Groaning as he comes.

He places the dishes in the sink. Grabs his laptop. Places it in front of me. "I can show you right now."

"Uh…"

"Or stream it to the TV."

"You want to watch porn with me?" I'm still dreaming. This is all one big sexual fantasy. I'm going to wake up sweaty and alone.

"Skye?"

I bite my tongue in the hopes I'll snap back to reality.

Nothing happens. I'm here.

This is reality.

I…

He…
What?
"You want to watch porn with me?" I ask.
"Gotta make sure you watch it."
"So you…" I don't even know what to ask. "Why?"
"Someone has to take care of you."
"Okay…"
His laugh is easy. "I'll send you the link. But I expect honesty."
"No, uh… maybe it's a good idea."
Disbelief streaks his expression.
"I got this offer." I unlock my cell. Hand it to him.
He reads every word. "Fuck."
"Yeah."
"This is real? Five grand?"
"I think so."
His eyes meet mine. "You have to do it."
"But that's… that's us."
"So?"

I bite my lip. How do I explain this to him? Forest has a perfect body. He has actual abs. Abs. I know how to flaunt my curves, sure. In carefully curated attire.

Everyone loves an hourglass figure.

The big boobs. The round ass.

But the not-so-flat stomach?

The cellulite? The stretch marks?

I don't care how many times people drop hashtags about real beauty. They want a fantasy.

"But…" He sets my cell on the counter. "Forget Diego. Forget Mack. Forget your love of showing off your tits."

"I don't—"

"Skye." He pulls up my Instagram on my cell. Goes right to the picture of the bralette. "We talked about this."

"Yeah, but that's…"

"Spank bank material, yes." He studies the picture. "If it wasn't you."

"Right." If it wasn't me. Because I'm… whatever. Not going there. "You'd be part of the new pictures. You'd be spank bank material."

"I already am."

"Oh."

"Oh?"

"I didn't know you realized that."

He looks at me like I'm slow on the uptake. "You were accusing me of fucking the entire state of California last night."

"Only half the state."

His laugh is big. Hearty. "That makes a difference."

"It does."

His smile spreads wider. "I know why women want to fuck me."

"Your sparkling personality?"

His laugh gets bigger. "Exactly."

God, his laugh is beautiful.

And his eyes. They're so dark and deep.

He's handsome, not beautiful, but his eyes are gorgeous.

He meets my stare. Raises a brow *what are you looking at?*

I shrug. "Looking for the visual evidence of your sparkling personality."

He chuckles *yeah right*. "It's the tattoos." He taps the broken heart on his chest. "I'm not complaining. I've used it plenty. But it's not because they think I'm interesting."

"You are very dull."

His laugh is easy. "Incredibly boring."

"Kind of brooding."

He nods *exactly*. "Girls see me as a damaged bad boy. I get it. I—"

"Fuck them?"

"I did, yeah." His eyes meet mine. "It's the same for you."

I'm a damaged bad girl? "How's that?"

"How guys see you."

"Guys don't see me." Not usually.

He looks at me like I'm crazy. "Is this about your dress size?"

"No..." Maybe.

"What, your pants size?"

"No, I..."

"You post bikini pics once a week."

"Yeah, because—"

"And you tag them all with 'body positive.'"

"That's not what it means."

His eyes flit to my chest. My bare thighs. "What does it mean? You want girls who don't have perfect tits to feel good too?" His voice is completely matter-of-fact. He really does think I have perfect tits.

God... I... I'm concentrating. On something. I need to stay focused here. "It's about being comfortable in your skin no matter what you look like."

"How is that different?"

"I'm not—"

"You know there are dozens of sites devoted to pictures of busty goth chicks."

I... Uh... What? "You go to them?" Because he wants to see me naked. Because he wants to fantasize about me. Because he wants to fuck me.

"Holden reminds me every day."

Oh.

"Sends me links sometimes."

"And you—"

He ignores my question. "Guys see you and think 'oh, there's this edgy goth princess. I bet she's a kinky sex goddess.'"

"Guys think that?"

He nods. "You and I know that you're too uptight to watch porn much less tie someone up."

"I am not uptight. You're uptight."

"How so?"

"You..." I've got nothing. "I'm not."

"You don't watch porn."

"So?"

"You can't talk about sex."

No, I just can't talk about it with him. Not without screaming *please, take off your clothes, I need to fuck you. I like you. I want you. It's all you.* "Let's not—do you have a point?"

"Yeah. You're hot, Skye. If you don't see it, you're blind. Because the evidence is right here." He taps the image on my cell. "You're the one taking the photos."

"But—"

"I'm gonna write back. Say yes."

"But—"

"We're doing this."

"Are you—"

"You can pay my model fee. The rest is yours."

"Your model fee?"

He offers his hand. "Lunch after."

"I should give you more—"

"It's the least I could do." He pushes his hand toward me. "Say yes."

"Uh…"

"Say. Yes."

"Okay." I shake his hand.

He beams with pride.

Or maybe it's desire.

Maybe he wants to take half-naked pictures with me.

Because he wants to be naked with me.

That's something.

It may not be much, but it's something.

## Chapter Sixteen

FOREST

This is simple. *Carpe Diem* surrounded by dandelions. All in black.

An easy tattoo.

No reason to think about Skye naked.

No reason to recall the taste of her neck.

Or the sight of her bare thighs.

Or those crimson lips wrapping around—

"Forest?" my client asks.

Fuck, I need to pay attention. I'm usually good at blocking shit out and focusing on work.

It's what keeps me sane. What's kept me sane since I was a kid.

And now Skye is—

Uh-huh. Not thinking that. Shutting all that down.

Yeah, she's going to strip to her lingerie and sit in my lap, but—

I'm so fucked.

"You ready to keep going?" I make my voice as firm as I can.

Sure, this tattoo is a little played, but that's part of the job. If the client wants something cliché, the client gets something cliché.

This design is badass. Even if it's a little obvious.

The way the petals float away from the words—

It just works.

And I—

"I am," she says.

I take a deep breath. Push thoughts of Skye to the back of my head. "On three."

She grunts an *okay*.

"You've got this. Trust me."

Her red hair shakes as she nods. It's not the fire engine red of Mack's hair. It's a natural shade of copper.

But it still threatens my concentration.

Which is more distracting?

The mental image of Mack's nails in Diego's back.

Or my fantasy of Skye touching herself to my porn selections. Thinking of me. Groaning my name as she comes.

Shit.

I need to get over this.

This photo shoot is a great opportunity.

I'm not letting her fuck that up.

I'm not fucking that up.

"Forest?" My client's copper hair falls to one side as she turns to me. "Count me down, okay?"

"Sure."

Deep breath.

Steady exhale.

"Three, two, one." I turn the gun on. Bring it to her skin.

She yelps, grips the chair harder, nods *I've got it*.

For a few minutes, my entire world is ink on skin. The curve of the script. The lines of the flowers. Black against alabaster.

Then I finish and the world rearranges.

Her breath comes into focus.

The music—some eighties jam Holden likes.

The conversation at the counter.

Copper hair falling over a slim shoulder.

A year ago, I'd have turned the charm to eleven, taken her home, fucked her.

## The Best Friend Bargain

She's interested. She's already looking at me like I'm her salvation.

There's nothing stopping me.

Nothing except my complete lack of interest.

She's not Skye. I don't care what her neck tastes like, if her lipstick will stain my chest, if her—

Fuck. Not going there.

"Oh my God, Forest." She turns from the mirror to me. Smiles wide. "It's so perfect." She jumps to her feet. Runs into my arms. Hugs me tightly. "Thank you."

"Sure thing." I pat her shoulder.

She lets out one of those *oh my God, you're so safe* sighs.

This is her moment. I marked her body. We exchanged something. She wants to believe it's more than that.

I'll let her believe that.

She steps backward. Looks up at me with a dopey smile. "I… uh… I should get dressed, huh?"

"I have to clean you up first."

"Oh. Right." Her eyes brim with love. They're blue. Softer than Skye's. And darker.

This girl needs someone protecting her.

She needs someone looking out for her.

She needs someone who understands her. Who loves her. Who knows how to love her.

Skye does too.

Sure, we agree that *carpe diem* is generic and boring. Yeah, we understand each other.

But I don't know how to love. And she deserves better.

After I finish cleaning her up, my client hugs me goodbye. She holds on like she'll never let go. "I love it. Thank you."

"Yeah." For a second, I close my eyes. Let my mind wander.

It doesn't go to Mack.

It goes to Skye.

Her bright blue eyes. Her wicked smile. Her lush body.

I shake it off—I can't think about her like that—and walk my client to the door. Then it's back to the counter.

Holden flashes me a shit-eating grin. "Didn't get enough action from Skye?"

I roll my eyes.

Holden just laughs. He rises from his stool—he's sitting behind the counter, working on a mockup—and surveys the room like he owns it. "Shit. She always seemed like the generous type to me. Don't tell me she's greedy."

Fuck, I hope she's greedy. I hope she demands to come on my face until she can't take it anymore.

Holden's laugh is knowing. "You're thinking about her naked, aren't you?"

Footsteps move closer. "He is going to hit you." Oliver's deep voice bounces around the room. It's his usual removed tone. *I don't really care what you do. You're an idiot. But I guess it's entertaining enough.*

"Got any stories to share?" Holden nods *hey* to his friend. He's completely unmoved by mentions of violence. "She as flexible as those pictures suggest?"

"Which pictures?" Why am I asking?

His grin gets wider. He pulls out his cell. Goes straight to a photo of Skye practicing a pole move. Something where she's doing the splits against the pole, her heels hooked to the metal, her legs almost flat against it.

"Fuck." Oliver chuckles. "She always look like that?"

"That's what I'm saying." Holden addresses his friend. "Forest keeps selling this story about how he's not into her."

"Maybe he's not," Oliver says.

"Maybe he took her to his place last night and finally fucked her." Holden raises a brow *don't hold out on me.*

Honestly, I'm not sure how sincere he is. He does love dirty stories. But it's not like I've ever shared any.

Oliver laughs. "You want him to hit you, right?"

"You feeling neglected?" He winks at Oliver. "I could talk about how hot your sister is."

Oliver's poker face cracks. It's quick, a second, then he catches himself. "Good one."

"Where's the joke? Those long legs and that light hair." He makes a show of licking his lips. "Someone needs to show her the ropes."

"Touch her and die." Oliver shrugs like he doesn't care.

Holden just laughs. He doesn't want to fuck Oliver's sister (well, he isn't planning on it), but—

Shit, when it comes to Holden, there's no telling what he wants. Or what he's going to do.

Oliver's sister is way too young for me. She's still in high school for fuck's sake. But she's gonna be a knockout one day.

I'm old enough I look at teenagers and think "one day, they'll be attractive."

Better than the alternative, I guess.

"What about if I touch Skye?" Holden asks me. "If you don't like her, you won't mind me making a move."

My stomach turns. No way is he touching Skye. She's mine.

Only she's not mine.

She's very explicitly not mine.

I try to think up a reason for the tension in my shoulders. "She deserves better."

"No doubt. But shouldn't the lady make up her own mind?" he asks.

I clear my throat.

"I'm being straight with you, Forest," Holden says. "I want to do this the honorable way. Declare my intentions to fuck your gorgeous friend."

"You can fuck yourself," I offer.

"Oh, she's into that?" He mimes writing a note. "Good to know. I'll make a video for her."

Oliver laughs *your funeral*.

"Here's the thing, Forest. I need your help. I've got the party planning started, but I'm not sure how to make it extra special for her," Holden says.

My shoulders relax. He isn't actually trying to fuck her. I *know* that. I'm usually better at ignoring his attempts to piss me off.

Right now—

It makes me sick, the thought of Skye in Holden's bed.

In Diego's bed.

Kissing him, touching him, promising him forever.

I need to get over it. That's what she wants. And I want that for her.

I want her to be happy.

More than anything, I want her to be happy.

"For Mack and Diego's engagement," Holden continues. "Since the four of ya are peas in a pod."

Oliver shakes his head *you're so dead.*

"You're trying to get her back, aren't you?" Holden asks.

"No." Hell no. She's the last thing I need. Even if I still feel sick when I think about her kissing her fiancé.

"You gotta sell your ruse somehow. So I figure a big party at our place. This Saturday doesn't work. Or next. But the one after." He smiles. "Lots of drinks." He winks at Oliver. "Some of those idiots who took Mack's side after the breakup. Skye in one of those outfits that shows off her tits."

"No," I say.

He laughs. "It's already happening." He holds up his cell. Shows off a text to Mackenzie.

*Holden: We're having a party the Saturday after next. We'd love if you came. Diego too. Be there or miss out on the best party of the year.*

*Mackenzie: Okay. What should we bring?*

Then a bunch of details. Exact time and date.

About two weeks from now.

About two weeks before the wedding.

Plenty of time for me to go crazy.

"You go off with Mack," he says. "I'll console Skye. She deserves better, sure, but if you're not gonna give it to her, someone is. Might as well be me."

"I swear, sometimes I can't tell how full of shit you are," Oliver says.

"When it comes to fucking a hottie? Never." My brother smiles at me. "I'm not an honorable man, Forest, but I do respect certain things."

"Bros before hoes?" Oliver laughs. "That's your code of honor?"

"If you don't want her, let her go. Someone will take her. Might as well be me." Holden raises a brow *how about it*.

*Fuck no. I'll kill you if you touch her.*

I suck a breath through my teeth. He's right.

She isn't mine.

She's going to be someone's.

Hell, she likes someone.

It might be Holden. Or Oliver. Or some other guy who doesn't deserve her.

There's no one who deserves her.

My phone buzzes against my thigh. It has to be Skye. And I need to see it now. I need to know exactly what she thinks about this party, about this guy she likes, about where she wants to sleep tonight.

*Stay in my bed, princess. Stay with me.*

Fuck, what's wrong with me? That isn't what we're doing.

"Is that my girl?" he asks. "Tell her I'm thinking about her."

"Uh-huh." I pull out my cell.

*Mackenzie: Sorry I got so tipsy the other night. I hope I wasn't over the line.*

I should reply. Accept her apology. Tell her to fuck off.

But I don't.

I check Skye's text.

*Skye: They just sent me a check for a thousand dollars.*

My chest gets warm. Then my stomach, shoulders, arms.

It spreads all the way to my fingers and toes.

"She's asking about my new ink isn't she?" Holden teases.

Oliver whispers something to him.

He whispers back.
*Forest: What are you doing with it?*
*Skye: I can't even.*
*Forest: Congrats.*
*Skye: Are you sure you're okay with this?*
*Forest: Are you kidding?*
*Skye: No.*
*Forest: Am I okay with you making five thousand dollars?*
*Skye: You'll be half-naked on the Internet.*
*Forest: Are you having second thoughts?*

*Skye: No. I'm ready. As soon as we get the lingerie. They're sending it express.*

*Forest: How fast is that?*
*Skye: Unclear. Is Holden serious about this engagement party thing?*

"I will be there," Oliver says. "But only because I want to see you make a fool of yourself."

"Daisy coming with you?" Holden asks.

"Fuck off," Oliver says.

Holden laughs. "Tell Skye I'm clearing my bed for her."

I flip him off.

*Forest: Unfortunately.*
*Skye: It is a good idea.*
*Forest: I guess.*
*Skye: I'll be there. Holden will supply plenty of booze. How bad can it be?*
*Forest: Holden is capable of a lot.*
*Skye: When do you think the party will start?*
*Forest: Eight or so.*
*Skye: In two weeks, right?*
*Forest: Yeah.*
*Skye: I'll have the lingerie by then.*
*Forest: You want to shoot the day of Holden's party?*
*Skye: Why not?*
*Forest: Why?*
*Skye: If he's busy with party setup, he won't be able to bother us.*

It's not a terrible point.

*Forest: I work until three.*
*Skye: That's more than enough time. Three thirty at your place?*
*Forest: Sure. I'll make you a key. Movies tonight?*
*Skye: Obviously.*
*Forest: What are we watching?*
*Skye: Is it my pick or yours?*

It's mine, but I'd rather watch something she loves.

*Forest: Yours.*
*Skye: I know the perfect thing.*
*Forest: Lots of talking?*
*Skye: Of course.*

Fuck, I can already see her eyes lighting up. Hear her laughing, gasping, sighing, crying.

I need to be on the couch with her.

Right now.

But first—

*Forest: This is a great thing, Skye. I'm proud of you.*
*Skye: Thanks.*

I'm also terrified of what it means.

It's hard enough keeping my head straight when we're dressed.

With her in lingerie?

Fuck, I'm not sure how I'm going to survive this.

## Chapter Seventeen

SKYE

For the third time, I adjust my bra strap. A little tighter. No, a little looser.

There.

That's better.

I take a steady breath. Push out an even exhale.

Happy thoughts.

Relaxed thoughts.

Easy thoughts.

Yes, I'm wearing two scraps of black lace. Yes, I have to wear this sheer lingerie in front of Forest. Yes, I have to roll around Forest's bed in—

No happy thoughts.

No relaxed thoughts.

No easy thoughts.

I. Can't. Do. This.

It's just... It's impossible.

It's not about my dress size. That's only a part of it. Yes, I'm nervous about dropping my clothes in front of a guy who sleeps exclusively with tiny women.

Yes, I'm terrified to show this much skin, this much sexuality, to hundreds of thousands of people.

Yes, I…

I'm talking myself out of this.

But that isn't an option. There's a big, fat check sitting inside the black satin lingerie box.

It's right there, wrapped in black tissue (they're really into black), bearing my name, a *lingerie promo* memo, and four figures.

One. Thousand. Dollars.

With four more to come.

I can't turn that down. It's simply not in the realm of possibility.

My gaze shifts to the mirror.

So what if I have to shop in the plus-size section (mostly, elastic is an amazing thing)? If I'm soft? If my skin is bearing stretch marks and cellulite?

This is my body.

I refuse to let these "imperfections" bring me down.

My body is good to me. It's strong—I can lift myself onto the pole. And flexible—I can nearly do the splits.

And capable of intense pleasure.

Even if, lately, that pleasure has been the results of solo activities.

It's still important, that I can feel good. That I can experience the pleasure of a great song, a delicious cup of tea, a beautiful sunset, an, ahem, intense masturbation session.

I take a deep breath.

Repeat a calming mantra.

*Five thousand dollars.*

*Five thousand dollars.*

*Five thousand dollars.*

A few hours rolling around a bed with Forest and I make five thousand dollars.

They're practically paying me to have sex.

They know what I look like. I edit my photos for composition and color-correction, but I never alter the shape of my body.

And I—

Well, Forest was right. I post lots of bikini pics.

This lingerie company wants me. There are a million fashion bloggers. Plenty of them are blonde size twos. Plenty of them fit perfectly into the "conventionally attractive" box.

They want me.

My soft stomach, my thick thighs, my large chest.

Okay. I can do this.

I can pose with Forest.

I can let my best friend see me in scraps of lace.

I can touch him without bursting into flames.

I can do this.

I can totally do this.

---

I can't do this.

It echoes through my head as I don street clothes, let myself into Forest's place, prepare his room.

As I apply makeup (I go by Princess Skye for a reason and that reason is not a natural, California beach babe vibe).

As I fix my hair.

As I stare at my cell, waiting for Forest's *I'm on my way* text.

I pace around the room. Move downstairs. Put on my favorite movie.

*Before Sunset*. It's the middle one of a trilogy, but I know these three movies like the back of my hand.

It's a magical series. In the first, *Before Sunrise*, two strangers meet on a train in Vienna. They spend the night together, talking about love and life and philosophy.

In the morning, they part ways with a promise to meet at the train station in exactly six months.

It's a sweet movie. Like my first year of college. Like teaching Ariel how to do a smoky eye. Walking on the boardwalk with ice cream (sorbet for me). Mackenzie and I hanging out in the pool during one of her parents' work-vacations.

A world full of possibilities. Perfect in its optimism.

In the next, *Before Sunset*, the characters meet again. It's half a decade later. The hero wrote a book about their night together (technically, it's fiction). He's on a tour, at his last stop in Paris.

And there she is. The heroine.

They missed each other at the train station. They moved on to new lives, new loves, new passions.

Or so they thought.

They try to act nice, make small talk, catch up. But their facades break. She can't stand what his book did to her. How it reminded her of who she used to be. She's become someone else in this time, someone out of touch with romance and optimism.

She lost some part of herself when she didn't see him again.

And here he is and she's found it. But she has a boyfriend. He's married with a kid.

Things are strained with his wife. They're only together for the kid.

She only makes it work with her boyfriend because he's away half the time.

They end the movie in her apartment, listening to music, lingering in this moment. He's watching her dance, his expression the picture of love, his posture finally relaxed.

She tells him he's going to miss his flight.

He knows.

An ambiguous ending. Answered by the third movie, sure, but perfect as it is. One moment of real connection, intimacy, love.

They know they own a part of each other's souls. That they have to choose between giving up their lives and giving up a piece of themselves.

It's real and raw and romantic at once.

It makes me believe in love.

That there's someone out there who will fill the emptiness in my heart.

Then the movie ends and I...

Forest is the only person I trust. And he...

It's not happening.

I push that aside. Focus on the snappy banter and the quaint charm of Paris.

The door opens.

Forest's eyes flit from me to the TV. He smiles. "You're a parody of yourself."

"And what were you listening to during your workout this morning?"

His lips curl into a smile. "That's different."

"How?"

"You're supposed to listen to music on repeat."

"So?"

"Who watches the same movie once a week?"

"People with taste." I hit pause on the remote. The TV freezes on an image of Jesse and Celine sipping coffee. "You'd like it if it had explosions."

"You'd like it better if I had *explosions*."

I can't help but laugh. "Is that your idea of dirty talk?"

He clicks the lock. Raises a brow. "No." His smile gets smug. "You can't handle my idea of dirty talk."

Yes, now, please. "Uh…" These lace panties won't survive that level of enthusiasm. "We should get started. While we have the light."

He nods *sure*.

"The boxers they sent for you are on the bed. And dark jeans over that. But not too tight. I don't want lines." My gaze drifts to his hips. That tattoo. I can't see it, but I still itch to trace every letter. "Those are a good fit. But darker. If you have that."

He nods *sure*. "Give me ten."

"Sure, yeah. Do you want coffee or something?"

"No. Chase brought in cold brews."

"What a nice boss."

He makes that *kinda* gesture. "Compared to you, maybe."

"We haven't even started."

"I know you, Skye. You're gonna work me hard." He motions to the fridge. "Stocked it with matcha and almond milk yesterday."

"Oh." My tongue slides over my lips reflexively.

"I'll make you one—"

"No, change. We need to start." I need to gain some semblance of sense before I literally tear his clothes off.

I mean, I am going to remove his clothes.

But it needs to be—

God, it's hot in here.

"I'll make it." Maybe I can figure out how to ice a matcha latte. Or maybe I can figure out how to ice my entire body.

Anything to keep me from melting.

Forest nods *all right*, moves up the stairs, shuts his bedroom door.

I put the kettle on. Move to Holden's room (he was so kind as to text me "please do get naked in my bed Skye. You don't have to share the pics, though I'd love to see them. I just want to picture you there."). Strip out of my street clothes. Don my black satin robe.

Clothes mean clothing lines.

I need those gone.

The instructions for this shoot are clear. Lingerie and jeans only.

Jeans aren't really my thing—it's impossible to find anything that fits both my hips and my waist—so it's all lingerie.

Maybe a denim designer will offer me five grand for topless pics in jeans.

Until then—

The kettle steams. I move downstairs. Lose myself in the rhythm of fixing a matcha. Sift. Measure. Whisk.

Pour into warm almond milk.

Stir.

Add honey and vanilla extract.

There.

Perfection.

Hot, yes, but that's a lost cause.

I take a long sip. Let the rich, sweet drink warm my lips, tongue, throat.

For a moment, my life is all green tea and honey.

Then Forest steps out of his bedroom in boxers and dark wash jeans.

Unbuttoned dark wash jeans.

He stands at the top of the stairs. Looks down at me like he's Juliette on the balcony, searching desperately for Romeo. "You ready, Skye?"

No. But here goes nothing.

## Chapter Eighteen

SKYE

Forest leans against his bedroom door, pushing it closed.

I turn to the window. Pretend to check the light. It's still afternoon. It's still bright. I need to diffuse this.

The new white curtains are in place. They're a little too sheer. They're letting in a little too much light. But I can make that work.

I pull them closed.

Turn back to Forest.

Soft light falls over his face, shoulders, torso.

Mmm.

Must.

Stop.

Staring.

"Too tight?" he asks.

Right. His jeans. I need to make sure they're okay. To make sure he doesn't have any lines from his clothes.

Lines are a bitch to Photoshop.

I have to get closer.

I have to touch him.

No, I get to touch him.

It's the same as pretending for Mackenzie. We're pretending for the camera.

No big deal.

Totally not a big deal.

At all.

"Skye?" he asks.

"Yeah?"

"My jeans?"

I'm leading this. I'm the photographer, the art director, the producer. Which means I need to push my lust aside. At least until I'm fully in model mode. "Come closer."

"Oh?" He raises a brow.

I fight my blush. "I have to check for lines."

He takes a step toward me.

Another.

Another.

His room is small. This is California. His house is a quarter-mile from the beach. It's a big room, by those standards, but it's not big enough for the desire racing through my veins.

I move closer. Until I can smell his soap. Mmm, pine needles. Of course, Forest smells like pine. It's too fitting.

My fingers brush his stomach.

My eyes flit to his waist.

His jeans are unbuttoned. His black boxers peek through. Then the light skin underneath that. The dark ink on his hip.

No clothing indents.

"Perfect." I press my palm into his skin. Fuck, he's so warm and hard. It's not like touching him for Mackenzie's sake. It's just us. It's my skin against his.

"Where do you want me?"

I force my eyes to the bed. "Lying down to start."

He raises a brow. "Having your way with me?"

"They're not actually interested in you."

"Oh?"

"Yeah." Kinda. I drop my hand. Move behind my camera. "They only want pictures of me or us together."

"My ego."

"Is it bruised?"

He nods. "Maybe you'll be the one rubbing arnica on me this time."

Rubbing… Forest…

Jesus Christ.

I'm going to melt. I'm literally going to melt. Paramedics are going to find me in a puddle.

Death by desire. What a way to go.

"You're uh…" Must. Focus. I look through the viewfinder. Adjust the angle. "On the bed."

He sits.

"Flat."

He raises a brow. "You never do what I ask."

"And?"

"Why should I do what you ask?"

"Because if you don't, I'll have to get Holden to help."

He chuckles. "Fuck, that's a terrible fate."

"Yeah." I watch him through the camera. "So learn some obedience. For my sake."

"You sure your title isn't Mistress Skye?"

"Oh my God."

He lies on his back. Stretches his arm over his head.

God, he's so long and lean and inviting.

*Click, click.* I snap a few pictures of him. "You're sounding more like Holden every day."

"You're underestimating Holden."

"Yeah?"

"Yeah?" He turns to the camera. Shoots it *fuck me* eyes.

*Click. Click.* My breath hitches. My limbs buzz. My sex clenches.

Photographer.

In the moment.

Acing this.

"I'll post some good ones of you," I say. "So Mackenzie can see what she's missing."

He nods *sure*. There's no enthusiasm in it. If anything, his posture stiffens.

I try not to question it. "Look at me like that again. But, this time, reach for your jeans."

"Oh?" He raises a brow.

It's perfect. *Click, click.* "You're going to take off the pants sooner or later."

"Usually women sound more excited about that."

"Do they?"

"Yeah." His voice is knowing. Like he's back in a memory. Or a particularly vivid fantasy.

"Oh." I am a photographer motivating a model. I don't care who he imagines. Only that he pictures someone he craves. "Think about one. Imagine there's a woman you want more than anything, staring at you, begging you to slide your jeans to your knees."

"Yeah?" He makes eye contact, through the camera.

"Imagine she's begging you to take out your cock. To touch yourself. To let her touch you."

The playfulness in his expression fades into pure desire.

He stares at the camera like he knows it wants him naked.

His fingers brush the waistband of his jeans.

*Click, click.*

He hooks his thumb on his belt loop. Peels his jeans back.

*Click, click.*

Lower and lower.

Black microfiber stretches over his skin.

Over his hardening cock.

*Click, click.*

My breath catches in my throat. I push out a shaky exhale. "She's looking at you like she wants you more than anything. But you keep teasing her. You want to drive her crazy. You want her to melt into a puddle of desire."

His hands go to his hips. *Click, click.* He lifts his ass. *Click, click.* Pushes his jeans to mid-thigh.

*Click, click.*

He falls back on the bed. Places one hand on his *ahem*. Brings the other to his head.

He turns like he's lost in bliss.

Like he's about to come.

Like he can't take the agony anymore.

*Click, click.*

"I…" Want to mount him. Right now. "Do you want anything in particular?"

"This is your shoot, princess." It's not the *princess* he used around Mackenzie. But it's not the way he normally says my name either.

It's heady.

Needy even.

Or maybe I'm out of my mind.

Maybe I need to lean into that. To step into my role as a model. To embrace how badly I want him.

I scroll through our pictures. They're good. Insanely hot. Hot enough women everywhere are going to be desperate to touch Forest.

If they aren't already.

Ahem.

He has what he needs. Now, I need—"Let's start with your jeans on." I adjust the camera so it's pointed at the front of the bed.

Forest slips into his jeans.

I direct him to the appropriate spot. Snap a few pictures to check the lighting. Pull the curtain back to let in a little more sun.

There. Perfect.

I wrap my fingers around my remote. Step out from behind the camera. Look Forest in the eyes. "Ready?"

"Yeah."

Here goes nothing.

I undo the sash holding my robe together.

The black satin falls off my shoulders.

Forest's pupils dilate. His jaw drops. His fingers curl into his thighs. "Fuck, Skye."

"It's a little—"

"Yeah."

"They want sexy."

He stares, dumbstruck.

"They want a perfume ad vibe. The two of us, half-naked, tangled together."

His eyes move over me slowly. He takes in my thick thighs, my lacy black panties, my sheer bra. "You look…"

I swallow hard. "Is that a good pause?"

"Yeah." His throat quivers as he swallows. "I… uh… You…" His eyes move over me again. This time, they stop at my hips. "Is that one of those—"

"It's a thong, yeah." I turn enough he can see the thick strap.

His eyes get wider. His jaw falls back to the floor.

There's no put on. No pretense. No faking of any kind.

He. Wants. Me.

Fuck, it feels good. I'm warm all over. My fingers curl into the remote. My thighs press together.

"Could you—" I motion to my heels, the ones sitting by the foot of the bed. My black boots. The lace-up stilettos.

For pole.

Or photo shoots.

Not at all practical as streetwear.

But for this—

"Yeah." He gathers the boots in his hands.

I move to the bed. Sit next to him.

He shifts onto the floor. Onto his knees. His eyes stay on my ankle as he slides my right boot onto my foot.

Then the left.

He laces carefully. Like his life depends on it.

Then he looks up at me.

*Click.*

His laugh breaks up the tension. "You don't have to trick me into posing."

"It just… Seemed like a good moment."

"Me between your legs?"

"Yeah. I…"

"Miss that?"

Ahem. "I don't not miss it." My gaze flits to the camera. It is in the perfect spot for this. It's a great shot too. "Do you… are you comfortable with that?"

"With eating women out?"

Oh my God. "With simulating the position?"

"Yeah." His eyes meet mine.

"Sure, let's um…" I spread my legs a little wider.

He moves closer.

"You, um, the foreshortening means you don't need to get any closer to—"

"Your cunt?"

My cheeks flush. "Yeah."

He holds my gaze. "You don't like the word?"

"No, I just—"

"I won't use it if you don't like it."

My blush deepens. "No, it's more…" The desire in his voice is too sexy. I'm already melting. If Forest says—I can't even think it.

"You do like it." His smile gets wicked.

"I… Yes." My blush spreads to my chest.

His eyes get wicked too.

God, I want to touch him. "Hands on my knees maybe."

"Or here." He rests his palms on my thighs. He's not that close, but he's close enough.

"And I'll—" I hook my leg over his shoulder. Then the other. "Is the heel okay?"

"Yeah."

"It can dig."

"You know from experience?"

I clear my throat.

"You're not gonna warn me?"

"No, I just—Let me know if it does."

He nods *sure*.

"Stay there." My thighs rest on his shoulders.

His palms dig into my skin.

His lips stay so, so close to where they need to be.

I reach for his head. Knot my hand in his hair. Place the other behind my back. To hide the remote. And keep my balance.

*Click, click.*

I lean back. *Click, click.* I throw my head to one side. *Click, click.* Then the other *click*.

Then back. *Click, click.*

His nails dig into my thighs. *Click, click.*

My chest heaves with my inhale. *Click, click.*

My eyes meet his. *Click, click.*

It's too much. Too close. Too real. Too intimate.

I unwind my legs. Shift backward. "That's good." Even breaths. Even voice. Even smile. "We should get some… where we can see the panties."

"True." He stands.

*Click, click.*

Again, his chuckle breaks up the tension. "You can ask me to pose."

"No. You're a natural. I don't want to over-direct."

"You don't think I'll listen?"

Both. Mostly my inability to articulate anything besides *Forest. Naked. Now.* "Why don't you sit? I'll sit on you. We'll get the front. And the back."

He sits next to me. Shoots me that same wicked smile. "Yes, mistress."

He's in character. That's it.

That must be it.

I move him into the center of the shot. Then I shift into his lap.

He looks up at me like I'm everything he wants. *Click, click.*

I run my hand through his dark hair. *Click, click.*

## The Best Friend Bargain

He copies my gesture. Pulls my hair aside. *Click, click*. Rests his palm on my cheek. *Click, click*. Turns my head, so my neck is inches from his mouth. *Click, click*.

I arch my back into the air. *Click, click*. Then I settle into his lap. *Click, click*.

He wraps one arm around me. *Click, click*.

I hook my legs around his waist. *Click, click*.

He slips two fingers under the strap of my bra. *Click, click*. Undoes the hook. *Click, click*.

The lace falls to my sides.

I shift back. Catch it. Redo the hooks. "We, uh… we need it in the shot."

He looks at me with confusion. Then he blinks and he's back to the Forest I know. A hard wall with a few soft places. And, uh…

Not thinking about hard places.

I shift off him.

Turn to the camera. *Click, click*.

He reaches for me. *Click, click*. Rests his hand on my hip. *Click, click*. Tugs at my thong. *Click, click*.

"Widen your legs," I say.

He does.

I sit between them.

He brings his mouth to my neck. *Click, click*.

His lips skim my skin.

Softly.

Then harder.

Harder.

My eyelids flutter together.

My fingers dig into my thighs.

He pushes my bra strap off my shoulder. *Click, click*. Wraps his arm around me. "Do you want to take it off?" He motions to my bra.

My body screams *yes*. I try to find logic. Artistry. Something besides my libido.

It's a good shot, the bra next to us, his arm covering my chest. Like the lingerie is so hot we can't help but fuck.

But that means...

He's going to see me topless.

I... Uh...

"Skye?" His voice is still heady. "You want me leading?"

"Yeah."

He nods *sure*. His hand goes to my mid-back.

Slowly, he undoes the strap of my bra. *Click, click.*

Slowly, he slides the right strap off my shoulder.

Then the left.

I hold my arm over my chest. Catch the fabric. *Click, click.*

Let it fall. *Click, click.*

Let my arm fall. *Click, click.*

His breath quickens. His lips brush my neck. His fingertips skim my stomach.

Higher and higher and—

He pulls his hand away. Brings it to my neck. Turns my head so I'm looking into his eyes.

*Click, click.*

His eyelids flutter together.

Mine follow suit.

Then his lips are on mine.

He tastes good. Like honey. And something all Forest.

His lips are soft. Sweet.

They close around my bottom lip.

He sucks softly.

Then harder.

Harder.

*Click, click.*

I mean to pull back; I do.

But instead my lips part.

His tongue slips into my mouth. It dances with mine. Commands mine.

He kisses me like he's claiming me.

Like I'm the only thing he wants.

The remote slips from my hand.

I don't stop to get it.

I kiss him back.

Kiss him harder.

Deeper.

He pulls me closer. Until I can feel his cock against my ass.

He's hard.

Not because of the shoot or his imagination or his need for his ex.

For me.

It's everything.

It's perfect.

Then there's this sound. Footsteps. A familiar voice.

The door handle turning.

Holden.

I jump off the bed. Scramble into my robe.

Forest tosses something at the door.

Holden's laugh fills the room. "Damn, I missed something good."

I cinch my robe. Turn back to the interrupter. "Go. Away."

"Sure." He smiles *no problem*. "Just thought you'd want to know Daisy is on her way."

I clear my throat.

Forest shoots his brother a death glare. "We're aware."

"Don't stop on my account." Holden moves into the hallway. "Seems like it was just getting good."

"We're only—" Words. They're impossible. "It's a photo shoot."

"Can I get those photos?" Holden winks.

Forest throws a pillow at his head.

Holden catches it. Blows me a kiss. "Hope you're wearing that to the party." He turns, closes the door, moves down the stairs.

Forest shakes his head. "Sorry, he's an idiot."

"Yeah, I mean… we're obviously just…"

"Right."

"It doesn't—"

"Exactly." His eyes stay on the floor. "Do you need the room?"

"No, I, uh… my clothes are in Holden's."

Forest nods *sure*. "Should we…" He motions to the camera. "Do you need more?"

"No, I think we're good. And… uh… I'll get dressed."

"Yeah."

I turn the camera off. Remove it from the tripod. Move to the door.

I try to stay focused on my very simple task, but my eyes roam over Forest's body.

He's still hard.

There are more pressing things to consider, but at the moment, there's only one thing in my head.

This voice groaning *he's still hard*.

## Chapter Nineteen

Sure enough, Oliver's sister Daisy is downstairs. With her blond hair and her cornflower blue eyes, she's every bit as adorable as her name.

She's pure California Babe. Not that she's a babe just yet.

It's not that she isn't gorgeous. She is. But she's so damn young. A kid who needs protecting.

Hell, she's looking at Holden like he's the guy who's going to protect her.

Daisy turns to me as I step onto the main floor. "Forest, hey." She smooths her peach dress. "You look good."

"He still hard?" Holden asks.

Daisy blushes. "Sorry, he's—"

"He's my brother. I should be the one apologizing."

Her nod is knowing. Her brother is... maybe her situation isn't as bad as Mack's. Oliver isn't an alcoholic. Just a guy who likes to party.

But he's gotten sloppy drunk enough times I've had to apologize for him.

She's probably carrying a lot of weight.

And now Holden is fucking with her. Or trying to fuck her. One of the two.

I study my brother's easy expression.

He looks at me curiously. "You already finished with Skye?" He shakes his head. "Shameful."

Daisy stifles a laugh. "I'm sure Forest... gets the job done."

"I'm not." Holden holds up a bottle of vodka *you want some?*

I nod *sure*.

He fills a cup with ice. Pours. "Maybe I was wrong about Skye. Maybe she is the generous type. Getting on her knees, unzipping your jeans, begging to suck your cock."

Daisy's eyes go wide. Poor girl has no idea what she's getting into hanging out with Holden.

Someone needs to convince her it's a bad idea. But a warning from me isn't going to help. I'm older than her brother. Practically an older brother.

Teenagers don't listen to adults.

If I ask her to stay away, she'll run right to him.

If I ask Holden—

Maybe there's some reverse psychology I can use here.

"How does she beg? Is it more of a high-pitched whine? Or more low and needy?" Holden asks.

My balls tighten at the thought of Skye's groan. Not where my head needs to go.

"Fuck, what about that lipstick she wears? Does it stay on her—"

"Shut the fuck up." I can't think about her lips. About how good she tastes. About how much my body is humming.

I want to kiss her again.

I need to kiss her again.

I need to feel her skin against mine.

Not just because I want to fuck her. Because I want more. I want everything.

Only I'm not capable of giving her everything.

He smiles, victorious. "Damn, you're on edge for a guy who just came."

Daisy stares at him with equal parts horror and interest. *Oh my God, how can he say that? It's so dirty. And so hot.*

I've seen this happen before. Way too many times. Holden enjoys corrupting the innocent.

Or so he claims.

Honestly, it's hard to tell when my brother means... anything.

"It was all acting," I say.

"You were acting like you had a boner? Uh-huh." He nods *sure, sure*.

"It happens." Daisy's voice is shy. "In my drama class, we were doing a kissing scene. And my acting partner... He... ahem." Her blush deepens. "It was awkward, but I managed to stay in character."

"You're as fast as a high school boy. That's impressive." Holden winks at me.

Daisy frowns. "I just mean... were you guys really taking pictures in lingerie?"

"Yeah," I say.

"For..." She looks to Holden. "I'm sure what your brother told me is wrong."

"She runs a fashion blog," I say. "The company is paying her to post their stuff."

"They give her the lingerie? And pay her to post it?" she asks.

"Yeah," I say.

Her eyes go wide. "That's awesome." She plays with the edge of her cardigan. "And you're helping her? What a good friend."

Holden hands over my drink.

I take a greedy sip. Vodka on ice. It's cheap enough it's shit, but not so cheap it burns. "Thanks."

"Mhmm." He hooks his arm around Daisy. "What are you drinking, gorgeous?"

She lets out a giggle. "If Oliver sees—"

"Tell him it's soda." He motions to the bottle of diet coke on the counter.

She nods *obviously*. " I don't really like the taste." Her eyes fix on Holden's.

"I have just the thing." He smiles, brings her to the bar, fixes her a rum and diet.

She takes a tiny sip. "Huh." Then a bigger one. "That's… really good."

"Don't let her get drunk," I say.

She fights a frown. Stops herself from saying something about how she's not a kid.

I'm not going to argue. I remember being that age. Thinking I understood the world.

Sure, I grew up fast. But I had a hell of a lot to learn too.

"You and Skye were awfully fast." Holden fixes himself a rum and coke. Turns to me. "Tell me you got the job done."

I flip him off.

He smiles. Turns to Daisy. "See, this is the kind of guy you want to avoid."

"Is it?" she asks.

He nods. "He gets all pissy if you question his ability to make a woman come. That kind of insecurity—it's a sign he can't rise to the occasion."

"He can't…" She clears her throat.

"No, he was the white flag." Holden laughs. "Black flag I guess, given the attire."

"Do you have pictures?" she asks.

Upstairs, a door closes. Skye's heels tap the hardwood floor.

She descends the stairs slowly. Like she's a princess showing off her ornate dress. I guess she is.

She's wearing something new. Hot pink with tiny black polka dots. It hugs her curvy body. Falls just below her knees.

Her blue eyes fix on me.

"Fuck, he's already hard, isn't he?" Holden asks.

Daisy rises to her tiptoes to whisper something in his ear.

He whispers back.

She laughs.

"Are you jealous we didn't invite you?" Skye steps onto the main floor.

"Always." He releases Daisy for long enough to fix Skye a Moscow Mule.

Skye takes it. Nods *thanks*. "Aw, baby, you know it's only because you don't have the stamina."

"Oh?" Holden raises a brow. "You think I can't make it?"

She nods. "It's sad. I mean, it's flattering, that you want me so badly you come in thirty seconds. But I need a guy who lasts long enough—"

"Skye, baby, are you daring me?" he asks.

"What if I am?" she asks.

"Then I'm gonna have to show you just how long I last." He sets his glass on the counter. Reaches for his jeans. One hand on the button. The other on the zipper. "Now, we have to set the terms."

"Oh?" She takes a long sip. Lets out a deep groan. That *oh my God, I need more groan*.

My balls tighten.

I try to shake it off. Fail.

Try to look her in the eyes.

Fail harder.

I don't know what to say. How to explain what happened in that photo shoot. How to deal with how badly I want to kiss her again.

If Holden hadn't interrupted—

I can still say it's acting. That it's nothing. That I'm not going out of my mind, wanting her out of that tight outfit—

I can say it.

But it's bullshit.

"Are you taking that off—" He motions to her tight pink dress. "Or just tempting me with how tight it is?"

Daisy frowns.

"You need all the help you can get, Holden," Skye says. "I wouldn't want to speed you up."

"I can do this on hard mode, baby," he says. "Show me those tits again. I'll be there fast."

Skye's cheeks flush. "You... uh..." She clears her throat. "I actually need to get dinner, so, uh—"

"Maybe you should go together," Daisy offers.

She wants to be alone with my brother. In an empty house.

I don't think so.

"Uh, well..." Skye stammers. "We should probably order something, for, uh—"

The door saves her from finishing her sentence.

The handle turns. Ariel steps inside. She looks at Holden and shakes her head. "You're too old for her."

Skye laughs. "I think that's the appeal."

Daisy turns bright red. "No, I... We... Excuse me." She rushes to the bathroom.

"Poor girl. She has no idea what she's getting into." Ariel crosses the room to me. Pulls me into a tight hug. "Are you okay? You look flushed."

Holden chuckles. "He and Skye were rolling around in their underwear."

Ariel squeals. "Really? You finally realized it and—" She takes in our expressions. "Never mind."

"How are you feeling?" My gaze goes to her stomach. She's showing more every day. I guess that's what happens at this stage of pregnancy. She's due in mid-August. It's less than three months away.

Three months until I'm an uncle.

I'm sure Chase is way too over-protective. That she can't stand the thought of another guy trying to protect her. But I don't care.

I'm not letting anything happen to my niece.

"Good. Uh..." Her cheeks flush. "Things you don't want to hear."

"Horny?" Holden asks.

"Why are you asking if your sister is horny?" I ask.

"Because that's clearly what she means. And, once again, I

don't live in some fantasy world where my sister is the only pregnant virgin since Mary," Holden says.

Skye laughs. "Is Chase coming?"

"Later. He's closing the shop." Ariel looks from Skye to me. "You were in lingerie?"

"For my Instagram," Skye says. "A company wanted to pay me for photos."

"That's amazing." Ariel smiles. "And you went with Forest as your model?"

"Well, um… we're kinda…" Skye looks to me. Her cheeks flame as soon as her eyes meet mine. "You didn't tell her?"

"Why would I?" I ask.

"Tell me?" Ariel frowns. "You don't think I can keep a secret."

"No, I know you can," Skye says. "But, uh… Forest and I are faking a relationship. For the time being."

"Oh, because he can't handle Mackenzie getting married?" Ariel asks, completely earnest. My sister does not understand normal social mores like tact.

Holden bursts into laughter. He doubles over, clutching his stomach as he cracks up. "About time someone called you on it."

"Was that supposed to be a secret?" Ariel frowns. "Sorry, Forest, but—"

"It's fine," I say.

"And Skye volunteered?" She looks at Skye knowingly.

Skye clears her throat. "Actually, I asked him to do it. Mackenzie is just…"

"She's awful," Ariel says. "But this is still stupid."

Holden laughs harder.

Ariel looks at me. "Should I lie?"

Skye blushes. "No, uh, you're right. It is stupid. But it's really a favor to me. I have to beg him—"

"Go on." Holden winks.

Skye rolls her eyes. "I had to beg him to do this." She takes a long sip of her Moscow Mule. "Come on, Ariel. Let's get dinner."

"Oh yeah, can we do Thai?" Ariel's eyes light up. "I've been craving Thai basil for three weeks straight."

"We made Thai on Sunday." We still do family dinner every week, whether Dad is in town or not. Right here. In this living room.

"Yes, and I'm still craving Thai basil." She looks at me *obviously*. "Just me and you."

The bathroom door opens. Daisy steps outside. She looks at the scene with that same wide-eyed innocence.

Ariel completely misses it. She nods. "Hey, Daisy."

"Hey." Daisy smiles.

"You want to get Thai with us?" Ariel asks.

"And talk about Charlotte," Skye says.

"And other things." Ariel shoots Skye a knowing look.

Daisy looks to Holden. When he nods *go for it*, she offers the girls a yes.

"You inviting us?" Holden asks.

"No boys allowed." Ariel hugs Holden. "But we'll talk later."

"We will?" he asks.

"Oh yeah. Someone has to tell you what a dick you're being," she says.

I chuckle.

"You too, Forest." My sister waves goodbye.

She wraps her arm around Skye. Immediately starts gushing about her baby daddy Chase. And about her baby. And how horny the pregnancy is making her.

Fuck, I'm crazy excited to be an uncle. It's the best news I've had in forever.

But that is too much information.

Holden waits until the girls are out the door, then he turns to me. "She asked you to do this, huh?"

"Yeah."

"Because she hates Mack?"

"Yeah."

"You really believe that?" he asks.

"Why wouldn't I?"

"Dunno... just seems like a lot of effort. For hate."

"What the fuck are you talking about?" I ask.

"Maybe there's a simpler explanation."

I stare at him, trying to figure out what he means.

"It is the chance to kiss you."

"And?"

"She's pretty into that. And you—you *were* waving the black flag."

"So?" There's no doubt I want to fuck Skye. Maybe she wants to fuck me too. But that doesn't mean anything.

Sex isn't always important, meaningful, beautiful.

Sometimes it's just a way to come.

Maybe that's all she wants from me.

Maybe she also sees me as a tattooed bad boy with a perfect body. A box to check before she gets with a guy who wears a suit to work.

"You ever wonder why Skye spends all her time with you?" he asks.

"We're friends."

"Think about it, Forest." He shakes his head *God, you're stupid*. Shrugs. Shifts back to *I am the most difficult guy in the universe* Holden I know so well. "I'm saying. If you're gonna continue being an idiot, I might have to change the odds on some of these bets."

"What are you talking about?"

"Look at the evidence. Figure it out. I have money on you being smarter than this. Money I don't want to lose."

I flip him off.

He shakes his head *it's sad how little you see*.

## Chapter Twenty

SKYE

The waitress smiles as she drops off our drinks. Thai tea with coconut milk for me. Water for Ariel. (Much to her eternal pout). A plain iced tea for Daisy.

She nods *thank you*. Takes a dainty sip.

She's dressed well for a high school girl, but it's still obvious she *is* a high school girl. I'm not sure why. Her posture is good—amazing for a teenager. Her dress is pretty. A simple wrap in a warm shade of pink that flatters her light complexion.

Her makeup isn't quite right—her lips are too red for her look, her eyeshadow is too light—but it's nice.

I guess it's all the little things, together.

Don't get me wrong. She's gorgeous. I can see why Holden is interested. If he is.

I really can't tell with him.

Besides, it's probably less her looks and more the whole *shy, innocent, soon to be legal* thing.

I tear the paper off my straw. Take a long, delicious sip of my Thai iced tea. It's not my usual drink—it's full of both artificial colors and flavors—but there's something about the creamy coconut milk, the rich tea, whatever it is that makes it this shade of orange.

My groan is too loud.

"Save something for Forest." Ariel laughs as she takes a long sip of water. She motions to the drink *can I?*

"Of course." I offer it to her.

"Don't tell him. Or Chase." She takes a long sip. Stifles her own moan. "He rides me hard about the caffeine."

"He rides you hard?" Daisy's voice is half joke, half question. She *is* shy. And she's not in the right environment to shine.

Ariel is… not the most tactful person. And I… Forest always says I fill the silence. Talk a lot. Not too much, since he likes it, and he's quiet, but a lot.

Ariel laughs. Then blushes. "He, um…" She looks to me for help. *Should we tell her this?*

I shrug. What do I know about interacting with teenagers?

"We, um, should probably not discuss that," she says.

"Oh." Daisy's nod is knowing. "If you don't want to talk about sex, don't. But don't act like I'm some innocent flower."

"Are you not?" Ariel asks, not at all aware of her bluntness. "You're even named after a flower."

"You're named after a mermaid," Daisy says. "Can you breathe underwater?"

I can't help but laugh. She's funny. And bolder than she looks. "I am not omnipresent."

They look at me like I'm crazy.

"Like the sky? It's everywhere." When they don't laugh, I move on. "When do you turn eighteen?"

"This summer." Her smile is warm. "I may not have a lot of experience with guys, but I'm not innocent."

Ariel shoots me a *yeah right* look.

Daisy catches it. Does nothing to hide her frown.

I nudge Ariel. "Maybe, uh, maybe that's true." I turn to Daisy. "Besides, there's more to life than sex."

"There is?" Ariel asks.

"Oh my God, you're so horny." I laugh. "All the time."

"I know." She pouts. "I can't work. Or watch TV. Or take walks. My head keeps going back to sex."

"Chase?" I ask.

"Or other guys?" Daisy asks.

"Always Chase." Ariel beams. "He's just so…" Her sigh is dreamy. "He is… We are… we can't be as rough anymore." She rubs her stomach. "Charlotte gets in the way." She looks to me. "Do you think you and Forest will have babies?"

"We aren't even—" I clear my throat. "We just kissed once."

"You did!" Ariel looks to Daisy. "Can you believe it? They finally kissed. Oh my God." She wraps her arms around me. "That's amazing."

"You've only kissed?" Daisy asks.

"Well… so far." I release Ariel. Take another sip of Thai iced tea. It's rich and sweet, but it fails to cool me off. Forest's lips… they're so soft. I want them again. All night. But we… he…

I have no idea what it means.

If it means anything.

Maybe he got caught up in the moment. Maybe that's all it is.

"I would have thought…" Daisy takes a long sip of her soda. "You two seem comfortable together."

"We are. Sorta." I can't think about it right now. "So you and Holden, huh?"

"We're just friends." Her cheeks flush. "He helps me out sometimes."

Disbelief spreads over Ariel's face. "You're a virgin, right?"

"Ariel!" I press my palm into my forehead. Laugh even though I shouldn't.

"What?" Ariel asks. "She is. Should I not ask?"

"I don't see why that matters," Daisy says.

"Do you like him?" Ariel asks.

Daisy turns bright red.

I clear my throat.

Ariel shoots me a *what* look.

"You're modeling now?" Daisy changes the subject. "When did

that start? Is it full time?" She stares at me like she's sure I'm a model. Like there's absolutely nothing weird about me making a living as a model. Like I'm not too short, too big, too weird.

"Not yet. But this job will... well, it's not enough to move out. Not yet. But soon," I say.

Ariel nods. Refuses to accept this change in subject. "You seem nice, Daisy. And smart. But Holden is very charming. It's easy to miss what a troublemaker he is."

"I know," Daisy says. "He's just a friend."

"But you do like him," Ariel says.

"It doesn't matter. I know where we stand." Her blue eyes fill with regret for a moment—she can't stand that he isn't hers, that he won't be hers, that he sees her as a kid—then she blinks, and her expression is pure acceptance.

God, I know that feeling.

Only when I try to find it—

It's gone.

I can't accept this anymore. I can't accept friendship and nothing more.

I need more.

I need everything.

Ariel continues. "Keep it that way. He sleeps with everything that moves. And he doesn't... there's nothing wrong with that. If you want that, go for it. But he's not the kind of guy who sticks around after. You know what I mean?"

It's surprisingly tactful for her.

Daisy nods. "I knew that after ten minutes of talking to him."

I chuckle. "It is obvious."

"What about you and Forest?" she asks. "He was looking at you like he couldn't wait to take you upstairs." Her blush deepens. "Back upstairs, I guess."

I don't know what to say, so I take another sip.

"Was he really—" She nods to her crotch. "The whole time."

"Not the whole time," I say.

## The Best Friend Bargain

Ariel clears her throat. "Please do not talk about my brother's boner. I don't need to hear that."

Daisy giggles. "Sorry."

Ariel looks to me. Mouths *oh my God, she wants him.*

She does. But there's nothing we can do about it. The more we tell her to stay away from Holden, the more she'll go after him.

"You're good friends?" Daisy asks.

"Great friends," I say.

"Oh my God, Skye. He practically lives at Dad's house now. He's never at his apartment," Ariel says. "Do you really think he's there because he likes it?"

"Yeah?" It's a huge house. With a basketball court. Who wouldn't like it? "Besides, he's only there for family dinners."

She shakes her head. "All the time. Because he wants to be near you."

"I'll go to his apartment," I say.

"Oh." Daisy's interest perks. "You go to his apartment."

God, she's such a kid. That's a big deal to her. Not something people do. "Yeah, we're friends."

"And where do you sleep? When you spend the night at his apartment?" Ariel asks.

"I take his bed." But—"He takes the couch. It's just—"

"And you're in his sheets and they smell like him?" Daisy's eyes go wide. "That's so romantic."

"I don't know which of you is more obvious." Ariel shakes her head *ridiculous*.

She turns to the waiter as he drops off our food. Basil chicken and eggplant for Ariel. Shrimp green curry for me. Pad Thai for Daisy.

Kind of obvious, but hard to knock. Not that I had such sophisticated taste at her age. Or now. Green curry has to be in the list of most popular Thai dishes somewhere.

I pick up my fork.

Drop it as Ariel jumps out of her seat.

I follow her gaze to Chase.

And—oh, God, poor Daisy.

Chase smiles. "Look who I found at Inked Hearts." He pats Mr. Flynn's shoulder. "He was talking to Oliver." Chase nods *hello* to Daisy. "Your brother says hi."

She hides behind her hands. "Hey, Dad."

Ariel practically skips to her baby daddy. She wraps her arms around him. Squeezes tightly.

He whispers something in her ear.

They whisper back and forth.

Finally, she pries herself away. Offers Daisy's dad her hand. "It's nice to see you, Mr. Flynn."

"Please. Gabe," he says.

"Gabriel?" she offers.

His chuckle is low. Knowing. "Sure, Gabriel." He shakes her hand.

She motions to us. "Come. Sit. We just ordered food. If you're hungry."

"It's actually no boys allowed." I nod hello. "But next time."

"Do you have everything you need?" He looks to Daisy.

"Yes, Dad, thank you." She takes a long sip of diet. Nearly chokes on it.

"Oliver is spending the night at Holden's place," he says.

Does he really believe that?

It's possible Oliver will get so drunk he crashes on the couch. But it's more likely he'll take someone home.

Though—

He is protective of Daisy.

"I'll make sure she gets home, Mr. Flynn," I say.

"Gabe." He offers his hand.

I take it. Shake. "Gabe." I won't say it—God knows I hate hearing it—but Mr. Flynn… Gabe is super hot. Like level ten hot. Easily as hot as Chase or Forest.

He's tall and lean with crystal clear blue eyes and ashy brown hair. There are hints of grey at his temples. He's obviously not twenty, but he looks good. Younger than his age—he must be somewhere around forty.

He *wears* his business casual look. And the tattoos that peek out from under his rolled sleeves are pure bad boy.

I shouldn't stereotype, I know.

But he really is—

"Don't worry about me," Daisy says. "You finally have a night to yourself. I thought you had a date?"

"I do." His voice is paternal. Firm and giving. The same as Forest's. "But how am I supposed to enjoy it if I don't know my baby girl is okay?"

"I'm fine." Her voice gets unusually curt "You should go. Get dressed. Aren't you going someplace nice?" she asks.

"She's trying to get rid of me." He chuckles. "Come here."

She stands.

He pulls her into a hug. "Be careful, okay?"

"It's just a party." She pulls back. "But I will."

He looks to me. "Take care of her." There's something about the way he says it. Like he'll know whether or not I mean it.

"I will." I'll do my best, at least. Holden is… well, he's a lot of things. But he won't let anyone hurt Daisy. Not physically. Not emotionally either.

I think.

Probably.

Honestly, it's really hard to read him.

"Okay." He hugs her one last time. Nods goodbye to Chase. Leaves.

Daisy sighs *thank God*.

Ariel laughs. "Oh my God, Daisy. Your dad is so hot."

I laugh too. "You're not supposed to say that."

"Don't worry, I still think your dad is hot." Ariel turns to Daisy. "He's got a real… um… who's that guy all the ladies like?"

"Me?" Chase offers.

She laughs. "That's it. You." She wraps her arms around his shoulders. "You look good today."

"You too." He kisses her cheek.

He whispers in her ear.

It's disgustingly cute.

It fills my head with all these ideas.

That could be us one day. Me and Forest. Him fussing over my pregnancy. Getting even more protective.

We used to talk about it, when we were younger, and our lives seemed full of possibilities.

Now—

God, I can see it.

Him in a tux. Me walking down the aisle in some over-the-top black and purple dress. His ring on my finger.

A big, beautiful life.

Shit, I'm getting way ahead of myself.

We barely kissed.

I want to kiss him again, but—

God, I really want to kiss him again.

## Chapter Twenty-One

SKYE

By the time we get back to the Ballard place, the party is in full swing.

Eighties pop music flows from the speakers. Streamers cover the walls. Tattooed men bump into—

Well, this is one of Holden's parties, so it's full of beautiful women. There must be two dozen hot chicks I've never seen before.

As soon as Daisy steps inside, the party boy appears. He whisks her to the bar. Points out her protective older brother, Oliver, who's sitting on the couch with Forest.

They're deep in conversation, hands around plastic cups, bottle of bourbon in front of them.

Daisy frowns at the sight of the bottle, then Holden slides his arm around her waist, and her discomfort disappears.

God, that poor girl. Her crush on the troublemaker is super-sized. She's so young. She's still in high school. And he's this cool older guy, with tattoos and experience and a devil may care attitude.

Ariel and I watch them for a minute. He's being nice enough. Introducing her to friends, filling her drink, asking about school.

Maybe it's innocent.

Maybe he's actually keeping an eye on his best friend's kid sister.

Maybe his whole *I live to cause you pain* thing is just for kicks.

"You think he'll..." I reach for a euphemism. Remember Ariel doesn't understand them. "He's not into virgins or something?"

Ariel's nose scrunches. "He's into anyone who moves."

I can't help but chuckle. "Anyone?"

"Anyone pretty." Her eyes meet mine. "Forest hasn't been with anyone in a while."

"Yeah, but..." I pull my arm over my chest. "He's still into Mackenzie."

"Maybe."

"Maybe? He fucked every girl with the same body type for six months straight."

Ariel frowns.

"And the ones with bright red hair..." God, there were so many.

"Yeah, but has he ever been with a cute goth chick?"

"Probably."

"A hot, curvy goth chick who isn't willing to let him get all woe is me?"

"How can you love Chase and hate your brother's brooding?" I ask.

"Chase is..." Her hands press together. Her lips part with a sigh. "He's protective. Sweet. Caring. Strong."

I know the feeling.

"It's not like I like his brooding. I mean, there is a certain appeal to the damaged guy, right? I thought I was beyond that, but I wanted to fix him. Every time he hurt, I wanted to soothe him."

"You did."

"Well..." She bites her lip. "He's made a lot of progress, yeah, but he's the one who did it."

"It wouldn't have happened without you."

She beams. "God, he's just so... have you ever seen his eyes when he smiles?"

"I have."

"And that feeling of melting into his arms?" She sighs. "It's the best."

"And the martyr complex?"

"He's getting there." Her eyes meet mine. "Forest isn't like that. He takes care of people, but he doesn't feel—"

"Yeah."

"He loves you."

"Not that way." I scan the room for Daisy. I am keeping an eye on her. Though… I'm terrified to say it, but I trust Holden to protect her.

That's truly horrifying.

And a much better focus for my attention.

Ariel follows my gaze. Shakes her head *you aren't distracting me.* "He's protective of you in a different way."

"Maybe."

"He kissed you."

"It was acting."

She raises a brow. It's the same gesture as Forest. Or Holden. "Oh yeah, it was acting when he kissed you? Holden said you were almost naked."

Why did I tell her that? "That's your brother."

"So?"

"Doesn't it bother you, thinking about that?"

She turns her head to one side. "Oh. You're trying to get me to change the subject."

"No." Maybe.

"You're uncomfortable about it."

Ahem.

"Because…"

"I'm—"

"You haven't talked to him about this like an adult."

"Why did I tell you I like him?" I ask.

"I already knew. Everyone knows."

"They do not—"

"Yeah, everyone but Forest thinks the two of you belong together," she says.

"His opinion is the only one that matters."

"True." She surveys the room. Waves hello to her brother.

As soon as he spots us, his lips curl into a smile. Then his eyes meet mine and his cheeks flush.

Fuck, I can't look at him either.

Ariel laughs. "I can see why Holden is so annoying. It's kind of fun being the one in control."

"Oh?"

"Well, not like *that*. Did I tell you about what Chase did last night?"

"Go on."

"Oh!" Her eyes light up. "You're trying to distract me again."

"You don't want to talk about the dirty things your boyfriend did to you?"

"Hmmm."

"He is the father of your child."

Her smile widens.

"You look good, by the way. You are glowing."

"So sweet of you to compliment me right when I'm asking you questions you don't want to answer."

"Am I?"

She nods *you are*. "And I'm huge."

"You look good."

"I feel like a whale." She rubs her belly. It is round, but she wears it well. "I'm afraid I'm going to knock over displays at grocery stores."

"Have you?"

She glares. "That isn't funny. And—Oh, you're still trying to distract me." She shakes her head *you're sneaky*. "He really took off your bra?"

I clear my throat.

"I bet he didn't need to do that for the shoot."

No, but—"He was acting."

"And you—"

"Were acting."

She raises a brow *really*.

"I can't let it be more than that, Ariel." I want it to be more. I need it to be more. But only if it is more. "He's in love with Mackenzie. He's not going to love me."

"No." Her eyes go to her brother as he stands and moves toward us. "He just doesn't know how to let go of her."

"Yeah."

"It sucks."

"Worked out for you."

She nods *it did*. "Maybe he needs a push."

"Love has changed you."

She just smiles.

Forest cuts through the crowd. Goes right to us. He hugs his sister hello. Whispers some warning about how Chase better be taking care of her.

His eyes flit to the door. Then to me.

They fill with deep, pure affection.

He blushes as he moves closer.

His hand skims my hip. My side. My lower back.

He rests his palm there. Applies the softest, lightest pressure.

Slowly, he pulls my body into his. "Hey." He looks down at me.

"Hey." I look up at him.

His fingers skim my temple.

He holds my gaze. Pulls me closer, closer.

He leans in.

Like he's going to kiss me.

I close my eyes. Rise to my tiptoes.

It needs to be real. Just us. No camera. No pretending. Nothing but our lips connecting—

"Hey." Mackenzie's voice breaks the moment.

He turns his head.

His lips brush my neck.

Fuck, that feels good. It's not the same as a proper kiss, but it's still hot as hell.

Is it for me?

Or for her?

"You make a lovely couple," she says.

I step backward, breaking our touch. "Don't sell yourself short." She's many things. Including pretty. "You look very stylish."

She smooths her red dress. Rubs her engagement ring with her thumb. "You do too." She looks to Forest. "And you…"

He nods *hey*.

She forces a smile. "Can we talk?"

"Where's Diego?"

"Parking the car. I, uh…" She bites her lip. "I have to ask you a favor."

My nails curl into my palms.

Forest looks to me for a split second. He opens his mouth to say something, but nothing comes.

He turns to his ex. "Yeah, sure." He nods *later*. "We'll talk later."

About the kiss?

Or is that some platitude for her sake?

I watch them cut through the crowd.

Ariel grabs onto my wrist so I won't chase after them. "He has to work through it himself."

"I know." But I don't have to like it.

## Chapter Twenty-Two

FOREST

Mack wraps her fingers around my wrist. She takes a half step toward me. Then another.

A familiar scent wafts into my nostrils. Her strawberry shampoo. It's too strong, too artificial, too chemical.

It hits every pleasure center in my brain. Every raw nerve. Every tucked memory.

Too many things flit through my head.

Then her red nails scrape my forearm and my thoughts scatter.

This is too much. I need to leave. I need to tell her I'm not interested.

But I don't.

I can't.

I'm frozen.

Mack moves closer. Brings her lips to my ear. "Can we take a bottle outside?"

"Is that a—" No, I'm not asking her if it's smart. If she needs to be sober. If she needs to stay lucid.

She's not my responsibility anymore.

"Sure." I step in front of her. Take her hand. Weave through the crowd, to the bar, grab a bottle of her favorite red wine.

"Outside?"

"Yeah." I lead us through the sliding glass door.

Despite the happening party, the backyard is quiet. There are two women sitting on the bench in the back, tangled in each other, kissing, touching, laughing.

It's too dark to see the details. But I get the gist. They're happy. In love as much as they're in lust.

Must be Holden's friends.

"Oh." Mack laughs. "Does your brother know he's missing this?"

"If he knew, he'd be here."

"Isn't he trying to bed Oliver's little sister?"

I motion to the patio table, the one next to the basketball court.

She ducks under the cream umbrella. Places her purse—and two wineglasses—on the glass table. Sits on one of the white cushions.

I open the bottle.

Maybe a drink will clear my head. It's not like it can make my thoughts any fuzzier.

I want to be inside, with Skye, holding her close, kissing her hard.

But I can't offer her my heart—I don't know how—and I can't let her accept less than everything.

"Here." Mack hands me a full glass of wine.

"Thanks." I take a long sip. It's strong. Astringent. Fruity. Not terrible. Not great either. Not that I appreciate wine.

"Is Holden trying to sleep with that high school girl?" She looks up at me, her big brown eyes wide.

The way she always looked at me. Like she trusts me. Like she wants me.

Like she needs to know exactly what I'm thinking.

"I don't know." I take another sip. "I can't tell with him anymore."

"Isn't she seventeen?"

"Turns eighteen soon."

Mack laughs. "God, his life is like a porno. Girl on girl in the backyard. Barely legal women waiting for his bed."

"Fuck knows what else."

Her laugh is soft. Easy. "Holden is... he's the only person who treats me the same."

"What do you expect?"

"I don't know. I..." Her eyes fill with frustration. Another look I know well.

Another look that begs me to comfort her.

She's still so tiny, like she's going to blow away in a breeze, like she might disappear if no one keeps an eye on her.

"To... uh..." She holds up her glass.

"True love."

"Okay." She shakes her head *that's ridiculous*, but she still clinks glasses.

I finish my wine in one gulp.

She takes a smaller sip. "You and Skye look happy."

"We are." I refill my glass.

Mack's gaze goes to the bottle. Her posture stiffens. Her lip corners turn down.

I take a long sip. Swallow hard. The second glass is better. Or I'm already getting drunk. Maybe that's what I need. To let my inhibitions dissolve. To lose myself in the moment the way I did upstairs. "You and Diego?"

She bites her lip. "Usually, yeah. We... it's stupid."

"Is it?"

She nods. "Tell me more about you and Skye. How did it happen? When did you know? It's just such a crazy story. I never thought you two would get together. You were so insistent you weren't interested."

Fuck, I wish I knew how it happened. When. It's obvious now. I want Skye. Need her. Can't have her.

Even if I was willing to let her accept less than she deserves, she wants someone else.

She isn't mine.

She won't ever be mine.

I take another sip. "It wasn't one moment, I guess. More an awareness that set in more every day."

She nods, listening.

"Skye and I were always friends, but we didn't get really close until after—" I finish my glass. Fuck, that's a lot. My entire mouth puckers. But I still pour another. "Until after you fucked Diego."

"I—"

"You want the story or you want to apologize?"

She plays with her engagement ring. "Go on."

"She took pity on my pathetic ass. But she never treated me like that. Like I was a loser for not moving on."

"But you did..." Her gaze stays on her shiny rock. "You moved on."

I don't know anymore. "I didn't realize it, at first. Skye became a part of my life. My favorite part. I'd be at the gym, counting down the minutes until I could get home and make her dinner. Or I'd be at work, smiling every time she texted back. Or I'd help her on some photo shoot. And... she gets this look when she steps behind the camera. Like she's exactly where she belongs. Like she wants to discover every inch of the thing, everything that makes it tick or purr." My chest warms. That is Skye. She is big and bright. Like the sun. Like the moon. Like the stars. "She asked me for help once. She needed a male model."

"Oh?"

"Yeah." A few hours ago, but it's still true. "It was a sexy shoot. We were pretending. But there was something about having her body that close. About feeling all her softness. Smelling her shampoo."

"When did you know?"

"I think I always knew. But when I kissed her... I couldn't deny it anymore." I can't deny it anymore.

Mack watches me refill my glass. Says nothing.

I offer her a top-off.

She nods *sure*. "Did it start then?"

It's been going on for a long time. I've wanted her for a long time. "It was physical at first. I thought that was it. That I needed to get laid. But then I'd see her dancing to her favorite song, groaning over her matcha, crying at the end of *Before Sunset*. It hit me a little at a time. Then all at once."

"And she felt the same?"

"Yeah." No. I don't know. There's another guy. But maybe… Maybe she's over him. Maybe she wants me more. Maybe I can make her forget. I swallow another sip. "It's hard to believe someone like Skye would want a guy who's such a mess."

"You're not a mess, Forest." Mack's nails tap the glass table. She watches them work for a moment then she looks up at me. "She gives you what you need?"

I study her face, trying to find her intentions.

She can't possibly mean—

But she does.

"Does she get me off?" I raise a brow. "Are you really asking that?"

"No."

"Then what?"

She stares at the floor. "It's just hard to believe that she'd fill your needs."

"What is it this time, Mack? Her style is too weird? Her clothing size is too big? Her employment status is too pathetic?"

"No, I don't…"

"How are you going to insult her today?"

"I'm not—"

"That she isn't kinky enough? Generous enough? Sexual enough?"

She swallows hard.

"Is that what happened with us? I couldn't make you come so you had to look elsewhere?"

"No."

"Was I not creative enough?"

"Forest, don't—"

"If you're going to insult one of us, it's me. So tell me. What was it? Was he bigger? Better? Did he last longer? Did he do things I wouldn't even dream of—"

"Forest—"

"What are you doing?" I refill my glass. "Why are you asking about Skye?"

"I worry about you."

"You worry about me?"

"Yeah. You… you didn't take our breakup well."

"You fucked someone behind my back. For months. How did you expect me to take it?"

She shrinks back, wounded.

Like I'm the one hurting her.

Like I'm an asshole for pointing out the facts.

"And now you're asking if Skye fills my needs?" I finish my wine in two gulps. "What the fuck is that?"

"Yeah… but, uh… it wasn't that."

"What?"

"The sex." She looks into my eyes. "He's not bigger. Or more creative. Or kinkier. That's not why he's better."

My stomach churns.

"It's because he tries to connect with me. To stay in tune with what I want now. And not what I wanted three years ago."

"What are you talking about?"

"You could never see it, Forest. You could never see past this idea you had of me."

"So you fucked him?" I pour another glass.

"You thought I was this mess you needed to clean up. You were so proud of how functional you were. Of all these ways you could take care of me."

My eyes go to the bottle between us. Is she going to make me say it? She drinks as much as her mom. I worried for a reason? "I was taking care of you."

"Because it made you feel superior."

"Because I loved you. And I wanted you to be okay."

## The Best Friend Bargain

"You loved how I made you feel."

What the fuck? That's what relationships are. What love is.

It's that warm feeling in your chest. That sense of satisfaction when someone melts into your arms. The bliss when her laugh flows into your ears.

"It's not like that with him. He loves me. He doesn't try to change me. He doesn't look at me like I'm some challenge he wants to fix."

"I never—"

"I… I didn't mean to fall for him. But I did. He saw me. The person I was then. The person I'd become. Not the stupid teenager he met a million years ago."

"I never thought you were stupid."

She takes a step backward. "I didn't like the person I was anymore. I didn't like the person I was with you."

"How am I—"

"That's why I left. Because I hated that version of myself." She slides her purse onto her arm. "I loved you, Forest. I really did. And I'm really sorry I didn't end things before I started with Diego. But it wasn't out of malice. It was… it just happened."

Every cheater's favorite phrase.

It just happened.

Like she didn't choose to kiss him, touch him, fuck him.

Like she didn't know what she was doing when she replied to flirty texts.

Or sent secret emails.

Or went to his place alone.

It just happened.

She just kissed him.

And I can't even argue.

Because this thing with Skye—it just happened.

"I'm sorry that you can't move on. But, I hope for Skye's sake that you do." Mack looks at me like I'm the world's biggest disappointment, then she shakes her head, turns, leaves.

It's just me and the girls in the corner.

At this point, they're up to more than kissing.

But I can't say I'm particularly interested in anything but clarity.

A few minutes of sitting in silence does nothing to clear my head.

So I pour another glass.

Maybe the wine isn't going to help me figure this out.

But it's not like things can get any fuzzier than they are now.

## Chapter Twenty-Three

SKYE

I swallow another sip of Moscow Mule. Nod *uh-huh* to whatever it is Oliver is saying.

Something about his sister. She's graduating next month. The first person in his family who's going to college.

He's proud of her.

It's sweet, really.

I finish my drink.

He chuckles knowingly. "You're worse than I am."

"No." I pop an ice cube into my mouth. Suck every drop of sugar, ginger, and booze. "That's your third one."

"I'm three times your size."

Ah, if only. I don't correct him though. Why point out those numbers?

"You want another?"

"Yes, thank you."

"You trust me to get it right?"

"I trust you to make it strong."

He chuckles *fair enough*, scoops our drinks, moves to the bar.

I cross one leg over the other. Smooth my dress. It's new. Cute. Retro sexy. Sexy, period.

But my fake boyfriend isn't here to appreciate it. The room is too crowded. I can't tell if he's still outside. If he and Mack are deep in conversation. If they're taking off their clothes, fucking on the cold concrete.

Not that I'm picturing it.

Not that I'm buzzing from Forest kissing me.

Not that I'm aching from him leaving.

Ahem.

A hand brushes my shoulder.

I turn, expecting Oliver. The man is a godsend when it comes to refilling drinks. Or shaded tattoos. Or quietly drinking without excessive conversation.

A man of many talents, really.

An attractive tall man with beautiful blue eyes.

But my heart does beat for him.

Only it's not Oliver.

It's Diego.

"Hey." He offers me a smile. That same million-dollar smile. "How have you been?"

"Good." I reach for my drink, but it's gone. "Busy." With my unemployment. "Lots of photography projects. The fashion blog. You know—"

"I do. Mack follows you."

"Oh."

"She misses you."

I don't know what to say to that. I try to smile, but it's half-hearted. My cousin misses me. Too bad. She knows what she did. "How are you guys? Good? Happy? Trouble in paradise?" My laugh is impossibly fake.

His is nervous. "We got into a fight on the way here."

"Oh."

"Mrs. Davis was drinking…" He looks around the room. Stops on Oliver, who's currently heading in this direction. "Your friend?"

"Yeah. One of Forest's friends."

He nods. "Another tattoo artist?"

"Yeah."

"Didn't think that was your type."

"Yours either."

"Fair enough." His laugh gets easier. "She… she really does miss you."

"Are you her keeper now?"

"No. She hates when I get involved." He scans the room, no doubt looking for Mackenzie. "I thought you'd want to know. You two were like sisters."

"I know."

He shrugs *none of my business*. "You look good, Skye."

"I am good."

"Forest treating you well?"

"Yes. Of course." I force a smile. Diego and I were friendly before Mack slept with him. But we weren't really friends. "And you and Mackenzie? Lying on the grass watching the clouds? Making out on the beach? Coming so hard you wake the neighbors?"

"No." He laughs. "She's not the loud type."

"Oh." That is too much information. But I'm the one who asked. "I…"

"Need another drink," Oliver interrupts. He nods *hey* to Diego. Hands over my drink. Takes a long sip of his. "How's uh, grad school was it?"

"Yeah. A PhD. Good. A lot of work." He offers his hand. "How's the shop?"

Oliver shakes. "It's great. Making a killing." He studies my expression looking for… something. I can't read him. "Your fiancée went outside with Forest."

Diego frowns. "I should find her."

"Do that." Oliver smiles, serene.

Which is weird as fuck. Oliver isn't a smiley guy.

He waits for Diego to leave, then he turns to me. "What's the deal with that guy?"

"Honestly, I don't know," I say.

"Mm-hmm."

"What's that mean?"

"He seems more like your type."

"He's obviously very engaged."

"Yeah." He takes a long sip. Raises a brow, suggesting something.

God knows what. I clear my throat. Try to think of some way to change the subject.

"You're doing this for Forest?" he asks.

"It's more about…"

"Getting in his pants?"

Ahem.

"He's a good-looking guy."

"Yes." I swallow a sip. Fuck, it's strong—almost all vodka—but not strong enough to save me from this awkward conversation.

"Tall."

"Aren't you?"

"That's how I know."

"Okay…" I stare at my drink.

"Holden has been giving him a lot of shit at the shop. Testing him."

"Sounds like Holden."

He nods *true*. "He keeps asking Forest for his permission to fuck you."

I choke on my drink.

"Not your type?"

"No, I…"

"Like quiet guys?"

"Yeah." I take another sip. "You, uh, don't talk about girls. Is there someone special? Someone not so special? Several women waiting for a booty call?"

He shakes his head *nice try*. "I don't really date."

"All wham, bam, thank you, ma'am?"

"Something like that." He downs his glass of bourbon. "You?"

"It's been a while."

"Because you're waiting for Forest."

Ahem.

"Why don't you find him? Make a point of making out in front of everyone? That's why you're doing it."

"I'm helping my friend."

"So you can kiss him."

"I'm still helping him." And we're not—he said no kissing anyway. But then he kissed me. And, God, it's confusing, and the vodka isn't helping.

He shakes his head *bad idea*. "You're helping him make his ex jealous. Who's going to help you make him jealous?"

"That's uh…"

"You want me to do it?" He pats his lap. "I'll be gentle."

Is he serious? I can't tell. At all.

First Holden. Now this.

Did I wake up with magic boobs? Are my pheromones now super-powered? Why are all these hot guys propositioning me?

"I, uh…" He takes my hand. Pulls me onto his lap. Motions to Forest.

Forest cuts through the crowd, wine bottle in hand. He looks right to us. Frowns.

Sneers even.

"He gets jealous easily," I say.

"Exactly." Oliver leans in to whisper. "Pretend I said something really funny?"

My laugh is fake.

"Funnier than that."

Uh…

He chuckles. "You're bad at this. Probably good. So you won't actually help him get her back."

"He doesn't want that." Maybe. In theory. I think.

"How do you want him?"

"Huh?"

"In your mouth? Your ass? Your cunt? You want him pressing you against the wall? Pinning you to his bed? Taking you in a swimming pool?" He wraps his arm around my waist. "Or do you want to climb on top of him and fuck him senseless?"

"Uh…" Fuck I'm blushing everywhere.

And Forest is staring at us, his eyes hazy, his fists curled.

He's jealous of someone.

Is this stupidity actually working?

God, men are such base creatures. It's always sex and possession and anger.

Forest crosses the room to us.

I slide off Oliver's lap. "Hey. How's Mackenzie?"

"Fine." He takes my hand. Pulls me closer. "You want another drink?"

"Okay." I look back to Oliver. When he nods *go for it*, I turn to Forest. "Are you okay?"

"Yeah. Come on." He leads me to the bar, grabs a bottle of vodka, cuts through the crowd.

Then up the stairs.

Into his room.

It still smells like him. Like us. Like the fresh lingerie.

Forest presses the door closed. He uncaps the bottle of vodka, takes a swig, passes it to me.

It's strong like this. Not my taste. But, hey, I'm not letting my best friend drink alone. "What happened?"

"Some bullshit."

"Bullshit how."

"I've been stupid, Skye."

"What?"

He sets the bottle on his desk. Turns his body toward mine. "I don't care if she's jealous."

He…

"I don't want her anymore."

"Forest—"

"I need to kiss you again." His hands go to my waist. "A real kiss. One that isn't for her. Or the camera. Or this guy you like—"

"I don't—"

"Come here." He presses one palm into my lower back. Pushes my body into his.

He looks down at me with those dark eyes.

But they aren't full of love or need or affection.

They're hazy.

Really hazy.

He's drunk.

"Skye." He holds my body against his. "I need to make you come."

"Forest—" I press my palm into his chest. To push him away. But my palm refuses to push. He feels too good. Warm. Hard. Safe.

"I need to taste you, Skye." He brings one hand to the back of my head. Knots his fingers through my hair. "You have any idea how often I think about that? I dream about you. About kissing you, touching you, making you come."

"You're drunk."

"Tell me you don't want that, and I'll go."

I shake my head. "I…"

His fingers brush the hem of my skirt. "Tell me you don't to come on my face. I'll leave. Right now. If you don't want that—if you don't want anything from me—I'll go."

*God yes. Right now. Right here. I don't care who sees.* "You're drunk."

"So?"

"You're only saying this because you're drunk."

"No." He tugs at my hair. "I'm saying it because you're the sexiest woman I've ever seen. Because I've spent the last two weeks fucking myself to the thought of you."

"You did?"

He nods *yeah*.

My heart thuds against my chest. I… He… No. Not like this. "Ask again when you're sober."

"It's not like that. I'm not—"

"No." Finally, I push him away. "I don't care what Mackenzie said to upset you. Or why you felt the need to get this plastered. I'm sorry about what happened. I'm sorry you can't get over it, but this—" I swallow the nerves that rise in my throat. "You don't use me to prove anything." I take a step backward. "You don't use me."

"Skye. It's not—"

"No." I turn and march out of the room.

I expect him to chase me. To apologize. To at least send a text. But he doesn't.

## Chapter Twenty-Four

FOREST

Fuck, it's bright in here.

Why is it this bright?

I close my eyes, but there's still too much light flooding my senses.

I stumble to the bathroom. Wash my teeth. Piss. Shower.

After three glasses of water, a handful of NSAIDs, and a cup of very shitty coffee, the pounding in my head fades to a dull throb.

Last night comes into focus.

Mack telling me to get over myself.

Too many glasses of wine with vodka chasers.

Skye blushing in Oliver's lap.

Skye looking up at me like I hang the moon.

Skye pushing me away, staring at me like I'm the scum of the Earth.

Fuck.

So much for not fucking up the relationship that matters most.

I down another glass of water. Hold my breath to keep my nausea at bay. Force myself to eat a slice of unbuttered toast.

Holden is up in his room. It's quiet. He must be asleep.

As soon as he wakes up—

That's too much.

I find my phone. Scan it for clues to Skye's mood. No new texts, emails, calls.

Nothing on her blog.

But on her Instagram—

A picture of us. Her sitting in my lap in that sheer black lingerie.

It's cropped at the nose. Her eyes aren't visible. But those berry lips—

Fuck.

I try to think of an appropriate apology. *I'm sorry. I'm an idiot. I drank too much. Let myself get carried away.*

*You're wrong, Skye. It's not about Mack.*

*It's about you.*

*I want to fuck you.*

*Skye, the things I want to do to you. It's all I can think about. The taste of your lipstick. The feel of your mouth against mine. Your soft thighs against my hands.*

*I want to kiss you for hours. Like we're back in high school, making out because we're so enamored with each other's bodies. Because we're too nervous to do anything else.*

*It's not about Mack. It's not about her wedding. It's not about this ruse.*

*It's my cock. He's a demanding mother fucker. He wants every inch of you.*

*He wants your perfect tits, your delicate hands, your pretty lips.*

*I know I shouldn't say this. I should keep it to myself. Keep things normal. So I won't.*

*But, fuck, somehow I need to make this clear. I need to explain. Yeah, I was drunk and stupid and jealous.*

*Maybe I have something to prove. Maybe I'm not over her. Maybe I'm an angry mess.*

*But that isn't why I want you.*

*It's you.*

I settle on something short and sweet.

*Forest: Fuck, I'm an asshole.*

*Skye: Accurate.*

*Forest: You get home okay?*

*Skye: I'm fine.*
*Forest: Did you?*
*Skye: It's next door.*
*Forest: It's a fair question.*
*Skye: Want to know if I stumbled into someone else's bed?*
*Forest: Did you?*
*Skye: Does it matter?*

My stomach turns.

I can't stand the idea of anyone touching her. Not Oliver. Not my brother. Not this guy she likes.

But that's the wrong thing to say.

She doesn't get that it's about her. That I can't stand the thought of anyone treating her casually. Tossing her aside. Using her.

*Forest: Are you home?*
*Skye: I don't want to talk.*
*Forest: Are you?*
*Skye: I'll see you later.*

She doesn't have to talk to me.

She shouldn't talk to me.

But I'm doing something.

I'm fixing this.

---

SKYE OPENS THE DOOR WITH A STERN LOOK. SHE PUTS HER FINGER over her mouth in a *shhh* gesture, steps onto the stairs, pulls the door almost all the way closed.

"Here." I brandish my thermos like I'm offering her my heart.

"Here?" Her gaze goes to the mint green container.

"Matcha with almond milk."

"And?"

"You drink it."

She eyes the drink tenuously.

"It's an offer, not a contract."

"Okay." Her fingers brush mine as she takes the thermos. She brings it to her lips. Takes a small sip. Let's out a big sigh. "Fuck, you're too good at this."

"Yeah." Goddammit, I need to hear her groaning like that again.

"It makes it harder to tell you to fuck off."

"You can."

She looks up at me *of course, I can, duh*. "I don't really want to talk to you right now."

"Okay."

"Okay?"

"Do you not want me to respect your decision?"

"Well…" She takes another sip. Stifles a groan. "You're usually more… fighting me."

"I'm sorry." I look her in the eyes. "If you don't want to hear it, I'll go. But I am."

She presses her lips together. "Okay."

"Can I buy you another?"

"I just started this one."

"All right, can I buy you another in five minutes?"

A laugh breaks up her frown. She shakes her head *what am I going to do with you?* Takes another sip.

"You don't have to talk to me. Or listen. Just take the matcha and go."

"Maybe."

"I was an asshole. An idiot. A—"

"Did you mean it?"

I stare into her eyes.

"Do you still want that?"

"Right here?"

"In general."

I try to study her expression. To figure out what she wants me to say.

Skye doesn't like me handling her with kid gloves. She wants the truth. Usually.

Does she want it now? Or does she want everything to stay the same?

Is she in love with this other guy?

"It's not a trick question," she says.

"I—"

"Is that Forest?" A booming voice interrupts. Mr. Kim pulls the door open. Offers me a hearty smile. "How are you, son?"

Skye clears her throat. "Dad, we're kinda—"

"Talking on the porch. Come inside. You want something to drink?" he offers.

Skye melts into her teenage girl form. It's the same thing that happens to me around my dad, though my teenage form is a lot more sulky.

She looks at her dad like *oh my God, Dad, you're embarrassing me.* "We're kinda—"

"You want to speak privately." He winks. "Your mother and I understand you have a sex life."

"Oh my God." Skye blushes. "Dad! Can we not?"

"Are you kids coming inside?" He pulls the door open wider. Motions *come in.* It's friendly. And demanding.

Mr. Kim is a nice guy. He's also huge. Not fat. Big. The dude is as tall as me and he's twice as built. He's a bodybuilder. And one of those doctors that works on bones.

"We're almost done actually." Skye clears her throat.

"Nonsense. I'll make tea." Mr. Kim leads us into the kitchen. He motions to the empty table.

That same round table that's been in here since I've known her. The same wooden chairs. The same shiny white floor.

Their house is always clean. Except for her room.

It's so familiar. Even this, Mr. Kim inviting me inside, giving Skye the third degree, insisting on fixing tea.

Besides being a doctor, the man doesn't fit many stereotypes about Asian guys. He's a former swimmer who can deadlift more than I can. He keeps up with fashion trends. He drives a flashy car.

But the man loves his tea.

"What are you in the mood for today, sweetie?" He snaps into paternal mode. "Jasmine or Gyokuro?"

"Dad, I'm—"

"Jasmine it is." He smiles, not at all bothered by her trying to push him out, and fills the kettle.

I take a seat.

Skye lets out one of those teenager sighs, but she does sit. "I have to edit more photos, so I don't really have—"

The whistle of the tea kettle interrupts us.

Mr. Kim smiles. "You too, Forest?"

"Yes, thanks, sir," I say.

"Please. It's David." He reminds me to call him by his first name, the way he always does. "Did you eat breakfast? I made Skye's favorite."

"Scrambled eggs with tomatoes and extra green onions?" I ask.

He nods. "He's a good kid. Knows your favorite breakfast."

Skye clears her throat. "We can brew the tea."

"I know, sweetie. But I'm talking to your boyfriend."

Her eyes nearly bug out of her head.

"Unless you have something to hide?" he asks.

"You know I'm twenty-five, right?" she asks.

"Yeah, but you'll always be my little girl." He turns to the pot. Scoops leaves. Pours water. Replaces the lid.

Skye uncrosses and re-crosses her legs as her dad brings the pot and cups to the table.

He pours carefully. Hands the first to her.

"Thank you." She takes a long sip of the jasmine green. She doesn't sigh the way she sighs over her matcha, but she still gets that faraway look, like she's lost in a world of pure bliss.

"How is work, Forest?" Mr. Kim sits across from us.

"Dad, can we not—"

"If you want to finish your editing upstairs, we can do that. Or we could talk about how you're posting half-naked pictures of you and your boyfriend on the Internet," he says.

Her cheeks flame red. "We're just—A lingerie company. We, uh…"

He looks to me. "I went to medical school. I understand biology. I understand that my daughter is a woman with needs—"

"Oh my God!"

"I'll support whatever you want, sweetie. But if that's posting explicit images on the Internet we need to talk about what that means for your future."

"It's my fault, sir." I fight a blush. Fuck, I'm twenty-eight and my fake girlfriend's dad is questioning my intentions. What the hell is happening to my life? "A lingerie company offered Skye a fee to post images of their products. I'm the one who suggested I model. I promised I'd keep it tame, but—"

"You did post that from your account, didn't you, honey?" her dad asks.

"It's just marketing." She blushes. "They want to sell sexy."

He nods with understanding. "And you don't mind strangers looking at your bare ass?"

"Dad!"

"You can show your ass to strangers but I can't ask you about it?"

"Can we just not?" She swallows the rest of her cup. "I'm helping them advertise a thong. That's part of it. I'm lucky they're offering money at all. Lots of plus-sized influencers aren't offered cash—"

"Sweetheart, you know your value better than that," he says.

"Am I in trouble for posting a picture of my butt or for not asking for enough cash?" Her brow furrows. "Are you really—"

"You're not in trouble." He looks to me. "Do you think there's anything wrong with me making sure my daughter understands how her decisions might affect her future?"

"With all due respect, sir, Skye knows what she's doing. She's been developing a following for years. She's an amazing photographer and a talented model. And her sense of style is unrivaled." I take a long sip. It wets my throat, but it doesn't chase away that sense that I'm suddenly back in high school.

Mr. Kim nods. "You understand some future employers will frown upon this?"

"My face isn't in the shot. If I decide to shut down my blog, no one will know it was me." She turns to her dad. "But, yes, I do realize that."

He nods. "And you, Forest? You're supporting yourself?"

"Oh my God." She hides behind her hands.

"He's always staying with his parents," Mr. Kim says.

"Yes, that would be so embarrassing, if he still lived with his parents." She sighs. "What a loser? Who would even talk to such a pathetic figure?" She shoots her dad a cutting look.

He returns a *watch your manners, young lady* look.

She has a point. She lives with her parents. Should he really be questioning whether or not I live on my own?

Her parents claim they love having her here.

Any suggestion that they don't is going to eat at her. She hates that she can't support herself. That she's still struggling to find a full-time job.

"Yes, I have an apartment in West LA," Forest says. "The shop is doing well. I could support Skye if she wanted that."

She lowers her hands enough to look me in the eye. "You could?"

"Yeah. If you wanted to live with me while you built your following." I turn to Mr. Kim. "Skye likes hanging out at my dad's place. She likes the basketball court."

He laughs. "Should we play a game, sweetie?"

"Is it *who can die of embarrassment first*? I think I'm winning," she says.

He just laughs. "We go through this every day. I've been asking about you, but Skye doesn't like to share."

"She can be tight-lipped. I try to respect that," I say. "I try to give her what she wants. Sometimes, I screw it up, but I'm learning." My eyes meet hers for a second, then she looks away.

"We, uh… we were actually leaving," Skye says. "So, Dad, thank you so much for the tea. It's delicious—"

"But no matcha latte?" he offers.

"Good in a different way. And, uh, I can't wait to make bulgogi tonight. I can bring home some more green onions." She lowers her hands. Forces her lips into a smile.

She's already wearing a full face of makeup.

Did she put it on after I texted? Is it for me? For herself? For someone else?

Fuck, I want to know.

I want everything in her head.

But one thing at a time. I still have to make this up to her. "We do have plans."

"When will you have her home?" he asks.

"Dad!" she squeals.

He laughs. "Just kidding. Why don't you join us for dinner tonight, Forest?"

"Oh, well—" I look to Skye for a clue. After she nods *okay*, I turn back to Mr. Kim. "That would be great."

"You're coming to the wedding?" he asks.

I nod. "Yes."

"You have something to wear?" he asks.

"I should." It's been a while since I've needed a suit.

"And you, sweetie? You have a dress your aunt won't criticize?"

"Is that even possible?" She sticks her tongue out in distaste.

Mr. Kim nods *true*. "She gets sensitive about—"

"Boobs. You can say boobs."

"I can say boobs but not ass?" Her dad challenges.

She cringes. "Mrs. Davis get upset if she sees too much of mine."

"That must be hard for you, sweetie. Since you enjoy showing them to strangers on the Internet so much," her dad says.

Skye clears her throat. "Yeah, I, uh—"

"If you need a new dress, you can borrow this?" He brandishes his credit card. "Or maybe your boyfriend—"

"No, that's—" She swallows as she takes the card. "That's very generous. Thank you. I appreciate it."

"Keep it under three hundred dollars," he says.

"What about shoes?" she asks.

"Three hundred total," he says. "If that can't cover the engagement party and the wedding, we can talk."

"Sure." She fights a frown.

His voice softens. "You don't have to go."

"I know." She slides his credit card into her purse. "I want to."

They exchange a look, one of those familial looks, where two people communicate everything without saying anything.

Skye turns to me. "I guess... we should head out. To our plans."

"And shopping," he says. "Bee said there's a sale at Nordstrom." He refers to Skye's mom by her nickname. Her name is Belinda. Most people call her Linda, but he always calls her Bee.

"Yeah, and Nordstrom." She hugs her dad goodbye. Grabs her purse. Heads to the door.

I follow.

"I love you, sweetie," he calls.

"Love you too," she says.

For a second, the words drift into my ears, my head, my heart.

For a second, I believe it's for me. That she loves me. Wants me. Needs me.

Then I blink and she's staring at me like I'm an asshole.

And I want her love, need, affection, trust more than anything.

## Chapter Twenty-Five

SKYE

"What happened last night?" I hug my purse to my shoulder. Which does nothing to slow my pulse.

My heart is beating so fast.

And so hard.

He's so close.

I want to slap him for last night. Then pin him to the wall and kiss him senselessly.

He motions to his car. "We can park in the garage."

"What garage?"

"At Nordstrom."

I stare back at him. "Are you serious?"

He shrugs *am I?*

I can't tell. I usually can. Okay, I sometimes can. Right now, my body and head are at war.

My body screams *just kiss him. Stop talking. Stop questioning. Stop worrying if he's thinking about her.*

*Take off his pants. Climb into his lap. Drive down on his thick cock—*

My head knows better. But *you'll regret this tomorrow* is a much less persuasive argument than *FUCK FOREST NOW*.

A laugh breaks up his poker face. "Nordstrom has nice menswear."

I just stare at him.

"Maybe I want to go."

"If you want to go, fine. But don't accuse me of shopping at a giant department store."

"Where do you get your shoes?"

I clear my throat.

"'Cause I remember something about Zappos having the best price."

"Do you want me to leave?"

"No." He offers his hand. "I want to buy you a matcha latte."

"We're walking?"

"It's a nice day." He motions to the bright blue sky. The lemon sun. "Horribly bright, but—"

"How much did you drink?"

"Too much." He dons his sunglasses. Takes my hand. "I'm an idiot."

"You are."

"The stupidest person on the planet."

"True." I follow him down the sidewalk. "But self-flagellation isn't an apology."

"I sound like Chase, huh?"

"Yeah, but Chase can pull off the whole tall, dark, and self-loathing thing."

"Dark? He has dirty blond hair and blue eyes."

"And?"

He chuckles. "He pulls off tall, light, and self-loathing."

"Don't even, Forest. Remember Halloween? You spent two hours laughing about how his Daredevil costume fit him perfectly, because 'Matt Murdock is the only self-loathing motherfucker more irritating than Chase is.'"

"I meant it with love."

It's true. And Chase wouldn't mind either. He wears his misery proudly. Or he did. Until he and Ariel got together.

I don't know him well, but she's like a sister. She's happy, so I'm happy for them.

Still. "What do you say about me when I'm not around?"

"Mostly 'Holden, stop talking about Skye's tits.'"

I clear my throat.

"You're right. Feeling like shit isn't an apology. But I am sorry. And I want to make it up to you." He lifts his sunglasses. Cringes as light floods his eyes. "I'll chauffeur you all day—"

"All day?"

He nods *yeah*. "To any shop in Southern California."

"What if I want to go that amazing pinup shop in Glendale?"

"If you don't mind traffic—"

"And I want to listen to No Doubt the entire way?"

He makes a show of cringing. "The pop ones too?"

"Of course."

"That's a fate worse than death. But, yeah, we can listen to every album they've ever made."

"Oh, please. If Gwen was a guy, you'd be worshiping her for writing so many songs about her ex."

"Would I?"

I nod *hell yeah*.

He motions to the green light a block ahead.

I try to keep up with Forest, but he's fast and I'm in platform boots.

The red hand flashes.

We run onto the street. Whiz through it. Hit the sidewalk just in time.

He looks down at me with a smile. A smile that says *yes, I did mean everything I said last night. I do want to fuck you. Because I like you. Because I am totally over Mack. Because you're the most beautiful woman on the planet.*

I try to find a coherent response. Settle on a non sequitur. "Actually… Gwen is too mature for you. She doesn't wish ill on her exes."

"Not a single line about how they should die in a car crash."

"Or drive off a bridge," I say.

"Or burn to death."

"Nothing about how he's a bastard for sleeping with a new woman," I say.

"What about her last album?" He motions to the red light.

"The one you call shit pop music? That you refuse to listen to?"

"Do I refuse?"

Yeah, he does. Not that I mind, exactly. I appreciate Gwen's pop career for what it is, but I don't love the sound. "Always."

"Play that."

"Really?"

He nods *yeah*. "If it's what you want."

The light turns green. I step into the street.

Forest steps after me. His hand brushes my lower back.

Then it settles there. He pushes gently, just enough I know he's leading.

It's intimate. Loving. Sweet.

I want more of it. All of it. All of him and his love and his affection.

Right now, it's me and Forest. No camera. No exes. No parents.

There's no reason to put on a show.

He's touching me because he wants to touch me.

Maybe he meant what he said last night. Maybe it wasn't a drunken attempt to use me. Maybe it was alcohol dissolving his inhibitions.

"Why do you like the bridge guy anyway?" I step onto the sidewalk.

He keeps pace with me. "I don't like him personally."

"No? You aren't following his Instagram? Sending fan mail? Writing fan-fics about the two of you running off together?"

"Fuck no. My fan-fics are gang bangs."

I can't help but laugh. "The whole band taking you?"

"Yeah."

"All at once? Or one at a time?"

"One at a time doesn't sound like a great gang bang."

My cheeks flush. It's hard staying mad at him. It really is. "Is this another one of your porn fetishes?"

"No."

"What, um…" I force my gaze to the shops in front of us. We're almost to the start of Abbott-Kinney. It's quiet for a weekday afternoon. No one to overhear this conversation. "What's your favorite?"

"You really want to know?"

"Why? Will it scare me?"

"Does porn scare you?"

"A little."

He raises a brow.

"Why do all these videos have a guy going at a woman's mouth like he's trying to fuck her skull?"

His lips curl into a smile. "No violent oral for you?"

I shake my head.

"Or none at all?"

Ahem.

"You don't like giving head?"

I clear my throat.

"You don't?" He chuckles. "Fuck, if Holden heard that—"

"No, I…" I pick up my pace.

He matches it. "He likes to torture me by asking if you're generous or greedy."

"Oh?"

"He thinks you seem generous."

"Please don't elaborate."

"Sometimes, he thinks you're greedy. Depends on the day."

I don't know what to say, so I settle on, "Oh."

"Are you?" He pulls me closer as we pass a family in Disneyland gear.

So. Not. Answering. It's way too loaded. "I also find your brother annoying, yes."

"You know what I'm asking." His hand goes to my hip. His fingers curl into the fabric of my dress.

It's thin. I can feel the pressure of his fingers. The heat of his hand.

"Skye?"

"Yeah?"

"We're holding up the matcha."

"Right. We should be walking." But I don't move. I stay inches from him.

His breath warms my ear.

His fingers brush my hip. Then they're lower. Pressing the fabric of my dress into my outer thigh.

"We should." He stays put too.

We stay frozen for a moment.

The sun warms my skin.

The wind ruffles my dress.

The passing traffic blurs together.

Then some driver honks his horn and I jump away from the street.

I turn. Move toward the matcha shop, the one with the pink walls and the palm tree pillows.

Forest follows me. "There's no shame in not liking something."

"What if your girlfriend didn't like it?"

"I don't have a girlfriend."

"But would you date someone who… didn't do that?"

"Someone? Or you?"

I clear my throat. "Hypothetically."

"Depends."

"On?"

"Why she doesn't like it. What else she likes. If she's open with me or not."

"Oh." God, it's hot today. It's not—the breeze is only getting stronger—but it is.

"But probably, yeah."

"Really?"

"Why wouldn't I?"

"I just thought… most guys are really into that."

"You mean your ex?"

No… just things guys say. "He was… too rough."

He nods with understanding. His expression gets protective. "Did he hurt you?"

"No, not like that. He just… got carried away."

He pulls me closer.

"I do like it." My cheeks flush. "Just not… violent."

His laugh breaks up the tension. "You don't want to gag on a cock?"

"Oh my God!"

"That's a fair request."

I say nothing.

"Has it happened?"

"Yeah… a few times. With… that doesn't matter" There have only been two guys. But that is not information I need to share. Not at the moment. Not with someone who's fucked half the women in the city. "Do you do that with your one-night stands?"

"No."

"No?"

"Never," he says.

"Why not?"

He steps onto the curb. Pulls off his sunglasses. "Never wanted to."

"So you don't…" I try to look him in the eyes, but it's impossible. "You don't go down on your one-night stands?"

"I don't."

"Ever?"

"Ever."

"And they—"

"I don't let them suck me off either." His voice is matter-of-fact. Like it's so obvious women want his cock in their mouths.

Not that I—

God, it's hot in here.

My cheeks flame. "You miss it?"

"Fuck yeah."

"You're that—"

"A woman tugging at my hair as she comes on my face." His eyes light up. "What's better than that?"

"Oh, I meant—" I nod to his crotch. "Receiving services."

"It's not where my head goes when I fuck myself. But I wouldn't turn it down."

"*You* don't like it?"

"No." His voice is loaded, like he can't pack how much he likes it into the single syllable. "I like it. But I'd rather give than receive."

"Oh."

"Oh?"

"Yeah. Oh."

"You?"

Uh… No comment. "Is it too personal? Or…" He loves giving head. Loves women coming on his face. Loves… Uh… Must. Change. Subject. "Is that it?" I stop at the red light. Almost there. It's right across the street.

The wall across from us is adorned with pink roses. And a sign reading *I Love You So Matcha*.

It's the perfect place to snap a photo. If I can stop blushing. Or make eye contact with something besides the ground.

"That's a good way of putting it," he says.

"So you, uh… what did you want? With your one-night stands? If you didn't want intimacy?"

"I don't know."

"You don't know?" I focus on the *don't walk* sign. "You were the one doing it."

He runs a hand through his hair. "Honestly, Skye, I don't remember. I guess, at the time, it felt like a way to control something. To prove something. To find some piece of me I'd lost."

"Did it?"

"A little. But, mostly, it was something to do." He looks down at me. "Mack said something last night."

"Yeah?"

"That it wasn't about Diego being better or bigger or kinkier."

"Did you think it was?"

## The Best Friend Bargain

His brow furrows. "Not exactly." His eyes fill with vulnerability. "But that had to be a part of it. You don't start fucking someone else if you're satisfied."

Maybe. "Women aren't like that. There's a reason Gwen isn't obsessed with who her ex is screwing."

"She's way hotter than him. Honestly, it's a miracle he ever bagged her."

Well, yeah. Gwen is a babe. Whereas the ex who inspired *Tragic Kingdom* is less conventionally attractive.

"The guy must be a fantastic lay to keep her around for so long."

My laugh breaks up the tension in my shoulders. "You really think that's it? That relationships are all about sex?"

"Only sex? No. But that's a big part of them. That's one of the things you share. That you don't give to anyone else." The light turns green. He takes my hand, pulls me across the street, leads me into the matcha shop.

It's quiet. Clean. Air-conditioned.

We move straight to the counter. Order our usual drinks. Matcha lattes with macadamia milk.

He always orders the same thing as me. So I can drink his.

He likes the latte enough, but it's not a passion. It's not something that sets his senses on fire.

We pay. Move to the wicker chairs across from the coffee table.

I sit.

He sits next to me. Leans in close. "It's not the orgasms. It's the intimacy. Kissing someone and feeling them in your soul." His gaze flits to the menu. "It's different when you love someone."

"Yeah."

"And I did. I loved everything about Mack. She understood me in a way I needed. When we were dressed. And when we weren't. For a while, at least."

"The sex got bad?" I've never heard that.

"We were going through the motions."

"Oh."

"Guess it should have been the first sign."

Maybe. I have a hard time giving Mackenzie the benefit of the doubt. "You think it was your fault?"

"I don't know."

"Do you still... want her?"

"Part of me does. But mostly—"

I don't let him finish. "You still want her on her knees, begging for forgiveness?"

He arches a brow. "On her knees?"

"Yeah, I mean, as long as she's begging for forgiveness, she might as well earn it on her knees, right?"

"You think I get off on my ex begging to suck my cock?"

"Don't you?"

He stares at me like I'm crazy.

"Think about it. Right now. Close your eyes. Imagine Mack in that dress she was wearing last night. She knocks on the door. Comes into your room."

"This is stupid."

"Close your eyes," I say.

He does.

"You're sitting at your desk, working on a mock-up. She comes in, undoes the zipper of her dress, tosses it on the ground. She's not wearing anything under it. She's naked. And you're dressed. She gets on her knees. Brushes that long red hair behind her ears. Places her hands on your thighs. Whispers *Forest, I'm so sorry I left. I'm so sorry I fucked him. It was a mistake. It was always a mistake. I want you back. Let me prove how much I want you back.*"

His eyelids flutter open.

"That... I mean..." I can't bring myself to look for evidence. What if that gets him off? What if he's raring to go right now? I can't... I can't...

My eyes go to his crotch.

He's not hard, but he's getting there.

Awesome.

So awesome.

The barista calls my name.

I jump to my feet. "I'll get those."

"Skye—"

"You don't have to explain. I asked a question. If I didn't want an answer—"

"I don't—"

"Please, if you do respect me, don't say another word." I don't want to hear it. I can't hear it. I'm going to throw up if I hear it.

"Skye—" His fingers curl around my wrist. "I don't want—"

"Please stop." I pull my hand to my side. March to the counter.

His eyes turn down. His brow furrows the way it does when I just don't get something.

But what is there to get?

It doesn't matter that we kissed. That I still ache for him. That I want him more than I've ever wanted anyone.

Not if he still wants her.

## Chapter Twenty-Six

FOREST

For three minutes straight, I will the frigid water of the sink to calm my cock.

The icy liquid chills my wrists and numbs my hands.

But my cock stays ready.

The mental image of Skye stepping into my room, slipping off her dress, dropping to her knees—

Her dark lips around my cock—

Her groan vibrating against my skin—

Fuck. So much for lowering the flag. I turn the off the faucet. Press my back into the wall.

The bathroom is as cute as the main store. Green walls. Pink accents. Neon sign reading *I Love You A Latte*.

It's sweet enough, but every goddamn latte place has the same sign.

Every matcha place has *I Love You So Matcha* somewhere.

I want to appreciate the cute sign. To repeat the words without cringing.

I want *love* to feel right on my tongue.

Instead, *I love you* sends my thoughts to Mack's red nails in Diego's back. His name on her lips. The room humming with pleasure.

She said it so many times. For months. The entire time she was fucking him.

That she was figuring out how to leave.

That she was done with me.

She still looked me in the eyes and whispered *I love you* like it meant something.

It used to mean something. To mean everything.

But now—

My stomach churns. My cock deflates. If Mack is good for anything, it's destroying my desire.

There's nothing less sexy than that horrible mental image.

I don't know why Skye thinks I still want Mack.

I don't know how to explain this to her. It's not like I can say *sorry I spent so long in the bathroom. I had to cool down after hearing you narrate that very dirty story. Have I ever told you how much your voice drives me crazy? The soft groans. That throaty whisper. The heavy exhales.*

*I'm already getting hard again thinking about you pawing at my jeans.*

*It has nothing to do with Mack.*

*It's you. I want you, Skye. I want to drag you in here, peel your panties to your ankles, dive between your legs.*

*Fuck this awkward conversation.*

*Fuck conversation, period.*

*Let me show you exactly how I want you.*

*Maybe I can't make you happy. Maybe I can't give you my heart. But I sure as hell can make you come.*

After another minute of cold water, and a few more thoughts of Mack's frustrated stare, blood returns to my brain.

I meet Skye at those wicker chairs she loves.

She motions to my half-finished pink takeout cup. "I drank some for you."

"I appreciate that."

Her gaze goes right to my crotch. She does nothing to hide it. Or to pretend she's looking me up and down. "You, uh… You're ready to go?"

*I will be if you keep staring.* "Go?"

## The Best Friend Bargain

"I decided about the dress. I, uh, I want to get an awesome pinup thing at the shop in Pasadena. But uh… that probably won't make Mrs. Davis happy."

"Right."

"So there's a cute store near the Nordstrom. And we can get you something in the men's store after. If you want."

"I have a suit."

"You sure?"

"Sure enough."

She nods *okay*. "Maybe, um… maybe I'll get lunch to go too. At that place with the yellow umbrellas."

"On me."

"Sure, yeah." She stands. Tosses her finished drink in the trash. "I guess we should get your car."

"Yeah."

"And, uh… It's okay."

"What's okay?"

"This… You… You don't have to explain anything. I know what I signed up for. I know you're… I know." She offers me a weak smile.

I study her expression, trying to figure out what she means.

I don't know what to say. I don't know how to help her. So I nod *okay*, follow her out the door, try to figure out what she wants.

---

After a ten-minute walk home, a fifteen-minute drive to *Tragic Kingdom*, and ten more minutes of parking (to the same album), I'm no closer to figuring out what Skye wants.

I can't blame her for keeping her cards close to the vest. That's Skye. That's me. That's us.

But it eats at me in some way it usually doesn't.

I hate that she's upset. That she won't tell me why. That I can't figure it out.

I follow her lead. Talk about tattoos and clothing design and upcoming shoots. She has a whole beach series planned. She already has a few of this season's hottest swim trends.

Apparently, clothes are always a few months ahead. She's already late on showing off the summer styles.

I try to carry on a coherent conversation as we leave the parking garage, but my head fights me. It keeps replaying yesterday's shoot.

Her body between my thighs.

Her lips against mine.

Her hand in my hair.

Fuck.

I need a cup of coffee. Or an entire bottle of wine. Or both.

I step onto the concrete of the strip mall. This place can paint itself as ornately as it wants. It's still a strip mall.

The sun bounces off the white concrete, making everything way too bright.

My stomach turns from the excessive light.

Or maybe that's the way Skye is closing off.

It's hard to say.

I reach for her hand.

She presses it into her side. "A pool would be ideal. The beach is nice. It's free. And it's more scenic. But the water is freezing until August. And by August it's crowded everywhere. I can go up to Malibu, but that's such a far drive." She steps onto the down escalator. Grips the rubber railing. "It might be worth it. And I can handle some cold water. But only some. I'm not that tough."

"You are too."

She shakes her head. "No... I only seem tough because I wear a lot of black makeup."

"Is that why you wear it?"

Her voice softens. "It just feels right."

"It suits you."

"You think?" She makes a show of rolling her eyes.

For a second, the mood is light. Then a thin girl passes us. Her Nordstrom bag smacks my thigh. And Skye's.

# The Best Friend Bargain

My best friend frowns.

"You need help?" I ask.

"Huh?"

"Up in Malibu. I can hold a reflector. Man the camera."

"You're going to man the camera?"

"You don't think I can?"

"Maybe if I want a shitty porno."

"Go on…" I arch a brow.

She half-smiles. "You never said what you like."

"You want to know?"

"Do I?"

"It's not gang bangs."

"Or violent skull fucking?" she asks.

"Or that."

"So…"

"Solo women."

She looks up at me. Stares into my eyes like she's looking into my soul. "It took you an hour to admit you like to watch women fuck themselves?"

"You didn't ask."

Her laugh lights up her eyes. "You really…" She turns to step off the escalator. "That's really what you watch?"

"Not the only thing. But my favorite."

"Really?"

"Are you gonna test me?"

"How would I even—"

"See how long I last on different videos."

"Oh my God." A laugh spills from her lips. Then another. A bigger, heartier one. "Is faster or longer better?"

"Faster."

"What if you draw it out more when you like something? Because you need more of it?"

"Is that what you do?"

Her hair whips her cheek as she turns her head. "I don't watch porn."

"What do you do?"

"Somehow, I stay busy." She laughs. Shakes her head *you're so ridiculous.*

I shouldn't ask this, I know, but I have to. "When you fuck yourself?"

Her cheeks flush. "I take my hand—"

"You have a vibrator?"

"None of your business."

"What do you think about?" I want to move closer, but even with her laugh, she's giving off *stay away* vibes. I slide my hands into my pockets so I won't touch her. Fuck, I want to touch her. "What do you think about when you fuck yourself?"

"Men I want to bed."

"Bed?"

"Yeah."

"Which men?"

"You know…" She clears her throat. "Instagram models. And guys I um…"

"Anyone I know?" *Who the fuck is he? This guy you like. Who doesn't see how great you are. Who doesn't deserve your attention.*

She fights a blush. "You, uh… I should really… find a dress. So, uh… Why don't you give me twenty minutes? Then meet me in the dressing room?" Her eyes meet mine. Her chest flushes.

Fuck, she really does have amazing tits. Her dress—a snug purple thing that hugs her chest and glides over her hips—is just low enough to drive me out of my fucking mind.

"You don't want to tell me?" I try to drag my eyes from her chest, but it's impossible.

"What kind of girls do you watch touch themselves?"

"Hot ones."

"Okay, same answer. Hot guys."

"Big tits."

"It's porn. They all have big tits."

"Yeah, but—" I bite my tongue. I can't take that back.

I certainly can't spring it on her when she needs a ride home.

When she can't run the fuck away from me if she's terrified of how often I think of her.

"Twenty minutes, okay?" Her gaze flits to my crotch then it's back on my eyes.

Or maybe I'm imagining things. Maybe I'm one of those guys who thinks every hot chick wants to fuck him. Maybe I'm completely out of touch with reality.

I nod *okay*, buy a cold brew at the Nordstrom coffee shop, pace around the mall as I drink.

I'm not into coffee the way some of my friends are, but I do love cold brew.

It's rich, strong, chocolaty.

Full of caffeine.

Not that I need the perkiness today.

I need the ice cooling me off.

I need the liquid running through my veins.

I need the caffeine constricting my blood vessels.

Or the opposite. Fuck knows how the science works.

I give Skye an extra five minutes, then I head to the store.

The sales woman nods *hey*, does nothing to stop me from walking straight to the dressing room.

Maybe she has a thing for tattooed guys in sunglasses.

Maybe she doesn't care about her minimum wage job.

Maybe she likes listening to customers fuck.

Not that we're going to fuck.

Just—that idea is in my head.

I swallow another sip. When it fails to cool me down, I pop the lid, suck on an ice cube.

"Forest?" Her voice is soft. "Is that you?"

I bite the ice cube in half. Swallow the pieces. "Yeah."

"Can you zip me?"

"Sure." I move to the sound of her voice. The third stall on the right.

The dressing room is like the rest of the store. Retro cute. Pastel colors. Classic patterns.

The walls are pink polka dots. The stalls are a complementary shade of teal.

It's adorable, yeah, but it's not Skye.

A lock unclicks. Her door falls open.

She's standing there in bare feet, in a pretty pink dress, her back exposed.

My fingers brush her skin.

She lets out a soft sigh.

Fuck, not what I'm doing.

I pull the zipper up. Step back. Give her room.

Her gaze goes to the mirror. "What do you think?"

It's a cute dress. A-line, I think. High neckline. Plenty of skirt. Tight on her tits. Loose around her waist. "Mrs. Davis will have a hard time calling you a slut."

"Will she though?" Skye asks.

I can't help but laugh. "Hard justifying it."

She nods *fair*. Rises to her tiptoes. Spins.

Her dress spins with her. It rises enough I see a flash of her panties.

Black lace.

From that lingerie company? Or something that's all hers? That she wears to feel sexy?

That she takes off before she fucks herself?

Wears as she fucks herself?

Maybe her vibrator is too much pressure. Maybe she has to keep her panties on.

Maybe I can pin her to the wall, pull her panties aside, lick her until she's screaming my name.

Skye stops, facing me. Looks me in the eyes. "How bad is it?"

"Bad?"

"Not me?"

"Isn't that what you're going for?" *Look at her eyes, Forest. Stop looking at her ass. Stop thinking about the taste of her cunt.*

"I don't know." She smooths the dress. "Part of me wants to show up in something really low-cut. So Mrs. Davis faints. But then I think about my mom and how she'll hear about it for months."

"Would she mind?"

"Not exactly. But… I don't want to put more on her than I have to. I'm already living in her hours. Eating her food."

"Keeping your room a mess?"

"It's my room." She brushes her hair behind her ear. "It's more the uh… other rooms. I try to clean up. I do. And I cook when they're working."

"You're a good daughter."

"I do okay."

"You look beautiful." I manage to bring my gaze all the way to her bare neck. She's darker than I am, but her skin is still so light compared to her dark hair. The contrast is all her. And it's fucking hot. "Not like Skye, but still beautiful."

"Like Mack?"

"No." I shake my head. "You're nothing like Mack."

"Nothing?"

"Okay, you both like clothes. And talking about tattoos. But beyond that—" I brush a stray hair from her cheek. "You're Skye. You're smart. Funny. Tenacious."

"I'm tenacious?"

"You haven't given up on me."

She stifles a laugh. "That makes me tenacious?"

I shake my head. "The way you work on your blog. Your following. You kept doing it even when it wasn't going the way you wanted. You never backed down. Or gave into bullshit."

"Maybe."

"You…"

"I should try on this one." She motions to a black dress with white polka dots.

It's cute, but it's not her. I nod *sure*.

She lets the door close, but she doesn't lock it.

I try to look away. To respect her privacy. To think about what a great friend she is and how much it will hurt if I lose her.

About how she deserves a guy who's capable of loving her with his entire heart.

About how I need to put her first.

"What do you think?" She pulls the door open. Smooths the flowing skirt.

"You know I wear the same thing every day?"

"It looks good on you." She gives me a long, slow once-over. Her eyes settle on mine. "You like it?" She takes a half-step toward me.

"It's not you."

"But do you like it?"

Fuck, the skirt is loose. Perfect for peeling off her panties and pulling her into my lap. "I'd like it better if it was you."

"You like the way I dress?"

"Yeah."

"I always thought... you always fucked girls who were conventional."

"So?"

"And thin."

"I didn't—"

"Never anyone like me."

"No one is like you."

"But you... the story about Mack. You got hard thinking about her... thinking about some revenge blow job."

"No."

Her fingers brush the waistband of my jeans. "Then what."

"You, Skye."

"What?"

"I was thinking about you." I bring my hands to her hips. "I don't want to fuck Mack. Or any of the redheads who come into the shop. Or any of Holden's friends. Hell, I don't want to fuck lingerie models. Unless they're you."

Her eyes go wide.

"I don't want anyone else, Skye. I want you."

## Chapter Twenty-Seven

SKYE

Forest shifts his hips, pinning me to the wall.

My eyelids flutter closed.

His lips connect with mine.

His kiss is hard. Hungry.

Pure need.

Pure desire.

My lips part.

His tongue slips into my mouth.

It swirls around mine.

It feels so good. So right.

I'm kissing Forest. I'm kissing my best friend. I'm kissing my favorite person on the planet.

My body is pressed against his.

His body is pressed against mine.

His cock—

He's hard.

For me.

Forest. Wants. Me.

I break our kiss. Suck a breath through my nose. Push out a steady exhale.

It does nothing to bring me back to Earth.

Who the fuck needs Earth?

Earth is a waste of time.

This—his dark eyes filled with pure lust—is way better than Earth.

He brings his hand to my cheek. Rubs my temple with his thumb. "You need to slow down?"

I shake my head so hard my hair smacks into my cheeks, chin, nose. "I need to go faster."

He motions to the door behind us. "Can you stay quiet?"

"No."

"They might call security."

"I don't care."

"Me either." He shifts his hips, keeping me pinned to the wall. "But your dad is right—"

"You are not bringing up my dad."

"I can't let you fuck up your future."

"You don't want to?"

"Fuck no." He shifts his hips backward, lowers me to the ground, wraps his fingers around my wrist.

He takes my hand. Brings it to his cock.

His jeans are in the way, but I can still feel him.

Hard. Ready.

Huge.

"I'm not leaving until I make you come," I say.

His pupils dilate. "Me either."

"So…"

"Stay quiet."

My tongue slides over my lips. "Or…"

"Or I'll have to stop." He slips his hand under my dress—

Though it's not actually my dress. I'm still wearing the shop's dress. A black and white polka dot number with thick straps. Cute. And not in a Skye way. In an adorable innocent virgin kind of way.

Though I shouldn't stereotype virgins.

I dressed like a goth princess when I was a virgin.

Now that I'm—

His hand brushes my sex. Over my panties. "You're wet."

My nod is heavy.

"You get wet thinking about me?"

"Yes."

"You fuck yourself to me?"

"All the time." My cheeks flush. It's weird, feeling shy given where we are. But I do.

He rubs his thumb over my cheek. "I love when you blush."

"Oh." My blush deepens.

"I can't always tell with your makeup. But when I can—" He presses the back of his hand against my sex, pressing the rough lace of my panties into my flesh. "It drives me insane."

"My blush?"

"And the way you groan over your drinks." He turns his hand over. Presses his palm against me. "The way you look at me when I take off my shirt."

"You do that on purpose?"

"Yeah."

"Bastard."

His lips curl into a smile. "And this?" He drags his fingertip down my cheek, chin, neck, collarbone. All the way to the neckline of my dress. "You telling me you aren't trying to drive me out of my mind?"

"I didn't think—"

"You always think."

"That you wanted me."

"I do." He pushes the right strap off my shoulder. Then the left. "I have."

"For how long?"

"A long time."

"But Mack—"

"Forget about Mack," he says. "I don't want to think about her right now. I don't want to think about shit right now." He presses his palm into my sex. Softly. Then harder.

Fuck, the pressure is intense. "Forest."

"Quiet."

"Okay." I try to lower my voice to a whisper. Get most of the way there.

"Fuck, Skye—"

"Yeah?"

"You drive me crazy. You know that?"

I shake my head.

He nods *yeah, you do*. He drags his hand over my sex. Until his fingers are on my clit, pressing the lace into my tender flesh. "You have no idea how long I've been dreaming about this."

"I have too. I mean, I do too."

"How long?" His eyes bore into mine. They're wide. Earnest. Completely without defenses.

"Always."

"Always?"

"Since we met. I… I always wanted you. I tried not to think about it. To step out of the way when you got together with her. But I—"

"Princess—"

"Yeah?"

"You always ignore what you want?"

"It wasn't like that." It was… complicated. Sisters before misters. Even if Mackenzie ignored that, I wasn't going to. It wasn't like there was a chance. It wasn't like he looked at me.

"Not anymore. Not with me." He rubs me over my panties. "I'm going to give you exactly what you want, princess. Before you realize you want it. When you're too caught up in bliss to even think about what you want."

Holy shit.

"That okay with you?"

I nod so I won't groan.

"Fuck, I want to make you scream." He presses his lips to mine. They close around my top lip. Then the bottom.

He sucks softly.

Then harder.

Then it's a scrape of his teeth.

Enough it hurts.

Enough I know I'm his.

Fuck, I want to be his. All his. Always.

He works me with soft, slow strokes of his fingers.

I tug at his t-shirt. It's not enough. I need to touch him. I need his skin against mine.

I break our kiss with a sigh. "Shirt off."

He nods.

I pull it over his head.

My palm brushes his chest. Then it's my fingers against the raised lines of ink.

I trace the tattoo on his chest. The glass heart shattered into a million pieces. "You've been through—"

"Princess, I love talking to you."

I nod.

"But right now, I need to taste your cunt."

My eyes go wide. "Oh—"

"Don't tell me you don't like it." He slips his hands under the dress. Hooks his thumbs into my panties. "Skye, don't tell me—"

"I do."

His lips curl into a wicked smile.

He stares into my eyes for a minute, then his eyes close.

He leans in. Kisses me hard. And deep. Like he won't get enough. Like he's claiming me.

Forest peels my panties over my ass.

He lowers himself to his knees as he pulls my underwear down my thighs, over my calves, all the way to my ankles.

I lift one foot. Kick the underwear aside. It's an extra from the lingerie company. A very expensive scrap of lace. But I can't say I care where it ends up at the moment.

Forest is between my legs.

Forest is between my legs, staring up at me like I'm the only thing he wants.

Like I'm everything he wants.

He ducks under my dress. Brings his lips to the inside of my knee.

A soft kiss.

Then harder.

Higher and higher—

Fuck, the pressure of his mouth is divine.

I can see him in the mirror. The white on black polka dot fabric swishing over his head and shoulders. The muscles of his back tensing and relaxing. The jeans slung low around his hips.

It's not enough.

I need more.

I reach around. Unzip my dress. Toss it over my head.

He slides a hand up my body.

I cringe as he touches my stomach. For a second, insecurity floods my senses. I have to look away from the mirror.

I'm too soft. Too much. Too different than what he's used to.

"You gonna watch, princess?" He nips at my skin. Then he does it harder. Hard enough it hurts.

I bite my tongue so I won't groan. "Yes."

"Fuck." He scrapes his teeth against my flesh. "You like to watch?"

"I don't know."

"I like thinking about you watching." He drags his lips higher and higher. "About you trying to watch pleasure spread over your face until it's too much. Until you can't take it anymore and you have to close your eyes so you won't scream."

"Forest—"

"Watch." He looks up at me for a second. His expression is a potent mix of desire and satisfaction.

He has me exactly where he wants me.

God, this is exactly where he wants me.

He groans against my thigh as his hand brushes my stomach. He reaches higher, higher. Until he's tracing the outline of my bra.

He slips his hand inside the cup. Draws circles around my nipple.

## The Best Friend Bargain

My gaze goes to the mirror. Fuck, it's such a beautiful sight. Forest toying with my breast. Nipping at my thighs. Pushing my legs wider.

I knot my hand into his hair. Hold tightly as he drags his lips higher, higher, higher—

There.

His lips brush my clit. It's soft, barely a touch.

He does it again.

Harder.

Harder.

Then softer. Softer. So soft I can barely feel it.

He uses one hand to press my thighs apart. Uses the other to toy with my nipple.

Works me with those same soft brushes of his lips.

Then harder and harder until—

"Fuck." I tug at his hair. "Forest. Please."

He pulls back enough to nip at my inner thigh. "I'll have mercy today. But I'm gonna make you beg next time."

My sex clenches.

"Fuck, Skye. You taste good." He doesn't wait for a response. Just dives between my legs.

No more teasing.

He licks me up and down. Slowly. Like he's savoring it.

He explores me. Scrapes his teeth against my lips. Flicks his tongue against my clit. Plunges his tongue inside me.

I press my palm to my mouth, but it's not enough to keep my groan contained.

He releases my breast. Traces a line up my neck and chin.

He hooks my bottom lip with his thumb.

I take his digit into my mouth. Suck hard.

Fuck, he tastes good. And having Forest's thumb in my mouth—

It fills my head with so many delicious ideas.

He toys with me as I suck on him.

I knot my hand in his hair.

My brow knits.

My lips part.

My eyes fill with—

Fuck, it's too much. I close my eyes. Groan against his hand.

His pressure gets harder. Higher. Higher—

There.

He flicks his tongue against my clit. A little to the right. Down. Up. Left.

Harder.

Softer.

Back and forth.

Up and down.

Circles.

Zigzags.

Sharp—

Fuck. I scrape my teeth against his finger.

He pulls back to groan. Then his mouth is against me and he's working me just right.

Those quick, hard flicks.

Again and again and again.

Every flick of his tongue winds the tension in my sex. He pushes it tighter, tighter, tighter.

Works me higher, higher, higher.

Until it's too much to take.

And not enough.

How can it be both?

How is he so fucking good at this?

He keeps that same steady pace. That same perfect pressure.

I wind tighter and tighter.

Then I'm there.

My world goes white. Nothing but pure, blinding light. Nothing but bliss.

The tension in my sex unravels. It flows through my torso, down my limbs, all the way to my fingers and toes.

My sex pulses.

# The Best Friend Bargain

My clit throbs.

My nipples pang.

I moan against his hand as I come. But that isn't enough either.

I pull back. Groan his name.

He looks up at me with fire in his eyes. It's pure demand. *I have you where I want you and I'll stop when I'm done with you. Not a second sooner.*

I press my back into the wall to steady myself.

He plants a kiss on my inner thigh.

I tug at his hair. To pull him up. I need my hand around his cock. I need him in my mouth. Between my breasts. Inside me.

It doesn't matter, as long as I have him.

He stays put.

I tug again. "Please."

He stands.

I reach for his jeans. Undo the button. Pull down the zipper.

Mmm. He's still hard. And there's only a thin layer of cotton between us. Only those black boxers.

His eyelids flutter together. "Skye."

"I lied before."

"Huh?"

"I think about sucking you off all the time."

His lips part with a groan.

"I think about you groaning my name as you pull my hair. And the way you'll taste in my mouth. And—"

"Ahem," a loud voice interrupts. "The dressing room is back through here. There's one woman trying on some new styles, but otherwise, it's empty."

I jump backward.

He motions *quiet*. Unzips his pants. Jumps onto the tiny chair. Crouches.

So his legs aren't visible. So only mine are.

The shopper says something to the saleswoman.

The saleswoman laughs. "Yes, she's been in here a while. I'm sure she'll buy a lot. Why else would she be in here?" She clears her throat. "No, no, no one will interrupt you. But I will be back in a few minutes to see if you need more sizes."

Forest stifles a chuckle.

I press my hand to my mouth so I won't laugh.

Fuck, the saleswoman has us nailed. And now... I guess I have to buy this boring dress.

But then again it's the dress I wore the first time Forest really kissed me.

The first time he—

Fuck, I'm hot just thinking about it.

He waits until the door clicks then he turns to me. Makes that same *shhh* noise. Mouths *I'll meet you outside.*

He slips out of the store with quiet footsteps.

I change into my street clothes, gather the polka dot dress, slip out of the dressing room.

The salesgirl is standing behind the counter, shaking her head *you think that's enough?*

Ahem. I stare at the wall. Uh... another dress. There. I grab the same thing, but in all black. And red sunglasses. You can never have too many pairs of sunglasses.

The salesgirl smiles from the counter. She grabs one of the rose pins sitting on the display. Sets it on top of my dresses. *You're buying that too.* "Attending a special event with your boyfriend?"

"Yeah. A wedding."

"Who's?"

"His ex's."

Her brow scrunches with confusion. "Reminding him why he chose you?"

"Uh..." I pull out my dad's credit card. Hand it over.

She uses a tissue to pick it up and swipe it then hands it back. "I don't mind activities if you two are alone. But let me know first." She makes the *money* sign with her first two fingers.

"Yeah... sure."

"I can keep the coast clear." Her gaze shifts to Forest, who's standing outside the store, the picture of confidence. "He's hot."

"He is."

"Girls with big boobs always get the hot guys." She sighs wistfully. Hands over my receipt. And a bright pink shopping bag. "You expecting a scene at the wedding? Or just more like this?"

"No, uh…" I don't know. I'm not going there.

"Good luck. Seems like he likes you a lot. But guys like that… The hot ones have so many options." Her gaze flits to my chest. "You'll be okay if he's a boob guy."

"Thanks." I scoop the clothes into the bag.

"He seems like a boob guy."

I stare at her dumbstruck for a moment.

She stares back like we're besties. Like she's giving me the world's greatest advice.

Okay…

Finally, I turn, rush out the door, meet Forest outside.

He shoots me that same wicked grin. "Offering her some tips?"

"She's jealous girls with big boobs get all the hot guys."

He laughs. And stares at my chest. "I'd say great tits. But they are huge, yeah."

I clear my throat.

"Fuck, princess, you have no idea how badly I want to taste your nipples."

My cheeks flush. "We need to—"

"Eat." He motions to the restaurant next door.

My frown is more pout than anything.

He laughs. "Don't worry, Skye. I'm going to take you home tonight and torture you mercilessly."

"That's in… we promised to have dinner with my parents."

"I know."

"That's eight hours away."

"You can't wait?"

I shake my head. Hell no, I can't wait.

He just smiles. "Come on." He nods to the restaurant. "You're gonna need your strength. Trust me."

## Chapter Twenty-Eight

FOREST

We finish lunch with twenty minutes of posed pictures. A second round of drinks. My sunglasses next to Skye's. Her hand on mine.

Her in my lap.

Her in my lap in sunglasses.

Her in my lap in sunglasses, smiling.

After a dozen shots of her in my lap, I'm hard enough to cut granite.

She blushes as she slides onto the chair next to mine. "Is that really—" She does nothing to hide her stare. Or her interest.

Her eyes go wide.

Her cheeks flush.

Her breath hitches.

*Princess, that's enough. Your cunt is too close to my cock. It's as greedy as I am. It wants your berry lips, your soft tits, your sweet cunt.*

Fuck. Not helping.

I suck another sip of cold brew. This is way too much coffee. It's good—rich and chocolatey—but it's not helping with my hangover.

I'm too old for hangovers.

But then I'm also too old to drink a bottle of wine by myself.

To give a shit about what Mack thinks.

At the moment, I can't remember why we're doing this. Why we're participating in this ruse.

I have a curvy goddess staring at my cock like she's desperate to devour it.

Everything else is irrelevant.

Skye is—

Fuck, I'm going to drag her to the bathroom at this rate. The need in her eyes. The heave of her chest. The purple fabric hugging her tits.

"You're off work all day?" she asks.

"Yeah." Thank God.

"So we can go to your place?"

"Can we?"

"Right now." Her eyes meet mine. "Or I'm going to take you in your car."

"It will be too hot."

"I don't care."

"We'll get heatstroke."

"Don't care."

"You will. When it happens. It would be a hell of a way to go, but I can't die yet. I need to make you come again."

Her blush spreads to her chest.

My heart warms. My limbs buzz. My cock—

Fuck, I need to stop teasing her. It's too tempting. I'm ready to ask her to go right here, on the restaurant patio, in view of everyone who walks by the mall.

"Forest—"

"Too far." I need to torture her, but I don't have the patience. Or the stamina. Not with her looking at me like that. "My dad's house."

"What if Holden—"

"He's working today."

"You're sure?"

"I can be." I pull up the Inked Love schedule on my phone. It's right there. An appointment until five. "We only have a few hours."

"You can last a few hours?"

"No. But I have other ways to make you come."

---

THE WALK TO THE CAR IS TORTURE.

The drive is worse.

I swear, we hit every red light.

Gwen Stefani groans about something. Her ex. Fashion. Music. I don't know.

Or care.

It takes all my concentration to keep my eyes on the road.

Finally, I pull into the driveway. It's empty. No Holden. No Ariel. No one to fuck this up.

I love my family, but now is not the time.

I need to fill the entire house with Skye's groans.

How loud is she when she doesn't have to stifle her groans?

Is she breathy? Low and needy? High and desperate?

Does she scream?

Fuck, I'm already hard.

I turn the car off.

Her tongue slides over her lips. "It would be wrong to unzip your pants?"

Yeah, but I don't have it in me to stop her. "I need a place to fuck you properly."

Her eyes go wide.

Goddammit, it's the best thing I've ever seen. Well, second best.

I reach for the door. "Inside. Now."

She nods *of course*, slides out of the car, gathers her stuff.

I grab the pink shopping bag.

She blushes as my hand brushes hers. "I'm not sure I'll be able to wear either of these."

"Yeah?"

"I'll spend every minute thinking about the dressing room."

"Good."

Her eyes go to her shoes. Platform combat boots. Pure Skye.

She's always wearing black shoes.

They're always hot as hell.

"Keep those on." I pull my keys from my pocket. Try to name the Dodgers lineup. Something to cool my cock. So I don't come the second I see her naked.

Fuck, I hate baseball.

I switch to the Lakers. The Clippers. The teams' playoff histories.

I slide the key into the lock. Push the door open.

"Forest, nice of you to join." Holden's voice flows from the living room.

Skye bites her lip. Presses her palm into mine. "I thought he was working."

"That you, Skye?" he calls. "I was working, but I finished early. And look who I found on his way home from the gym? We just finished a round of free throws."

We trade a knowing look.

He didn't.

Did he?

I push the door open.

He did.

Holden is sitting at the table with Ariel and Mr. Kim.

Ariel's in her usual all-black outfit. (She's not goth or emo, just practical). A snug maternity dress. She's about five months now and she's glowing.

Holden and Mr. Kim are in their workout gear.

"Ariel made chai lattes." Holden beams with pride. Not over our sister. Over fucking with me.

Or maybe I don't give him enough credit.

No, I give him plenty of credit.

"With almond milk?" Skye asks.

"I'll make one." Ariel stands. She surveys us with a knowing smile. "You look different today."

"Me?" I ask.

"Both of you." She looks at Skye. "I wonder what it is?"

Skye clears her throat. "We, uh…" She looks at me *help me out here?*

"You think I know what to say?" I whisper.

"I can't think," she whispers back. "Is there any way to lose them?"

"It's Holden. He won't leave until we admit we need the space to bone."

She bites her lip, considering it.

"If you want to tell your dad—"

"Right." She turns back to my family. And hers. "I'll help."

"I'll make two." Ariel moves to the counter.

"Should you be having more caffeine?" I ask.

My sister makes a show of rolling her eyes. "Hmm… I've been pregnant for more than half a year. You think I don't know?"

"Someone has to look out for Charlotte," I say.

"You think I'm not worried about Charlotte?" She shoots me a cutting look. "If Skye wasn't here, I'd hit you for that."

"You can't hit back either. Not if you're worried about Charlotte," Holden says.

"Why would I hit Ariel?" I ask.

He shrugs *you would*.

Mr. Kim chuckles. "I remember when Skye's mom was pregnant." His smile gets wide. "I was worried all the time."

"Yeah?" Ariel fills the kettle with water. She makes a show of grabbing the box of decaf chai and placing two bags in one mug. "About her? Or Skye?"

"Both. I was still in med school. I'd just finished my obstetrics round. I was terrified of all the things that could go wrong," he says.

"Did you get over it?" she asks.

He shakes his head. "It only got worse when Skye was born. She was an easy baby. Barely cried. But I'd worry about that. Worry she didn't know how to use her voice."

"That isn't a problem," I say.

"Oh?" Mr. Kim asks.

"She loves telling me I'm an idiot," I say.

"Only when you're being an idiot," Skye says.

"Oooh, I love telling him he's being an idiot." Ariel scoops chai leaves into the steeper. Drops the mesh ball into a plain white mug. "He's usually pretty responsible though."

"Go on," Mr. Kim says.

"Or don't," I say.

"No, do." Holden crosses one leg over another. "I never hear about Forest's fuckups. Only mine."

Mr. Kim laughs. "I don't think Skye realizes it, but her mom and I still worry about her."

Skye clears her throat.

"Sweetie, I'm your dad. I have to say this." He takes a long sip of his drink. "Ariel, you make a mean cup of tea."

Ariel smiles. "Thank you."

He turns to Skye. "Skye got more headstrong as she got older. She was so smart and so creative. Her art teachers always wanted to give her extra work. For a while, I thought maybe I didn't have to worry. She was getting straight As. She was helping with dinner. She was cleaning up after herself. Mostly." He looks to me. "I didn't realize she had only changed so much." He turns to Skye. "She doesn't always use her voice."

Skye clears her throat. "I, uh…"

"I won't embarrass you too much sweetie. I just want your boyfriend to know. He has to be careful. To make sure he's really listening. It's easy to look at you and see the strong, smart woman you are," he says.

"Thank you," she says.

"But the makeup is deceiving," he says.

"Oh my God." Skye shakes her head. "We are not having this conversation."

"Okay." His laugh is knowing. "She's so much like her grandma. She looks just like her too."

# The Best Friend Bargain

"I wish I'd met her." She refers to her grandma. Supposedly, that Mrs. Kim was a rule-breaker. She had an affair with a soldier. Found out he was KIA the same day she found out she was pregnant. Or so the story goes.

"She would be impressed by everything you've done," he says. "And more understanding of those pictures than your mother is."

"Oh God." Skye turns bright red. "I thought we—"

"We did. But your mother stumbled on them during her lunch break." Mr. Kim chuckles. "She's... concerned."

Skye hides behind her hands. "Please wake me when this nightmare is over."

"Which pictures?" Ariel asks.

Holden pulls out his cell. Goes right to Skye's Instagram.

There are new pictures from lunch.

And the two lingerie shots.

"Damn, Skye..." Holden looks at her dad. Thinks better of going into his usual *I want to suck on your tits* thing. "You sure you want to waste your time with my brother?"

"You should be sure you're with a worthy man." Mr. Kim looks to me. "No offense, Forest."

"None taken." I'm the same way with Ariel. I wasn't exactly happy when I found out she and Chase were dating, much less making a baby. She had good reasons for asking him. And I can't exactly fault her for falling for someone with piercing blue eyes.

I don't appreciate Chase's. But Skye's?

Those bright blue eyes find mine. "Forest is... sometimes he's difficult. He has some baggage, yeah, and he has an unusual job. But he's handsome—"

"He is handsome, sweetie, but looks fade," Mr. Kim says.

Holden doubles over with laughter.

"Mr. Kim," Ariel says. "I hope you don't mind me saying this, but you're an older man."

Holden laughs harder.

"It's true," he says.

"But you're still very handsome. And in great shape too." Ariel's voice is matter-of-fact. "Maybe looks don't always fade."

"You have your whole family backing you up," he says. "I like that."

"He does." Skye smiles. "He's a family man, even if he doesn't realize it. And, well… he always looks out for me. Makes sure I have extra green onions. And matcha lattes. And the right shoes for the occasion."

Her dad raises a brow.

"He treats me well. I trust him. What else is there?" she asks.

"Sweetie, I like Forest too, but love is more than green onions," he says.

"Yeah, also matcha lattes." She shoots her dad a knowing look.

He nods *true*. "Did you get the green onions?"

She mouths *fuck*. "I'll get them now."

"Let's go together. So we can talk. Before your mother gets home." He exchanges her look.

"Yeah, sure…" Skye cringes. "After tea."

Mr. Kim smiles. "Tea always comes first." He looks to Ariel. "You don't mind making me another?"

"Never." She leans in to whisper in Skye's ear.

Skye laughs. "Trust me, you don't want details." She turns to me. Mouths *sorry*.

I pull out my cell. Tap her a text.

*Forest: I can wait to torture you.*
*Skye: It won't be until after dinner.*
*Forest: I'll make you pay for that, princess.*
*Skye: How's that?*
*Forest: You ever get so close you're begging to come?*

She looks up at me with wide eyes.

"You know we all realize you're sending dirty texts," Holden says.

"I hope you're not sending any nude pictures, sweetie," her dad says, easy breezy. "Your mom won't take that well."

"Uh…" She grabs her tea. "Let's just…"

"Talk more about the pictures," Holden says. "How many more are you posting? And how explicit will they be?"

She flips him off, but she still takes a seat at the table.

I sit next to her.

She interlocks her hands with mine.

It's torture waiting to fuck her, but it's perfect too.

## Chapter Twenty-Nine

SKYE

Even though we only need green onions, Dad makes a point of driving to the Asian market on the other side of the freeway.

It's a stupid decision in traffic. Or maybe it's smart. It gives him plenty of time to lecture me.

Only he doesn't. He puts on one of my Garbage CDs, makes his usual Dad joke *Skye, the music you listen to is garbage*, laughs like it's the funniest thing anyone has ever said.

He makes innocent small talk the whole drive there, the entire time shopping (which is like one minute. We're only buying green onions), the ride out of the parking lot.

He waits until we're almost home. Then he asks, "Do you really trust him that much?"

It's a good question. Easy to answer. "I do."

"And you're sure about pursuing modeling?"

"I'm not modeling?"

"Sweetie, you're posing in lingerie on the Internet. You're modeling."

"I'm a fashion blogger."

"You take pictures of yourself in clothes. That's modeling."

"Photography."

"And modeling." He makes eye contact through the mirror. "Your mom and I are happy to have you home. We'll be happy if you live with us forever. And never get married."

"What about grandchildren?"

"Who said you wouldn't have grandchildren? Ariel's only twenty-four and she's pregnant. Ballards are probably hyper-fertile."

"Does it work like that?"

He chuckles. "No. But you wouldn't be the first woman to have an accident."

"Ariel didn't… it was on purpose."

He nods. He knows the whole story. We were all there when Ariel and Forest's mom died. We saw how much it hurt them. "Your mom likes Forest. She's worried he's pushing you with modeling—"

"He wasn't."

"I know. But your mother—"

"She still thinks I'm sweet and innocent."

He laughs. "Exactly." He turns onto our street. "I'll back you up if you're sure. She'll be upset, but she'll respect it."

"Respect what?"

"Her daughter posing in lingerie on the Internet."

"I'm not… it's not a new career."

"Are you sure about that?" he asks.

I… well… no. The photos are getting a great response. The lingerie company is happy. I have a check for four thousand dollars on the way.

It's possible.

Yeah, it's scary being so, well, naked, but it's exciting too. And it's… okay, it's not exactly heroic, but I want other bigger girls to feel beautiful too. I want to prove I'm just as sexy as any size two swimsuit model.

Even if I don't believe it all the time.

"I am sure," I say.

He offers me a fist bump. "Then we've got this."
I tap my fist with his. "You're such a dork."
"Yeah, but your friends still think I'm hot."
"Oh my God." I hide behind my hands.
"Hey, those are good genes you inherited."
"So not talking about this."
"Asian women age well."
"Mom is white."
"Your mom is as beautiful as the day I met her."
I roll my eyes. "Should I tell her you said that?"
"Sure, but I tell her every day."
He does. It's sweet. And cheesy.
They're sweet and cheesy.
I check my cell as he parks. I have a text from Forest.
*Forest: Probably won't get a real chance to talk for a while. I'll be at my dad's place after dinner. In my room. Waiting. Come without underwear.*
"Your boyfriend?" Dad asks.
"It's nothing."
"Your sexuality is—"
"We are so not discussing this."

---

DAD PUTS ME TO WORK COOKING.

Holden and Ariel keep Forest busy. Then Mom gets home and she tells me we'll talk later.

She's polite during dinner. She asks Forest all the usual questions. Like he's a stranger and not the guy who's been my best friend forever.

*What do you do?* (Tattoo artist) *How is work?* (Good, the new shop is doing super well) *Where do you live?* (In a one-bedroom in West LA) *And how much do you make?* (He has to check his tax returns) *Do you want children?* (Yes) *How many?* (It doesn't matter, as long as they're loved) *Will one of you stay home?* (Probably not).

Even though Forest answers flawlessly, it's pure torture.

After many servings of marinated beef and many cups of after-dinner tea (dessert is reserved for special occasions in Korean culture), my parents dismiss Forest.

Then Mom turns to me and brings up the pictures.

It's a long, long, long lecture.

Yes, she respects my choices and she wishes we lived in a world where women could show their body without consequences, but that isn't our world, and I need to be sure.

Is this boy really good for me?

Do I know what I'm doing with my life.

I wait for her to finish. Then I say it.

For the first time, I say, "I'm going to take photos. And model. I'm going to be a plus-size model."

She looks at me, impressed. "You're sure?"

"Yeah." For once, I am. For once, I know what I'm doing. For once, I have direction.

"Then I'm happy." She hugs me. "And this will pay enough for you to move out?"

Dad chuckles. "Bee, if she moves out, she'll have more time with that boy."

"Remember when we were her age? Nothing stopped us," Mom says.

Gross.

Then they're trading sweet nothings. And probably dirty nothings.

I say goodbye and practically run to Forest's place.

It's quiet downstairs. I slip out of my panties, drop them in my purse, move to his room.

My knock is soft.

He doesn't answer.

So I knock louder.

Still nothing.

I push the door open.

Sure enough, he's spread out over the bed in only his boxers.

Sleeping.

I find a spare t-shirt in his drawer. Then I change into my favorite pajamas and I climb into bed next to him.

## Chapter Thirty

FOREST

Light streams through the window. It falls over my black desk, my white walls, my plain sheets.

Skye's curvy body.

Shit.

So much for my promise to fuck her properly.

Not that I can complain about sleeping next to hear.

I slide my arm around her waist. Pull her body into mine.

She melts into my chest like she belongs there.

She does. Right now, it's obvious. Right now, it's the most obvious thing in the universe.

I need to make her smile.

I need to make her laugh.

I need to make her come.

"Mmm." She stirs as I pull her closer.

"Go back to bed, princess." Yeah, I want to fuck her. God how I want to fuck her. But I want this too. Skye relaxed, happy, at peace.

The way she is when she drinks a matcha latte. Or when she steps behind the camera. Or when she watches *Before Sunset*.

God, she loves that movie.

After a dozen viewings, I get the appeal. But it doesn't hit me the way it hits her.

I love it because she loves it. Because every time we watch, I see her eyes light up. I hear her laugh, gasp, cry.

Right now, that's—

Well it's not better than making her come. But it's good in its own way.

She arches her back as she yawns. "No… I…" She shifts her hips, rubbing her lush ass against my crotch. "Oh."

"Oh?"

"You're hard."

"Yeah." I can't help but chuckle.

"What's funny."

"You've never slept next to a guy?"

"I'm aware of the mechanics. I can still appreciate the result."

I bring my hand to her hip. Pull her closer. So her ass is against my cock.

"Fuck." She reaches for something. Gets the sheets. "Are you going to—"

"Am I going to?" I hook my thumb in her panties. "I told you to skip these."

"I did. You were asleep when I got here. So I put on my pajamas."

"Hmmm."

"Hmmm?"

"Might have to take them off now," I say.

"I wouldn't object to that."

"You wouldn't object?"

"Yeah, I… uh… I'm not good at dirty talk."

"Princess, you told me you've been daydreaming about the taste of my cock—"

Her cheeks flush. Her face is bare. She washed off her makeup last night.

She's religious about skin care.

I see her without makeup all the time. I don't prefer it. Or prefer the makeup.

Both are Skye.

She looks fucking hot with the dark eye makeup and the crimson lips.

But there's something about seeing the girl no one else sees—

It makes my chest warm.

It makes my everything warm.

"If that's bad dirty talk, I'm not sure I can handle good dirty talk," I say.

"You're complaining?"

"Fuck no." I rock my hips so my cock grinds against her flesh. I have to piss before I fuck her properly. But I'm never going to lower the flag if I keep her this close. "Just warning you, I might come too fast."

"Is that usually a problem?"

"No. But I'm not usually with someone this sexy."

Her blush deepens. "You mean I'm—"

"Don't bring up anyone else."

"You started it."

"I didn't mean it like that." I press my lips to her neck. "More that you're the sexiest woman I've ever seen."

"You've seen a lot."

"None of them are you."

"So it's because I'm—"

"Take off your panties."

"The question?"

"I'm answering it." I slip my hand between her legs.

She shudders as I drag it higher.

As my fingers brush her clit.

Fuck, those panties are sheer. I can almost feel her. I need to feel her.

"Forest." Her lips part with a groan. "Fuck."

"That?"

"What...?"

"Your groan." I run my finger over her clit so the lace brushes her skin.

She tugs at the sheets as she groans.

"It's the best thing I've ever heard."

"Better than—"

"Better than anything." I scrape my teeth against her neck as I rub her over her panties.

Her groans get louder.

She arches her back, rubbing her ass against my cock.

It's sweet torture.

The best kind of torture.

"Forest…" She turns her head away from me. "This is uh…"

"Yeah?"

"I want to kiss you. But I… morning breath."

I chuckle. "You want to stop to brush your teeth?"

"Is that a problem?"

"No." I rub her a little harder. "More time to torture you."

Her smile is shy. Fuck, it's something else seeing Skye shy. She's usually as loud as a firecracker.

It's something else, seeing her like this, period.

It's still hard to believe.

"You're evil." She sighs as she pulls away. It's pure whine. Pure need. Pure anticipation. "I think you might kill me at this rate."

"Too much?"

She shakes her head *not at all*.

"Come back without panties."

"I will if I want."

My balls tighten. Fuck, I've always loved her sassy comebacks, but this is something else.

I watch her saunter, then I get up, head to the bathroom in the master, piss, wash my hands, brush my teeth.

When I return from the hallway, she's at the sink, digging through her purse.

She pulls out her lipstick. Turns to the mirror. Purses her lips as she applies it.

Her cheeks flush as her gaze goes to my reflection.

"You need makeup for this?" I move into the bathroom.

"Well..." She presses her lips together. Checks her reflection. Drops the makeup. "I've had this image in my head."

"Yeah?"

"Of my lipstick on your cock."

Fuck.

"If that isn't a problem." She turns to me.

I back her into the counter. "Later."

"Later?"

"I need to be inside you." I pull her t-shirt over her head and toss it aside.

Her expression gets shy, nervous even.

"Fuck, princess." It's the first time I've really seen her topless. The first chance I've had to savor her.

God damn, she's better than I ever imagined. And I imaged plenty.

Round tits, perky nipples, sloping waist, lush hips.

She looks up at me. "You..."

"You're perfect." I bring my hands to her hips. I pull her body into mine as I bring my lips to hers.

She groans against my mouth. Parts her lips.

Her tongue dances with mine.

It's music. Somehow, we both know the notes, the rhythm, the steps.

We're in synch.

Or maybe that's no mystery. Skye's been my best friend for a long time. She knows me better than anyone.

I rock my hips, grinding my cock against her stomach.

She groans as she pulls back.

My eyes find hers. "Are you safe?"

"Yeah. The IUD and I... it's been a while." Her fingers dig into my bare chest. "You?"

"Yeah." I push her panties off her hips. "Turn around."

She nods *okay*, spins on her heels.

I peel her panties to her knees. Leave them there. So they're binding her legs. So she's at my mercy.

Skye groans as I pin her to the counter.

She places her hands on the tile. Arches her back, thrusting her ass into the air.

Fuck, she has a great ass.

I take a moment to admire it, then I do away with my boxers, bring my hands to her hips.

I hold her in place as I bring our bodies together.

My cock brushes her cunt.

She groans. Rocks back, driving onto me.

Fuck.

Pleasure floods my senses.

My eyes close.

My nails dig into her skin.

My cock pulses.

Her soft cunt envelops me.

I pull her closer. So I have all of her. So she has all of me.

"Fuck." She reaches back. Scrapes my hips with her nails. "You're big."

"Too much?"

"No. Just." She sucks in a deep breath. "Slow at first."

I nod. Bring my lips to her neck.

She groans as I suck on her tender skin. Her head falls to one side. Her hair falls over her eyes.

Her lips part with a groan.

Fuck, there is something about that berry lipstick. It's Skye.

And it's fucking hot.

I scrape my teeth against her neck. Softly. Then harder. Harder.

Hard enough she yelps.

I keep one hand on her hip. Bring the other to her chest. Cup her breast.

She feels right in my hand. Like she belongs there.

She does.

And this—
Fuck.
I pull back slowly.
She groans as I drag my thumb over her nipples. "Forest."
"Yeah, princess?"
"That's... keep doing that."
"Watch."
"It's too much."
"Try." I bite her harder.
Her groan is equal parts agony and ecstasy.
Her eyes blink open. Go to our reflection. She takes in everything. My lips against her neck, my hand around her chest, my body behind hers.
I hold her in place as I fill her with a slow, steady thrust.
Her tits bounce as I fill her.
Through the mirror, her eyes find mine.
She stares like she can't get enough.
Maybe she can't.
Fuck knows I'll never get enough of her.
I dig my fingers into her skin. Drive into her again and again.
"Fuck." She presses her palm into the counter.
"Too much?"
She shakes her head. "More."
I nip at her neck. "You sure?"
"Yeah," she breathes.
"Tell me if it's too hard."
She arches her back, driving me deeper.
"Promise you'll tell me, princess."
She nods. Then she turns her head toward mine.
I bring my hand to her cheek. Pull her into a soft, slow kiss.
Fuck, she tastes good. Like mint toothpaste and Skye.
She knots her hand in my hair, holds my head against hers.
Her kiss gets harder.
Like she wants me to know I'm hers.
I am.

But does she know that?

She breaks our kiss with a sigh.

Her eyes find mine. She nods *go*, turns to the mirror, watches as I drive into her.

As I toy with her nipples.

As I nip at her smooth neck.

She gasps as I press her hand to the counter. "Fuck. Forest—"

I keep her pinned.

Then I move faster.

Harder.

Harder.

There—

Her groan gets louder. Her eyes close. Her chest heaves.

She's exactly where she needs to be.

I watch pleasure spread over her expression for a moment, then I drive into her.

Again.

And again.

Until she's groaning and panting and writhing.

"Fuck." Her fingers slip from the counter.

"Touch yourself," I groan into her ear. "I want to watch you come."

Her nod is heavy. Needy. "Don't stop."

Like hell.

She slips her hand between her legs.

I drive into her with steady thrusts.

She brings herself to the edge.

Then I push her over it.

Skye groans my name as she comes. Her brows relax. Her eyes close. Her teeth sink into her lip.

I thrust through her orgasm. Then I bring my lips to her ear. "Keep going, princess."

"Fuck." She turns her head to mine. Her eyes fix on mine for a moment. They promise love, affection, need.

They promise everything.

Then her eyes close and her lips are on mine.

I kiss her as I fill her.

She kisses back with everything she's got.

We stay locked together.

It feels like forever passes. Like we're finally in this perfect space where we belong.

Like we've reached fucking Nirvana.

I don't need a physical form anymore.

I'm pure bliss.

And she's—

She's everything.

Skye pulls back to groan.

Her head falls to the right as she comes.

Her cunt pulses around me.

It pulls me over the edge.

With my next thrust, I come.

I groan her name into her neck. Work her until I've spilled every drop. Until we're both a sweaty, panting mess.

Slowly, I untangle our bodies.

She looks up at me with hazy eyes. "That was—"

"Yeah."

"You…" She rises to her tiptoes and brings her lips to mine.

This kiss is different. More affection than need. More tenderness than rawness.

It still fills me everywhere.

It's still everything.

## Chapter Thirty-One

SKYE

After we shower together, we dress (him in only jeans; me in last night's purple dress), head downstairs.

He goes straight to the kettle. Fills it with water. Sets it to 175.

My stomach flutters. Which is ridiculous. He does this every day. I spend the night all the time. He always fixes my matcha latte before he does anything else.

It doesn't normally fill my stomach with butterflies.

Only, right now, nothing is normal.

He's...

We...

I...

Forest looks back to me with a smile.

My heart melts.

It's such a beautiful smile. It lights up his eyes, softens his brow, erases the tension in his shoulders.

It makes me warm all over.

"If you look at me like that, I'm going to have to take you again." He turns to the fridge. Fills a mug with almond milk. Slides it into the microwave.

"Like what?"

"Like you're picturing me naked."

Mmm… not a bad idea. "You're not wearing a shirt."

"And that?" He turns and motions to my dress.

"What about it?"

"The skirt is begging for my hands."

"Oh?" I tug my skirt up my thighs. An inch. Then two.

His eyes go straight to my exposed skin. His tongue slides over his lips. "Do that again, and I'm going to fuck you so hard you see stars."

"I don't have a problem with that."

His eyes move over my body slowly. Stop on mine. "Yeah?"

I nod. "Can you?"

"Can I?"

I clear my throat.

He raises a brow.

I motion to his crotch. "Can you go again so fast?"

His laugh is big. Hearty. He has to hold on to the counter to steady himself.

"It's a fair question."

"It is."

"So why are you—" My cheeks flush. "Why are you laughing at me?"

"It's not"—he struggles to get the words out—"that."

I clear my throat.

"It's just—" The steam of the kettle interrupts him. He shakes his head. Sucks a breath through his nose. "You're so matter-of-fact."

"And?"

"You're usually so sure of yourself."

"Are you laughing because you can't?"

"See." He straightens himself. "That's the Skye I know."

"The Skye you know insults your dick?"

"Is there something wrong with taking a while to rebound?"

"Well…" I'm not sure, exactly. I don't have a ton of experience in the dick department. "No."

# The Best Friend Bargain

"Then it's not an insult."
"And you?"
His smile widens.
"You are laughing at me."
"No." He taps *keep warm* on the kettle, crosses the room, wraps his arms around me. "I love that you're asking about my dick."

"Oh." He slides his hands down my hips, over my ass. "He loves it too." He pulls my body into his, so I can feel his hard-on.

Fuck, it's hot. But I have to stay strong here. "He's a he?"
"Yeah."
"Does he have a name?"
"No." He laughs.
"He's personified, but he doesn't have a name?"
"Yeah… he's the one in control, not me."
"Oh?" I slide my arm around his neck. "You let your dick lead you around?"
"No, but he tries."
"Like…"
"You." He digs his fingers into my ass, pressing my dress into my bare skin. "He makes a lot of demands for your tits."
"Oh?" I raise a brow.
He nods *hell yeah*. "And your lips."
My cheeks flush.
"He's way into your dark lipstick."
"Go on…"
"Princess, if I go on I'm going to take you right here."
"Where's the problem?"
His smile widens. "I need to feed you first."
"That's really not necessary."
"The matcha?"
"Even that."
He slides his hand over my ass, down my thighs, all the way to my bare skin. "You'd rather fuck me than drink matcha?"
"Of course."

He beams with pride. Motions to the table. "Sit down. I'm making you breakfast."

"But—"

"What did I tell you yesterday about needing your strength?"

Uh…

"Was I right?"

"Well…"

He laughs. "We got cockblocked, yeah. But I've got the whole morning free today."

"All morning?"

He nods. Takes a step backward. "Trust me. You'll need the energy."

I trust him… but I'm fine waiting for the energy. Sure, matcha lattes are the greatest beverage in the world.

But can that really compare to his lips or his hands or his cock?

I'd much rather have him in my mouth.

Ahem.

He spins on his heels, grabs the matcha tin from the fridge, starts fixing it.

God, there's something about watching his shoulders tense and relax.

It's just… beautiful.

It really is.

I need to touch him.

I need to rip his clothes off.

I need to… uh…

No. Fuck anything else.

I really do need to rip his clothes off.

I give him enough time to whisk the matcha, pour it in the heated almond milk, stir.

It gives me time to add another coat of lipstick.

Then I unzip my dress and pull it over my head.

I back up to the couch. Grab a pillow. Place it exactly where I need it.

"See—" he turns to me. Drops his jaw. "Fuck, Skye—"

"Come here."

"I—"

"You said later. It's later."

He gives me a long, slow once-over. "You'd rather—"

"Suck you off? Yeah." I reach around my back. Unhook my bra. Slide it off my shoulders.

His eyes go wide. "Skye—"

"Come here."

"Your—"

"Or you're going to make me think you don't want it."

"Fuck no." He sets the mug on the counter. Takes three steps toward me. "But you have to know something, princess."

"Yeah?"

"I've been dreaming about your mouth for ages."

My sex clenches.

"About watching those pretty red lips stretch over my cock."

I stare into his eyes.

"You want me coming in your pretty mouth?" He moves closer. Until he's close enough to touch. "Or maybe here." He cups my breast with one hand. Runs his thumb over my nipple.

Softly.

Then harder.

"On those perfect tits." His touch gets harder and harder until—

Fuck. My eyelids press together. My lips part with a groan. "I want to taste you."

He brings his other hand to my cheek. Catches my lip with his thumb.

I flick my tongue against his digit.

Then he slides it into my mouth.

I look him in the eyes as I suck hard.

He stares back at me.

His dark eyes are on fire. Demanding and needy at once.

It's intense. Almost too much.

Intimate in a different way.

He toys with my breast until I'm groaning against his thumb, then he moves to my other nipple and teases it just as mercilessly.

My hands go to the waistband of his jeans. I'm not smooth the way he is, but I still manage to unbutton and unzip him.

To push his jeans off his hips.

Rub him over his boxers.

His eyes flutter closed.

Anticipation spreads over his face.

Fuck, it's beautiful. It's the best thing I've ever seen. It really is.

I push his boxers off his hips.

Mmm.

It's the first time I've *really* had a good look at him. He's every bit as thick as he feels.

And there's something about seeing him hard and ready for me.

It makes me hot all over.

I wrap my hand around him as I release his thumb. "Not too hard."

He nods with understanding.

I press my lips to his chest.

He helps me onto my knees. Onto the pillow.

His hand knots in my hair.

My lips brush his tip.

Then it's a slow flick of my tongue.

He tastes good. Like Forest and soap.

I place one hand on his hip. Use it for balance as I wrap the other around him.

God, he's warm and hard and mine.

I know he isn't, that this is still messy and confusing. But right now, he is.

Right now, he's entirely at my mercy.

It's thrilling.

I look up at Forest as I brush my lips against his tip.

His fingers dig into the back of my head. He stares back at me, eager, wanting, needy.

# The Best Friend Bargain

I take my time exploring him. Dragging my lips over his shaft. Flicking my tongue against his tip. Tasting his soft skin.

He groans as I take him into my mouth.

I wrap my lips around his tip. Press my tongue against the underside.

"Fuck." His breath gets heavy.

It bounces around the empty room. It fills me everywhere.

I grip him tighter. Suck on his tip until his groan gets low and deep.

Then I slide my lips over my teeth and I take him deeper.

Deeper.

As deep as I can.

He reaches for me. His fingers brush my neck. Shoulders. Collarbone.

Chest.

He takes my breast into his hand. Rolls my nipple between his thumb and index finger.

Fuck. His touch sends desire racing to my sex.

I groan against him.

He toys harder.

I pull back, take him again.

"Fuck, Skye." He pinches my nipple. "You're too good at this."

In response, I wrap my hand around his base. I keep it there as I pull back and take him again.

He tugs at my hair, pulling me back. Then it's his palm against the back of my head, pushing me forward.

The desperation of his gesture makes my sex clench.

I work him as he guides me.

Deeper—

Harder—

Fuck. It's too hard.

I gag. Pull back. Cough. "Not so—"

He nods *I know*. Offers his hand.

I take it.

Forest helps me up. "You lead, princess."

The desire in his voice makes my sex clench. I nod. Bring one hand to his hip. Wrap the other around his thick cock.

He shudders as my lip brushes his tip.

This time, I go slowly. I taste every inch of his tip. Bring him into my mouth. Tease him with my tongue.

Soft flicks against his base.

Then harder ones.

Slow swirls of my tongue.

He groans as I toy with his tip. His hand knots in my hair. It tugs.

But it doesn't push or pull.

He rakes his nails over my shoulder. Takes my breast into his hand. Toys with my nipple.

It's hard in the best possible way.

I toy with him until he's groaning, then I take him as deep as I can.

Softly at first. Then harder. Harder. There—

His groan is pure ecstasy.

I work him with a steady pace.

He toys with my nipple.

Every brush of his fingers sends a pang of desire straight to my sex.

The feel of his flesh against my lips—

The taste of him in my mouth—

Fuck, I'm on fire. I really am.

I look up at Forest as I work him.

He stares down at me with heavy lids. Then his eyes close and his lips part with a groan. "Fuck, Skye." He rolls my nipple. "I'm gonna come in that pretty mouth."

My sex clenches.

I keep my pace.

My pressure.

His groans get lower, louder.

He shifts his hips, pushing deeper. Deeper.

There—

He tugs at my hair, groaning my name as he comes in my mouth.

I wait until I have every drop, then I swallow hard.

His eyes blink open. He looks down at me like I'm heaven-sent. "Fuck."

My cheeks flush.

"On the couch."

"On the couch?"

He offers me his hand.

I take it.

He pulls me up. "On the couch. On your back. You're coming on my face again."

"I—"

"Now."

"You—"

"Now, princess." He doesn't wait for a response. He wraps his hands around my waist, guides me to the couch, helps me onto my back.

And I—

Well, if this is what he wants, I'm not about to deny him.

## Chapter Thirty-Two

SKYE

After, I clean up in the upstairs bathroom. Return to a kitchen that smells of coffee and green onions.

Forest looks up at me with a hazy smile. "Warned you about needing your strength."

"You have another one in you?"

His smile is wicked. "You shouldn't bait him like that."

"I shouldn't?"

He nods. "He likes to prove shit."

"Like…"

"How many times he can make you come."

Oh. My cheeks flush. "So you…"

"If you keep looking at me like that, yeah." He motions to the mug on the table. "I warmed it up."

"Thanks."

"I can make another if you'd—"

"Maybe after."

His smile shifts into something pure affection. "I love the way you drink matcha."

"Oh?" I descend the stairs.

He nods. "Not just because you moan like you need it in your mouth."

Despite our earlier activities, I blush. What is it about Forest? He's been my best friend forever, but he still makes me feel shy.

"Cat got your tongue, princess?"

Uh… I step onto the main floor.

His smile widens. "You get this look in your eyes. Like you're exactly where you're supposed to be. Like, for a single moment, the world is perfect."

"It is."

"It is." He offers his hand.

I move closer. Take it.

Forest pulls me into a tight hug. He brushes my hair behind my ear. Rests his palm on my cheek. "In your makeup already?"

"You don't like it?"

"Do you care?"

Usually… no. Today, I'm all fluttery and awkward. I want him to like me. To think I'm pretty. To think I'm sexy. To think I'm girlfriend material.

It's ridiculous. We've been friends forever. He knows me.

He knows exactly who I am.

"Princess?" He strokes my temple with his thumb. "Where are you going?"

"You're right. I don't care."

"Then why'd you ask?"

"Well…" I look up into his eyes. "Maybe I care a little."

His laugh is soft. "I love it."

"Yeah?"

"It's you." He brings his thumb to my wine lips. "Though… I'm not sure I'm ever going to be able to concentrate again. Not when you're wearing this lipstick."

"Oh?"

"Gonna think about those pretty lips around my cock."

My sex clenches. "Is that a problem?"

His smile is easy. "Fuck no." He releases me. Moves to the stove. "Sit. Drink." He scoops scrambled eggs onto ceramic plates, grabs forks, brings them—and sriracha—to the table.

I take a seat next to my matcha latte. It's lukewarm, but it's still good. Sweet, creamy, rich. The perfect complement to the bite of green onions and sriracha.

"That enough green onions?" He offers me a napkin.

I look up at him like he's crazy. "Enough green onions?"

Forest chuckles. "It's possible."

"Blasphemy."

"There was that one time. At the ramen place on Sawtelle."

"I don't recall this."

"The waiter offered to bring more green onions and you said, no, this is enough."

"Because I didn't want to put him out."

"Uh-huh."

"He'd come back three times already."

"Uh-huh." He shakes his head *sure*.

"It's not that—" My eyes meet his. God, there's something about his look. Not just the affection. The familiarity. He does know me well. He knows my routine, my life, my dreams. "Uh…"

"You don't have to admit it." He moves to the counter. Brings over a tiny cutting board full of chopped green onions. Sets it next to my plate. "That's all we have in the house."

"Ah."

"Didn't plan for this last time I went shopping."

"Oh."

"Could have asked your dad to grab extra last night."

I clear my throat.

"What did he say to you anyway?"

"The usual. Don't chase after a boy unless he's good enough. Make sure you trust him. Your mother is upset about the half-naked pictures."

"Ah."

"Yeah." I bite my lip. God, this smells good. It's brimming with green onions. But more is still better. I take everything that's left on the cutting board. Then I add sriracha. Stir. "But she came around, I think."

"How'd you manage that?" He picks up his fork. Takes a bite. No hot sauce.

"How do you eat that without sriracha?"

"I take the fork, bring it to my mouth, chew, swallow."

"It's so much better."

"I like it this way."

I shoot him some side-eye.

"I can taste the green onions better."

That is an excellent argument.

"Want to tell me why you're trying to change the subject?" He wraps his fingers around his mug of coffee. Brings it to his lips. Takes a long sip.

"Well, uh…"

"Your mom. What happened?"

"Well, I…" I force my eyes to his. "I kinda told her I'm going to officially pursue modeling and photography."

His eyes go wide. "You are?"

"Yeah… I think so."

"You think so?"

"No… I am." My cheeks flush. "It's just—"

"No just." He stands. Takes my hands. Pulls me up and into a hug. "That's fucking amazing."

"You think?"

"Fuck yes."

My blush deepens. "It's just—"

"You're an amazing photographer."

"I'm new at it."

"And you rock everything you wear."

"But I—"

"Have perfect tits?"

"I'm not what models look like."

He pulls back enough to give me a long, slow once-over. "Maybe that's fashion's loss."

"Yeah, but it's still—"

"I know." He squeezes my hand. "You're gorgeous, Skye. And

## The Best Friend Bargain

your body is fucking amazing. You don't have to agree. But I'm not going to let you say anything less."

My chest warms. "It's more… what other people will say."

"Where are they? Can I hurt them?"

"What will that solve?"

"It will feel good." His eyes meet mine. "You never want to hurt people who hurt you?"

"Sometimes." In the moment, sure. When I get a comment about how I'm too fat to wear a bikini. Or some dumb John Hughes kinda ching-chong racist bullshit. Or all those girls in high school who looked at me like I wasn't good enough. And the guys who spread rumors… "A lot of times."

"Go on."

"It doesn't accomplish anything." I stare back at him. "When have you ever hit anyone?"

"Been a while. But I would. If someone hurt Ariel. Or you. Or Holden even."

I can't help but laugh. "You'd fight for Holden?"

"Fuck, I'd die for Holden."

"Really?"

"He's my little brother."

"*He* needs *you* looking out for him?" I ask.

"Isn't he hitting on Oliver's underage sister?" Forest asks.

"I, uh… I actually think he's just helping her out."

Forest's eyes fill with doubt.

"I think he's a good guy, deep down."

"Very deep."

"You'd die for him even though you think he's a… what do you think he is?"

"An instigator. But he means well… Usually."

"That's sweet."

His cheeks flush. "Anyone would—"

"They wouldn't."

"They… I've been helping them out a long time. After Mom… it was hard. Dad could barely get out of bed for a while."

His eyes meet mine. "But you're not getting me started on that, princess."

"No?" I want to hear it. He doesn't talk about his mom's death. Or the time after it. But he wears the scars from it. They're everywhere.

"Not until we finish this."

"Finish how."

"You're officially pursuing photography and modeling?"

"God, does that make me an influencer?"

"It makes you exactly an influencer."

My nose scrunches in distaste.

"Is it such a bad thing? Influencing other women to find amazing clothes."

"Well..." I bite my lip. "There is a real lack of fashionable plus-size clothes."

"And..."

"There could certainly be more non-white influencers." God, the word still makes me cringe. "It's just... no one looks at me and thinks model."

"I do."

"You know what I mean."

"It's scary, putting yourself out there."

"Yeah."

"People might reject you. They'll probably say rude shit about you. That's what people are like."

"Yeah." I bite my lip.

"As much as I want to threaten to kill them, I'm not sure that will accomplish much."

"Probably not," I say.

"But I promise, when it's within my power, I'll do whatever I can to protect you. If you'll let me."

"Yeah?"

"Fuck yeah." He squeezes my hand. "You're my best friend, Skye. Even if you weren't the sexiest woman in the universe, I'd still want to protect you."

My blush spreads to my chest.
"You're really going to pursue this? Full time?"
"I think so."
"That's big."
"It's not—"
"We have to celebrate."
"No, we don't—"
"You don't want to drive around Los Angeles, getting the best of everything matcha?"
"Well… when you put it that way."
His smile is big, broad, pure love.
It makes my stomach flutter, my chest warm, my limbs buzz. Does he really have all that love for me?
It's hard to believe.
But I want to believe it.
I really want to believe it.

---

After breakfast, we drive to my favorite ice cream place—the vegan one that uses cashews and coconut as their base. (It's amazing, as good as "real" ice cream, not that I've had it recently).

I get half vanilla, half matcha.

Forest gets all chocolate.

God, the way he licks that cone—

It's beautiful torture.

And the way he watches me eat my scoop—

That's even better.

After we finish, we walk to the coffee shop next door, talk about nothing, take pictures for Instagram.

For the first time all day, I think about Mackenzie. Is that why he's doing this? Is he still gunning for her? Am I some space filler?

I should ask.

But I'm too scared to hear the answer.

I post a sexy-cute ice cream picture. His arm around my waist.

Our cones next to each other. Light colors with my black dress as a background.

Out of habit, I check comments, likes, messages.

There's something.

*Dear Princess Skye,*

*We love your latest sponsored posts. I know it's late in the season and you may be booked, but we're ready to offer you three thousand dollars to post our swimwear.*

*The details are up to you. We know you'll do something creative and amazing. We need six images, spread over the next few months, ending with something on the Fourth of July.*

*We're happy to send the swimwear ASAP. Let us know your exact sizes. We see you in something retro, like that amazing purple dress you're always rocking.*

*XO,*

*Beau Tied Swim*

Forest's fingers brush mine. "Some guy send a dick pic?" He pries my index finger from my phone. "I'm gonna get jealous if you don't say you like mine better."

I laugh. "Really?"

He shakes his head *hell no.* "Do women like dick pics?"

"Am I supposed to speak for all women?"

"Yeah, you have a line on womankind as a whole, don't you?"

"Mmm, I'll just call it up, yeah." I pretend to dial a number. Bring my cell to my ear. "Hey, womankind, what are your current thoughts on dick pics? I know you were against it a few years back. Have you softened any, no pun intended?"

His laugh is big, hearty. "Fuck, I love how funny you are."

My blush deepens.

"No one makes me laugh like you do."

"You're not too bad yourself."

"I'm okay. But you're really fucking good."

"Thank you." I pretend to end the call. "The, uh, the women have spoken. Still not into dick pics, unless specifically requested."

"Then?"

My eyes meet his. "Are you asking for my opinion? Or all women's?"

"Yours."

"Are you going to send one?" My eyes go to his crotch immediately. God, his lap is sexy. He's wearing his usual dark wash jeans, sitting with his legs spread, just inviting me to climb between them.

"Is that a yes, princess?"

"Well, uh… I think the male anatomy is attractive in a proper context."

"The male anatomy?"

"Yeah?" I try to force my gaze to his eyes. Get as high as his chest. Mmm, that broken heart peeking out from behind his t-shirt. Can I be the one to fix it? To save him? Fuck, what am I trying to save him from?

That isn't me. That isn't how I think.

I know people don't save each other.

But I still…

Ahem. "Yes, the male anatomy. I wouldn't say I find it stimulating on its own. But in the context of an attractive man I want to fuck? I'm interested."

"You're interested?" He motions to my flushed cheeks. "That's all?"

"Well… it depends on the, uh—"

"Craft of the image?"

"Exactly. I need beautiful composition. Lighting. Mood. Cropping."

"Cropping?"

"Mm-hmm." Finally, I manage to look into his eyes.

They're wide with enthusiasm. "Go on."

"If it's just a dick, well… how am I supposed to know who's dick it is?"

"The 'sent from' isn't enough?"

I shake my head. "I want to see the rest of him. The narrow hips. The strong thighs. The—"

"Tattoo?" He peels his jeans down his hip, showing off the lyrics tattooed to it.

Mmm. "Yeah, the, uh, context. I mean, ideally, it's a full body shot." Must stop staring at tattoo. "So I can see his face. See his expression. See exactly how he feels."

"Besides horny?"

"Yeah." My laugh is nervous. "So uh—"

"I'll make a note."

My eyes go wide. "You're going to send me—"

"Maybe. If you ask."

"Have you ever?"

"No." His eyes meet mine. "But there's a first time for anything."

"Oh."

"Oh?"

"Yeah. Sticking with oh."

He smiles. "What was that message? You had a look."

"Oh, it's… I'm still on you sending me a naked picture."

"You could take one if you want."

"What?"

He nods, the picture of confidence. "If it would help you—"

"Fuck myself to it later?"

"Well, yeah. But I was thinking your photography." His smile is wicked.

"Right." It's so obvious now. Forest is evil. How could I miss it for so long?

"That's a thing. Nudes."

"Yeah…" Naked pictures. Of Forest. "The guys aren't usually hard."

"Who needs usual?"

"Right." Naked pictures. Of Forest. Hard. "You're going to—"

"What was the message?"

"The what?"

"Let me." He motions for my cell.

I think I hand it to him, but honestly, I'm not sure.

Yes. It's there. In his hand. And he's looking at it. Smiling wider. "Fuck, Skye. That's amazing."

"You want to be hard in the—"

"How soon will you have the swimsuits?"

"Uh…"

"I'm going to write back, okay?"

"Uh-huh."

"I'm gonna negotiate. Ask for five grand. Hope they meet us at four."

"We… uh…" Forest. Naked. Hard. Pictures.

"I don't want to push if you'd rather take the sure thing. But you deserve more than three."

"Sure, yeah."

"And I'll ask them to send stuff ASAP. So we can shoot it at Mack's hotel."

Trance broken. "Mack's hotel?"

"In Malibu. She's renting it for the weekend of the wedding. We've got rooms Thursday, Friday, Saturday, Sunday even."

"After the wedding?"

"It's a thing, apparently."

Of course, it is. "How do you know?"

"Holden." His nose scrunches. "The thing is…"

"Yeah?"

"She won't do it if I ask. I kinda… said some shit I needed to say. That she didn't want to hear."

"Oh."

"We can do it at the beach if you want. Or, fuck, I think one of the Inked Hearts guys has a pool. But I want to take you to that hotel pool, drag you into the water, tear off your swimsuit."

Okay, trance back. "Won't other people be there?"

"Not if you ask to keep it private."

Private skinny dipping with Forest. After a photo shoot that's earning me several thousand dollars.

What the hell happened to my normal life?

"Okay." I suck a breath through my nose. Try to find some semblance of sense. "I'll ask her."

"Good." He offers his hand.

"What are we shaking on?"

"Me fucking you after the shoot."

I shake. "You drive a hard bargain."

He smiles. "Princess, you have no idea."

## Chapter Thirty-Three

FOREST

Today, the world is beautiful.
Bright blue sky, soft white clouds, blowing palm trees.
Even the shop is beautiful.

Morning light. Hardwood floors. Hot pink string lights.

As soon as the door swings shut, Holden jumps—actually jumps—onto the desk.

He brings his hands together with a slow clap. "Didn't realize you had this kind of stamina." He winks. "I'm proud of you."

I flip him off, but it's just for show. I don't have any anger, frustration, irritation in me today.

Life is good.

It really is.

"Damn, pissy for a dude who spent the last day and a half getting laid. Unless…" Holden shakes his head. "Don't tell me she's not generous."

"You've used that one." I try to stifle a laugh, but I can't. My brother is too ridiculous.

"It really is old material." Oliver moves out from his suite. Slides a palm-sized sketchbook into his back pocket. "Maybe you should try something about how she must be kinky, what with her penchant for corset lacing?"

"Oh, that's good." Holden blows his best friend a kiss. "You've been studying my techniques, haven't you?"

Oliver chuckles. Shakes his head *the horror* then turns to me. "You two figure it out?"

"You could say that," I say.

"She was upset at the party. But…" He smiles. "Jealousy does work."

"Yeah." I run my hand through my hair. It's hard to believe that was less than two days ago. It feels like it's been a million years. Last night with Skye was perfect. We cooked dinner together—a Korean dish she wants to practice, so she'll make it as well as her dad does—then we watched one of those indie movies she loves, walked on the beach, fell asleep in my bed.

Well… after doing lots of other shit in my bed.

My chest warms at the thought of her smile.

My cock quivers at the thought of her moan.

Holden clears his throat. "Forest, dude, how many times do we have to go over this? If you're going to replay fucks, you need to narrate."

"You run out of porn or something?" Oliver asks.

Holden shoots him a *get real* look.

"Let me guess. You've got so many women pawing at your jeans that you don't need porn?" Oliver offers.

Holden chuckles. "Nobody *needs* porn. But I enjoy it, sure. Lining up some newbie friendly videos. In case any inexperienced women ask for pointers."

Oliver's smile disappears. "If you touch her, you die."

"What did I say about touching?" Holden shrugs. "Only video recs."

Fuck, they're ridiculous. But that reminds me—"I picked out a video for Skye."

"Go on." Holden turns to me.

"Not over this whole you showing my sister porn thing," Oliver says.

The bell rings as the door swings open. Chase steps inside. Surveys the scene. Raises a brow.

"Could be worse," Holden says. "I could have gotten your sister pregnant."

"Don't joke about that." I know Ariel wanted to get pregnant. She's over the moon. Honestly, Chase did her a huge favor. But the reason why she needed to get pregnant at twenty-four, the possibility she'll suffer the same fate our mom did—

It's not funny.

I know joking is Holden's way, but I can't stand laughing over it.

"Would you rather she not have a rec?" Holden asks. "She might stumble on some gross shit."

"I hate to admit it, but he's right," I say. "That's why Skye doesn't like porn. Too violent."

Holden's eyes go wide. "So she doesn't like it rough."

Fuck, I've said too much. That's what I get for arriving at work pre-coffee. Not that I regret spending that time making Skye come instead. "None of your fucking business."

"Maybe she does," he says. "Some people like watching shit they'd never do in real life. Or vice versa. But I promise I'll send Daisy something vanilla. Classy. Made for women." He holds up his hand *scout's honor*. "On her eighteenth birthday."

Chase chuckles. "Does he actually want to fuck her? Or is he just fucking with you?"

"I'm not sure either." To me, Daisy is clearly a girl. But Holden is barely twenty-one. He's only a few years older than she is.

If she wants to celebrate her eighteenth birthday in his bed—

It's really none of my business.

"If it blows up in your face, I'm taking Oliver's side," Chase says. "He's a better artist than you are."

Holden mimes offense. "That's fucking cold. Suits you." He turns to me. "We're getting off track here. Skye doesn't like porn. All porn? Or just violent porn? What if the two of you make a video?" He smiles wide, so, so happy to fuck with me.

I smile back. Holden is Holden. When things are good, it's fun, sparring with him, teasing him, telling him to fuck off. It's how we connect. How he connects with everyone. "Then I'd have some great material in my spank bank. And you'd have nothing."

"It's all up here." Holden taps his forehead.

"What's up there?" Oliver motions to Dare and Patrick, who are in the back, talking about something in hushed tones. "You guys think there's anything in Holden's head?"

"Like a brain?" Patrick glides into the main room. "No."

"More than you have," Dare says.

"Oh yeah? Should we put that to a test, Darren?" Patrick asks.

"I don't know, Trick—" Dare says his friends nickname like it's an eye-roll in audio form—"should we?"

They do this every day. Insist we call them by ridiculous nicknames. Then constantly throw their real names in our face.

Not that I blame them. Darren especially. It's hard to make that name sexy.

Poor women trying to groan *oh Darren*.

Dare has a certain mystique. Yeah, it's trying too hard. But they're young enough to get away with it.

Holden's friend's.

This whole shop is Holden's friends.

My little brother has the world eating out of the palm of his hand. And he uses all that charisma to piss me off.

"Skye's the goth hottie with the big tits?" Patrick looks to me. "You finally fucked her?"

"Yeah." Not that it's his business.

"Nice." He offers me a high-five.

I shoot him serious side-eye.

Holden takes the high-five instead.

Chase shakes his head. "Five minutes, then you're leaving or working. Got it?"

Everyone groans—the way kids groan at teacher's commands—but they do nod. Chase is a good boss. He commands authority well.

Not that I want to think about the implications.

"You know, you really are more of a Patrick," Holden says.

"At least I'm not even more annoying that Holden Caulfield." He rolls his eyes.

"You know what, you're right. Trick is good. 'Cause you only have one trick, then the ladies move on." Holden laughs.

Dare does too.

"Yeah, and Dare works for you, because someone has to dare a woman to fuck you," Patrick says.

He and Holden crack up.

Then the three of them are moving toward the suite in the back, trading barbs, cracking each other up.

Thank God. Holden is like a heat-seeking missile. He moves to the nearest person he can torment.

Skye is right. He means well. Deep down.

Very, very deep down.

Chase slides behind the counter. Oliver heads to the front. Motions *come here*.

I do. "How's Ariel?"

"Didn't you see her at the party?" Chase asks.

"She doesn't tell me stuff," I say.

He smiles. Beams, really. "Good. Happy. It's getting close."

"Not even two months," I say.

"And she's—" Chase chuckles. "Shit, that's not something you want to hear."

"It's making her horny." Oliver laughs. "She talks about it all the time."

Chase blushes, suddenly sheepish. "It happens." He presses on. "She's getting an ultrasound tomorrow. It's not bad. Standard prenatal screening."

"Will she kill me if I crash it?" I ask.

He nods *she will*. "She gets scared. An audience will only—"

"Yeah." My kid sister wants her boyfriend's comfort. She needs him, not me. If there's any time where she should need him, it's this.

But it still feels like a loss. Like I'm not needed anymore.

It's weird.

Empty in some way I can't explain.

I'm happy for her and Chase. I wish the circumstances were different, but I'm over the fucking moon. And, fuck, I'm going to have a niece.

It's amazing.

I just—

It's hard, respecting the lines they're drawing. Respecting her boundaries. Her independence.

"You and Skye finally did it." Oliver offers his hand to shake.

I take it.

"Congrats," he says.

"Thanks." I guess.

"You figure out what you're doing with her?" he asks.

"Yeah, we're…" Best friends. We're always going to be best friends. Beyond that—fuck, I don't know. I don't know what she wants. Or if I'm capable of being what she wants. What she needs. "We're getting there."

He shakes his head *that's not good*.

Chase backs him up. "You're still going to the wedding?"

"Yeah." It's what she wants. And she's right—she has to go to this wedding, or she'll hear about it forever. I'm happy to be her shield. "Mack is her cousin. What choice does Skye have?"

Oliver nods *maybe*. "And you?"

"What about me?" I ask.

"Why are you going?" he asks.

"She needs me," I say.

His expression gets incredulous. "But what do you want?"

"To help her," I say.

He shakes his head. "Help her by keeping her away from that."

"He's right," Chase says. "Sometimes, support doesn't cut it. Sometimes, your friends or family need tough love." His eyes flit to Oliver. That same knowing look of his. *This guy's drinking is going to catch up with him one day.*

But that's just Chase being Chase. His brother is an alcoholic. He's paranoid about that shit.

"Don't think about what Skye wants. Think about what she needs," Chase says. "Figure it out before you lose her. Because—"

"You didn't knock her up. You don't have nine months to figure it out," Oliver says.

Chase just chuckles. "It did help."

"Don't remind me," I say.

"Let me ask you something, Chase." Oliver turns to Chase, suddenly disinterested in my dilemma. "Does she like to call you Daddy?"

"Why would she—"

"Is it in a *you're the daddy of my baby* kind of way? Or more of a *Daddy, punish me* kind of way?" Oliver asks.

"You're too much like Holden." I shake my head. "Leaving before I hit you."

"Fuck, if he hits you." Chase shakes his head. "He's never hit Holden."

"It's the latter, isn't it?" Oliver asks.

Chase just laughs.

I make good on my word.

They keep exchanging—

Fuck, I don't want to know.

I settle into my suite. Try to focus on a mock-up.

But Chase's advice keeps flitting through my head.

*Don't think about what she wants. Think about what she needs.*

What if she needs someone who knows how to love? Someone who isn't a fucked-up mess?

Someone who isn't me.

I know how to protect her. How to take care of her. How to make her come.

But maybe I don't know how to love her.

Maybe I can't be what she needs.

# Chapter Thirty-Four

SKYE

I toss my bag on the leather sofa. Not that the couch is real leather.

It's cheap, from Ikea. Not at all well-made. Total trash compared to the several-thousand-dollar couch at Forest's dad's place.

Or the modern sectional at my parents' place (Mom loves "modern" furniture).

Hell, the damn thing is a little lumpy.

Torn in all the wrong places.

But it's perfect.

It's Forest's.

A couch we bought together. Okay, that I helped him buy. God, I still remember that day at Ikea, dragging him through the tiny rooms, trying to snap him out of his *she's fucking someone else* haze.

Nothing inspires a move like walking in on your soon to be ex with another guy.

But it also—

Well, I'm not sure what Forest would say, but as far as I could tell, he was a simmering ball of hurt and anger for the first few weeks. Months even.

It was hard, getting all this shit together. But we did it. And now it's ours.

Okay, it's his. But my mark is here.

Black blanket with a spider print. Movie posters in black frames. Some of his favorites—both dumb action movies and animated features his mom loved—and mine.

All three of the *Before* movies. On the wall with the TV. The main attraction.

"Princess, you really are a parody of yourself." Forest wraps his arms around me. Brings his lips to my neck. "Could you love those movies anymore?"

"No."

"At least you know."

"I know?"

"What you love."

"You don't?"

He sucks on my skin. Softly. Then harder.

Hard enough my thoughts scatter.

We're talking about something. But it can't possibly be as important as this.

It can't possibly be as interesting as this.

Is anything?

He drags his lips down my neck. To the space where my neck and shoulder meet. "I tell you how much I like this dress?" His fingers brush the strap.

"Mmm." Maybe. Probably. What are we talking about?

"I've been thinking about taking it off since I picked you up."

At my parents' place. Then we went out for ramen (with extra green onions, of course). And sake.

Now, we're at his place. And I'm buzzed. And ready to rip his clothes off.

He sucks on my skin.

Softly.

Then harder.

"You wear it to drive me crazy?" he asks.

I nod. "Wait until you see what I have under it."

He pulls my body into his. My back against his chest, my ass against his crotch.

He's hard.

God, it's the best feeling in the world. I'll never get tired of it.

"I will." His fingers dig into my hips. "I have something for you."

"Forest," I breathe.

"Yeah, princess?"

"I need you."

"How do you need me?" He rocks his hips, grinding his cock against my ass. "Here?" He slips his hand over my thigh, between my legs.

It's over my dress. He isn't touching me properly. But it still drives me insane.

"Here?" He drags his hand up my torso, neck, chin, all the way to my mouth. "Or here?"

"Is there an all of the above?"

His laugh is loud. Full. It makes his body shake. "Fuck, Skye."

"It's not a joke."

"I know." He steps backward. Spins me around. Looks me in the eyes. "You're so charming."

"Yeah?"

"Yeah." He brushes my hair behind my ear. "We need to celebrate more."

"We've been celebrating for the last two days."

"I have matcha ice cream in the freezer from that place in Culver City."

Mmm, the perfect mix of creamy coconut, sugar, matcha. Not as good as him but damn good all the same. "Why didn't you lead with that?"

His smile spreads over his cheeks. It's easy. Free. Gorgeous.

He has such a beautiful smile.

It lights up his entire face. Especially those coffee eyes.

I want to stare at them all day.

He takes a step back. Motions to the couch. "Sit."

"Take your shirt off."

"How are those two things related?"

"You ask me to do something. I ask you to do something."

"How much did you drink?" he asks.

I hold up my thumb and forefinger *a little*.

He raises a brow *you sure about that?*

"Very sure."

"Sit."

"Shirt." I motion *take it off*.

He doesn't. Which is cruel. But probably for the best. I'm already dying to fuck him senseless. If he starts losing clothing—

Ahem.

I smooth my dress. Take a seat on the couch.

He fills two mugs with ice cream. Then two glasses with water.

He's right there—his apartment *is* small—but he's still too far away. I want to touch him, hold him, kiss him.

"How come we never hang out here?" I ask.

"There?" He turns back to me. Motions to the couch. "Or here?" He draws a circle in the air, like he's saying *the entire apartment*. "Or there?" He nods to his bedroom.

My cheeks flush. God, I'm so ready to fuck him. It's ridiculous.

I'm not usually this... Well, horny. But it's been forever. Since yesterday morning.

Stupid parents wanting to hang out with me.

No, it's nice. They're supportive. Too supportive sometimes, but I'm the same as Forest. Family comes first. Always.

Which is why—

Ugh, not thinking about her. She gets the entire weekend of her wedding. Until then, I'm enjoying my time with my best friend.

Hopefully, without his clothes.

He laughs. "Princess, you're staring."

"No..."

"Yeah." He crosses the room. Hands me a glass of water. "You're drunk."

"Tipsy."

"That's good."

"Good?"

He nods. "You'll say yes to my request."

"Go on…"

"Drink first." He holds up his glass of water to toast.

I do.

He sets his glass on the coffee table. "You look good here."

"Is it the dress?" I tug my skirt a few inches up my thighs. It's a hot dress—another freebie from a designer—and it's black. Like the couch.

"Yeah. But more than that."

"We should come here more."

"It's not next door to your house."

Is that why he's always at his dad's house? Because he's closer to me? "True."

"Or near any good matcha shops."

"Also true. But you make a good latte."

His lips curl into a smile. "Only the one bedroom."

"Did you need a second?"

"Fuck no. I just mean—"

"It's kinda small."

"Yeah." He runs a hand through his hair. "I do pretty well. But I'm not a doctor married to a consultant."

"I'm not a—whatever your dad does in sales."

"Yeah, but—"

"You're a guy so you have to provide?"

"Not exactly." He moves into the kitchen. Grabs the mugs of ice cream. And spoons. "More that I—"

"Love to take care of people."

He nods *yeah*. "I'm never going to have the kind of money your parents' have."

"I know."

"You deserve that."

"Maybe I'll make it myself."

"Oh?" He slides onto the couch. "You're going to be that big?"

"I hope so." My fingers brush his as I take the ice cream. "I got another offer. A hair salon. It's not much, only a few hundred dollars, but it's something."

"Are you changing it?" He runs his fingers through my hair. Along the ends. Then along my neck.

"Just a trim… I think." Fuck, his touch feels good. "I like this style."

"It suits you."

"Thanks."

"It's hot too."

"Yeah?" I set my mug in my lap. Wrap my fingers around my spoon. "I always thought… Mack has such long hair and you're always with girls—"

"I'm with you."

My blush deepens. "So, I uh… I like your apartment. Even if it's too close to the freeway. I'd live here. I mean, I know you're not inviting me just yet. Or maybe you never will. But if you wanted to—"

"Good to know."

"Yeah." I bring a spoonful of ice cream to my lips. "It's a good size. Not too small. Or too big."

He raises a brow.

Oh. "I didn't mean that."

"Uh-huh."

"You sound like Holden."

"That's my favorite thing about this place." He turns his body toward mine. "No Holden."

"It is nice."

"Listen to this." He wraps one hand around my wrist. Brings the other to his mouth. Makes the *shhh* gesture.

The room falls silent. Nothing but the hum of the air-conditioning. The passing traffic outside. "Listen to what?"

"Quiet."

"Oh." I can't help but laugh. "It is different."

"No one to interrupt when I tear your clothes off."

"Or cockblock us by inviting my dad to dinner."

He nods *hell yeah*. Takes my spoon. Brings the ice cream to my lips.

I suck the treat off the spoon.

He watches me with rapt attention. Then he brings another spoonful to my lips.

Fuck, it's good. Rich and creamy. Just enough sweetness to balance the matcha. "When did you get this?"

"Yesterday."

"You drove all the way to Culver City after work?"

"It's three miles."

"On the other side of the freeway." That's the ultimate LA compliment, crossing the 405 for someone. "Thank you."

"You like it?"

"Yeah."

He brings another scoop to my lips. "Me too."

I lick it off the spoon. "You're not eating it."

"This is better."

"It is." I shouldn't feel so shy. I'm still buzzed. But there's something about the way Forest looks at me. He makes me nervous in the best possible way.

"Princess Skye... it has a nice ring to it. You could take over the world."

"I hope so."

"You have your swimsuit shoot figured out?"

"Not yet. But I... I don't want to think about her for a while."

He nods *yeah*. "One question."

"Okay." I take another bite of ice cream. "But only because you're feeding me matcha ice cream."

His smile is wide. Easy. "Fuck, Skye..." His fingers skim my temples. "I really like you."

"I really like you too." More even. I mean, I've loved Forest as a friend for a long time. For a million years.

"You sure you want to go to the wedding?"

Huh. That's... not the question I expected. I stare into his eyes, trying to figure out his intentions.

He's worried.

About me?

Or about how much he still loves her?

The thought makes me sick. There are so many ways this can go wrong. Him standing up during the ceremony and saying *yes, I know a reason why you can't wed. I'm still in love with you.*

Her sneaking out of the engagement party for one last tryst.

Him breaking down in tears when she and Diego say *I do*.

It's horrible.

But if that's what's going to happen—

It needs to happen. I need to know. And he needs the closure. To release her or... not.

If not...

"Yeah," I say. "I'm sure."

"You still have something to prove to her?"

Not exactly. "She's family, Forest. I have to." I stare into his eyes. "Do you still want to?"

"I never wanted to."

"Oh."

"But if you need me there, I'm there."

"Because you... you don't want to see it?" I swallow hard. "To see her get married?"

"I don't want anything to do with her."

"You're over her?" I wrap my fingers around the mug. It's cold. Soothing in a strange way. Like I'm preparing for my entire world to go cold. Only I—"don't answer that."

He just stares back at me.

"I, uh... it's only been a week. You don't have to know."

"But another week and a half will clinch it?" He raises a brow *really*.

Maybe. Better than nothing. "Things are different. We've uh—"

"Fucked?"

"Yeah, and we... we're something."

"We are."

"You're my... boyfriend." I try to say it with confidence. Get halfway there.

"Yeah."

"Okay. Good." I reach for another spoonful of ice cream. This time, I bring it to his lips.

He sucks on the spoon like it's some part of me.

My sex clenches. He's just so... uh...

"I do want to be your boyfriend, Skye." He steals the spoon. Feeds me a scoop of ice cream. "But you have to know something."

"Okay." I don't want to know anything. I want to stay with *I want to be your boyfriend*. But that isn't life. There's always some clause.

I know Forest well, yeah.

I care about him.

Love him in... in ways I can't even begin to describe.

I also know him well. And, he...

He's not the most functional when it comes to relationships. So I should listen. Hear him. Believe what he's saying.

"You know the song *I Will Survive*?" he asks.

"Of course."

"Holden set it as my ringtone for Mack," he says.

"Of course he did." That's classic Holden.

"There's this line that always gets me." He feeds me another scoop.

I swallow hard. It's still good—rich, creamy, sweet, comforting. "Okay."

"About being okay, because you still know how to love. Because you're ready to give your love to someone who loves you back."

"It's good advice." But what does it have to do with us?

His brow furrows. "Yeah, I just..."

"What?" *Please don't say "I still love her." Anything but that.*

His voice is matter-of-fact. Accepting. Like he's sure of his fate. "I don't know if I'll ever be there."

"You don't know if you'll get over Mackenzie?"

"No." He shakes his head. "If I'll ever know how to love again."

Oh. That's worse. Or maybe the same. Would I rather he love neither of us? Or both?

No, it doesn't matter.

I need all his love.

"I care about you, Skye. I... you're the most important person in my life. You're family. And you know I'd die for my family."

"Yeah."

"But I—."

"It's only been... like a week." I want all his love, yeah, but I can be patient. Patient ish.

"True."

"You don't have to know now."

"You sure?"

"Yeah."

"Good. Because I have something way more fun than this conversation."

"What?"

"Close your eyes."

"But—" I hold up the ice cream.

"Do it anyway."

"What do I get?"

"Trust me."

I set the ice cream on the coffee table. Place my hands over my eyes. "Should I count?"

"Sure. To ten." He moves around the apartment.

One, two, three—

He grabs something from the desk.

Four, five, six—

The TV turns on.

Seven, eight, nine—

Light flashes.

Ten.

I open my eyes.

Look straight to the TV.

To the adult video on the TV. It's paused at the moment. On a frame where things are... just starting.

It's actually really nice. All bright and white and light. An attractive couple in a clean bedroom. Framed beautifully.

Not what I expect from porn.

"Do you want to?" His fingers brush my thigh. "I won't cry if you say no, but I really, really want to watch you watch."

"Oh."

"What do you say, Skye? Will you watch with me?"

## Chapter Thirty-Five

FOREST

Skye's eyes stay glued to the TV. She stares, transfixed by the frozen image.

Probably judging its composition.

It's nice—as far as I can tell.

A director known for creating videos specifically for women. Apparently, that means more beautiful images, more story, more emotion, more affection.

As Skye would say, no violent skull fucking.

Not what I normally watch.

Not because I dig violent skill fucking. Or facials. Or big fake tits.

Because I can't stomach the kind of intimacy on display in this video. Not usually.

But now that I'm with Skye—

Fuck, I'm really with Skye.

"You really think I'll like it?" Her voice is shy. Timid. Not at all like her.

Or maybe she's finally showing me that side of her.

I like it.

Don't get me wrong. I love that Skye is a sassy, confident,

badass. But I also love that she'll let her guard down, show me where she hurts, admit she's embarrassed.

Fuck, the flush in her cheeks—

It's everything.

"You won't hate it," I say.

Her laugh is nervous. "Quite the recommendation."

"If you don't want to—"

"No, I do. But, uh—" She motions to the remote. "I want the power to turn it off."

"If you're too overcome with desire?" I tease.

"Of course."

"And you have to jump me right away."

"Since when do you say 'jump me.' Is it 2005 again?"

"Princess, I live in 2005."

This time, her laugh is big. Hearty. "True." She shifts into my lap. Runs her fingers through my hair. "You just need the emo bangs."

"Exactly."

"You'd look cute with long bangs."

"I'll consider that." I look up at her. Stare into her gorgeous blue eyes. Fuck, this is a perfect view. Why stop to look at anything else?

"Hey." She smiles at me.

"Hey." I smile back.

It's sweet. Innocent even. Like we're kids about to kiss for the first time.

It feels like the first time with her. It's been so long. Forever.

But my body knows hers. My lips know hers. There's something instinctual about it.

I bring my hand to the back of her head and I pull her into a slow, deep kiss.

Her lips part.

My tongue slides between them.

I claim her mouth. Like I'm claiming her. I want to. I do—

But I can't.

She deserves everything. All the love in the world.

If I can't give that to her—

It's a problem for another day. For once, I'm not drowning in my inability to mend my broken heart.

I've got a knockout in my lap and she's promising to watch a dirty video with me.

Maybe she'll make one later.

Maybe she'll fuck herself for my viewing pleasure.

Fuck, I'd watch that all day, every day, for the rest of my life.

She pulls back with a groan. "Can we go right now?"

Fuck yeah. "We can. But I want to make you wait."

She makes a show of pouting. "Pure. Evil." She taps my chest. Slips out of my lap. Onto the couch cushion next to mine. "You should know something, Forest."

"Oh yeah?"

"If you make me wait, I might... who knows what will happen?"

"You won't fuck me?"

"It's possible."

"I'll take that risk." I can't help but smile. She's bluffing, but she's not good at it. She's not a good liar.

Skye bites her lip. She knows she's caught, but she doesn't let on. She just shrugs. "Okay, well—"

"Well?"

She clears her throat. "I'll give it a chance. But only because it means so much to you."

"I appreciate that."

"I know." She pulls her legs under her. Smooths her dress. Places the remote on the couch cushion.

Her eyes meet mine for a second. Then they're on the remote.

She presses *play*. Looks to the screen.

The actors meet in front of the bed. A built white guy in a suit and a curvy white woman in a cocktail dress.

She whispers something about how it's been forever.

He nods. Promises he misses her. Needs her.

She undoes his tie. Unbuttons his shirt.

He spins her. Unzips her dress. Peels it off her shoulders.

Skye's fingers curl into her skirt. She pinches the fabric between her thumb and index finger.

Her eyes go wide.

Her lips part with a sigh.

I know that sigh. It's the sigh she makes when she takes her first sip of matcha latte.

She wants more. Needs more. Needs everything.

For a second, I consider calling her on it. Teasing her about her interest. Making her admit she likes it.

I swallow the impulse.

I don't want to say anything to stop her.

I don't want to do anything but watch her.

Skye shifts to her other side.

Her fingers tug at her dress.

Her heels tap together—she's wearing her heeled combat boots on the couch.

Fuck, I love those boots. I need her wearing them when she comes.

She stares as the actors strip to nothing, climb onto the bed, roll around the sheets.

Her gaze shifts to me.

She watches me watch her for a moment. "You're not—"

"I am."

"You should—" She motions to the screen.

"Watching something better."

Her cheeks blush. She bites her lip. Turns back to the screen.

This is it. Where things get, well, pornographic. Where I might lose her.

Skye looks at sexy half-naked people all the time—lingerie ads, perfume ads, actors in foreign films.

It's easy enough to write this off as typical eroticism.

But this—

Her eyes go wide as the male actor flips over the female actor. He arranges their bodies so they're facing the camera from the side. So we can see all the action.

Slowly, he pushes into her.

Quick close-ups. The penetration. His hands on her hips. Her hands curling into the sheets.

Surprise spreading over her face.

Then pleasure.

Then back to the wide shot as he drives into her again and again.

Skye doesn't close her eyes. Or look away. Or get off the couch.

She watches carefully.

Interest spreads over her face—the kind she gets when she's watching a great movie—then it shifts to something better.

Desire.

"I… Uh…" Her eyes flit to me then they're back on the screen. "You like it?"

"It's um…" Her voice gets stronger. More confident. "Yeah."

"You want to keep watching?"

She turns to the TV as the male model pins the female model to the bed. "Um…"

I need to lead this. "Come here."

She nods *okay*. Turns enough to shift into my lap. Fuck, it's the perfect position. But it's no good. It means she can't watch.

"Turn around." I tug at her skirt.

She shifts off my lap. Pulls her skirt up her thighs, over her ass, all the way to her waist.

My fingers curl into her panties. Slowly, I peel them to her knees.

She kicks them off her feet.

I pull her into my lap. Slip my hand between her legs.

She's already wet. Ready. Needy.

I stroke her anyway. Softly. So softly her groan is more whine than anything.

"Forest," she breathes. "Please."

"Please what, princess?"

"Fuck me." She rolls her hips, grinding her ass against me. "I want to come on your cock."

My balls tighten.

"Please."

How can she be so demanding and polite at the same time? It defies reason.

I want to make her come first. To make her come until she can barely breathe.

But my body disobeys my mind.

It needs her now.

It needs the two of us connecting.

As one.

It's ridiculous—I haven't wanted that in so long—but I do. I want it with Skye.

I want everything with Skye.

She shifts onto the other couch cushion. Her hands go to my jeans. Her eyes meet mine.

She holds my gaze for a moment, then she watches herself unzip my jeans.

I do away with my t-shirt. Lift my hips enough to push my jeans and boxers to my thighs.

Her gaze flits to the screen for a moment. Then she turns to me. Crawls into my lap.

Her knees plant outside my legs.

Her thighs squeeze my hips.

Her fingers curl into my neck.

Slowly, she lowers her body onto mine.

My cock brushes her cunt.

Then she takes me deeper, deeper—

Fuck.

My eyes close.

Pleasure floods my senses.

And something else too. This satisfaction. This wholeness. Like

I'm exactly where I'm supposed to be.

This is more than her coming on my cock.

It's her body against mine.

I knot my hand in her hair then I pull her into a slow, deep kiss.

Her lips part for my tongue.

Her hips shift.

She raises herself up then drives down on me again.

I slip my hands under her dress. Use one to guide her. Bring the other to her clit.

I rub her softly.

Then harder.

Higher.

There.

She groans against my mouth. Drags her teeth against my lip.

I keep that same pressure, same speed.

She drives down on me again and again.

We kiss hard and deep.

Our bodies know something our minds don't.

She's mine.

I'm hers.

We stay locked together—kissing, groaning, moving together—until she's there.

She pulls back to groan.

Her nails dig into my shoulders.

They rake against my chest.

It's hard. Violent almost.

Hot as fuck.

It pushes me to the edge.

I pull her down on me again.

Again.

Then I'm there, groaning her name as I spill inside her.

She waits until I'm done, then she collapses on top of me.

I hold her close.

We catch our breath together.

And, for one moment, I know.

Whatever happens later, this is perfect.
I need her to be mine.
Forever.
I need to give her everything.
Always.

## Chapter Thirty-Six

SKYE

After, we shower together, clean up—somehow, there's melted green tea ice cream everywhere—watch one of *my* favorite movies.

It's considerably less erotic but amazing in its own way.

Forest doesn't even complain it's all dialogue, no action. He keeps his arm around my waist, holds me close.

We sleep together in his queen-sized bed.

I wake up in his arms.

Sure, there's a lot of ugly shit on the horizon.

But this, right now—

This is perfect.

---

FOR A FEW DAYS, I AVOID THE UPCOMING DISASTER.

I hold film screenings in my parents' living room. All Linklater. Then Jim Jarmusch. Nicole Holofcener. Ava DuVernay.

I only break to fix dinner with Dad.

Or to text Forest—as long as it has nothing to do with Mackenzie and her wedding.

When my package of swimsuits (and a check for $2500, half

upfront—I guess Forest's negotiation went well) arrives, I run out of excuses.

There's barely a week until the wedding.

Until Forest breaks down crying because he's really losing Mackenzie this time.

Or until he realizes he's over her.

Until he's all mine.

Either the worst thing in the world or the greatest.

No pressure.

Uh…

Well, I need her help with the pool either way. I don't want to be her friend. Or her confidant. Or her anything.

But I do want this favor.

I can talk to her.

Really.

I fix another matcha.

It fails to inspire courage. Or constitution, really. It's not that I'm scared to talk to my cousin.

It's more all the hate in my stomach.

Deep breath.

Slow exhale.

Happy thoughts.

I pull out my cell. Dial her number.

*Ring, ring—*

Fuck. I can't do this. I go to end the call, but she picks up first.

"Skye? Is that you?" she asks.

"Yeah."

"Is everything okay?" Her voice drips with vulnerability. She really does care what I think. If I forgive her.

Which I don't.

I mean, she hasn't even said sorry.

"Yeah, good actually." I shift my cell to my other ear. "I have to ask a favor."

"Sure," she says.

"You're renting out the hotel in Malibu for the weekend, right?"

"Yeah." There's a smile in her voice. "It was Daddy's idea. He wants his family to fly in easily. They're all in New York. And they're used to nice places."

"It looks nice. Online, I mean."

"It's beautiful. Do you have a room?" she asks.

"Oh, well… I don't know. My parents are taking care of that."

"I'll ask Mom to make sure you have a good one."

I clear my throat. Mrs. Davis doing me a favor? Unlikely. But that isn't why I'm calling. "It has a nice pool, right?" I act as if I don't know. As if I haven't spent hours staring at the pool. Which is completely perfect for this shoot.

"Yeah. Two, actually."

"Would it be possible for me to reserve it for a few hours?"

"You want to reserve the pool?"

"For a photo shoot."

"Oh." Her voice shifts. "Something with Forest?"

I try to read her tone. Is she happy for me? Jealous? Angry? I can't tell. "No. These are just me. For a swimsuit company."

"Oh." Her voice gets easier. "That's great. A plus-size swimsuit company?"

"Yeah." Why does that matter?

"Like with the lingerie?"

"Yeah."

"That's great, Skye. Your pictures are beautiful. I mean, the ones with Forest are a little much. But still hot."

"It doesn't bother you?"

"Hmm?" She feigns ignorance.

"Seeing your ex-boyfriend with someone else?"

"No." Her voice is matter-of-fact. "I'm happy for you. I miss you, Skye. I miss him too, sometimes. But not like that."

"Oh." Yeah right.

"I know you… you have every right to be mad. I know you're avoiding me. Honestly, it means so much you're even coming."

"Yeah." I bite my tongue so I won't add *fuck you for even inviting me.*

"I'm really sorry. I... I didn't mean for this to happen. I know that isn't an excuse, but... In the end, it worked out, right? I'm happy. You're happy."

I guess.

"You and Forest... it seems right. Is it right?"

"Yeah." I think so. I hope so. "He's a great guy."

"He is. Just... Be careful."

"Huh?" What the hell is she doing?

"Never mind. I shouldn't have said anything. There's nothing I can tell you. You know him better than I ever did." She makes that *hmmm* voice. "I'll book the pool for you. If you do me a favor in return?"

"Yeah."

"Mom's been driving me crazy. Especially complaining about your clothes. Promise you'll wear something—"

"Slutty?"

"Yeah."

"Sure." I laugh. For a second, I forget our frost. I forget that she stole my crush. That she went years without apologizing.

I'm laughing with my cousin, joking about our parents.

God, I miss that. I miss her being my friend.

But that bridge is ash at this point.

There's no fixing it.

"Friday afternoon work?" she asks.

"Yeah, thanks." My stomach flip-flops. It's weird. I still want her approval. The way I did when I was a little kid. "I'll, see you—"

"At the rehearsal dinner. That night. You won't have a ton of time to change."

"Sure, yeah."

"We're doing a bachelorette party after. In the suite. I think someone ordered a stripper. If you want to come—"

"Maybe."

"Oh." She does nothing to hide her disappointment. "I, uh, I should go. There's so much to do. Don't have a big wedding. Not that you would. Not your style."

It means something, but I don't what it is. And it doesn't matter. She's not getting to me. I clear my throat. Make my voice as pleasant as possible. "Yeah. I'll see you later."

"You too. I… uh… I miss you, Skye. Take care."

I end the call. Place my cell on the kitchen table. Stare into my empty mug.

Mackenzie misses me. She wants to help me. She wants to warn me about Forest.

I don't know what she's after. But then I don't care.

And it doesn't matter.

Mackenzie does what she does. She's not doing it to me anymore.

I have the pool for a few hours.

Sure, the rest of the weekend might be a train wreck, but at least I'll have my photos.

That's something.

## Chapter Thirty-Seven

SKYE

I tie my robe a little tighter, but it does nothing to chase away my goose bumps. Between the fluffy clouds and the breeze, it's a cool day.

Which is good. The soft light is flattering. It's bright enough our surroundings look beachy but not so bright my pics will be overexposed.

Hell, if the sun comes out, I can really sell the idea of multiple swim sessions on multiple days.

My plan is set. Four images. As if I spent four different days lounging in swimwear.

One in the water.

One by the infinity pool in front.

One at the secluded pool around the corner.

And one mid-party. Or at least mid-toasting with my boyfriend.

Not that I can consider the implications at the moment. I have a job and limited time. I need to focus.

It takes half an hour to set up. Tripod, reflectors, props. Attire. Hair and makeup check.

There.

If I start really rolling in it, I'm hiring a hair and makeup team.

Or maybe not. After a dozen years of honing my "dramatic look," I'm pretty damn good at it.

I even know which products are truly waterproof.

Thankfully, this swimsuit company gets me. They understand I go by Princess Skye because I'm dark and loud.

A retro bikini in a deep shade of eggplant.

A modern one-piece in dark black.

A red bikini with a ton of cleavage.

An old school one-piece in hot pink, with black polka dots.

My black combat boots are sitting by the pool chair. The ones with a chunky heel thick and heavy enough to bash a skull.

And sandals.

I bought actual sandals. Three pairs even. Black. White. Red.

It's ridiculous. I haven't worn sandals since… forever. But they feel right.

The combat boots are going to be fierce with the black bikini.

But the red sandals are sexy in their own way. They're something a California Beach Babe would wear.

It's not me. But that doesn't mean I can't borrow the look.

This is a photo shoot. Not a reflection of my soul. Though—

Everything I shoot is a reflection of my soul.

Ahem.

"Hey." A deep voice interrupts my thoughts. Forest. He's in jeans and a white shirt (as I requested), holding two take-out cups. A milky cold brew. And an iced matcha latte.

"Hey." I bite my lip. It's weird, being here. Like there's a Mackenzie aura weakening my resolve. It takes all my attention to stay on task. Photos. Awesomeness. Done. "You look good."

"I brought a darker pair too." He motions to his medium wash jeans.

"And the swimsuit?"

"Yeah." He chuckles. "Under this."

"Oh."

He nods. Moves around the pool—it's a long, rectangular

thing, surrounded by picture-perfect chairs. Cream and sand. Pale pink towels. Palm trees everywhere.

He sets our drinks on a glass table, next to a stack of props (mostly sunglasses). "Where do you need me?"

I reach for my matcha latte. Take a long sip. It's a little cold, but it's still delicious. Sweet, creamy, comforting.

"After this." He closes the distance between us. Wraps his arms around me. Pulls me into a slow, deep kiss.

His lips close around my bottom lip. He sucks softly. Then harder. Then it's the slow scrape of his teeth.

Again and again—

Until my body is buzzing.

He pulls back with a sigh. "Fuck, you taste like honey."

"Oh."

He smiles. "You always taste like honey."

My cheeks flush.

"The other day, I ordered an iced matcha for myself."

"Oh?"

"It tasted good. 'Cause it tasted like you. Of course, the barista looked at me funny when I started groaning over it."

"You what?"

He laughs. "I thought about kissing you. Then about—" His eyes travel down my body. "Princess, you look divine."

"Thanks."

"I need to taste you properly."

"Right now?"

"After this."

"I'll taste like chlorine."

His smile gets wicked. "You like the taste of chlorine."

I clear my throat.

"You'll want to taste it too."

I swallow a sip of my matcha so I won't overheat. It doesn't help. At all. But it's still good.

"Might let you this time."

"You might let me?"

He nods. "If I'm feeling generous."

"If you're feeling generous you'll *let* me suck you off—"

"Is there a question in there?"

Fuck, there's something so hot about the commanding tone to his voice. Like he knows I want it that badly. Like I want him that badly. "Uh… no."

"Good." He grabs his coffee. Takes a long sip. "Where do you need me?"

"Let's do the ones with you first. Before I get wet."

"Before, huh?"

Oh. My blush deepens. Which is good for this set, actually. I'm in the black bikini. The most revealing one. And the sweetest one. And the one least like Mackenzie.

But I'm not thinking about that.

Not at all.

I take another sip, set my drink on the counter, sit on one of the cream chairs.

Forest drops to his knees to help me into my sandals. His fingers linger on my ankles.

He looks up at me with a goofy smile.

Then he leans closer and he presses his lips to the inside of my knee. "Later." He stands. Offers his hand. Helps me up.

Somehow, I maintain my composure.

I slip on my props. Arrange the camera. First the bench on the other side of the pool.

He sits.

I move the tripod. Get the angle just right. Slip the remote between my fingers.

Sit next to Forest.

I rest my head on his shoulder. *Click, click*.

He slides his arm around me. *Click, click*.

I stare at him like I'm madly in love. *Click, click*.

He stares back. *Click, click*.

Then he moves closer, closer, until his lips hit mine.

## The Best Friend Bargain

He presses his palm into my bare back, holding my body against his, as he slips his tongue into my mouth.

He kisses me like he's claiming me.

Like I'm the only thing he wants.

I forget about the shoot. About the wedding. About everything but kissing back.

Mmm, he tastes good. Like chocolate and honey and Forest.

*Click, click.*

My palm digs into the cushion, pressing the button on the camera.

He pulls back reflexively.

At least, I think it's reflexively.

His expression gets sheepish. "Got carried away."

"That's okay." More than okay.

"You look so fucking sexy, Skye."

"Thank you." My body buzzes. Right now, I believe it. That he wants me. Only me. That the rest of this weekend means nothing. That it doesn't matter.

Is that true?

God, I need it to be true.

"Am I messing up your lipstick?" He catches my lip with his thumb. Slides the digit into my mouth.

Mmm. I look up at him as I suck hard.

He looks down at me with that demanding stare. One that says *I'll fuck up your lipstick if I want. I'll split you in half, princess.*

Slowly, he pulls his thumb from my mouth.

"No." I can barely speak. "It doesn't rub off." My gaze flits to his crotch. "We've already tried that."

His smile gets wicked. "Princess, you keep looking at me like that and this shoot is going to get pornographic."

I shake my head.

He raises a brow.

"I'm in charge." I stand. "You're my model. You do what I say."

"Yeah?"

"Yeah." I turn. Sit on his thighs.

"I'll do what you say."

"But…"

"He won't—" He pulls me up his thighs until my ass is against his crotch. Against his hard cock.

Mmm. "I don't have an issue."

"That's the tone you want?"

"Why do you think I'm sitting here."

He chuckles. "And I'm the evil one?"

"Maybe we're both evil." I motion to the camera. "Smile."

He turns to the lens. Wraps his arms around my waist. *Click*.

I shift around the bench. Snap photos in a dozen different positions.

Then we toast our cans of soda, get a dozen like that.

I switch to my combat boots. Repeat our poses. Then do a set of solo photos.

Forest watches with rapt attention as I slip on my robe, slip off my swimsuit, pull on another. The purple one-piece.

He helps me tie the halter top. Traces the low neckline all the way to the v below my breasts.

His fingers linger on my skin. He looks down at me, asking for permission.

I nod.

He slips his hand into my bikini. Pulls my body into his. Toys with my nipple as he kisses me hard.

I slip my hand into the back pocket of his jeans. But it's not enough. I need more.

I tug at his button. Cup him over his jeans.

He groans against my lips. Pulls back with a sigh. "Not yet."

"Not yet?"

He nods. "Work first."

"You're pure evil." I use his words.

He just smiles. "Well, yeah." He adjusts my swimsuit so it's covering me properly. "I learned from the best."

## Chapter Thirty-Eight

SKYE

The purple swimsuit is pure torture. There's nothing wrong with the design. It's stretchy, cute, comfortable.

But Forest keeps looking at me like he's about to devour me.

Even as he follows my instructions to hold reflectors or move chairs or do away with my sunglasses.

This isn't a lingerie shoot. It's not supposed to be sexy.

I mean, it's not supposed to be unsexy. But I can't post a bunch of topless images where I'm pawing at my boyfriend's jeans.

I certainly can't post images of his hands on my chest. Or my hands on his thighs. Or my lips around his—

My entire body blushes.

The pool is cold. I should be shivering. But I'm not. I'm on fire.

I close my eyes. Take a deep breath. Think of unsexy things. My parents flirting at dinner (so gross). Their *hey, maybe head to Forest's place, or at least use headphones* wink. Them climbing the stairs, turning up their Prince music, and well…

Too many details.

So gross.

So, so gross.

Okay, that's better. Ish.

"You okay?" Forest asks. He's standing at the side of the pool, all tall and beautiful in his jeans and white t-shirt, his hands around a gold reflector.

Fuck, it's hard shooting blind. I need to expand beyond self-portraits. Or find a photographer for my self-portraits. Though I guess they'd just be portraits then.

My chest tightens at the thought of giving up my role behind the camera. Yeah, I love rocking fashionable attire. I love finding confidence in my body. I even like the attention, mostly.

But framing a photo, getting the lighting and the cropping just right—

That's bliss.

"Trying to cool down." I can't help but smile. "Someone keeps—"

"Revving your engine?"

"You sound like Holden."

His nose scrunches in distaste. "I usually think about the Lakers."

"You love the Lakers."

"They're terrible now."

"Still. They inspire passion. When you and Chase watch games... well, it's pretty quiet, because it's you and Chase, but—"

"I should think about our rivals?"

"Yeah, the, uh..." I try to remember which team in the uh... league? Division? Region? "Sports team."

He chuckles. "Yeah, the sports team."

"Fuck those guys."

"They are the worst." He laughs so hard his sunglasses slide down his nose. He drops one hand to fix them. Returns it to the massive gold reflector.

"A little to the left." I try to focus on the cropping. There must be an easier way to do this. Some way to get a remote feed from the camera. So I can pose as I compose.

Maybe I can train an assistant to explain the photos to me. Something.

I need to get better at this.

Fast.

To expand beyond "influencing." Into headshots or boudoir or commercial photography.

To finally make enough money to move out of my parents' place.

I will.

I want to.

But, first, this shoot.

It's amazing.

And not just because Forest keeps feeling me up. Though that is...

Ahem.

Focusing. Composing the image. Concentrating.

There. I turn so I'm in three-quarter profile. Tease the camera. "One more foot left."

He moves.

"One foot higher."

He raises the reflector.

I think that's it. Probably. I shoot the camera my best come-hither look. *Click, click*.

Then playful, sassy, sweet.

I blow a kiss.

Turn and place my hand on my hip.

Move to the edge of the pool. Place my hands against it. Like I'm about to get out.

Then I do get out. I take a dozen casual (ish) photos. *Hey, look at me, just happening to capture the perfect post-dip shot*.

Then I lie back. Let the sun fall over my body.

"Fuck, Skye." Forest's voice drips with desire. "You trying to kill me?"

"Maybe." I turn to the camera. Blow it one more kiss. Take one more picture.

Forest drops the reflector.

I check the images. They're good. A little flushed, but that only sells the whole *I'm swimming today* vibe.

This covers this pool. Now I need something on the beach.

"Five minutes," I say. "I'm going to change and touch up my makeup." I motion to the lounge in the hotel.

"You mean twenty minutes."

I flip him off.

He laughs. "I'll get water." He pulls me into a tight hug, kisses me hard.

I hold him tightly for a moment, then I release him. Step backward. Motion to the lounge.

He nods. "You can torture me, but I'll torture you back."

"Counting on it." I blow him a kiss.

He catches it.

My chest warms. It just feels good.

I grab everything I need, move into the hotel, ignore all the signs of Mack's wedding.

Red, red everywhere. Her colors are red and silver. Because why not?

Okay, red is a perfectly reasonable color. A bold choice for a beach wedding even. Most people do shades of blue-green. Teal, turquoise, mint, cerulean.

Something summery.

Something that reminds of the ocean.

Not something that screams of a winter holiday. Or a backstabbing—

Ahem.

Not going there. Today is good. Tomorrow is—I don't know. But today is good.

I change into my third swimsuit. Touch up my eye makeup. My lipstick. My hair.

It's a basic straight look. For this one. Then into the water. For a fully... submerged look.

Or maybe some sort of swimsuit catalog sexy, wet vibe. I want to get it all.

After one more hair and makeup check, I head back to the pool.

Forest is sitting under the umbrella, fingers curled around a water bottle, eyes on Mackenzie.

She spots me and offers a big, friendly wave. She's wearing a white sundress (of course) with tall silver sandals (surprising). Her lips are as red as her hair and her sunglasses.

She looks happy.

Like she wants to see me.

To torture me, probably, but I'm not thinking about that either.

"Hey." She meets me halfway around the pool. "You look great." She turns to Forest. "How'd you land such a knockout?"

I shoot him a *what the fuck* look.

He shrugs *fuck if I know*. "You know what they say—"

"Girls like guys with a big dick." I hold my straight face for as long as I can. A laugh rolls up my chest and throat, spills from my lips, knocks me sideways.

Forest laughs knowingly.

Mackenzie's laugh is more… awkward. "I'll get out of your way." She offers me a hug.

I take it.

It's weird. Uncomfortable. And familiar.

I miss when we were friends. When we were nearly sisters. That summer she stayed with us, before the whole Forest thing—

God, it was like stuff I saw in the movies. We stayed up late watching chick flicks, trading gossip, eating cookie dough.

She took me shopping, taught me how to curl my hair (not that it holds it), convinced me to upgrade from drugstore makeup to premium stuff.

She helped me dye my hair medium brown, when I wanted to look more like Mom.

Then blue-black (it's naturally more of a dark, dark brown), when I wanted to look like Dad.

"Are you guys good for a while?" She pulls back with a smile. "The hotel wants this space free in forty-five." She motions to the tables by the pool. "They have to set up for the party."

"Sure." It's so weird, watching my cousin explain practicalities like she never stole my crush.

I can feel that bond we used to have.

And the loss of it.

It hurts. But I still hate her.

I hate that she has any of my attention. But she does.

Is this how he feels too? Only with all the extra baggage of sex and romance?

Ahem. She isn't ruining my mood. She just isn't. "Sure. I'll move the stuff. We're going to head to the other pool anyway."

"Oh yeah?" She raises a brow. "Getting some privacy?"

"Maybe." Forest laughs. "If I feel merciful."

My sex clenches.

Mackenzie... laughs. It's this knowing laugh. Like she remembers some time they fucked in the pool.

Not that it matters.

I know they had sex. A lot of sex. But that was a long time ago. And even if it wasn't, I'm not a cavewoman. I'm not obsessed with sex.

Only my stomach is churning.

This is...

UGH.

"We're hitting the beach first." I move to our stuff. Gather everything I can. "So we'll see you at the party."

"Sure." She smiles. Waves goodbye.

Forest helps me collect our stuff. He follows me to the secluded pool.

It's all kinds of sexy, the way it's hidden between shrubbery and the hotel wall, but it also means the whole thing is cast in shadow.

A shadow that isn't going anywhere.

Okay, sticking with the plan. Beach. Now. I pick up my tripod. Motion to the reflector. "Let's make these fast."

His smile is wicked. "Why's that?"

"Hmm, I wonder?" I try to tease, but there's a heaviness in my shoulders. She's so there. No wonder he's all moody and jealous. Or he was. I don't know. It's confusing.

I try to push it aside as I lead Forest along the stone path. All the way to the sand.

It's windy as hell—way too cold for a bikini—but it looks gorgeous.

I set up the tripod. Direct him to the proper spot.

Then I go. Pose as quickly as I can. A dozen super posed shots. A dozen natural ones.

Yes, I'm just running toward the ocean. That's normal!

I'm hanging on the sand. Like everyone does.

I'm waving at a friend.

He drops the reflector. Moves to me.

Then I'm hugging my, uh, something. Kissing him. Sliding my hands into the back pocket of his jeans.

And he's untying my bikini top, tugging the cup until my breast is exposed.

*Click*.

"You gonna record all this, princess?" He slips his hand between my legs. Rubs me over my swimsuit.

The damn thing is too thick. I can only get so much of his touch. "I… uh…"

"Should order you to take that top off right here."

My body buzzes. "You should."

"Order you onto your knees, so I can come on those pretty tits."

Holy fuck. "You should."

He shakes his head. "We have one to go."

Right. One to… Uh… pictures. We. Take. Pictures.

Fuck. He's way too good at this.

I press the heel of my hand into his chest. "Back. Behind the camera."

"Oh?"

I nod *yes*. "You can't be trusted in front of it."

He smiles, but he does move back.

Thank God. I'm ready to rip his clothes off. Which is such a bad idea.

The beach is empty, sure, but it's *the* view. Anyone anywhere in the hotel can see us on the sand.

Maybe if we go in the ocean…

No, it's too cold. And how am I going to—

Ahem.

I recall my parents disgusting flirting again—it's very effective—shift back into *fun beach day* mode.

Then a little sexy goth princess mode.

Forest keeps staring like he wants to consume me. But when I nod *we're done here*, he picks up the camera, makes a point of holding it in front of his face.

"You follow orders?" I ask.

"I'd rather give them, but if that's what you're into…"

"No, I… I'd rather that too."

He smiles that same wicked smile. Leads me back up the path, past the hotel crew setting up the party, around the corner to the secluded pool.

We're completely out of view of the party.

Though we're… right there. Around the corner.

It's illicit. And hot as hell. Not that we're… uh… still picture time.

I set up the camera. Stall by re-checking the shoot requirements on my phone. It's surprisingly broad. Whatever I think will sell swimsuits.

It can be sexy, fun, sweet, silly, scary.

But the shop's website is decidedly family friendly. It's not going for a *buy me and you'll want to bone all night* vibe.

They're cute swimsuits. Not sexy ones.

Though that's really a false distinction.

Forest is adorable when he gets all contemplative. And he's sexy as hell.

## The Best Friend Bargain

It's possible to hit both.
It's possible to work and not fuck Forest immediately.
I mean, in theory it must be possible.
Somehow.

## Chapter Thirty-Nine

SKYE

"Can you get us some waters?" It's a weak excuse, but it's all I've got.

He nods *sure*. "Anything else?"

A moment to cool down. "That's it."

He nods *sure thing*, kisses me goodbye, moves around the corner.

I do away with my third swimsuit. Pull on the sexy red bikini.

It fits like a glove. What I expect from bra-sized swimwear. But still rare enough I appreciate it.

With Forest gone, and the shade following over the pool, I cool down enough to concentrate.

I need to knock out the cute photos before he returns. Because once he's here—

He's impossible to resist. He really is.

I arrange the camera just right, grab the remote, step into the pool.

Static poses. *Click, click*. Action shots. *Click, click*. Cute expressions. *Click, click*.

He turns the corner with our water bottles. Tosses one to me. Smiles as the water bottle lands in front of me.

"What?" I pick it up.

"That was a perfect shot."

"I don't do sports."

His laugh gets louder. "If you wanted me to leave, you could have said that."

"I was thirsty." I uncap the bottle. Take a long swig. Swallow. I *am* thirsty. That's true. I'm melting.

Surrounded by water and I'm melting.

He's too sexy. It's wrong.

"Where do you want me?" He uncaps his bottle. Takes a swig.

God, his lips look so beautiful wrapped around the bottle.

"Skye?" he asks.

"Here."

"In the pool?"

I nod.

"Not behind the camera?"

I nod.

"You know what that means, princess?"

My tongue slides over my lips.

"It means I'm going to make you groan so loud the waiters wonder if they should come to watch."

My sex clenches. "I know."

He pulls his t-shirt over his head. Kicks off his shoes. Pushes his jeans off his hips.

He's wearing a black speedo. Only a black speedo.

It's just…

He…

I…

My body buzzes.

He slips into the pool. Closes the distance between us.

"I, uh… I need some photos of us. You know… like a happy, sexy couple." My fingers brush the soft skin of his stomach. Then his hip. The lines of his tattoo.

I want to be that tattoo.

To mark his skin, his heart, his soul.

Do I have that sway over him yet? Do I take up that much space?

I want it so badly.

I want him so badly.

"Are we not?" He stares down at me, his eyes wide with affection.

"Uh…" Right now, sure? But after this weekend… I can't answer that. So I move closer. Arrange my hand just so. *Click*.

I cheat toward the camera.

He follows my lead.

For a dozen pictures, we stay appropriate. Hands touching, arms locked, my body in front of his.

His arms around my stomach.

His lips on my neck.

His cock against my ass.

He's hard. It feels so good. It's wrong, how good it feels.

Forest turns me around. He tugs my bikini cup aside until my breast is fully exposed.

He looks down at me, equal parts needy and in control. "You gonna get that one?"

Fuck.

"'Cause I was hoping to fuck myself to it later."

I just barely nod. And press the button. *Click*.

He cups my breast. Rolls my nipple between his first two fingers.

Softly. Then harder. Hard enough to hurt.

I let out a needy groan.

He watches himself work as he toys with me. He pushes my other bikini cup aside.

I reach around my back. Undo the clasp. The knot.

The top falls onto the pool.

Forest scoops it between his fingers. Tosses it onto the concrete. "Come here."

"Huh?" I glide to him.

He wraps his arm around me. Pulls my body into his, until my breasts are against his chest.

He takes the remote from my fingers. Taps the button. *Click, click.*

Oh. Right. The photo shoot. We're still doing that.

He brings his hand to the back of my head. Tugs at my hair. *Click, click.*

He turns me, so we're both facing the camera, covers my breasts with his arm.

*Click, click.*

With his hands.

*Click, click.*

He drops his hands. So I'm on display.

*Click, click.*

His lip brushes my ear. Neck. Shoulder. "Princess, you have no fucking idea what you do to me." He shifts his hips, so his cock grinds against my ass.

Then his hands are on my chest and his lips are on my neck.

He sucks on my skin as he toys with me.

*Click, click.*

We're taking dirty pictures. Sure, they're R, not NC-17, not yet.

They're classy. Like the video we watched.

We could do that. Make our own video.

For the world to see.

Or just us.

Fuck. It sets me on fire.

Desire overtakes me. I stop thinking. I lose control of anything but my desperate urge to touch him.

My body melts into his.

He forms around me. Becomes exactly what I need. Or maybe he already is exactly what I need.

He toys with my nipple until I'm panting, then he turns me around, brings his lips to mine.

He kisses me hard. *Click, click.*

It's my bare back, my swimsuit-clad ass, his barely-clothed front.

It's a perfectly framed shot. But I don't care.

I only care about touching him.

"That thing have a video function?" He nips at my ear.

I nod. "I... should we go upstairs?"

"We should do it here." He doesn't say it, but it's there in his voice. *Where we can get caught.*

Because the risk is hot as hell.

Because it's driving me insane.

Because. Just because.

I nod *yes*.

He nips at my neck. Harder. Harder. Hard enough I groan.

Forest toys with my neck until I'm tugging at his hair. Then he drags his lips over my shoulder, collarbone, breasts.

He takes my nipple into his mouth. Sucks softly. Then harder. Harder.

There—

"Forest." I reach for something. Get his stomach.

It's strange, touching him under the water. Smooth. There's too little friction. Too little connection.

I need more.

But I have no time to consider it.

The way he flicks his tongue against my nipple—

Fuck.

He tortures me with slow flicks.

*Click, click.*

We're recording this.

It's so...

Fuck.

I tug at his wet hair.

He toys with me. Slow flicks. Fast ones. Hard. Soft. Circles. Zigzags.

The soft suction of his mouth.

The rough scrape of his teeth.

"Forest—" I dig my fingers into his chest.

"You taste like chlorine." He moves to my other nipple.

Tortures me with his soft, wet tongue. "You taste like that everywhere, princess?"

Oh my God.

"Come here." He guides me to the edge of the pool.

I press my hands onto the wall. Push myself up.

He helps me onto my back. Spreads my legs wide. Until my thighs are pressed into the concrete.

I don't care that I'm splayed out on the concrete.

Only that he's between my legs.

That he's mine.

*Click, click.*

My breath catches in my throat. I need him so badly. I need him now. I need him more. I need every bit of him.

He undoes the tie holding my bikini bottoms together. The right. Then the left.

The suit falls into the pool.

Then his lips are on my thighs. He tortures me with those soft scrapes of his teeth. Higher and higher.

Almost.

Almost.

He gets so, so close, then he pulls back. Presses his lips to the inside of my other knee.

He works his way up again. Then down the other side.

Then up again.

Up the other side.

Again and again.

Until I'm dizzy.

Until I'm panting.

Until I'm tugging at his hair, squirming, digging my heels into his back.

His lips brush my clit.

The anticipation inside me unravels. Bliss spreads through my body, taking over every single inch.

It's intense. Like it's the first time he's touched me. Like it's the first time anyone has touched me.

His lips close around my clit.
He sucks softly.
Then harder.
Hard enough the world goes white.

There's nothing but the big sun, the bright sky, the bliss spilling through me.

I'm unraveling and winding tighter.

It shouldn't be possible, but it is.

"Fuck." I claw at his shoulder. He's still wet. Slick. My hand glides over him. I can't get a grip.

Forest takes my hand, brings it under the water, to his swimsuit.

To his cock

He's hard.

The Lycra stretches over him. Begs for my hands.

I slip my hand into his swimsuit. Wrap my fingers around him.

I can't move—not in this position—but I don't care. I can feel him. That's what I need.

He keeps me pinned.

Sucks softer and softer until—

I whimper.

He keeps that pressure.

It's intense. It winds me quickly. Pushes me right to the edge.

I'm brimming with pleasure. It's too much. I'm going to burst.

His nails scrape my thighs.

The hint of pain pulls me back.

It's so much. Too much. But I still need more.

I run my thumb over his tip.

He groans, but it does nothing to slow him. Or speed him. He's endlessly patient.

He works me exactly how I need him.

The pressure gets tighter and tighter.

Until I'm wound as tight as I can go.

Everything releases as I come.

My sex pulses. His name spills from my lips.

I claw at his shoulder. Rub his cock. Dig my heels into his back.

My orgasm crashes through me like a wave. Pleasure rolls through every inch of my body. Leaves me spent. Slack.

Forest looks up at me with a satisfied smile.

I reach for him again. He's still hard. I need that. "Speedo off."

"There." He motions to the wall behind us.

The wall directly in front of the camera.

He picks up the remote—it's right next to me.

He's a genius.

An evil genius.

I nod *hell yes*.

He climbs out of the pool. Pushes his swimsuit aside.

God, that's a glorious mental image: Forest naked, sopping wet, hard.

I need it.

I need to know if he tastes like chlorine too.

I don't tease him. I just go.

Couch cushion on the ground. Knees on the cushion. Hand around his cock.

He groans as I take him into my mouth. "Fuck, Skye."

I take him deeper. Deeper. As deep as I can.

*Click, click.*

Then I pull back and do it again.

Harder.

And harder.

*Click, click.*

He tugs at my hair. "You're gonna make me come, princess."

I don't stop.

I want to make him come. I want to taste him in my mouth. Or feel him on my chest.

Anywhere.

I don't care. As long as I get every ounce of his pleasure.

I grab onto his ass. Take him deeper.

He tugs at my hair. Pulls me off him. Pulls me up.

"Hands. Wall. Now."

## The Best Friend Bargain

He doesn't wait. He guides me to the wall. Places my body in front of his. His body behind mine.

He turns us enough to cheat to the fucking camera.

My hands slip from the wall.

He helps them back. Wraps his arm around my waist. Holds me in place as he brings our bodies together.

His cock strains against me for a moment.

Then he pushes in.

*Click, click.*

Slowly at first.

Then harder.

*Click, click.*

It's intense. Almost too much.

Then he shifts deeper and it's not enough.

He pins me to the wall. Drives into me with steady thrusts.

It's fast. Hard. Perfect.

"Fuck." He scrapes his teeth against my shoulder. "Skye."

His chest melts into my back.

My body melts into his.

He drives deeper.

Deeper.

"Forest." Fuck, that's a lot. In the best possible way.

He rocks into me with that steady pace. Again and again and again.

Until he's shaking. Groaning into my skin. Holding me closer.

He groans my name as he comes.

His cock pulses inside me. Sends waves of pleasure through me.

God, there's something about feeling him come.

It's everything.

He thrusts through his orgasm. Then he untangles our bodies. Brings me back to the towel. Helps me clean up.

Fuck, it's so intimate. I can barely look at him.

Forest helps me into my robe.

He dons his jeans. Pulls me into a tight embrace. "I tried to warn you, princess." He presses his lips to my ear. "You made me come too fast."

"Are you complaining?"

"No, but it means I have to take you upstairs and make you come." He takes my hand. "Right away."

## Chapter Forty

SKYE

Forest makes good on his promise. He uses my vibrator (okay, I packed my vibrator) to make me come three times. Then he tosses it aside, throws me on the bed, fucks me so hard I see stars.

After, he holds me close.

Our bodies stay connected. In a different way. One that's softer, sweeter, more love than lust.

It feels right, like we really do belong together, like this isn't going to end in disaster.

Eventually, my phone buzzes with *you're going to be late* warnings from my parents.

Forest heads to the shower.

I arrange my outfit. Fix a tea. Sip it on the balcony.

She's there, dipping her feet in the pool.

In a red bikini.

Just like the one I was wearing.

It shouldn't be surprising—Mackenzie only wears red. It should make my stomach churn. It shouldn't fill my throat with jealousy.

But it does.

It echoes through my head. *Has she worn it before? With him? For him?*

*Was he thinking about her? Replaying some fuck with her? Proving something about her?*

*Is he still in love with her?*

Diego comes up to Mackenzie. Pulls her from the pool.

He must say something about how she needs to dress, because she follows him to the lobby.

"You okay, princess?" Forest's footsteps move closer.

I swallow my envy. "Yeah, just…" They're gone. There's no evidence. No reason to believe he was thinking of her.

But what if he was?

What if he's still in this for her?

I turn to Forest. Look up in his eyes. Try to find the courage to ask.

Fail.

"Just tired." I force a smile. "You wore me out."

He beams with pride. The way he used to when he won a basketball game. "How much time do you need?"

"Why?"

"Holden." He shakes his head *he's ridiculous*. "I need to keep him occupied."

"Go. I'll meet you there."

"No. I'll be here. Just want to know how long I have to do battle. Five minutes requires a different technique than thirty."

"I don't mind."

"I do." He presses his lips to mine. "Go. Or I'm going to make you come again."

For a second, all that tension dissolves.

Then I move into the shower and it hits me.

It stays with me as I shower, dry, dress.

As I fix my hair and makeup.

As I step into my shoes.

*Is all of this for her?*

*Is all his love for her?*

*Will he ever love me?*

## Chapter Forty-One

FOREST

"Fuck, Skye, you're wearing that dress." Holden blows Skye a kiss. He makes a show of fanning himself. Then pretending to check the state of his boner. "Why are you hanging out with this loser?"

"I don't know." Her fingers brush my tie. It's hot pink. To match her dress. "He cleans up pretty nice."

"And I?" He motions to his suit.

As much as I hate to admit it, Holden looks good. His grey suit and teal tie suit him. The blue-green color brings out his light eyes. Highlights his sandy hair.

He's the only one of us who inherited Mom's coloring. And the only one—

He was so young. I'm not sure he remembers her.

"Hmm, I've seen better." Skye gives him no satisfaction.

"Better? Than this." He spins. Stops. Strikes a model worthy pose.

She nods *yeah*.

"Oh, those times you creeped into my room and watched me fuck myself." He winks at her.

"Yes, that's exactly what I meant," she deadpans. "I installed a camera in your room so I can watch you masturbate."

"Our secret." He mimes *my lips are sealed*.

"Yeah, it's too bad you come so fast," she teases. "Disappointing."

"Baby, only 'cause I'm thinking of you." He takes her hand. Drops to one knee. Places a kiss on the back of her hand. "I won't lie, Skye. The first time we're together, I might not be able to control myself. But round two—"

"You think I'm staying for round two after round one was so disappointing?" she asks.

"You're still with Forest."

"Forest is skilled."

"Go on…" He raises a brow. Looks to me *are you going to offer details?*

"We should say hi to your parents," I say.

"That means he's sick of my bullshit." Holden scans the room. But he can't be looking for Skye's parents, because they're clearly at the bar, toasting, staring into each other's eyes.

Oh. That's it.

His gaze stops on Mack. She's talking to someone I don't recognize. A friend of her dad's. He's friends with everyone. Though friend is the wrong word.

It's more that he wields considerable influence.

He's well—

There's a reason her mom is always drinking.

Holden nudges Skye. "Let's mingle. Me and you."

"I'm ditching Forest?" she asks.

"Who would you rather have on your arm?" He raises a brow *come on, look at me.*

Across the room, Mack turns to us. She nods *hey*. Makes eye contact with me.

What the hell can I say to her? Besides *get the fuck out of my head?*

I don't want to think about her anymore.

I don't want to be here.

But it's what Skye needs.

I'm going to have to get through it.

"How about we get a drink?" Skye looks to me. Mouths *is that okay?*

I nod *yeah*. "I'll meet you there."

Holden smiles. "Moscow mule?"

"Of course."

He offers his arm.

She takes it. Laughs at some joke he makes. Blows me a kiss as she walks away.

It's with my permission. It's because Holden is trying to spare Skye a scene.

Trying to protect me from myself. Well, from the person I become around my ex-girlfriend.

But it feels so fucking familiar.

It's there, in the pit of my stomach. *She's going to leave you too. She's going to find someone better. She's going to fuck him like she never fucked you.*

Which is ridiculous.

The last few hours—

I'm still sore. I don't have anything left. There's no way she has another round in her.

If she does—

I should leave. Take her back to my room. Make her come until she begs me to stop.

That's exactly what I need. Her groan bouncing around the room. My name rolling off her lips. Her hands tugging at my hair.

The world fucking perfect.

I try to stay locked in the memory of her body against mine, but it's not enough. Dread still rises in my throat.

*She's leaving too.*

*You're not enough.*

*You're never going to be enough.*

*You're never going to figure it out.*

*She's going to find someone who knows how to love. Who really can give her everything.*

I turn to the bar. Watch my brother order my best friend a drink.

The bartender stares at her tits. Her parents say something about her outfit.

She shrugs. Takes her drink. Downs it quickly.

Her parents kiss. Really kiss. Like horny teenagers.

They're always like horny teenagers.

Fuck, Skye looks so much like her dad. Except for those eyes. She has the same bright blue eyes her mom does.

Her mom is lithe, blond, subdued. She wears soft makeup and styles her hair in a no-nonsense bob. Even now, at a formal event, she's wearing flats and a practical dress. Skye says it's from Nordstrom.

She always rolls her eyes when she says it. Not that I get her feelings. Yeah, she prefers independent boutiques. But I've seen her leave that particular department store with a bag full of stuff plenty of times.

Fuck, some of the stuff in the lingerie section—

"Forest, hey." Mack's voice flows into my ears. Pulls me from my dirty thoughts. "You're not drinking?"

Does that bother her? Is she that insecure about her problem? "Not yet." I turn to her. Offer my hand.

She shakes. "Last time—"

"It was a party."

She nods *it was*. "I was out of line. But, uh—"

"We both had shit we had to say."

"Yeah." Her smile is soft. "Are you and Skye okay?" Her fingers brush my arm, over my suit cuff. Then the bare skin of my wrist.

"Yeah."

"I hope I didn't cause any conflict."

I study her expression, trying to pick it apart. Does she mean it? Or is she secretly living to tear us apart?

Maybe she's like me. Maybe she's not over what happened.

Maybe she has an ugly part of herself she can't control. She always did. She was always jealous of Skye.

It must kill her that we're together. I don't care how much she says she's happy for me. I don't buy it.

I know Mack. At least, I know who she used to be. That girl would be overflowing with jealousy. Even with her wedding tomorrow.

She just—

She could never quiet that voice.

I sympathize, I do. In the abstract. At the moment, it's hard to feel anything but dull nausea.

"We worked it out upstairs." I smile at my ex.

She laughs nervously. Turns to a passing waiter. Grabs two glasses of champagne.

My fingers brush hers as I take one. "Thanks."

She takes a long sip. Swallows hard. "It's good to see you."

"Yeah?"

"After everything… this is a lot. I thought I'd see more people who knew me… who don't think I'm some bitch who doesn't appreciate her privilege. Who doesn't realize she needs a real job."

I wouldn't say that. Or the opposite. She's somewhere in between. "You support yourself?"

"Mostly." Her eyes turn down. "Daddy helps with the rent sometimes. Diego is still getting his PhD, so he's not—"

"He'll be a biotech billionaire one day," I say.

Her frown turns upside down. "Yeah. I hope so." She takes a long sip. "That isn't why I'm with him."

"It's really none of my business." I don't want to know. What if the fear in my stomach is true? She might say *the truth is, you didn't know how to love me. You never loved me enough. You never were enough. You won't be enough for her either.*

"Right. I just… You look good." She finishes her glass. "Handsome. Happy." There's something in her voice. Something between bitterness and nostalgia.

"You do too." I motion to her cream dress. "Very bridal."

"Yeah." Her laugh is awkward. "It's so much. And it's tomorrow. I… I'm freaking out a little."

"You need another drink?"

"Usually, you tell me to stop."

"I'm not your keeper anymore, remember?"

"Yeah." Her expression gets apologetic. "You're right, I… uh… I actually wanted to ask you something."

"Oh?"

"Tonight. Will you mind if I borrow Skye?" She holds her glass to her chest. "My maid of honor is doing a bachelorette in the suite."

"I'm not her keeper either," I say.

"You're past that?"

Sorta. "Getting there."

"Good." Mack presses her lips together. "And you… you aren't trying to fix her?"

What the fuck? "What do you mean?"

"Nothing. Just… everyone has issues."

Sure…

"Forget I said anything." She bites her lip. "I hate to drive a wedge. I just… I didn't know if you knew. Why Skye hasn't talked to me all these years."

What is she talking about?

"I, uh, I guess it worked out for her."

"What worked out for her?"

"She always liked you. She wanted to be the one… I told her I wouldn't. I meant it." Her fingers brush my wrist. "But I couldn't help myself."

"What do you mean?"

"When we started. Skye had a crush on you."

Okay…

"It wasn't even a crush, exactly. She wanted you." She drops her voice. "Sexually."

"Sexually?"

"Yeah, she talked about it a lot. Didn't you know?"

I shrug like I do.

"I guess it worked out. Since you're together now. And it's

about more than that."

Skye's wanted me forever.

It's not surprising, exactly. She more or less admitted. Hell, it's flattering.

But this whole ruse was her idea.

Did she have ulterior motives?

Has she been manipulating me for the last month and a half?

Has all this been an attempt to get in my pants?

It's not like her.

She's not a liar.

Fuck, I'm the one who put my foot in my mouth. Blurted out that we're together.

I'm the one who started this.

I swallow hard. "You know, I don't think she'd appreciate you talking about it like this. Behind her back. In public."

"Right." She fakes an apology. "It's out of line. I just… I get worried. Big moments… sometimes people have big reactions and when she drinks a lot—"

"Yeah."

"I'm sorry. And, Forest, I… I am sorry about how everything ended with us." She wraps her hand around my wrist. Lifts to her tiptoes. Presses her lips to my cheek. "Take care."

"Congratulations."

She nods. "I'm gonna—" She motions to the bar. "Details to work out with your girlfriend."

"She's yours."

I watch Mack cross the room. Join Skye.

I watch them hug hello, discuss something, laugh at some bad joke Mr. Kim makes.

Skye turns to me. Motions to her purse.

She pulls out her cell.

I do the same.

*Skye: Apparently, there's a stripper heading to Mack's room in twenty.*
*Forest: And you want to stick dollar bills in his g-string?*
*Skye: Might be entertaining.*

*Forest: Go for it.*
*Skye: Will you be okay?*
I will. I'll get there.

I'm being stupid. There's no way Skye would do this to manipulate me.

There's no way she'd lie to me. Not on purpose.

There's no way this is an elaborate way to fuck me and throw me away.

That isn't like her.

But it still echoes through my head.

*Maybe that's all your good for. You sure as hell don't know how to love her. So why wouldn't she take the one thing you have to offer and leave?*

*It's not like you can talk. You fucked half the state.*

*She's just following your lead.*

*Can you really blame her? You're the one who can't love her.*

*You're the one who's not enough.*

## Chapter Forty-Two

SKYE

As promised, three fellows in fireman costumes burst through the door.

They dance to an old pop song. Cavort around the room, thrusting their crotches, shaking their hips.

After a lot of gyrating, they sit Mackenzie in a chair in the middle of the room. Dance around her.

Strip out of their suspenders and yellow pants. Down to tiny red g-strings.

They're attractive guys, sure. Tall, fit, without an ounce of fat on them.

But it's so... fake.

I try to make conversation with the maid of honor. By the third time she giggles *Diego wouldn't like this*, I need another drink. Then a second. A third.

You know what Diego wouldn't like? Mack sleeping with another guy.

He's getting off easy, her leering at a few over-the-top guys in fireman costumes.

Forest got his heart broken.

Forest got thrown away.

Diego—

Well, I guess he's the one who has it worse. Since he's marrying the spawn of Satan.

But I doubt he sees it that way.

I drink until the maid of honor is interesting. Until the strippers are cute. Until the music is rocking.

The room starts spinning.

Someone helps me to the couch. Yes, that's good. Stable. Secure.

I rest my legs on the cushion. Lie back. Stare at the ceiling.

The same white ceiling in our room.

This room is so much like ours. Same pale pink walls. Same palm print pillows. Same silver fixings.

It's nice for a hotel. Expensive. Usually, even the priciest hotel is a little bit tacky. (I would know. Mackenzie's hotel magnet Dad used to invite me to join them on trips. Since Mackenzie didn't have anyone to play with). But this place is nice.

It's no abandoned pool, but—

I push off the couch. Move to the balcony.

Wind whips the sheer curtain in every direction. It blows my hair over my eyes. Ruffles my dress.

It's cold. But I'm still buzzed enough I barely feel it.

Maybe I need more. Maybe the solution to this horrible weekend is very strong, very large Moscow Mules.

I've never drank my way through problems, but now seems like a good time to start.

One more day and this horror is over.

One. More. Day.

Either Forest realizes he's totally over Mackenzie.

Or…

UGH.

I try to focus on the view. It's beautiful.

The moon casts a soft glow over the sand, the ocean, the hotel's concrete.

The party is still going. Half in the lobby. Half at the pool deck.

Well-dressed people toast, laugh, dance. I'm too far away to make anyone out. To see the pool cast highlights over faces.

The pool. It was ours. It was perfect.

Now?

Who knows.

I shift my gaze to the ocean.

A voice interrupts. "Aren't you cold?" Mackenzie asks.

"A little." I try to offer her a smile. Get most of the way there. "Aren't you supposed to have a stripper in your lap?"

She laughs. "I'm letting the maid of honor have a turn."

"It's not her last night of freedom."

Her gaze shifts to her engagement ring. "True."

"You scared?" I'm not sure I want to know. There's a part of me that misses her. But mostly… well, if she's happy with Diego, if she's sure—

No, it doesn't matter.

If Forest loves her, he loves her. Even if she won't have him. His love is still for her.

Maybe.

I mean, maybe I'm too drunk to think straight.

No. If I was drunk, I wouldn't realize it. But if I'm thinking I'm not drunk—

"Yeah." Her voice is honest. "It's weird, thinking about how I'll never have anyone else. I'm excited but… mostly it's a lot."

"Maybe you need another drink?"

She smiles as she brandishes a bottle of vodka. "You first?"

I take the bottle. Drink straight from it. Fuck, it's strong. But smooth.

Mackenzie laughs as she takes the bottle. Takes a heavy swig. "Damn." She coughs.

"You never drink it straight?"

She shakes her head. "You do?"

"Not usually," I admit.

She joins me at the railing. Looks at the view. "This is a nice place."

"It is."

"Forest seems... like he's grown."

Okay...

"I'm really glad. I just... I worry."

I bet. "What about?" I don't wait for her response. I take the bottle back. Take another swig. Wooh, drinking. It is a bachelorette party. I'm having fun.

"I think I..." She presses her lips together. "I just, I hope he's with you for the right reasons."

"What do you mean?" My stomach churns. From the vodka or the conversation. Both maybe.

"He... I swear, Skye, I'm only telling you this because you're my friend."

That's overstating it. I nod *go on* anyway.

"Don't you think it's really convenient? You two start dating as soon as I announce my engagement. Maybe it's a coincidence... or maybe he's using you."

"He's not." I can't say it was all bullshit. But he's not. Is he?

I'm the one who pushed him to do this.

Sure, it was his idea, but he wanted to pull back.

He wanted to run a million miles away.

I more or less begged him.

"I hope not," she whispers.

"Are you jealous?"

"No." She shakes her head *that's ridiculous*. "Don't get me wrong. I'll always love him. But I want you two to be happy. I want him to deserve you. Does he?" She turns, looks me straight in the eyes. "Are you sure he's here for you? I know you care about him, but he's a bitter guy. He'd think nothing of using you to get back at me."

"If you're not jealous, how can he get back at you?"

"I'm not, but... that's how his mind works. It's always sex. Always who's better off. Who wins."

That's...

No...

He wouldn't.
She's fucking with me.
She's trying to hurt me.
She's trying to ruin this. To ruin us.
But she is right about one thing.
If he's here for her—
If he still loves her—

"Excuse me." I set the bottle on a glass table. "I should…" I don't bother to think of an excuse. I head straight to Forest's room.

## Chapter Forty-Three

FOREST

A fist pounds at the door. It's frantic. Needy. "Forest." Skye's voice flows through the wood. "Are you there?"

"Yeah." Fuck, it's late. What is she doing up? I flip the light on. Climb out of bed. "Hold on."

Her knock continues. "I have to…" Her voice is slurred. Drunk or maybe tired. Or both. "I have to talk to you."

I pull the door open.

She barrels inside. Paces between the bed and the wall.

"Princess, are you okay?"

"No, I…"

"You want to sit?"

Her hair whips her cheeks as she shakes her head.

"You want a drink."

"Yeah." Her gaze shifts to the mini-bar. "A—"

"Water?"

Her lips curl into a smile. "No, I… I guess I'll just say it." Her pacing ceases.

Her eyes meet mine.

She stares at me like I'm holding her heart. "Are you in love with me?"

"What?" Where the fuck did that come from?

"Are you in love with me?"

"Skye, we kissed for the first time two weeks ago."

"But—"

"I thought that it was new. That I didn't have to know yet." I can't know yet. She has to see that. I need more time. I need to figure this out. To figure out what the fuck love means. What it means to offer someone your heart.

She closes the distance between us. Places her hands on my bare chest. "Are you in love with me?"

"I don't know."

"You don't know?"

"Fuck, I still can't wrap my head around you wanting me."

She swallows hard. "But you do?"

"I what?"

"You want me?"

I bring my hands to her hips. "Princess, let me get you some water. Something to eat. You're drunk."

"It was a party."

"So?"

"People drink at parties." Her fingers dig into my skin. "It's an easy question, Forest. You love me or you don't."

" I—"

"Don't say you love me as a friend. Don't tell me that bullshit."

"I—"

Her voice is needy. Desperate. "It's an easy question. You love me or you don't."

"Skye."

"What? Are you like all the other guys? You'll fuck the fat chick because she's the grateful type but you won't—"

"You're the one who pushed for this."

"But—"

"You'll fuck me, but you won't wait for me?"

Her chest heaves with her inhale. "That's not fair."

"It isn't."

Her frown deepens. "It wasn't like that. I love you." Her inhale is sharp. "I love you, Forest. I've loved you for a long time. I need you to love me back."

"Skye—"

"Just admit it. Look me in the eyes and tell me that you don't love me. That you'll never love me."

She's probably right.

I'm not Gloria Gaynor.

I don't know how to love again.

Sure, she's here because she's drunk and scared. But that doesn't change the facts.

I'm not enough for her.

I can't offer her what she needs.

I'm not capable of it.

"I'm sorry, Skye." I reach for her, but she pulls away. "I still don't know what it means. Or how to do it. Or what it feels like."

She steps back.

Her eyes go to the ground.

Her body curls inward.

God, she looks so hurt. I want to wrap my arms around her. Hold her. Soothe her.

But there's nothing I can say.

"Because you love her?" Her eyes meet mine. "You still love her?"

"No."

"But you don't love me?"

"I don't know. I don't know what that feels like."

She takes my hand. Pulls me into her.

Her lips collide with mine.

It's fast. Reckless.

She kisses me hard. Then she releases me.

Her eyes find mine. "You'd know. If you loved me, you'd know."

"Don't go."

She blinks back a tear. "I have to."

"Skye—"

"I'm sorry, Forest. I... thought things would be different." She turns and walks out the door.

# Chapter Forty-Four

FOREST

It takes twenty minutes to arrange everything with Holden.

My head is racing. There's no point in attempting sleep.

Instead, I head to the bar downstairs.

The party is over, but the bartender is still serving.

I take a seat. Order a Moscow Mule.

It's too sweet, but it tastes like Skye.

Fuck, I already miss her.

My heart is already breaking.

It's ridiculous. It was already broken. How can it break more?

I don't know if I love her.

But I still feel the ache of losing her.

Maybe that's enough to convince her. *Princess, there's a hole in my gut right now. Come back. Fill it.*

*Maybe that's not love. Maybe I'll never be enough for you.*

*But I'm going to be selfish for once.*

*I need you.*

*Stay because I need you.*

*Even though I'm not enough.*

*Even though I don't give you what you need.*

No. I could never ask that of her.

But, fuck, it's nice to imagine for a minute. I could have a big, beautiful life with Skye. She could move into my apartment. Do all sorts of dirty shoots on my bed.

In our bed.

I could help her until she made enough to hire a real assistant.

We'd get a bigger place. Get married. Have a few kids.

I'd teach them to play basketball. She'd teach them photography. We'd argue over which art they should learn—photography or drawing.

I'd tell them to go to college, but they'd argue that I didn't need my college.

We'd get old and gray (she'd finally dye her hair hot pink) and retire in Mexico, where we'd spend all our time swimming.

Even though I hate the beach, I'd love being there with her.

And the whole time, she'd be missing something she needs.

Because I'm not enough.

I finish another round. Savor every drop of the bittersweet drink.

Order another.

Then I see the last person I need.

Mack sits next to me. Drops her credit card on the bar. "Can I get this round?"

## Chapter Forty-Five

SKYE

For once, I'm glad my parents are over-involved. They can deal with my stuff, so I can get out of here as soon as possible.

I pack the, uh, more sensitive items. And makeup. I may be a heartbroken mess. But at least my mascara is in place.

I change into something warmer. Don shorter shoes.

Stop at the sound of a knock.

"Skye, baby, I'm here for you." Holden's voice is bouncy. But sympathetic too.

"What do you want?"

"Forest sent me."

"Oh." Figures. He's breaking my heart in style. I'll give him that much. "I'm leaving."

"I'll take you home."

"You're sober?"

"Had two drinks four hours ago."

It's not completely implausible. I saw him have that first drink. Then he went to flirt with... someone.

He probably spent the last few hours getting laid.

Good for him.

"I can call a cab," I say.

"No can do."

"Are you going to physically restrain me?"

"Sounds kinky. I'm game."

"What if I'm not into it."

"Then why'd you suggest it, baby?" He laughs. "You could open up. Follow me to my car. I'd rather throw you over my shoulder and carry you. Throw you on the hood, maybe."

I can't help but laugh.

He's so ridiculous.

He doesn't mean any of this.

Maybe.

I think.

It's really hard to tell with him.

"Fine." I let him in.

He looks around the room—it's at full-on tornado state at the moment—and shakes his head. "You're still drunk."

"You can finally take your swing." I motion to the bed. "Get me on the rebound."

"Finally?" His laugh is soft. "I proposition you all the time."

My laugh breaks up the tension in my chest. Not enough. But some. "True."

"You could stay here. Talk to Forest when you sober up."

"No thank you," I say.

"What happened?"

"What if I said *I'll only stay if you fuck me*."

"You wouldn't." He takes my overnight bag and slings it over his shoulder.

"What if I did?"

"No."

"No?" Really?

"You really think I'm gonna sleep with the woman my brother loves?"

Well… maybe. I don't know. "He doesn't love me."

Holden scoffs *okay, right*. "He does. He's just an idiot. But we both know I'm not gonna convince you." He motions to the door. "I'll suggest you stay one more time."

I shake my head.

"If you need a guy, I know a few."

"A guy who will fuck anything that moves?" That's the last thing I need.

"Fuck no. All the guys I show your Instagram. Heard a lot about how they want to come on your tits."

Oh my God.

"Already, I hear myself say it. But it would be hot. You have to admit." He grabs my purse and coat. Opens the door for me.

I move into the hallway. Check that the coast is clear.

No sign of Forest.

Good.

I mean, it should be good. Because I'm sure. I'm done. I'm leaving.

Even if it makes me empty.

Even if it hurts like hell.

It's just…

Happening.

"Are you into that?" he asks. "Not that they'd object to coming other places?"

"Please stop."

"Always thought coming on the back was underrated."

"Oh my God."

"Fucking some hottie doggie style and you're pulling out—"

"That isn't—"

"It's almost as effective as condoms." He chuckles. "Not that I do it."

"You're just Mr. Sex Ed?"

"Women ask." He leads me to the elevator. Presses the button.

"The seventeen-year-olds you flirt with?"

"You mean Daisy?" he asks.

"Yeah."

He laughs. "It's not like that. She just needs a friend."

"Uh-huh."

"I have a code."

"The bro code?"

"You could say that." The elevator dings. Holden holds the door open. Motions *after you*.

It's empty. No sign of Forest. He's not here. He's not waiting for me. He's not begging me to stay.

Of course, he isn't.

He doesn't love me.

Why would he beg me to stay?

Why would he want me to stay?

Now I'm gone and Mackenzie is jealous and he has everything he wants.

His picture-perfect revenge. Reconciliation. Whatever.

I press my back into the wall. Fuck, the elevator is *moving*. Or maybe it's the vodka.

Either way, I need to hold on to the railing to stay upright.

Holden notices. Warps his arm around me to lead me to the parking lot—also empty.

Then to his car.

The passenger seat.

He leans over me to click my seatbelt. "Gotta say, this is a nice perk." He winks, gets into the driver's seat, turns the car on.

"You really wouldn't fuck me?"

"You know you wouldn't ask."

"You're flirting right now."

"So?" His gaze shifts to the hotel. "We can stay. Go back to his room—"

"No."

"You sure?"

"Yeah."

He shakes his head *you're being an idiot*, but he still pulls onto Pacific Coast Highway.

## Chapter Forty-Six

FOREST

**M**ack twirls her cocktail straw.

Ice clinks against the glass. Bounces off the maraschino cherry. Sends amber liquid spiraling.

She's drinking an old fashioned. She always did. She always liked the mix of richness and sweetness.

"Skye ran out of the party." She brings the glass to her lip. Takes a shy sip. "Is everything okay?"

This whole thing started because… I don't know anymore. I'm not sure what I was after. If I was doing this for her. Or if it was for me. If I needed revenge or closure or something in between.

I'm a clueless mess.

But I know one thing: I haven't got any patience for this bullshit. "Don't pretend you care."

Her eyes turn down. " I do."

I swallow my vodka. This is my second glass of straight vodka. My fourth drink of the—it's past midnight, so I guess that makes it morning. My head is spinning. My heart is heavy. My stomach is in knots.

But my inhibitions?

Those are long gone.

"What the fuck did you say to her?" I swallow another sip. Let the booze warm my mouth and throat.

"I didn't—"

"You did."

She stares at me with mock horror. We've spent the last hour making small talk, dancing around this bullshit, replaying her twenty-third birthday.

The birthday where we snuck out of her party so we could fuck like rabbits.

Maybe Skye is right. Maybe I'm a caveman. But I'm not an idiot.

I know what Mack is doing.

"What did you say?" I finish my drink in one long gulp. Suck every drop of vodka from an ice cube.

"Only that… I'm worried about her. About you." She meets my gaze. "The timing is coincidental."

"Oh?"

"Yeah, and Skye is my cousin. My friend. If you're using her—"

"Are you fucking kidding me?"

Surprise streaks her face. "Forest—"

"You're here, flirting with me, the night before your wedding. After cheating on me with the asshole you're marrying. And you want to accuse me of using her?"

"Those things aren't… I'm not flirting." She takes a long sip. Sets her drink on the counter. "I'm just…"

"It's scary. I get that. And I don't blame you for flirting. Fuck, I don't blame you for wanting more."

"I'm not—"

"I don't know what you're after, Mack, but I—"

She leans close enough to grab my wrist.

Fuck, that strawberry shampoo.

For a second, memories flood my head. Our first kiss. The bonfire on the beach. The smile when I told her I loved her.

Then I smell her shampoo—that same shampoo—and my stomach turns.

Ugly memories replace the pretty ones. Our empty apartment. The pale pink sheets. Her red nails in Diego's back.

His name falling off her lips.

"Forest, I…"

"Whatever it is, don't."

"But—"

"I don't care, Mack. I don't care if you're scared. If you're looking for an out. If you're about to say 'take me to my room' or 'I'm sorry I hurt you. It was the worst thing I ever did, and I'd never do that to Diego.' I don't care anymore."

Her eyes fill with disappointment.

I don't want to hold her.

I don't want to comfort her.

I don't want to help her.

She's hurting and I don't give a fuck.

She doesn't have my heart anymore.

"I don't care if you hurt me. I really don't." I stand. Pull three twenties from my wallet. Drop them on the bar. "But if you try to hurt Skye again, it will be the last thing you ever do."

"Is that a threat?"

"Yeah. It is." I would kill for Skye. I'd do anything for her. "She was right. She needed me. As a shield. And I'm going to protect her."

Mack pouts.

"Stay the fuck away from her."

"We're family—"

"Show up at Thanksgiving. Say hello. Carve the turkey. Then stay the fuck away from her. Don't ask if she's okay. Don't pretend you care what's wrong. Don't say you want to be friends."

"I do."

"Too bad. You're done." I slip my wallet into my jeans. Take a step backward. "You're not hurting her again. Not on my watch."

"I don't want to hurt her."

"Then don't." I take another step backward. "Congratulations, Mack. You're going to be a beautiful bride." As for the rest of it?

I don't give a fuck.

As long as she stays away from Skye. It's going to be hard to make sure that happens if Skye's done with me.

But I—

Maybe I don't have the right words yet. Maybe I'm not enough for her yet.

But I can get there.

I just need time. I need to convince her to give me time.

Even if she won't, I need to make sure she's okay.

I go straight to the parking lot, call a ride share, text my brother while I wait.

*Forest: Is she okay?*

*Holden: She's in bed, yeah.*

*Forest: You're at her place?*

*Holden: Yeah. We just fucked. She's better than I ever hoped. And that mouth? God damn, I can see why you're into her. Get real, Forest. I'm on the couch.*

*Forest: I don't know with you.*

*Holden: That's how I like it.*

*Forest: Is she okay?*

*Holden: She's hurt, but she'll get there.*

*Forest: I have an idea.*

*Holden: That's new for you.*

*Forest: You remember when I caught you doing the spade on your ankle?*

*Holden: How could I forget?*

*Forest: Remember where I put it?*

*Holden: You have a point?*

*Forest: Got one in you today?*

*Holden: There was a hottie asking me that a few hours ago.*

*Forest: Yes or no?*

*Holden: I'll tell you the same thing I told her. Of fucking course. I'd be offended you asked if I was the type who got offended.*

*Forest: A yes is sufficient.*

## The Best Friend Bargain

*Holden: And boring.*
*Forest: You have it all figured out, huh?*
*Holden: No. But more than you.*
*Forest: I'm getting there.*
*Holden: We'll see.*
I guess we will.

## Chapter Forty-Seven

SKYE

Fuck, my head is pounding.

I guess that's what I get for drinking my weight in vodka. Hooray, alcoholism.

Is this how drunks feel all the time? Between the pounding head and the churning stomach, it's too much. I quit. Day two of my addiction and I'm already out.

I already know it won't help.

The shower is warm. It should feel safe, comforting, cleansing. It washes the booze from my skin, rinses the last remnants of chlorine, erases the scent of the hotel's shampoo.

I step out of the shower clean. Physically. But mentally? Emotionally?

Everything hurts.

A glass of water and a pain killer push the headache away, but they do nothing to ease the weight in my chest.

Forest is… I'm not sure what he is. Only that he isn't mine anymore.

God, I can only remember half of what I said. A lot of crying. A desperate plea. That sad look in Forest's eye. *I'm sorry. I don't love you. I wish I could say I love you, but it's just not the case.*

I can't blame him. The heart wants what it wants. His heart wants Mackenzie. He's probably in her hotel room right now. Finally getting the best kind of revenge—her, on her back, moaning his name.

Or is it her on her knees, begging for his cock?

Though, I—

God, I don't know what I think anymore. That isn't the Forest I know. He's hurt, sure. Angry, yeah. But he isn't petty or vindictive.

He doesn't even want her.

Does he?

Honestly, I'm not sure anymore.

I head downstairs. Fix a matcha latte. Add extra honey.

Sweet, creamy perfection. But it's empty. It's nothing.

The couch is clear. Except for the pillow and the folded blanket, there's no sign Holden was ever here.

Maybe he wasn't. Maybe this was a bad dream. Maybe if I pinch myself, I'll wake up.

No such luck. I'm still sitting at the kitchen counter, squinting from the too bright sun, seeking comfort in my tea.

At least Dad gets that. He's a smart guy. He knows what matters. Love. Family. Tea.

I mean, there's the whole medical school doctor salary thing too.

But, really, the love of tea is the biggest sign of his wisdom.

Besides, my life is going somewhere. Sure, it took me a while, but I'm getting there.

I have another twenty-five hundred dollars on the way, come July fifth.

And I have another hundred thousand follows. Since I started posting sexy lingerie pics. They're popular.

I guess a lot of people want to see bigger girls in sexy underwear.

Or maybe they want sexy underwear.

Or something to fuck themselves to.

Or even a designated ugly fat friend (Instagram star?) to make themselves feel better.

Hey, if seeing a chubby goth chick makes them feel better about themselves, who am I to judge?

It's still a follower. Still a way to demand more from the next brand who asks me to "influence."

Hell, I can start approaching brands myself. Find an agent. All that stuff.

I will.

And I'm going to expand my photography.

And move out of this house.

But not today.

Today is for wallowing.

I fix another latte. Stare out the window as I drink it.

It's too bright. It's a beautiful day—big lemon sun, clear blue sky, homeless guy sleeping on our porch?

Huh?

This is Venice, yeah, but this part is all residential. The neighbors are quick to call the cops.

If this guy—

At least I can warn him the cops are probably on their way.

I push the window open. "Hey." But that isn't some random hobo.

It's Forest.

He's leaning against the front door, his head resting on the railing, his hoodie lying on his lap like a blanket.

What the fuck?

"Neighbors call the police when they see strange men sleeping in doorways," I say.

His eyes blink open. He stirs. For a moment, his eyes meet mine and his lips curl into a smile.

Then everything hits him and his smile disappears.

Yeah, I know that feeling.

"What about strange hot men?" His voice lifts.

"Can they tell you're hot from here?"

"Maybe if I do this." He stands. Drops his hoodie. Pulls his t-shirt over his head.

There's—

His—

What—

"You..." My eyes go to his chest. I... He... But...

"I did."

"But?"

"You eat breakfast, princess. Let me make you something. You must have a hell of a hangover."

"But—"

"You can see it better if I come inside."

"But Mackenzie... it's—" I check the time on the microwave. "She's getting married in an hour."

"I know."

"You're supposed to be there. Unless you burst into her room last night and told her it was her last chance, that she could run away with you now or lose your forever."

"I did that then came here?"

"Maybe she rejected you."

"You really think you're second choice?"

"Well..." Not usually. But—"Sometimes."

"You gonna let me in?"

"When did you—"

"This morning."

"It's barely—"

"It's nearly noon, princes," he says.

"But—"

"Would have done it sooner, but I had to sober up."

Alcohol is a blood thinner. Getting a tattoo drunk is a bad idea. "What... what happened?"

He taps the door. "Let me in."

"Or?"

"Or I'm putting my shirt on."

"That will hurt your case."

"Even so."

It's a compelling argument.

I open the door.

Forest steps inside.

He's close. And he smells so good. Like the soap at his house. Like A+D Ointment and fresh ink.

God, it's even better up close. The other half of my tattoo, the one he did for me. Another line from the song. It wraps around his broken heart.

It's ours.

It's just for us.

Delicate, subtle, perfect.

God, he hates that movie. He hates it, but he still—

"Can I?" My fingers brush his chest.

"You don't need permission to touch me."

"Never?"

"Never."

"What if I tell you to get lost? To go back to Mackenzie and beg her to have you?"

"I won't."

"What will you—"

"If you really want me to leave, I will. I'll hate it, but I'll leave. I respect you, Skye. You are my best friend. You always come first." His thumb brushes my palm. "Is that what you want?"

I shake my head. "What happened?"

"After you got drunk and freaked out?"

I want to argue, but I can't. It's fair. Accurate. Kind even. He's giving me an out. I think. "Yeah."

"I got drunk and… figured things out, I guess." He takes my hand. "Mack was at the bar."

"What?" Jealousy rises in my throat.

"Let me finish."

"If you—"

"She was saying all this bullshit, and I snapped. I can take her hurting me, but not hurting you." He moves closer. Until he's close enough I can smell his shampoo. "I was pissed. I told her I'd kill her if she hurt you again."

"You did?"

"Not in those words, but yeah."

"Would you?"

"If you want me to." He squeezes my hand. "I told her to stay away from you. Because you deserve better, Skye. You deserve a happy life where no one ever fucks with you."

"She—"

"I don't think she realizes it, but I don't care. I can't watch her hurt you."

"Okay."

"And I… I don't have everything figured out. But, fuck, Skye the thought of losing you—it hurt worse than anything ever has."

"Yeah?"

"Not just because you're my best friend. Though you are." His voice gets soft. "Because—I'm still not sure what the words mean. If I have it exactly right. But I'm getting there."

"What the—"

"I'm not the smartest guy. Or the richest. Or the most… the least fucked up. But I'll love you more than anyone will." His eyes meet mine. "I love you, Skye."

"You love me?"

"Yeah. It was obvious after you left. There was this hole in my gut and nothing could fill it. Nothing but making sure you're okay. But trying to make you happy."

"This?" I trace the lines of his new tattoo.

"Yeah. Holden did it." His expression fills with vulnerability. "You like it?"

My nod is heavy. Like isn't a big enough word. "I love it. I love you." I stare up at him. "I…"

"I want to hear anything you have to say, princess. But right now, I really need to kiss you." His hand goes to my cheek. He looks down at me, asking for permission.

I nod a yes.

## The Best Friend Bargain

He leans in. Presses his lips to mine.
It's soft, slow, sweet.
Mine.
Right now, he's mine.
No, he's finally mine.
Forever.

## Epilogue

SKYE

Ariel pulls the door open. "Is it really eight?"

"Yeah." Forest hugs his sister.

She hugs back. For a second, she crumbles with exhaustion. Then she shakes it off, steps into the living room, draws a circle around Charlotte's crib. "She's fed and changed, but she—"

"I've got it," Forest says.

Her eyes bore into his. They question him. She's as protective as Chase is. "Can you do an hour?"

"I can do all night." He goes straight to the crib. Leans over it. Lets Charlotte wrap her tiny hand around his finger. "She's an angel."

Ariel shoots me an *is he for real* look.

I laugh. Of course, he is. Forest hasn't been as doting as Chase. But he's been obsessed with Charlotte since the day she was delivered. Four months ago.

Ariel is madly in love with her daughter. But she's also exhausted. It's all over her face.

"Take his word for it," I say. "Make him babysit all night."

He pulls Charlotte from the crib. Holds her to his chest. "All week. All month. Forever." He looks into his niece's eyes. "She's the sweetest thing."

"She is." Ariel softens. "But she's also an evil little sleep thief." She crosses the room to her daughter. Leans in to plant a kiss on her head. "I'm going to miss you, baby."

"You'll be in the next room," Forest says.

"Even so." She tears herself away from her daughter. Takes a single step toward the bathroom. Then another. Another.

I swear, it takes her five minutes to cross the living room. And it's not a huge one.

This is Chase's apartment. Well, it's their apartment now. It's been their apartment for a solid six months. More even.

But it is a one-bedroom. Yes, there are signs of Ariel everywhere—the framed movie posters, the bold purple blanket, the math pun pillow—but it's a lot smaller than her dad's place.

I fix tea for us. Chai, since it's all Ariel has. Thankfully, she does have some almond milk stocked.

I love Charlotte too, but I have to agree with Ariel. The adorable four-month-old is a sleep thief. If we're babysitting, we're going to need the energy to stay awake.

Ariel needs the night of sleep. I'm glad to do it.

Besides, there's something about watching Forest with his niece. He lights up.

He's happy, sure, confident, completely in his element.

A family man, plain and simple.

I've always wanted to have kids, but it was an eventually, someday kind of thing. After watching the two of them—

They're just so perfect together.

"Come on, Charlotte, let's say hello to Aunt Skye." He brings my, uh… I guess she's more or less my niece, to the couch. Slips her into my arms.

Charlotte stares up at me with those wide blue eyes. They're the exact same shade as Chase's eyes, but they're always—always—full of joy and curiosity. (Okay, the days of Chase's misery are pretty far in the past. He's not exactly happy-go-lucky, now, but he is… he's not miserable. And he is happy. Just in his way).

God, she really is the sweetest thing. So tiny and adorable and in need of protection.

I offer her my finger.

She wraps her hand around it. Slips. Does it again.

"She likes you," Forest says.

"I like her too." I laugh with Charlotte. She's a happy baby. Always laughing.

Don't get me wrong. She cries plenty. And God those cries— she has the lungs of an Olympic swimmer. The girl can scream.

"You want one?" He rests his head on my shoulder.

"This one? Are you going to steal her?"

His laugh is big, hearty. "We wouldn't get away with it."

"She looks too much like Chase."

"She does."

She shifts in my arms. Her eyes close. Her movement slows. She falls asleep.

As gently as I can, I stand, bring her back to her crib, lay her down.

She stirs for a second, but she stays asleep.

I return to the couch.

Forest pulls me into his lap. He turns me so I'm facing him. Brushes my hair from my eyes. "Do you want one?"

"One day. But not for a while." Whiny ovaries be damned. I have too many things to do. Sure, lots of Moms maintain high-powered careers, but that's not what I want.

I want to slow down when we have kids. To take six months off. To cut my workload in half. At least for a little while.

I'm lucky that I can do that. I still work for myself, set my own hours, make my own rules.

But that also means I'm the one in charge of everything. All the decisions, responsibilities, ideas fall in my lap.

It's a lot.

It's the greatest thing in the world, but it's a lot.

In the last few months, my career as an "influencer" really took off. I started getting weekly offers for posts.

Then daily.

There was even a bidding war over my Halloween costume. Two companies were very, very keen on having me promote their plus-size costumes exclusively.

I made more in October than I made... ever before.

It's still new. Tenuous. Hard. But it's expanding. Blossoming.

It's taken over my life. So much so that I haven't found time to move out. Finding a place, packing my stuff, signing the paperwork—

It's too much.

Sure, my parents drive me bonkers, but they're actually kinda sweet. And Dad's cooking is the best. Almost worth watching my parents sneak upstairs after dinner, turn on their Prince album and—

Okay, it's not worth avoiding listening to my parents' have sex.

But Forest *is* next door. He basically lives at his Dad's house now. Which is nice. Even if it means dealing with Holden more often.

(Besides, he has his hands full with Daisy. That's a can of worms I'm absolutely not opening).

"You can advertise maternity clothes." He presses his lips to my neck. "Then baby clothes."

I stifle my laugh. He's right. It would be a huge business opportunity. But that reminds me—"Will Ariel kill me if I change Charlotte's onesie?"

"If you wake her up."

True. I motion to my purse.

He reaches for it. Hands it to me.

I pull out the tiny wrapped present. Leave it on the coffee table in front of us. "Poor Charlotte is always in those math puns."

"Maybe she likes them," he says.

"What if she's terrible at math?"

"Maybe the puns will inspire her."

"Maybe."

He stares up into my eyes. "I guess I can't tear your clothes off here."

"We'll wake her up."

"That's a tragedy."

"It really is."

"Worst news I've had all day." He pulls me into a tight embrace.

I kiss him softly. Then harder. Hard enough I have to fight my groan.

It is tragic, that I can't touch him properly.

But this is good too.

This is great, actually.

I love being here for his family. They're basically my family. No, they are my family. I love Ariel like a sister.

And Forest—

Somehow, I love him more every day. I don't know how it's possible—I already feel like I could burst from all the love in my heart—but I do.

"I'll make it up to you later." He presses his lips to my neck.

"Is it later yet?"

He chuckles. "No. But it will be here faster than you think."

———

FOREST AND I SPEND AN HOUR LEAFING THROUGH CHASE AND Ariel's graphic novel collection. Between the two of them, they fill a bookshelf and a half with graphic novels and comic books.

Thankfully, there are a few coming of age stories. I settle on *Ghost World*. Forest skims some extremely violent comic book.

Eventually, the door handle turns and Chase steps inside. I guess it's about eight now. He must have come straight from work.

Ariel is still a PhD student. She's doing a half-load this semester, so she's home more. Even though Chase works full time(someone has to pay the rent), he's just as doting as his baby momma.

He nods *hello* to us. Goes straight to his daughter. He stands by her crib, watching her sleep for a moment, then he meets us at the couch.

He motions *go home*. "I've got this."

"Don't you want to sleep?" Forest asks.

He shakes his head. "I'll wake Ariel."

I'm not sure about that. Even if she's usually a light sleeper, she looked dead tired. "You sure?"

He nods *yeah*. "Go. You two look like you're desperate to tear each other's clothes off." His grin is knowing.

God, it's so weird seeing Chase grin like that. I guess I should be used to it by now, but I'm not.

He's just so… happy.

It looks good on him.

Different.

But really good.

"You sure?" Forest asks. "We don't mind."

"If you could come and watch her Saturday night," he says. "I made a reservation. And—" his expression gets sheepish, "we could use a night out."

"Sure." Forest stands. Pulls his friend into a hug.

Chase pats his back. Whispers something in Forest's ear.

Forest's laugh is nervous.

That's not like him.

He must be up to something.

He steps backward. Motions to the door. Puts his hand over his lips in a *shhh* gesture.

"Until Saturday." I hug Chase goodbye.

He whispers in my ear. "You're good for him."

"I know," I whisper back.

"Good." He releases me.

I follow Forest out the door. Down the street. All the way to my car.

"You mind if I drive?" he asks.

"No." I toss him the keys.

## The Best Friend Bargain

They veer to the right—way to the right—but he still catches them. "Princess, I'm going to have to take you to the basketball court."

"You say that every time we're at your dad's place."

"It's going to happen one day."

"Fat chance." Some things change. Some things stay the same. My lack of interest in sports is one of them.

He taps the lock on the car. Opens the door for me. Helps me inside. Even clicks my seatbelt.

I'd usually complain it's too old-fashioned, but it's nice having him this close.

I dig my hands into his hair. Pull him into a slow, deep kiss. Mmm. Forest. My boyfriend. My best friend. My everything.

He pulls back with a sigh. "Hey."

I look up at him. "Hey."

We stay there, staring at each other for a moment. He has such pretty eyes. Deep coffee with flecks of honey.

I could stare into them all night.

Well, almost all night.

We can't exactly *ahem* here.

He presses his lips to mine one more time, then he pulls back, shuts my door, gets into the driver's seat.

"Your place?" I ask.

"Yeah.." His voice is nervous. Shy even.

It's adorable.

Curious.

But adorable.

He laughs as my favorite Garbage CD fills the car. "Classic."

"It was playing on the way here."

"Even so."

"If I made fun of you every time you listened to that car-crash loving—"

"You do." He pulls onto the street. "Every time."

"Every time I hear it."

"How could you make fun of me if you're not around?" His

eyes flit to me for a moment. "Never mind, I'm sure you have your ways."

"I could text you."

"No doubt."

"Mock you to Ariel."

He nods as he turns at the light. "Mock me to your followers."

"Oh. I really underplay that."

He chuckles. "I shouldn't have told you."

"I'd have figured it out eventually."

"You're pretty sharp."

"I do all right."

His chuckle gets louder. "Just all right? You made five-figures last month."

That's true. It's been wild. Amazing, thrilling, and completely exhausting. I feel like Ariel. So in love with what I'm doing, but still in constant need of rest and relaxation.

"You've already made more than me this year, and you started in May."

That's also true.

"Next year, you'll make enough to take me to Hawaii."

"Since when do you want to go to Hawaii?"

"Since you posted the topless picture in the black bikini bottoms."

My cheeks flush. God, that picture was hot. And the look on his face when I took it—like he was going to fuck me right there, in the freezing cold water.

It was early October. The beach was empty—what kind of weirdo goes swimming in October—but it still felt illicit.

We waited until we were in the car.

But, uh…

Shit, what were we talking about?

"You okay, princess?" His laugh is knowing.

"Huh?"

"I'm thinking about it too."

"Uh-huh."

"You tasted like salt."

My sex clenches. "We, uh… how far is it to your place?"

He rests his hand on my thigh. Then he drags it higher, higher, higher—"you know how far it is."

"I know things?"

"A lot of things."

"Not sure about that at the moment."

His laugh fills the car. "I love when you're tongue-tied."

"Uh-huh."

He pulls his hand away.

I let out a whiny sigh.

"And that. Best sound I've ever heard." He stops at a light. Turns to me. "You make my life so much better."

"You do too."

"It's like I can finally see the sun."

"You hate the sun."

"But I don't. Not anymore. I want to feel it on my skin. I want to bask in its warmth. That's because of you, Skye. You… fuck, it sounds so cheesy, but you really did teach me how to love again."

"I did?"

He nods *you did*.

"How?" It's not like I was doing that intentionally. Sure, I wanted Forest to love me. I wanted to mend his broken heart. But it's not like I had a strategy. Or a lesson plan.

"You loved me."

"It wasn't on purpose."

"Maybe. But you could have tried to stop loving me. You could have moved to Seattle."

"Why Seattle?"

"It has that vegan ice cream you like."

"That's enough to move?"

"If you're looking to move anyway." The light turns green. He looks to the street. Focuses intensely on it.

Turns left instead of right.

This is the way to his dad's place. To my parents' place.

Not the way to his apartment.

Huh.

I watch the scenery as he turns into the neighborhood. Left. Right. Left.

All the way to the end of a street lined with bungalows and palm trees.

He parks in front of a cute one-story house. Turns the car off.

"Forest—"

"See it before you say anything."

"But this is—"

"See it."

I nod *okay*.

He helps me out of the car, clicks the lock, slides the keys into his pocket. Then he leads me into the house.

It's a house.

A freaking house.

Sure, it's not the size of my parents' place. Or his parents' place. But it's way bigger than his apartment.

And it's pure old-school Venice.

Hardwood floors in the living room. Tile in the kitchen. Box windows.

A sliding glass door to the backyard.

Light bouncing off the pool.

Wait.

The pool?

I move toward the glowing cerulean water. It's cool outside. Cold even. But I'm buzzing too much to feel it.

"There's a pool." I turn back to Forest.

He crosses the backyard. "There is."

"It's... I love it. But it looks expensive."

"It is. But we're just leasing for now."

"For now?"

He nods *yeah*. "The owner is willing to sell. If we like it."

"You want to buy a house together?"

"One day." He pulls something from his pocket. Places it in my palm. "I want everything with you, Skye."

"Me too. I mean—" I stare at tiny metal key. "For this place?"

"Yeah. I want to live here with you. But if you aren't ready… I can afford it on my own."

"You can?" This place is huge. Beautiful. Expensive.

He nods *yeah*. "But I'd rather be here with you. Save up for a down payment."

"Save up for a down payment?" My eyes meet his. "That's so grown up."

"You're twenty-six now."

I clear my throat. "You're not supposed to bring up a lady's age."

"You're a lady now?"

I nod *uh-huh*.

He nods *nuh-uh*. Presses the key into my palm. "I know you're just starting your career. You're still focused on that. I don't want that to change, princess. I love watching you soar. It's my favorite thing in the world."

"Yeah?"

"Hell yeah." He runs his fingers over the side of my hand. "I want to see it every day. I want to wake up next to you. Fix your morning matcha. Listen to you groan over it. Kiss you goodbye on my way out the door. Watch you set up shoots."

"Oh."

"Oh?"

I run my thumb over the back of his hand. "You want to see me topless in the pool."

"Hell yeah."

"That's the whole reason you did this."

"The main reason yeah."

"I understand." My eyes meet his. "I'm mostly here because you're beautiful."

"I know." His lips curl into a smile. "It's my gift. And my curse."

"It really is."

He pulls his hand away. Stares at the tiny metal key. "Will you?"

"Of course." I slide the key into my purse. "I want that too." I look up at him. "I love you so much, Forest."

"I love you too, princess." His hands go to my waist. He pulls my body into his.

I rise to my tiptoes.

His lips brush mine.

He kisses me softly.

Then harder.

Harder.

I groan against his mouth.

He presses his palm into my lower back.

I pull back with a sigh.

He looks at me with the world's biggest smile.

God, his joy is beautiful.

It's everything.

But, right now, I need something else.

I tug at his t-shirt. "Inside. Against the wall. It's too cold out here."

"Is it?"

I nod *yeah*. Motion to the door. "I need to have my way with you, now."

"What if I need to have my way with you?"

I take a step toward the living room. "Then you probably shouldn't keep me waiting."

---

## Want more Inked Love?

Sign up for my mailing list for an exclusive bonus scene from *The Best Friend Bargain*. What are Skye and Forest up to a few years after their happily ever after? Find out!

Holden's book, *The First Taste*, is now available.

In the mean time, get to know brooding bad boy Chase and

feisty heroine Ariel in *The Baby Bargain*, a sexy baby making romance.

## Already read all my tattoo artists?

Check out *Dangerous Kiss*, a sexy second chance romance featuring a dirty talking rock star hero and the math geek heroine who refuses to get out of his head.

## Author's Note

I've loved the "friends to lovers" trope for a long time. Before I ever read an adult romance, before I knew adult romance was a thing, before eBooks existed! There's something relatable about crushing on your best friend. They're so close, but so far, and it's so hard to contemplate risking an intimate relationship.

I've always loved the fake relationship. There's something about fake feelings turning real. Pretending to want someone, actually kissing them, really wanting to kiss them again--what's not to like?

When I started *The Best Friend Bargain*, I knew I wanted to write about my two favorite tropes. I wanted to hit all my favorite "Crystal Kaswell" beats. A broody tattooed hero, a bad ass heroine with an alternative style, tons of jokes about emo music, delicious tea and coffee, the intimacy of found family.

In a way, the book was a goodbye. I was twenty-nine, Forest is twenty-eight. If I want to keep writing new adult--and I do--I'm not going to write any more heroines my age. Heroes… maybe. If I write age gap books. Those are fun--just wait until you meet Daisy and Oliver's dad!!!--but they're *about* the hero's age. *The Best Friend Bargain* is about two friends in their late twenties, who are a little behind on their "adult lives."

This book was the last time I'd write a hero about my age. Which meant it was the last time I could reach for cultural references with ease. I wanted to make the most of it. To bring in movies, albums, TV shows I loved, that worked into the plot, without justifying why a character loves something more appropriate for someone ten years older.

I mock boys who sing about their ex's car crashes to amuse myself, yes. But, mostly, I bring pop culture into my books because it's how I relate to the world and other people. I grew up watching movies with my dad, watching Dawson's Creek marathons with my sister over the summer, blasting emo music in the car with my best friend.

Even now, as an adult with a business and a house, I wear a band shirt every Monday, I talk about movies with my dad, I mock emo musicians with my husband. Pop culture is a mode of communication.

I never make references for the sake of it. I never bring up songs, books, movies, etc. because I need to express some idea about them. It's easier to listen to a signer decry their ex, even though they're so clearly still obsessed with them, than to admit you feel the same way. It's easier to admit you love your best friend's favorite movie than to admit you love them. And it's easier to tell someone a book broke your heart than to explain exactly which stitches it snipped.

I hope you enjoyed watching Skye and Forest relate. I know I loved watching them dance around their feelings. They tried so hard to avoid the truth, didn't they?

I hope to see you back for Holden and Daisy's book. Holden is every bit as fun as you imagine him. And Daisy is exactly what he needs. Sweet, earnest, and working up the courage to ask him to punch her v-card. Is there anything more fun than a forbidden virgin? You know, besides a fake relationship? Or two best friends who are oblivious to how much they should be together?

I hope to see you soon for Holden's book *The First Taste*. It's every bit as delicious as it sounds.

As always, thanks for reading. If you enjoyed this book, please tell your friends (and your enemies! They might realize you're brilliant), leave a review on Amazon or Goodreads, get to know Ariel and Chase in <u>*The Baby Bargain*</u>.

Please do stay in touch.

Sign up for my mailing list to get exclusive bonus scenes, and be the first to know about new releases. You can also like my page on Facebook, join my fangroup, follow me on Instagram, follow me on Twitter, or friend me on Facebook.

Love,
Crystal

## Acknowledgments

My first thanks goes to my husband, for his support when I'm lost in bookland and for generally being the sun in my sky. Sweetheart, you're better than all the broken bad boys in the world.

The second goes to my father, for insisting I go to the best film school in the country, everything else be damned. I wouldn't love movies, writing, or storytelling half as much if not for all our afternoon trips to the bookstore and weekends at the movies. You've always been supportive of my goals, and that means the world to me.

Thanks so much to my amazing audio narrators, Kai Kennicott and Wen Ross. You always bring my characters to life in a way that blows my mind.

A big shout out to all my beta readers. You helped give me the confidence to put out a book a little more heartbreaking than usual. And also to my ARC readers for helping spread the word to everyone else in the world.

To all my writer friends who talk me down from the ledge, hold my hand, and tell me when my ideas are terrible and when they're brilliant, thank you.

Thanks so much to my editor Marla, my assistant Gemma, and my cover designer Melody Jeffries. As always, my biggest thanks goes to my readers. Thank you for picking up *The Best Friend Bargain*. I hope you'll be back for Holden's book, *The First Taste*.

## Stay In Touch

Sign up for my mailing list. (You'll get first notice on cover reveals, teasers, and new releases, and a bunch of awesome bonus content like the extended epilogue to *The Best Friend Bargain*).

You can also like my page on Facebook, join my fangroup, follow me on Instagram, or friend me on Facebook.

Made in the USA
Las Vegas, NV
19 December 2022

63486373R00236